AIR SERIES BOOK 3

BROKEN PATHS

AMANDA BOOLOODIAN

DEDICATION

Dedicated to silver for supporting and encouraging my dreams.

CONTENTS

I hate having a gun pointed at me. Having two aimed in my direction made me downright cranky. The man in front of me shifted his aim to Rider, and that pissed me off.

Sure, as a werewolf, he'd likely survive a bullet or two without a problem, but he was my partner and my best friend, so I never wanted that theory tested. Lucky for me, as a Reader, I could arm myself without anyone else knowing. My control was shaky, but when guns were involved, I had to chance it.

"You're on private property." The woman who spoke was human and short in stature, but there was nothing like a weapon in the hand to make a girl loom over others.

Mentally, I stretched out and grabbed the Path. Everything in this world left its mark and with the Path roaring around me, I could read that residual energy.

I made sure my voice was clear. "We're from the Treasury Department. Drop your weapons."

The man's eyes flickered to me, then back to his target. "Let's see your ID."

"Rider, show him," I said.

With my eyes on the guns, I molded the turbulent Path into a more solid line, shielding Rider and me from the strangers. The effort of keeping air solid burned through my strength fast.

The woman craned her neck to glance at Rider's credentials. "I'm putting away my weapon. We didn't recognize you."

I kept things formal. "And you are?" They put the guns away, but I was tense and didn't drop my guard.

"I'm Sable, and this gentleman is Doctor Wes Taylor. We're with the Mythological and Terrestrial Humanitarians. We own this property."

The Path peeled apart the wall that I had created once I stopped pouring energy into it. While working for the Agency for Interdimensional Regulation, the organization known as MyTH had come up a few times.

The Path showed the myriad of colors that swirled around Sable, indicating emotional upheaval, but she appeared to be trying to rein herself in.

"No one at the office mentioned this was MyTH property," I said. "Can I see your ID? Both of you?"

While Doctor Taylor got out his ID, I dragged myself out of the Path. It wasn't easy. I'd ripped open the Path, and my mind wasn't ready to let it go.

When I dropped myself back into the natural world, I took his credentials. Looking it over gave me an excuse to hide a few deep, steadying breaths, as the world grew dull around me.

There was some unwritten rule that badges and licenses must have horrible pictures. Dr. Taylor was one of the rare exceptions to that rule. His pale brown skin, rounded teardrop eyes, and short, stark black hair, looked almost as good in the picture as in person. He looked like he wanted to ask something, but I nodded and handed him back the piece of plastic.

"I'm Cassie Heidrich with AIR." I extended my hand to Doctor Taylor and then to Sable. "This is Rider. I think my usual partner Logan Seale may have worked with you in the past."

"Logan, yes." Sable smiled but didn't look at ease. "Is the old elf here?"

"He's back at home today," I said.

"And what brings AIR out to the woods?" Sable asked.

I realized that while Sable was talking, the doctor was sizing us up.

"We received word that there was a disturbance," I said.

"With the gnomes?" Sable asked.

"Yes. Doctor Taylor, is everything okay?" He'd been peering at me for far too long, which was starting to get unsettling.

"Please, call me Taylor," he said. "Sorry, I was trying to place you. There's something off, and I can't put my finger on it."

People always thought there was something off when they met me, but very few openly spoke about the feeling. Still, it was better than some reactions.

Sable shot a look at Taylor. "The gnomes have had a death in their family."

"It appears to be natural causes," Taylor said.

Things in my job were rarely clear-cut. "What do you mean appears to be?"

"There are no signs of trauma," Taylor said, "but the gnomes are insisting that the death wasn't natural."

"So you've examined the body?" AIR maintains a working relationship with MyTH, but I wasn't sure where medical examination falls in our lines of communication.

"Yes," Taylor said, "but they have refused to allow me to take her back to the lab. I took blood and tissue samples to check for toxins and poisons."

Death wasn't what I had expected to find out here, and I was sure if the office expected it, they would have sent someone else. I'd only been in the field about a year, and technically, Rider was in training.

"I'll have to call this in," I said, "but first, can you lead us to where the death took place?"

"Certainly." Sable's tension was noticeable as Rider and I followed the pair.

Her reaction made me wonder if MyTH would have called AIR about this type of incident, or maybe, like Taylor, she was put off by meeting me.

The trees had begun to put out buds, but brown was the dominant color until we arrived near the gnome hollow. The holes were nearly indistinguishable from the rest of the environment. However, as we moved closer, the air became more vibrant.

A tiny blur came from the direction we moved. It circled us and went back the way it came. Soon there were more. It was like being surrounded by an indistinguishable swarm.

We stopped. How do you avoid stepping on one of these little guys?

"Nord," Sable called.

A blur came to a stop in front of her. It was hard to tell if the gnome was male or female. Despite their speed, they were plump little creatures that never reached a foot tall.

"This is Nord, who speaks for the family," Sable said. "Nord, this is Cassie and Rider with AIR. They would like to see Am."

Nord peered up at us from the ground for a few moments before nodding curtly and disappearing.

"This way." Sable moved deeper into the woods.

Moss clung to rocks, and the trees were becoming noticeably greener. The air smelled of moist soil.

Whistling rang out around us as we approached the home of the gnomes. It sounded like a flock of birds, only most of the chittering was at ground level. Every now and again, a tiny person would come to an abrupt stop and look at us before moving on.

"You won't step on them," Taylor said. "They don't get underfoot, and if they did, they are fast enough to move."

Looking back, I saw that Rider had fallen behind and was watching the ground closely as shapes swirled around him.

Sable fell back, and Taylor led me to where a tiny body lay on the ground. "This is Am." Taylor knelt on the ground next to the unmoving shape.

My heart felt squeezed when I bent down next to Taylor and looked at the body of Am. She looked fragile, and her skin was as pale as chalk. Trying to keep my mind focused on the job, I took in the surroundings. A long slit in a rock shelf had many eyes peering out of it, which made me assume the gnome tunnels opened there. They probably had burrows below us, but there was no telling how many.

I cleared my throat twice before I trusted my voice not to break. "Was this where the gnomes found Am?"

Taylor kept his focus on the tiny figure. "This is where Nord led us. They said they didn't move her since it wasn't a natural death."

"And you think it was natural?" I asked.

Taylor looked uncomfortable. "I can't be certain without an autopsy, but they've refused to let me take her."

Gnomes held a very strict set of beliefs that said the dead must remain in contact with the ground of the hollow. From what little I knew, it was difficult to work around.

"But you're taking an educated guess?" I asked.

"From a cursory examination of the remains, it appears that she suffered a heart attack."

I paused to think that over. "That's a normal death for us, is it normal for a gnome?"

"It is," Taylor said, "although they don't know that's what it's called."

Nodding, I leaned back. "Have you worked with anyone besides Nord?" I asked.

"Nord speaks for the whole family," Taylor said.

"Nord?" I blinked in surprise when the small man appeared beside me. He must have been close by and listening. "What about Am's death makes you think it was unnatural?"

Nord cocked his head and looked at me. So far, the gnomes hadn't taken the usual aggressive stance against me. "Am died in an unnatural way. There was no age, no illness, no famine, and no fight."

"Could it be that her body gave out?" I asked.

"No signs," Nord said.

"Did anyone see anything out of place?" I asked.

"Only Am. Something not right. Still not right. Something came here." He was silent for a moment. I was about to ask my next question when he spoke again. "You are not right."

I could feel the heat creep into my face. "I'm going to do what I can to help, though. Tell me, what came here?"

"No one knows," Nord said.

"Did anyone see anything?" I asked.

Nord shook his head.

I studied the area again, and when I looked back down, Nord was gone. Logan would know what to do. He'd been at this much longer than I had, which was what made him a good mentor. Rider was even greener than I was, and I was out of my depth.

"Is there anything else you can tell us?" I asked Taylor.

"Not until I get the test results back," Taylor said.

"Did you see anything in the area when you arrived?"

"Nothing." Sable joined our conversation. "While Taylor examined Am, I looked around. Nothing looked disturbed. The only footprints were our own."

"Rider, can you check around a bit, see if you can pick up anything that is out of place?" I asked.

Rider frowned. "We are out of place. They are out of place."

I rolled my shoulders. "Agreed. See if you can sniff anything else out. Maybe one of your new friends can help you find your way around."

Rider looked around at the tiny figures at his feet. He bent over at the waist until he was nose to nose with a gnome. "What is your name?"

"She no English," piped up another figure. "My name is Indi. I show you."

Then they were off. Rider didn't seem to have any trouble following. He looked more comfortable with putting his feet down.

I stood and examined the ground around Am. We'd already trampled anything that might be a clue, but I had to look.

Taylor slowly rose to his feet next to me. "What did Nord mean by you're not natural?"

I raised an eyebrow at him and ignored the question. "Did anyone else give you additional information?"

"Actually, you got more out of him than we did," Sable said.

Taylor was eyeing me again. I tried not to glare in return. It wasn't professional to glare at a pseudo colleague, but staring at me wasn't professional either.

I turned my back to him and continued to survey the area. Rider looped back into view, and I was relieved. Taylor's eyes were becoming a physical weight.

"Did you find anything?" I asked.

"I did not. The area feels unsettling, but there are no traces of anything but forest," Rider said.

"Hmm. I'm going to take a look around as well." I caught Rider's eye, and he nodded. More than anyone else, I trusted Rider to have my back. "Why don't you have Sable and Taylor tell you what they know?"

Rider spoke to Sable and Taylor while I stepped away.

Taking my time, I closed my eyes and peeled back reality until the vivid Path was on display. Rider felt like something was off, so I didn't hold back.

Opening my eyes left me in shock. Thousands of trails covered the grounds. Bright yellow strands crisscrossed every inch of the clearing. They even climbed trees and led to holes I hadn't noticed with my normal sight. Turning on the spot, I followed the shimmering yellow tapestry.

When I looked towards Rider and the others, I could see them clearly. Rider was throwing off waves of inquisitive energy, warm blue wrapped around Sable and it hid traces of purple and black throughout, but Taylor was something altogether different. Earlier, my focus was on the guns, and I had assumed he was human, which was stupid. My partners were an elf and a werewolf. Gran even kept a fairy in our backyard. Then, when I meet someone new, while standing yards from a gnome hole, I assumed they were human.

I was as gullible as ever.

TWO

When I turned my focus back to work, I tried not to berate myself for making such a rookie mistake. Looking into Doctor Taylor could wait until I was back in the office. He wasn't human, but he also wasn't a threat now. The browns and blues with sparks of orange that flowed around him told me he was anxious, but no threat.

Moving my focus to the gnomes, I looked down at the body of Am. Everything left a mark on the Path: people, animals, objects we used, and plants. The dead left a reminder of themselves on the Path. Where they died usually held an imprint that was long lasting, as if the person was unwilling to go.

Am had no imprint. No part of her pressed against the Path in memory. Am looked so small, surrounded in bright yellows and radiant shimmers. A small pocket of air around her was void of all Paths. Nothing rippled or glided over the area. The unnaturalness of the empty space made my skin crawl.

Leading away from Am, and away from the gnome hole, there was a larger empty spot in the Path. Eyeing the space closely, I reached out to it, but when I neared the emptiness, goose-flesh broke out on my arms.

Hollow. The Path had been hollowed out.

The idea of forcing myself to touch the blank spot made me shudder, so I dropped my hand.

The Path was everywhere. The air was full of glimmers that represented the currents of the Path. It was a constantly flowing moving force. Except here.

My eyes rested on Am again, and my stomach twisted. She was sitting in that deadened space. The thought chilled me.

"Nord," I called. A race of yellow color stopped at my feet. Tiny twists of pale blue wrapped themselves around his yellow core. "It's important that you move Am's... It's important that you move her." I almost said Am's body, but I didn't think that would be well received.

He hesitated and puffs of blue-green issued from him.

"Not far," I said. "We can do it if you'd rather."

"It will be done," Nord said formally. Moments later, three gnomes raced up and then stopped next to Nord. In a slowness that I didn't think gnomes could possess, they reverently picked up Am and moved her on top of a nearby rock.

Once she was moved, the Path flowed over her. A sigh of relief escaped, and I rubbed the goose-flesh from an arm. At my feet, the bubble of emptiness stayed stubbornly in place.

Glancing up, I saw that Taylor was watching me intently, despite the fact that Rider was trying to keep his attention.

Ah, well, it couldn't be helped. I put Taylor out of my mind. I put my hand against a nearby tree for support and tried to move upstream against the Path. A few minutes of the past ghosted by, but it wasn't enough. I needed to dive back much further.

The powerful flow surged and tried to roll me back to the present. It wasn't long before I sagged against the tree, while reading the area ate away at my strength. Determination took me further, but I could tell it was wasted energy. A person could only do so much, and I had pushed myself to that limit. I let the current sweep me back to the present, and once solidly in the present, catching my breath took a few moments.

Rider had Sable distracted, but Taylor's attention was on me, watching as though he were trying to analyze the situation.

Anything that could leave those blighted holes in the fabric of the Path wasn't natural, and that was one certainty. Inspecting the emptiness again, I could see that the Path had gained a little ground, making the void smaller. I dropped the Path and hoped that the damage wasn't permanent.

"Rider." I'm not sure what he heard in my voice, but he was next to me faster than I expected. "We have a new case. Take statements from the gnomes. Get Taylor and Sable to help."

He looked me over before setting to work.

"Nord," I called out. The gnome arrived, and Taylor came up beside me. I crouched down, getting closer to gnome level. "We are going to look into Am's death. If it was unnatural, we'll find out."

"Something came," Nord said, repeating his earlier statement.

"We're going to look into this," I said, "and the doctor might be able to find some clues."

Nord knew what I was asking, and he looked sad. "You will search and find. Am stays here."

Taylor squatted down to talk with Nord. "I'm far too big to be able to see over Am here. You've been to our office before. I could take her there and be back tomorrow."

Shuffling his feet, Nord looked at the ground.

"We know it is important for Am to connect with the ground. Could we take a part of the earth with us?" I asked.

Taylor looked momentarily taken aback by the suggestion, but with a glance at Nord, he knew that this was the opening he needed. "I would ensure that she never lost contact with the ground."

"You will wait here." There was some distress in the voice before he disappeared.

"What do you think of this death?" Taylor asked.

"There's definitely something odd going on here. If you'll excuse me for a minute, I need to call the office." I stepped away without waiting for a response.

Hank, our handler and voice at the office, answered the phone. After relaying the information, I asked him a few procedural questions involving MyTH. Not only did Sable and Taylor have clearance, but they also had more training than I did, not that that's saying much.

No wonder Taylor had been watching me so closely. I'd probably screwed something up along the way.

Once I was sure Hank had our location and status logged, he transferred me to Dr. Yelton. The doctor assured me that Taylor's samples would be sufficient, but he would go to Taylor's lab to oversee the autopsy.

When the statements were wrapped up, Nord appeared. Eight gnomes carrying a large piece of tree bark followed behind him. Am lay on top of the dirt that covered the bark.

"You will have her back tomorrow," Nord said.

Taylor looked reverent. "You have my word."

The gnomes sat down their burden, and then each one patted the bark reverently. After that, they disappeared.

Nord was the last to go. "Tomorrow, before the sun goes from the sky."

Taylor agreed, and Nord was gone. With extreme carefulness, Taylor lifted the bark, and we left the gnome hole.

Gnomes don't have the best hearing, so we didn't have to

walk long before we figured it was safe enough to talk without being overheard.

"We'd like to be involved in this case," Sable said.

"You are involved," I said. "Taylor has Am and the samples. Dr. Yelton, the AIR doctor, will meet you all at Taylor's lab to work with you."

"The investigation part happened on MyTH property. Our benefactor will want to know what happened," Sable said.

MyTH was a private organization that helped acclimate the Lost when they entered this dimension. They helped the Lost find jobs, heard complaints, and helped the interdimensional community in a way that a government facility couldn't keep up with.

"We're all on the same side," I said. "Since the city is closer to this location than the Farm, it's likely we'll work together." AIR and MyTH had worked together for some issues, especially in the city. With the gnomes being on MyTH property, I doubted they would be too far out of the loop on this case.

That didn't mean they'd have a front row seat in the case. They were civilians after all.

Sable looked relieved. Taylor was bleeding anxiety, which ratcheted up a notch when I agreed to bring them into things. Even with the Path closed, I could feel his emotions pressing into me. I kept a close eye on him and noticed that Rider was already doing the same.

"Would you like to join us at the office?" Taylor asked. His anxiety hadn't died out, but he didn't let it slip into his voice.

"We need to get back to the Farm. Here's my card." I took one from my back pocket. It was a little bent, but it almost passed as professional. "Let us know if you all hear anything."

Rider and I walked back to the truck. Well, we called it a truck, but it was more like a SWAT vehicle. It had two rows of seats up front to hold a team, and the back was comfortable and strong enough to transfer the Lost. Relocation was the biggest part of our job. Fairies, gnomes, trolls, centaurs, and countless others are all real. Either Portals opened to other dimensions naturally, or someone would open one on purpose, and the Lost would find their way into our dimension. Most of the mythological legends around the world came from people spotting someone from another dimension. Sometimes, the Lost wanted to stay in our world, and at other times, there was no way to get them home. If they stayed, we located them where they were likely to go unnoticed. With the human population on the rise, it was getting harder and harder to find out-of-the-way places for the Lost to live, but so far, we managed.

When we reached the truck, I sighed. After spending so much time in the Path, I felt bleary eyed, but I still slid into the driver's seat. I had let Rider drive once, and I never wanted to repeat the experience. He was fine in a car, but get him into a larger vehicle, and he swerved through traffic appearing to expect other cars to jump out of the way.

He had far more fun than someone should have while driving.

"What did you think of Sable and Taylor?" I asked, as I drove us towards the interstate.

"They are interesting."

"Do you know what Taylor is?" I asked.

"You mean, he is not human?" Rider asked.

CHAPTER

THREE

"When are you going to learn to use contractions?" I asked. "No, *he's* not human."

"His smell was a little off, but I thought he was human," Rider replied. "He was a bit twitchy, though."

"Twitchy?"

"Yeah, like he had a bug under his tail."

The mental image gave me a good laugh.

Rider beamed. "It is good to hear you laugh. It has been a while."

My laughter died away as Rider's words sank in and sobered my mood.

"Sorry." Rider's whole face fell. "He took a part of you with him. I know that is difficult for you."

The 'him' was one of our partners: a Walker named Vincent Pironis. To save lives, he dragged a monster into the world between dimensions. This was part of a Walker's everyday skill set, so it shouldn't have taken more than a few days to return. That was more than five months ago.

"It's okay. He'll be back." I repeated the sentiment often,

but I was beginning to accept the idea that things went wrong or that he came back, but he didn't make contact. "Let's go over the day."

Rider grabbed the laptop. "Are we going to the Farm?"

"Yeah, we need to get together with Hank, but it's pretty late in the day. If we finish the reports while we drive, it'll save time."

Knowing how painfully slow Rider was at typing, I almost wished he were behind the wheel. This made sense, since he came from another dimension, which meant he didn't have much experience with a computer, and he was translating from his own language as he went. He recounted the report aloud as he worked so that I could make suggestions and add details of my own.

The typing continued as we reached the outer gates of the Farm. I waved my ID over the scanner. The Mid-West office of AIR was composed of more than one thousand acres of rolling hills, trees, and fields, with government buildings and housing clustered together in lumps. We housed and trained the Lost that were making our dimension their home, getting them ready to live among people.

The next gate held an empty guard post, but every time someone approached, surveillance cameras would narrow in on the car. Fences ran off in either direction, disappearing into the trees. They surrounded the Farm and had security cameras and motion detectors, along with razor wire. Nothing could come in or go out without being detected.

At the guard post, I leaned out and let my eye be scanned. The surveillance cameras picked up my identification decal on the car, and off we went. The road snaked around trees before we turned into the parking lot of the main office, far out of sight from the road.

In the building, we went through more scanners and used

our identification cards a few times to get to the command room. Technically, I had an office, but my mentor and usual partner, Logan, liked to be in the center of everything, so we rarely used the space.

Hank reigned in his usual spot next to a bank of large monitors on one side of the room. Logan leaned on the edge of Hank's desk, and as Rider and I approached, Logan tipped an imaginary hat in our direction.

"How was the tux fitting?" I asked.

Logan grinned. "I thought the woman doing the tailoring was going to cry. Gerald moved so much that he was repeatedly stabbed by needles. How were the gnomes?"

I glanced at Hank and raised an eyebrow, surprised that he hadn't filled Logan in.

Hank cleared his throat. "We hadn't gotten as far as the case yet."

"It's a case now, is it?" Logan asked.

Worn out from a day of Reading the Path, I pulled up a chair and told Logan and Hank about Am.

Logan's face fell. "Sorry to hear that. Not natural?"

"We're not sure yet. It happened on MyTH property," I said.

"I've worked with a few people from MyTH through the years. Sable has a good head on her shoulders," Logan said. "Another gal, though, her name was Angel, was a hellcat. Not literally, I'm pretty sure she was human. Maybe human plus, like you, but human all the same."

"It always struck me as odd that we work with an outside agency," I said.

"Most government agencies contract out at some point," Hank said. "It's cheaper to hire civilians."

"The main benefactor of MyTH used to be an AIR agent," Logan said. "He set up the whole thing."

"It's like an advocacy group for the Lost, right?" I asked.

"For the most part," Logan said, "but they also train much like we do, to help out in emergencies. Have you ever seen a domestic-abuse situation with the minotaurs?"

I leaned back in my chair and blinked tired eyes against the harsh florescent lights. "It's good to know more about them since we'll probably be working with some of them on this case. Dr. Yelton is at MyTH working with Dr. Taylor now. They only have a day to find out all they can."

"No clues at the scene?" Logan asked.

"There were a few things that weren't quite right, but nothing that I could put my finger on." My eyes flicked to Hank. AIR wasn't exactly in-the-know about the extent of my powers now. My partners thought that was best kept under wraps. Thankfully, Hank's eyes were on his computer screen.

"I smelled no one in the area that was not accounted for," Rider said.

Logan looked thoughtful. "Could be natural then."

"According to the file, the gnomes were insistent that it wasn't natural," Hank said.

"It's possible either way. We'll see what the labs say." I looked around the room. The night crew was already settling in. "I'll finish up the report."

"I will take care of that," Rider said. Before I could argue, he added, "This will be good practice since this type of case does not often come along."

My brow furrowed. "Are you sure?"

"I am," Rider said.

"I'll be going home shortly," Logan said. "If you leave Rider the truck, I'll give you a ride."

"Sure." I stood and stretched before following Rider to a desk, giving Logan and Hank a chance to finish whatever Rider and I had interrupted.

It didn't take Logan long. After I made sure Rider didn't need anything else from me, Logan and I went home.

Logan had helped Gran and me find the perfect house. It was in a nice neighborhood, but well outside of our bustling town. It was about an hour drive to and from the office, which wasn't terrible. It was also directly behind Logan's house. He and his kids were regulars in our kitchen. I think that had more to do with the amount of baking that Gran did, than with Logan and me being partners.

Logan dropped me off out front.

"Gran, I'm home." I made a beeline to the lit kitchen.

"Evenin.'" Gran's voice, like herself, was all southern belle.

"Did you have a good day?" When I entered the kitchen, the microwave chimed. Gran's psychic powers had a direct line to my stomach.

"Quiet today, but Dee Dee and I are going shopping tomorrow. How are things at the office?"

Settling down at the table, I told Gran a little about my day.

"Does that mean you'll be spending a bit more time in the city?" Gran asked.

"It's possible," I said.

"Well, don't work yourself too hard. I've hardly seen you around here."

Instantly, the guilt set in. "I may not have to go too often with MyTH working that end."

"You have to go see the Palm Reader when you go back."

So much from Gran came out of left field, but this was new. "Palm Reader?" I prompted.

"No idea," Gran said, "only that you need to go see her when you're back in the city."

If Gran said I had to go see a palm reader, I'd go see her. It was always best to follow Gran's advice. When I grew old, I wanted to be like her, a sweet old lady who took in strays and kept the elven neighbors stocked in sweets.

Not that I'd ever call Gran an old lady.

After dinner, I cleaned up and found a piece of cake in the fridge.

I grabbed a fork. "I've got some notes to go over."

"Your mom called today," Gran said.

I almost dropped my plate. Mom never called. Since I quit my normal, safe job as an accountant, and began using my powers on a regular basis, she broke almost all ties with me. She had suppressed her psychic abilities for years and thought I made a mistake by not doing the same. We saw each other at holidays and other special occasions, but mostly, Mom had her world, and I had mine.

"Mom called? Did something happen?"

"No," Gran said, "I think she was checking up on us."

"Is she coming over?" I asked.

"She mentioned this weekend, but I'm pretty sure she isn't comin' over." Gran winked at me. "If she ever does, we should keep her out of the back garden. She'd have a fit if she saw that we kept a fairy in the backyard. I don't think she'd like my cat much either, come to think on it."

"It'd be fine. Mom would put up with the fairies, cats, and elves, or she can stay home." I stopped. "We could go visit her, if you want." If Gran wanted to see her daughter, I'd tie Mom up in a bow and hand her over.

"And risk getting stuck talkin' to that dull husband of hers? I had enough of him at Christmas. We'll see her soon enough, though. Go take care of your notes and get a good night's sleep."

With my cake in hand, I went up to my room. There were files waiting for me to review on my tablet, and gnome research had to happen at some point. Tonight, I had other things on my mind, though. I ate the cake while I waited for the laptop to boot up. I could have checked my email through my phone, but I didn't want this email address on AIR equipment. In the past few months, I've been more careful about keeping my work separate from the rest of my life. Not that I had much of another life.

As expected, there was an email waiting for me from my friend, Quin. I didn't know much about her life, and she knew very little about my own. The shared aspect of our relationship was our talent. Quin was a Reader, like me. In fact, she was the only other Reader I had discovered. We had been sparse about personal facts, but I gathered that she was closer to Gran's age than my own. I was also sure she was lying about her name, but I didn't care. I used my middle name when talking to her. To have someone experience things similar to me was like finding a tiny spark of life on Mars. I hadn't known I was looking for the spark, but now that I'd found it, I coveted the shared experiences.

DEAR ANALA,

It was good to hear from you again. I tried your meditation methods this week. It brought a whole new perspective to my own practices. I'm happy you shared that one with me. Speaking of new perspectives, have you ever read the Path while it was raining? I'm stretching a bit more as a Reader since we've started talking, so I thought I would give it a try. It was amazing, the ripples of colors remained, but each ripple sparked its own rainbow. Words can't describe the sensation. Give it a try the next time it rains.

I saw a shadow of something on the Path while in the woods. Any ideas on what would cause a shadow?

I hope to hear from you soon,

Quin.

I REPLIED IMMEDIATELY.

DEAR QUIN,

I haven't watched the Path in the rain, but now I'm looking forward to trying! It also makes me want to try going swimming and checking the Path underwater. Once summer hits, I will be adding that to my list of things to do.

I've seen a couple of shadows on the Path. The ones that I saw came from different things. Once it was where an old building had been torn down. The building stood for over one hundred years, so it left an odd shadow on the Path, even though it was long since gone. The other time, I was in the woods. It's hard to explain. There was an old tree by me. The tree was there, but when I entered the Path, I caught a glimpse of its future. At some point, the old tree was going to die and leave a shadow in its wake. Since you were in the woods, maybe something like that caused the shadow.

Speaking of seeing new things on the Path, have you ever seen a hole in the Path? Almost like a tiny blank spot where the Path didn't touch. It was an odd thing to see, but I have no idea what caused it.

I hope to hear from you soon. Can't wait for it to rain!
Sincerely,
Anala

FOUR

"You remember when we used to saunter into the Farm at nine o'clock? I miss those days," Logan said.

"There's no line of cars at the gates at seven," I replied. "Besides, I have a report to check over and we need to spend time at the gun range today."

That perked Logan up. "I've got my six-shooter loaded and ready to go."

Rewards should be given out for the amount of effort it took not to roll my eyes. Elves get bored easily and jump from subject to subject. Every now and again, they wander into an area that doesn't bore them. It quickly invades their lives. Logan's latest obsession was with Westerns. It had taken almost a year, but now I was beginning to see why Logan's old partner had shot him over show tunes.

"First, you need to look over the report," I said, pulling up to the first gate of the Farm.

When we made it to the office, Logan and I went straight down the middle of the control room.

"Anything new?" Logan asked Hank.

"Everything is clear. Is she starting to drag you in early too?" Hank asked. "I'm beginning to think she lives here."

"It's a busy time." I purposefully avoided looking at the empty desks. "I better get to it."

Logan stuck around, talking with Hank while I claimed my usual desk and opened yesterday's report. It didn't take long to add a few comments and close it up again. After that, I poured myself into gnome research. Specifically, instances of death.

"We've got a case," Logan said.

I looked up from my computer and discovered that the day was passing me by. More desks were filled, and Kyrian, our boss, had arrived and was more or less looking over Hank's shoulder.

"Anything new on the monitors?" I asked.

"No portal build-up anywhere in the Mid-West, nothing suspicious on thermals, and Farm security is tight," Logan said. "We didn't watch a satellite sweep, but I think Kyrian is having Hank pull that up now."

"Do we have a relocation?" I asked. Usually, we relocate people when they've been spotted. When rumors fly around about mythological creatures, we're called in to take care of the issue.

"Criminal case," Kyrian said walking over, "suspicious deaths overnight."

Kyrian handed a tablet over to Logan, who immediately passed it over to me. We used to use actual files, but Kyrian was upgrading everywhere. Files or computer screen, it was all the same to Logan, and he always passed it to me. I didn't mind, though. Elves were curiously strong for being so tall and thin, so he did all the heavy lifting and I took on the paperwork.

I signed into the tablet and opened the only file it contained.

"Three deaths overnight," Kyrian said. "One was the victim of a hit-and-run, one fell down the stairs and broke his neck, and the other died of natural causes, an aneurysm."

"Are they Lost?" I asked.

"Human," she said, "they all lived together, and there's a fourth roommate. The police have him in interrogation. He's one of ours, and we need to take care of him."

Kyrian turned and left without a glance back. I grabbed my bag on my way out.

"Have you seen Rider today?" I asked without looking up from the file.

"He dropped the keys off earlier. He's in training for the day."

"Driver's Ed?" I asked.

Logan let out a whoop of laughter. We poke fun at Rider's driving, but for good reason. When we reached the truck, we did a thorough check. No new dings or paint scrapes and the tires held air, so we were good.

"There's nothing much beyond what Kyrian already told us," I said as Logan drove us to the station. "Four college kids, all roommates. Three of the four died overnight. The fourth one swears he didn't do anything, and didn't know his friends had died until the police showed up this morning. He hasn't been arrested, but he has been detained for questioning."

"They know we're coming?" Logan asked.

"Excellent question." I called Hank. He said he'd take care of the details before we made it to the station.

"What type of Lost are we working with?" Logan asked, after my call.

"He's a lar, named Bill. What do we know about lares? I've never heard of them."

"Hard to say really. I've only read reports on them. They were once believed to be protectors."

"Like what?" I asked.

"An area, a river, a family. You name it. The Romans thought they were heroes."

"The Romans? They go that far back?"

"Almost everything goes that far back," Logan said dismissively, "further even."

"Why did they think they were heroes?"

"See if there's a picture of him in the file."

I swiped through pages on the tablet. "Here's one. He's...oh." His hair was blond and a tiny bit longer than most men could get away with. His striking features drew your eyes to his face. Handsome wasn't enough to cover it. "He's beautiful."

Logan laughed. "They all are. It's in their genes."

"He looks like, if he smiled, you would hear a 'ting' when the light bounced off his teeth and glimmered through his hair."

If anything, Logan laughed louder. "I imagine in the times of the Romans, they were a bit overwhelming."

"Maybe." Dragging my eyes away from the picture, I swiped to other pages. "Are they warriors or do they protect people?"

"Not especially. I'm sure some of them were. They're usually pretty smart, but they can manipulate people to get what they want. Not on purpose mind you. They assume it's the way things are done."

"They expect people to do things for them?"

"Yeah, but in their defense, it's because people usually do what the lares want."

"You know, I've never worked with the local police. How does this work?"

"They're going to see us as feds. We go in, ask our questions, and get our Lost out of there if possible."

AIR was a government agency. The Department of the Treasury paid us, and the job came with a clearance level high enough to make your nose bleed, but it had never felt like a government agency.

"How do they feel about working with the federal government?" I asked.

"Usually, they don't care much. We're all on the same side. They don't always like that they don't know which agency we work for. They're not thrilled when we can't give them details either. But, it's not like we're the IRS."

There was a little anxiety on my part when we arrived. Our reception wasn't as congenial as Logan made it sound. We walked into a small waiting area and talked to a man behind bulletproof glass. He inspected our IDs with a great deal of scrutiny, and I received a sneer or two before he let us know someone would be with us shortly.

While we waited to be buzzed back to the inner areas of the station and the interrogation rooms, Logan rocked back and forth on his heels whistling, *Home On the Range*. I almost stopped him—he was whistling in a way that I've never heard a human whistle before, with two tones seemingly sounding out together in harmony, but I decided to let it go. The sound was enchanting—who cared what these people might think.

Time crawled by while we waited. Logan appeared unconcerned and waited patiently. I, on the other hand, checked the clock a few times every minute.

Ten minutes later, we heard a loud chink of metal against metal and then the door opened.

"Sorry to keep you waiting, I'm Lieutenant Parker." He caught Logan's infectious smile and shook his hand, while Logan introduced us.

Lieutenant Parker was maybe a few years older than me, and he was cute enough that he made my toes want to curl up.

It's too bad his face fell when he looked in my direction. He stiffened and didn't offer me his hand.

The curse of a damaged soul. Since my soul had been ripped out last fall, and then shoved, broken, back into my body, there was no way I could ever make a good first impression.

"Follow me this way," Lieutenant Parker said, leading us through a small maze of hallways.

"We're going to need to speak with the gentleman alone," I said when Lieutenant Parker stopped outside an ugly green door.

"That's what we were told over the phone." His voice had an edge to it. "Cameras are off, and the room behind the glass is empty."

"Would you show us?" Logan asked.

Lieutenant Parker shrugged and led us to the next door and opened it. Sure enough, it was empty.

"He's all yours," Lieutenant Parker said.

Logan stopped for a minute when we entered the room. "Yep, sounds empty."

We turned our attention to the lar in front of us. He was less beautiful in person. Mostly, he looked like a kid that had a hard night.

I introduced Logan and myself. "Tell me about last night, Bill."

"I've told you all again and again," Bill said.

"We're with AIR," I said.

This didn't make Bill any happier. Looking uncomfortable, he went into his story. "It was a normal night, or at least I thought it was. I went over to my girlfriend's house, and we hung out for a while. Met up with some friends at a bar—"

"Were any of these friends your roommates?" I asked.

"Nah," Bill said, eyeing Logan who was leaning against a wall.

It looked like Logan was watching, but I couldn't tell if he was actually paying attention. His head was bouncing slightly up and down as if he had a song stuck on replay.

"They had other plans for the night," Bill said.

"Any idea what those plans were?" I asked.

"Oliver had a date, and Zeek and Raj were going to a club."

"Did Oliver go home with his date?" I asked.

"He wasn't home when I came back and crashed out. Zeek and Raj never made it home either."

I casually tapped a finger against my temple, and Logan came forward. Our partnership was like a well-oiled machine. One of us would indicate for me to read and Logan would slide in and take over. I closed my eyes while Logan asked questions.

"Tell me a little about you," Logan said. The elf was so genuine in his interest that Bill didn't hesitate.

While they talked, I concentrated on opening my mind to the smallest bit of the Path I could manage. When I opened my eyes, the room took on a new texture. The room contained layered scars of past emotions. It took longer than I expected to sort through them.

"I'm majoring in English," Bill said. "Moved here about three years ago from Chicago. Got the apartment with the guys last year."

"Do you believe in ghosts?" Logan asked.

"Um, I— Ghosts?" Bill asked.

"Do you think they're real?"

"I guess so. I mean, I'm here, so I guess there are things that can't be explained," Bill said.

I watched the conversation unfold through the rolling imprint of the Path. The old influences in the room stopped becoming an issue when I concentrated on Bill. He was scared and nervous, which was to be expected. I would be, too, if I were on his side of the table.

"Tell me about the unexplained," Logan said.

"Um, it's, well, things happen. Bumps in the night, lights in the sky. You see all sorts of things on the Internet. I'm not like some crazy guy who hunts things down. I don't think Bigfoot is hiding out in the woods of the North West or anything. We talk about things from time to time, that's all."

I'd hate to break the news to him, but the closest Bigfoot lived in southern South America. They had moved out of North America about thirty years ago.

Bill's Path looked odd. I wasn't sure what I was seeing, but it appeared as though the Path was pressing in on him. I could read everything coming off him, but things were falling towards him almost as much as they were drifting away. Was the Path imprinting on him instead of the other way around?

"Do you take drugs?" Logan asked.

"I told you, I'm not some crazy person. I don't believe in aliens, and I don't expect zombies to rise from graves." Sparks of orange popped into Bill's Path, but we didn't need that to see that he was anxious about the question. I tapped the table, seemingly lost in thought. Logan took the hint and grilled Bill on drugs until he admitted that he, along with his roommates, smoked a little pot from time to time.

Logan kept him talking, switching the subject as often as he felt like it. I think that's why he liked interrogations so much. You're supposed to switch topics to throw the person off. Logan was a natural.

"What time did you get home?" Logan asked.

"Around twelve-thirty. They weren't there when I got home."

"Anyone else around that knows where you were?" Logan asked.

"I don't think so, only my girlfriend."

"What classes did your friends take?"

They were talking about classes and school when Logan flipped subjects. "What's that around your neck?" Logan asked.

I, too, had noticed that Bill kept touching something under his shirt.

"It's ah, nothing, a necklace." Floods of orange and browns filled Bill's Path, strong enough that the room would hold another layer of emotion for a long time to come.

FIVE

Taking a closer look at the necklace, I saw that it held a Path of its own that had extended itself. This wasn't the dim Path of an object that moved through an area, this held power on its own. It was possible that my imagination was running away with me, but my fingers itched to investigate the piece further. Since we were in a police station, taking evidence without a proper procedure was frowned upon, so we'd have to work through the locals to get what we needed.

We stood and thanked Bill for his time. Some officers at the door appeared to be eager to get back in, and barely took the time to point us in the direction of Lieutenant Parker. Actually, it was Logan that was pointed in that direction. They were trying their best to ignore me.

"Are you all taking him away?" The lieutenant asked when we approached his desk.

"I don't think he's done anything," Logan said.

"Are you all holding him?" I asked.

"Everything looks normal," Lieutenant Parker said, "but

each of the victims disappeared for about thirty minutes before they turned up dead. We're trying to piece things together."

"We do want to investigate a little further, but we don't want to step on any toes," I added.

"What do you need?" The lieutenant's voice had sunk a level. Maybe he was being overworked.

"He's wearing something around his neck," I said. "We'd like to hold it for testing."

The lieutenant raised his eyebrows at us. "You want his necklace?"

"Yes. Taken into evidence with no one else laying hands on it," I added.

"We know how to take evidence." There was an edge to his voice. "Why didn't you collect it?"

I shrugged. "If you'd rather we take—"

"We'll take care of it." Lieutenant Parker left us standing.

Logan introduced himself to an officer at another desk. The man looked surprised at first, but the elf could manage to make friends anywhere he went. The man offered Logan a seat and before long, they were chatting.

I stood awkwardly, feeling completely out of place. People walked by, and I tried to stay out of the way.

A man bumped into me on his way by, despite having loads of room to walk. I almost apologized, but I bit my tongue. He walked into me; there was nothing for me to apologize for.

"Watch it, lady." His eyes and attitude dripped with disdain. He looked so young that he had probably walked out of the police academy yesterday.

I'd had enough aggravation for one day. "I'm pretty sure you have enough space to move around."

The man crossed his arms. "You don't belong in here."

"Right now, I'd rather be about anywhere else." I tried to

keep the derision out of my voice. I can't say that I was particularly successful, but it's the thought that counts.

"You have an issue with us?" He dropped his arms and stood up straighter.

"There a problem, officer?" Lieutenant Parker asked.

I looked over at Logan who had stood watching the debacle, but he took a seat and grinned before going back to his conversation.

"She's in the way." The officer smirked in my direction.

Lieutenant Parker frowned at him. "Before you say anything else, officer, it takes a minute to walk across the room. It's pretty obvious how you two bumped into each other."

The officer glared at me and walked away.

"Sorry about that," the lieutenant said, as he watched the officer walk away.

My aggravation drained away, leaving gloom in its wake. "It's okay. I'm getting used to it."

He raised an eyebrow and looked at me. "You shouldn't have to get used to treatment like that."

"I've had a charming reception all around so far," I said, feeling dejected.

Lieutenant Parker started to talk, and then stopped.

Logan joined us, and I tried to look professional.

"Don't worry about it," I said. "I'm sure it was a misunderstanding."

"I have your evidence." Lieutenant Parker was addressing both of us for the first time. "Sorry it took so long, but it had to be documented."

They probably took pictures from every angle and recorded the object in meticulous detail, all because we wanted to take a look.

Logan took the necklace and signed for it. "We'll send it

back your way as soon as we're done with it. Are you releasing the kid?"

"In a few minutes. He's looking over his official statement now."

"To follow up, we'd like to take a cursory review of the victims," I said.

"Sure, I'll call ahead and let them know you're coming," Lieutenant Parker said.

"Thank you," I said, my smile not as forged as it had been.

Lieutenant Parker looked like he was stuck in his own mind when he walked us out, but then with three possible homicides in one night, it was no wonder.

"Do you have all you need?" Lieutenant Parker asked.

"Yes," Logan said, "but it doesn't look like we have a case here. We'll ask someone to drop the evidence back to you in a few days."

"Feel free to stop by if you need anything else," Lieutenant Parker said.

"We don't do much work in town, but it was nice meeting you," Logan said.

Lieutenant Parker shook our hands. "It was nice to meet you, Agent Seale, and you, Agent Heidrich."

"Okay," I said, but my mind was already on our next stop, the hospital.

Logan didn't look bothered about going to the morgue. Standing next to me waiting to be let out, he was humming, and this time, it was music that humans could mimic.

A buzz and a loud clunk announced that we could leave.

"Agent Heidrich, can I have a word with you, in private?" Lieutenant Parker asked.

Logan winked at me. "I'll wait out front."

Wondering what Lieutenant Parker wanted, I waited until the door locked again.

"I wanted to apologize," Lieutenant Parker said.

I shrugged but softened the attitude by giving him a friendly look. "Like I said, it's no problem."

"I'd like to make it up to you."

"Really, there's nothing to make up for."

He looked me straight in the eyes. "I'd like to anyway."

I wanted to say there really was no need, but I didn't manage to get the first word out.

"Would you like to meet me for drinks tonight?" he asked.

Drinks? That was not the direction my mind had been working towards.

"If you're free," he added after I'd been silent for too long.

Was my face going red? "Um, sure. I mean, yes. I'd like that." Yep, it had to be red now.

"Do you know Royce? Over on 10th street? We could meet there around seven."

I'd heard the name, but was completely unfamiliar with the place. Thankfully, the Internet was my friend. "Sure, I'd like that."

Had I already said that?

"I'll see you at seven." Lieutenant Parker stepped around the corner, and the door buzzed again.

Walking out, my mind was far from the hospital. Had I been asked on a date, or was this him feeling bad for being rude?

I guess I'd find out tonight.

"Are you two getting together at some point?" Logan asked.

"You knew he was going to ask me out?" I asked.

"Well, I had to make sure he knew this might be his only chance. I wasn't sure how your side of the conversation would go. I know last fall—"

"We're meeting later tonight." I didn't want Logan to

move our discussion to last fall, so at the truck, I snatched the tablet up, and started discussing the case while Logan drove.

Hank let us know the victims were in the same morgue, and Lieutenant Parker called to tell them we would be stopping by.

In the basement of the hospital, I looked over the bodies while Logan talked to the man who had shown us around. The morgue had some vestiges of deep blue showing grief, but for the most part, the Path was as sterile as their cleaning fluids. The usual day-to-day Paths of people at work circulated through currents.

The hit-and-run was messy, so I concentrated hard on avoiding the damage and reading only Zeek's Path. It was fading, but everything appeared normal. There were no traces of anger or betrayal lurking around. Oliver was the same way, but Raj was another story. The Path peeled away from him as though afraid to touch him. An unnatural pocket of nothingness surrounded him.

"I was told it looked like this man died of natural causes. Is that what you've found?" I interrupted.

"Preliminary reports show no external causes of death, but he did suffer a small aneurysm. We ordered a tox screen, but that will take a couple of days. Too early to say it was natural, though, at least not with certainty."

I braced myself before opening the floodgates of the Path, allowing it to pour over me, amplified a thousand fold. The sterile morgue turned into a tapestry of color. Shapes moved around as the past came into view, overriding the present. Blurry images of doctors and nurses walked around, and sheeted gurneys were moved in and out of the room.

Pulling myself towards the present, I watched ghosted images of the three boys being brought into the room for us.

Raj's Path was a gaping hole, and worse. As his body was moved around, other patches of voided Path had sprung up.

Shivering, I moved the Path further forward into the present. It was more difficult than I anticipated, but the blank spots drove me forward. This read too close to what had or hadn't surrounded the gnome, Am. Once I managed to get close to the present, I saw that the Path regained its typical flow. It was lighter in texture and color, but it had reclaimed the empty spaces.

Closing my eyes, I shoved the Path aside. When I opened them, I blinked rapidly as the dull colors of the real world returned. Logan and I left, thanking the man for his time.

"What did you find?" Logan asked.

"It's like Am. The Path around him is a blank slate. Do you think Raj knew about the Lost?" I asked.

"Most people wouldn't be able to keep the Lost secret if they stumbled into it. Bill swore that no one knew about him, apart from another Lost on campus. I doubt that Raj knew anything. We can have Hank dive into his background to be safe."

Logan called it in as we left the building. Once in the truck, I added to the report that Kyrian gave me, giving the agency an instant update on the investigation.

"According to the report," I said, "Raj and Zeek disappeared after entering a club downtown. Let's go there and see if we can find out where they might have gone."

"Is this town big enough to have a club?" Logan asked.

"We're turning into a city, at least when all the college students are around," I said. "Haven't you noticed that businesses and subdivisions have been creeping toward our neighborhood in the country?"

"Might be time to consider moving further out. Get a few more acres, spread out a bit," Logan said.

"What you mean is that you want a place large enough to get your own horse."

Logan laughed. It had such a musical quality to it that it held me briefly entranced.

Feeling lighter, I looked back at the case file. "Should we bring Rider in on the case?"

"We can ask him to check it out later."

Downtown wasn't busy, and we were able to park the truck on the street.

Logan hummed and watched people pass by as I struggled to pull up the Path and coerce it to flow into the past. In the morgue, the past popped up without trying. Here, it fought me every step of the way. The weather was cool, but it didn't take long for me to break into a sweat.

Since hundreds of people had walked through this area, each leaving their mark, the past would help me pinpoint which flowing trail we needed to follow. By the time I sifted through the evening, I was fatigued from the effort. Too much use of the Path in one day was draining me.

Once in the past, it was easier to focus what I was looking for and follow the flow without burning as much energy. Zeek and Raj left the club. When they parted ways, I followed the ghosted past of Raj. He walked towards campus, pausing a few times briefly on the way. University Park held many old Paths, but as he continued through, he appeared to be alone. We moved past stately old buildings used for lecture halls and classes, but I barely noticed them. When we reached the front of the law library, Raj's Path stopped.

He was there and then gone with nothing in between. No

one else was around, and the Path held no memory of him after that time.

I walked around in circles, catching stray bits of Path, trying to see if they tied to our case. It wasn't until Logan put a hand on my shoulder that I fell into the flow of the Path, moving to the present. For the first time in a long while, I was able to stop Reading the Path without much issue.

Well, it wasn't any trouble until it was gone. When the world turned ashen, I swayed, and then sat down hard on the ground having worked myself into exhaustion. There are records of other Readers following Paths into death. Thankfully, my partner knew when I'd had more than I could take.

"I sent Rider back for the truck," Logan said. "You look more tired than a cowboy at the end of a long drive."

"When did Rider get here?" I asked. My eyes felt like they were burning.

"I called him after we left the club. He stopped by the morgue to catch some scents. He joined us on Raj's trail. When I saw you were about done for the day, I sent him back for the truck. He can track down where Oliver went through the evening, then come back to follow Zeek's trail."

Logan stared as I hauled myself to my feet.

"I think I may have let you go too far today," Logan said.

"I'll be okay," I lied. Exhaustion leaked out of my pores, and the chilled weather was sinking back in its place.

We heard screeching tires and looked up in time to see Rider swerving around a car. The front tire of the truck jumped the curb and Rider came to a stop in front of us—half was on the street and half on the sidewalk. I must have looked worse than I thought because he jumped out and came around to meet us.

"You look like a ghost," Rider said. "Let me help you into the truck."

"I can make it to the truck on my own," I said.

Rider kept moving towards me.

"Boy, you are never going to learn," Logan chuckled.

"Rider," I snapped, "if you pick me up and put me in the truck I am going to tranq you."

Rider stopped and looked from me to Logan, confused. Logan laughed louder.

"You're not helping," I said to Logan.

I teetered, but there was no way I was letting anyone see me fall. If I couldn't control what my power did to me, I wasn't much use in the field. I certainly didn't want one of my partners to feel the need to save me from myself.

"I'll drive," Logan said, patting Rider on the back and taking the keys.

Rider looked confused and climbed in next to me. I decided to ignore the confusion and move on.

"Did you find anything on the trail?" I asked.

Logan turned the heaters up full blast and drove back to Rider's car.

"Nothing," Rider said, "since one of the deaths was similar to the gnome death, I thought I might find the same oddity in the area, but it was clean. There was no one around him when he died."

"Maybe we should check the Path where they died as well," I suggested.

Logan raised an eyebrow but didn't say a word.

Right, I thought. Stupid idea. "Tomorrow?" I suggested.

"We'll put it on the agenda," Logan said.

"Meet us at the house?" I asked as we drove up to Rider's car.

"I will meet you there," he said as he got out.

"Can we grab some coffee on the way back? I need a large dose of caffeine." I stretched out in the seat.

"Thinking of staying up late tonight?" Logan asked.

I sighed. "I should file this report. Plus, I want to pick Rider's brain more about the gnome scents and the trails here."

"You may be forgetting something. At around seven tonight," Logan said.

The reminder caused pixies to riot in my stomach. "There's a lot to do. I should probably call and cancel."

CHAPTER

SIX

"All that work will be there in the morning," Logan said. "Go out. Have some fun."

Biting my lip, I flipped through a few pages of the case file without paying attention. "I haven't been out with someone in ages. I'm not even sure what adults do when they go on dates."

Logan snickered.

"Okay, a first date, what do they do on a first date?"

"It's drinks. Talk and get to know him. You're both in similar fields, you have stuff in common."

Shrugging was the only response I gave.

Logan switched gears. "We need to go out and check on Essy this week."

This was a much safer topic. "Sure. The fairies have had a long winter. Maybe we can run out and see her tomorrow. *After* we go through the Paths of the other victims."

"Maybe we can take the horses out this time," Logan said, ignoring my comment.

"Hmm, maybe."

We ordered my coffee in a drive-thru and went home.

"Gerald is taking another art class," Logan said.

"How does he like it?" I asked.

Gerald was Logan's youngest son. The youngest of three children. From the conversations we'd had, I was able to glean that Logan's wife died not long after Gerald was born. Not long was a relative term. It could mean up to twenty-five years or so to an elf.

"He came home with an easel, a bunch of canvas, and about thirty different tubes of colors. He's pretty enthusiastic."

"What is he painting?" I asked.

"Anything that will hold still long enough," Logan said.

Laughing helped to relieve some of my dating apprehension. I downed the caffeine hoping to stimulate some brain cells so I could have a decent conversation that night. The drink perked me up, but I went straight to the kitchen when we got home. Gran already had a pot of coffee brewing.

"How you can drink caffeine in the afternoon is beyond me," she said as way of greeting.

"I need to make sure I'm awake this evening," I said.

Rider was pulling out plates and setting the table.

Gran beamed. "Dinner is ready for that very reason."

"Any idea if it's going to go well?" I asked, willing Gran to have a premonition of my evening.

"No idea." The look Gran gave me didn't hint if she was telling the truth or not.

Logan and I helped set the table.

Not wanting to think about this evening, I switched our conversation to the case as we settled into dinner. "I wanted to ask you again, Rider, about the trip to the gnome hole. You said the area was off, but you didn't smell anything?"

"I find it hard to explain. It is almost as if something should have been there, or had been there, and was then taken away."

Rider paused as though thinking that over. "That is not quite it either."

"Have you ever experienced anything that you could compare it to?" Logan asked.

"No," Rider said.

"And you didn't sense anything like that again today? Not even the last part of the excursion?" I almost said the last body, but stopped for Gran's sake.

Gran wouldn't care if we talked about bodies. If guests wanted to talk about corpses, then she'd be happy to let them, but I didn't want her to be too deeply mixed up in AIR work. I'd been loose about it in the past, but I was trying to keep work at work.

"Nothing like it," Rider responded.

While I mulled over what Rider said, I changed the subject. "How was your day, Gran?"

"Susan and I went shopping and then out to visit Morgan. I invited him to dinner on Sunday."

Morgan Renner was a troll that Gran got together with from time to time. He was smart for his species. Actually, almost any species would call him smart. He worked as a software development consultant. From home, of course. Smart or not, he looked like a troll, so he didn't go out often.

"It'll be good to see Morgan again," I said.

"You'll see another person from your past soon," Gran said.

I waited for more, but it didn't come. Thinking of Vincent, my heart beat faster.

"Any idea who it will be?" I asked, trying to sound casual.

"Sorry," Gran said, "I don't think it's him."

"It could be anyone," I said, trying to hide my disappointment. "I've had lots of friends."

That wasn't exactly true. My powers came on late in high school, and I wasn't able to keep many friends. Being a Reader made college a living hell. A person's Path said a lot about them, and I made and lost friends because of it.

After dinner, as I washed the dishes, I thought of the friends I had made since working at AIR. Even some of my casual friends knew about my gifts, accepted them, and accepted me.

Once the dishes were done, I excused myself. Time was moving on, and I had to get ready. Thoughts of Vincent flickered past as I went upstairs, but I mentally shoved them aside.

LIEUTENANT PARKER ASKED me to call him Ethan when we met. Once we were seated, with drinks in hand, we tried to make small talk in that awkward way people do when they don't know anything about each other.

"Do you live in the area?" Ethan asked.

"Yeah, I'm from here actually. I live outside of town now. You?" It was so much easier if he asked a question and I asked him to answer the same one.

"My family owns some land outside of town. I lived here for a while as a kid and moved back a few years ago."

I latched onto that. "Did you go to school in town?"

"East End Elementary. We moved when I was in second grade."

"I went to Crates for elementary."

He nodded, smiling. It was a nice smile, one that I wouldn't mind watching for a while.

"How about college?" he asked.

"I started here. They have a good accountancy program, but I transferred out of state for my senior year."

"You're an accountant?" He looked surprised.

"I used to be, but I was looking for a new line of work before my first year of work was up. How about you?"

"I went into the Navy for a few years and went to school while I was in service for the most part. When I got out, I went straight into law enforcement."

"How did you like the Navy?" I asked.

"It wasn't quite what I was looking for, but I like working for the local police department. How's your current job?"

Knowing that I should have steered clear of questions about jobs, I cleared my throat to stall for time. "Most days, it's good, and when they're not, at least I know we're working to make things better."

"I've never met someone who worked for the Department of Treasury unless they were with Secret Service. I didn't realize there were other agencies."

Once again, I found myself struggling with what to say. "It's, uh, specialized." It was lame, and I found myself studying my drink.

"So, what else do you do? Outside of work, I mean."

I'm sure Ethan noticed the grateful look I flashed him. "Not much, to be honest. Visiting friends, hiking, cooking, well, mostly baking really." Trying to think of anything else was impossible. Was that really all I did outside of work?

"I went to Tennessee a few weeks ago, and they have some great trails in the mountains."

"Hey, Parker!" A few men walked up; the one talking was obviously drunk. "How are ya?"

"Evening, Ike." Ethan looked less than thrilled.

All the men, except Ike, moved on to another table and waved down a waitress.

"Come have a drink with us," Ike said.

Ethan looked embarrassed. "Thanks, but I'm already having one."

"With her? She's cute, but..." Ike apparently had a problem getting beyond that.

"Excuse me for a minute," Ethan said to me. He stood up, took his friend Ike, and led him over to the other table.

The words, 'She's cute, but,' started playing in my mind. Ike's reaction to me had been better than Ethan's, better than most really, at least out of the people that don't ignore me completely. It wasn't exactly the words I wanted to hear while out with someone, so while Ethan's back was turned, I took a large drink, trying to shorten my visit.

"Sorry about that." Ethan sat back down across from me, looking abashed.

"It's no problem." It sounded fake, even to me.

Ethan leaned in. "He lost his wife about a month ago. He's a little lost, I guess."

"Oh, I'm sorry to hear that. If you want to go—"

"No," Ethan said quickly, "no. Only, I didn't want you to get the wrong impression."

His worried expression and sincerity made me want to take his hand. "No wrong impressions," I said.

"Can I get you another drink?" Ethan asked.

Crap, in theory, it had been a good plan.

I wanted to say something clever about only having one alcoholic drink, but I had nothing, and the way he looked at me, made my stomach flutter. "I wonder if they have coffee."

Before I could get the words out, Ethan was frowning, but he was looking behind me.

"Parker." It sounded like Ike was right behind me.

I turned and then there was beer. Not the good kind, like oh, say, anything in a glass. This was the bad kind that ended up all over me.

Gasping, I turned fully towards Ike. He appeared confused by what had happened, which made me wonder if it had been an accident, or if he was confused because he couldn't believe he had done it on purpose.

Ethan jumped up with the two napkins we had at our table, Ike babbled while one of his friends tried to pull him away, and I began to realize that people were turning to watch. Even without the Path, I felt the mixed bag of emotion begin to weigh me down.

My face began to turn red, and I felt the need to get out of there before drawing any more attention to myself. I grabbed my jacket, thanked Ethan, assured Ike on the way that I knew it was an accident, and then got the hell out of there.

The temperature had dropped, and as much as I didn't want to get my jacket soaked with beer, I was well aware of how cold wet clothes can get in the early spring. I had a momentary pang of guilt about leaving so abruptly, and without paying, so once I ruined my jacket, I moved a short way from the door and leaned against the building, waiting. It was surprisingly peaceful with the turmoil and noise trapped in the bar. It was too cold for many people to be outside for longer than necessary.

After a few minutes, I figured Ethan must have been talking with Ike. I pushed myself off the wall and tried to remember where I parked my car.

"I didn't expect you to be out here," Ethan said.

Embarrassment tried to creep up, but I nudged it away. After everything had already gone wrong, it was much easier to relax. How much worse could it get?

"It seemed rude to leave," I said.

Ethan grinned. "My friend just poured a drink on you, and you're worried about being rude?"

"It's not like you asked him to do it." I gave him a wry look. "I mean, you didn't, right?"

Ethan chuckled. "No, but I keep some clumsy friends around. You must be freezing. Can I walk you to your car?"

"Sure. I'm, um, that way."

We moved up the hill in silence.

"Tonight didn't go well, did it?" He sounded hesitant.

I laughed, not sure if he meant it as a question, but I answered him anyway. "It most certainly did not. I mean, I don't go out often, but I'm pretty sure this was not a successful first... time out for drinks." I almost said date. Did drinks count as a date?

"I'm around the corner," I said.

"Do you want to try again?" Ethan spoke quickly.

I looked down at the ground and thought about it. He was cute, friendly, and there was a chance we might have things in common. Now that he was familiar with me, my soul didn't affect him at all.

I crossed my arms across my chest as though cold, so Ethan wouldn't see them shake with nerves. "No beer involved?"

Ethan's eyes caught mine. "I promise I will not send you home smelling like a brewery next time."

"Don't make promises you can't keep," I said.

"Dinner?"

"Let's give dinner a try."

"Tomorrow night?"

"In a hurry?" I gestured across the street in the general direction of my car. "I'm over there."

"I'm afraid you'll really start to think about tonight and change your mind."

I laughed. "That's not a bad idea."

"Are you free?" Ethan asked.

"I am now, but work can be... tricky."

Ethan nodded and looked up and down the street. "Work

could pull us away at any time. We could agree now, not to let it bother us when we're called away."

"Even if it leaves one of us twiddling our thumbs at a restaurant?"

"I'll always call you," Ethan said.

"That might work. I'll do the same."

"Are you okay to drive?" Ethan asked.

"Yes, not that any cop in the world is going to believe me if I happen to get pulled over."

Ethan chuckled. "Flash your badge and I'm sure you could probably explain and get out of it."

"Oh no, if I get pulled over, I'll have them call you to explain."

He flashed a grin that made my heart beat faster. "I'll wait by the phone."

I had no idea how to say goodbye at the end of a date, but since I was freezing, I figured I could get away with leaving in a hurry. "See you tomorrow night." I slid into my seat, cranked up the heat, and then drove away.

Logan, Rider, and I decided to begin our day early in the spot where Oliver had broken his neck. Despite our destination, I had a smile that I couldn't quite shake.

Logan took notice and on the drive over decided to ask, "Last night go well?"

"Not at all." I laughed behind the words. "A beer spilled over me, and I left smelling like I had been at a frat party gone bad."

"Why the good mood?" Logan asked.

"We're trying again. Dinner. Tonight."

"Good to hear," Logan said.

When we arrived, there was no crime scene tape, and everyone was walking around, business as usual. I didn't waste any time diving into the Path. Since I was trying to pressure myself into the past, I let the full power wash over me. Too little sleep and too much coffee made my stomach agitated, as the flow of colors and shapes rushed by. After a struggle, I found the time I was looking for. Standing still in a surging river wasn't easy, so I could only stay rooted to the spot for a few seconds before being tossed back into the present.

The turbulence had taken my breath away, so I took a few moments before letting the others know what I saw.

That also gave me time to sort through the fragments I witnessed. "It was almost as if the Path jumped into his way."

"I am not sure what that means," Rider said.

"Neither am I," I admitted.

"Have you ever seen anything like it?" Logan asked.

I tried to think of a comparison. "No, it's almost like someone made a wave on the Path and that landed on the victim."

"What can do that?" Rider asked.

"I'm not sure," I said.

"Let's go check the other site, see if there are any similarities," Logan said.

We drove across town to where the hit-and-run occurred. All the while, I tried picking apart what I had seen. Once we arrived at our suspected crime scene, apprehension hit me. The roadway was busy, and our spot was right at the edge.

"We won't let you wander into traffic," Logan said.

I'm sure Logan couldn't read minds, but there were times, like when he answered a worry before I formed the question, when he made me wonder.

After briefly meditating, I jumped into the Path.

The raging current caught me up and propelled me

forward. Rider made a grunt of surprise, and when I looked at him, he was clearly standing in front of me. Logan, however, disappeared and cars zipped by faster than a gnome.

I tried to gain control and move back to the present, but the Path was persistent. Cars dissolved from view and the sun fell and rose so fast it was impossible to follow. As the roadway crumbled beneath me, I fell to the ground. Rider, still solid, knelt down next to me. We stared at each other as trees rose and died around us and then he spoke, but the sound was lost before it reached me. He cocked his head, reached out, grabbed me, and then tugged me into his arms.

With a slingshot motion, my world pitched. The Path went from some distant future into the present in an instant, and then it abandoned me altogether.

My stomach took longer to catch up. I shoved myself away from Rider and lurched far enough away to lose my breakfast. Eyes clenched shut, I rubbed my temples against the buildup of throbbing pressure.

It was a while before I could stand again. Rider was leaning against the truck, not looking at me. Logan, on the other hand, was pale and rigid.

"Whatever you did, let's not try that again." It was rare to hear so much tension in the elf's voice.

I shook my head. Vertigo threatened to toss me back to the ground, so I closed my eyes again until I was steady. "It wasn't something I tried. The Path dragged me along for the ride."

"Your gran would have had my ears if not for Rider," Logan said.

Looking from him to Rider and back again, I said, "I couldn't get back to the hit-and-run. I went forward instead." I'm sure I didn't want to know what happened, but I couldn't be left in the dark either. "What am I missing?"

Logan looked uncertain. "I wish I could say for sure. You got hazy around the edges, and then you were gone."

"I'm not sure I follow." I rubbed my forehead, trying to throw off the ache and take in what Logan was saying.

"I need to go to the Sanctuary," Rider said. Not looking at us, he got into the back seat of the truck without another word.

"For the case, we can work with what we have for now," Logan said, "but we need to talk about this."

"When you say disappear, do you mean... gone?" My voice was lower, and I watched Rider.

"As in no longer here."

"Did Rider?"

"No, he was as solid as you should have been."

"He was for me too," I said.

"What I want to know is where you went?"

"I didn't move. Not really anyway." Logan didn't look satisfied, so I grabbed a guess out of the air. "Maybe the Path hid me? It was strong."

Logan appeared to mull that over. "What happened didn't have anything to do with the case, right?"

"No." I wish I were as certain as I sounded, but the truth was, I had no idea what happened or why. "Not a thing."

"Leave it off the report." Not waiting for a response, Logan walked away.

SEVEN

"We'll check in on Essy," Logan said when I joined them in the truck.

Rider said nothing.

Worried about Rider, I kept an eye on him. "I'll call Travis and let him know we're on our way."

The Sanctuary was a government-owned area in the middle of nowhere, and we relocated the Lost there on a temporary or permanent basis. Essy was the Speaker for a tribe of fairies that were permanent residents.

After calling Travis, I could have begun my report, since other than Logan's humming, things were quiet in the truck. I felt shaky, though. I had no idea what had happened at the second crime scene, or why. The Path can take a Reader forward or back, but moving forward in time was rare, and either direction you go, you're in the real world—only the overlaying Path changes.

Except for today.

We made one stop so I could pick up a piece of fruit for the fairies, but it wasn't until we reached the Sanctuary that I felt steadier, although the sight of the horses didn't help. My limited experiences riding had been less than stellar.

Without a word, Rider walked past the horses, which bucked and moved out of his way, and then he disappeared into the woods. Travis tried to calm the horses while watching Rider retreat.

I passed a worried look at Logan who shrugged. Once the horses were calm, we approached and took the reins from Travis.

"I take it Rider won't be going," Travis said.

"No, he'll meet up with us later," Logan said. "Want to join us?"

"Sure, we're not expecting anyone out here until this evening," Travis said.

Logan patted the horse. "Let's saddle up."

I eyed my horse suspiciously before getting on. "Is someone relocating here?" I knew the horse was tame, but my heart thumped harder as I clumsily jumped into the saddle.

Travis flicked his reins and led the way. "Not yet, but another team wants to test temperature and conditions at the lake. I'm not sure what for yet."

"How's Essy doing?" Logan asked, changing the subject.

"The family is doing well," Travis said.

The ride took us through woods and stretches of fields filled with prairie grass. By the time we reached trees with denser foliage, my headache was gone, but my thighs were protesting from the ride. We dismounted, tethered the horses loosely to the trees, and then continued on foot. Spring was stretching into the area, and the canopy of branches above us was starting to fill back in with greenery. There was a chill saturating the air, but the warmth was nudging it away. In fact, the further we went into the woods, the warmer it grew and the denser the greenery became.

Whispers of wings on the wind, which could be mistaken for the buzz of bees, began to override other forest sounds. The further we walked, the louder the noise became.

Logan stopped. "We seek an audience with the Speaker."

There must have been enough fairies around to state our purpose.

From the left we heard, "Logan, I recognize you as keeper of the AIR treaty." Essy had arrived.

Some treaty, I thought, as dust drifted down onto me. The greatest defense a fairy had was the woods they lived in. The dust that I was trying very hard to ignore was a powdered form of poisonous plants from the area. They hadn't found anything I'm allergic to, but have been persistent in their efforts ever since we met.

Even though I knew the answer, I looked to see if Travis and Logan were getting the same welcome, but there were no fairies hovering above them.

"We will oversee any complaints or requests," Logan said, maintaining the proper greeting.

"We have neither complaint nor request."

With that out of the way, Logan dropped the formality.

"How was your winter?" Logan asked.

Essy landed on a small branch. "It was difficult, but we prevailed."

I stepped forward and held out an orange. "I brought something for you." Fairies loved sweet foods, and the orange would be exotic since they couldn't forage for them locally.

Essy glared at me and made angry chirping noises.

Feeling deflated, I handed the orange off to Travis and tried not to be too upset by the exchange. No fairy wanted to talk to me since my soul had been ripped out last fall. Essy knew me long before the incident last fall, but there was no changing how she felt about me now.

In the end, they took the orange from Travis after he ate two pieces to prove that it wasn't poisonous. A walk with Rider would have been more productive, even in his mood.

While Logan and Travis finished their visit with fairies, I took a step back, wiped the dust off the shoulders of my jacket, and watched my partner interact with Essy. I was relieved when he wrapped the visit up, and we walked back to the horses.

"Sorry about Essy," Travis said.

"She'll come around eventually." I held no real hope for that to happen, but I didn't want Travis feeling sorry for me.

We rode back, and I tried to hide my disappointment with the fairies, and my disdain for horses by talking with Travis.

Rider was leaning against the truck when we returned. He was sweaty but wasn't breathing hard. I'd never seen Rider in any other form than the one he wore every day, but I was curious if he ran on two legs or four. It sounded like an invasive question, so I raised the subject.

As soon as the horse stopped, I jumped off.

Logan remained in the saddle. "I'll help Travis with the horses, and then we can go to the office." He was always reluctant to leave the saddle. I'm sure he'd keep a horse in his backyard if he had space.

I thanked Travis and handed off the reins. Logan was humming when the two rode away.

"How was Essy?" Rider asked.

"Everyone was okay," I said.

Rider wrinkled his nose. "Poison Ivy?"

Sighing, I wiped off my shoulders again. "Probably." Rider looked more amiable than he had when we arrived. "Uh, I'm not sure what went on earlier, but I wanted to thank you."

"I was able to help, so I did," Rider said.

"You're okay, though?"

"It was—there were no side effects," he said.

I glanced towards the stables to see if Logan was on his way. "Do you know what happened?"

Rider hesitated. "I do not."

Werewolves have a distinct view of friendship, so I was fairly certain Rider wouldn't lie to me. It was hard to get into their inner circle, but once you were there, you were friends for life. Each of us held up our end of the friendship and always assumed that the other would do the same. I was learning what that meant.

I think he was holding something back, but I didn't press the issue.

When we made it back to the office, Rider went to the command room to check in with Hank, while Logan and I went to the clinic upstairs. No major catastrophes had befallen field agents or the Lost that day, so the doctor was available.

"I'm assuming you all are not here for a checkup," the doctor said as we walked in.

AIR had a few medical rooms on the second floor of the office. When field agents get hurt, there is not always a way to explain the injuries. You can't go to the hospital when a demon injects you with their venom, so we see Dr. Yelton. He also oversees care of the Lost.

"Good morning, Dr. Yelton," I said. "We're here to see what you have on Am. What can you tell us?"

"There's not much to tell, really," he said pulling out a folder. "The report will be entered tonight, but I expected the lack of information would pull you into the office."

"Lack of information?" I asked.

"I oversaw the gnome autopsy that Dr. Taylor performed at MyTH. They have a good facility, and Dr. Taylor did a fine job. The problem is that there was nothing to find."

"I'm not sure I'm following you, Doc," Logan said.

"We screened for toxic chemicals, did a thorough examination, and autopsy. We couldn't find anything wrong with the gnome," Dr. Yelton said.

"What did she die of?" I asked.

"Nothing," Dr. Yelton said. "There was nothing that she died of."

I blinked a few times, unable to process. Logan appeared to struggle too.

"What could do that?" Logan asked.

"I'm looking into other cases. It appears that her heart slowed down and stopped without causing any trauma to the organ or blood vessels around them. When anyone dies, you can see the damage that death causes on the body."

"Could it be a gnome thing?" I asked. My gnome research hadn't made it far.

"Nothing that we're aware of, but we are researching the issue. There is a problem with that line of logic as well, though. Yesterday, a file came across my desk. The preliminary looks the same."

"Raj?" I asked.

Dr. Yelton flipped over a file. "Yes, that's the name."

"What about the other two? Did their autopsies seem normal?" I asked.

The doctor leaned back in his chair. "His friends died from trauma caused by their accidents. We've received several blood and tissue samples from the bodies. We are going to continue to test for lesser-known toxins as well as toxins related to the Lost. I'll let you know if I find anything new."

"Thanks, Doc," Logan said.

"Thank you, Dr. Yelton." I followed Logan back downstairs, running the facts over in my mind, trying to figure out what it meant.

Rider was waiting for us in the control room. "Clancy filed

his report on the necklace you received from Bill. He did not find anything."

"Nothing?" I didn't mean to sound unbelieving. "Sorry, but this case is running into a brick wall."

"Has it been released?" Logan asked.

Rider looked unsure. "The report ended with currently in evidence and was followed by the word release."

"It sounds like it's still with us. Let's take one last go at it while it's here," Logan said, "to be thorough."

We went down a few flights of stairs, past the basement and into the first sub-basement. There were cavernous rooms, including one that held evidence. Another sub-floor down held our man-made portals, which must have been closed. When they were open, the air vibrated and set me on edge. I don't notice it much upstairs, but down here, it would be obvious, even with my mind churning over the case.

"Nothing gets thrown away here, does it?" I asked.

The evidence room wasn't tall, but it was enormous in length and width.

"Mostly, I think it gets shifted around," Logan said. "Twenty years ago or so, I saw them load a bunch of stuff and take it away. I think it went to a different storage area."

A musty scent that reminded me of stale old books wafted over us.

"I'm never down here much," I admitted. "It looks like the rows are dated, though."

Rider looked at the ceiling. "I am not sure that I like being so far below the ground."

I read a note card held in a silver plaque, with the dates 1992.7-1993.2. "We'll make it quick, if we can."

Logan led the way. "Oldest to the left, moving to the newest on the right."

Old fluorescent lights buzzed overhead as we walked the length of the room. Each row was marked with dates.

"Here's the current year." Logan turned down an aisle.

There were boxes and tagged bags lining the shelves. A few of the boxes had our names on them from other cases. I lingered on the box that was signed with Vincent's name, before silently berating myself and moving on. He'd contact me or he wouldn't. There was no reason to dwell on it.

Obviously, my heart and head were in two different places.

Moving further down the aisle, I focused again on the current case.

Logan stopped in front of a tiny evidence bag. "No finger-prints, no lingering residue."

"Clancy looked the item over. There was nothing he could use from it," Rider said.

"Clancy's good," Logan said, "if there were anything there, I would expect him to find it. But, even clairvoyants can be fooled."

Rider picked up the evidence bag and turned it over and over in his hands. "Can we open this?"

"Feel free," Logan said, "it's been released. Don't touch it, though."

Rider opened the bag. His nose wrinkled after sniffing the contents. "It smells like Clancy and..."

"And?" I asked.

"Sterile is the best description I have," Rider said.

"It was worth a try," Logan said.

"Yeah, I guess it was a dead end. Still—" I closed my eyes and took a few steadying breaths.

"You sure you want to do that again today?" Logan asked.

"It's fine," I said, concentrating. The Path flared up around us.

Each item on the shelf radiated color. When I turned

around to look at the shelves behind us, I could see that many items held a distinct Path. In a far corner of the room, brilliant blue stood out like a volcano, even from this distance. A bright incessant Path spread up from the floor, but I ignored it, thinking of the portals below.

A well of gold sprang from Logan's core, like a small glittering sun, and wrapped itself around him. Worried blues and greens twirled through.

"It's fine," I repeated again, and gave him a look that I hoped was reassuring.

Rider was a fluctuating flow of greens and browns that flickered between instinctual animal and human.

"What's the necklace look like?" Logan asked.

Focusing on the small package that Rider had put back on the shelf, I could see the trail he had left behind, but concentrating hard, I looked back further.

"It's blank," I said. "I can see where other people have been near it, but Clancy's right, the necklace doesn't tell us anything."

Sliding the Path away, the real world came into clearer focus, but with color drained away.

"Let's get out of here," Logan said.

The sterile carpet hushed our footsteps as we exited. We didn't shut off the lights. I'd hate to think someone else might have come in while we were here. The thought of trapping someone in this vault with the lights out made my skin crawl.

"Remind me to bring a flashlight next time we come down here, just in case."

⁂

"It's good to see you again." Ethan stood to greet me when I found him waiting at the restaurant. "You look nice."

"Thank you," I said, taking a seat. "It's good to see you too."

Trying to find the thin line between looking nice and looking like you were trying too hard was one I was never proficient with. Lately, though, my work attire had improved along with my work ethic, so it wasn't too hard to find an outfit to wear.

The waitress appeared at the table with a pitcher of ice water and asked if Ethan would like some, poured his water, and left the pitcher on the table. Then she said she'd be right back with a menu.

My good mood faltered, but Ethan poured me a glass of water and didn't appear to give it a second thought. When the waitress came back with one menu, for Ethan, he handed it to me and asked for another. She apologized, looking genuinely sorry, and later, when she brought Ethan a drink and forgot my coffee, she also appeared very apologetic.

Ethan watched the waitress walk away, presumably to get my coffee, and he looked nervous.

We hadn't had the chance to talk yet, so I dived in. "How was your day?" It was an awful question, but it would hopefully get the conversation started.

"It wasn't bad. We closed the case your team was interested in, so I have a light caseload right now. How was yours?"

My mind flashed on this morning, being thrown forward in the Path and disappearing in time, but I shoved it firmly away and replaced it with smaller facts that I could talk about. "We mostly drove around today and spent some time at the office."

Ethan began to talk, but our waitress appeared.

"Would you like to order?" Her voice was friendly, but she did not come bearing coffee.

"Oh, are you ready?" Ethan asked me.

"Sure."

We gave our order, and I checked after the coffee. The waitress apologized again and took off for the kitchen to place our order. Ethan tapped his fingers on the table and watched her walk away.

Grabbing another harmless detail of my day, I threw out, "My partner did manage to convince me to get on a horse."

"A horse?" Ethan's fingers stopped moving, and his good humor returned. "Do you keep those around the office?"

I laughed, but then I thought, didn't we have horses at the Farm? "We weren't at the office, we had to go off road and Logan will take any excuse to be around horses."

"He's a fan of riding?"

"Yes, but I'm sure he also gets some entertainment value out of watching my attempts."

"I'm sure you can't be too bad with horses."

"My first experience was, oh wow, about a year ago now, and things didn't go well. My horse ended up at the stables long before I did."

"You fell off?" Ethan asked.

"Bucked off."

"Ouch. Were you hurt?"

"Bruised pride and embarrassment more than anything else, it was practically my first day... uh, in my current position." My awkward stammer made me shift in my seat.

"Sorry to hear your first time on a horse went so badly. Maybe, if you'd like some tips, I could take you riding. Only if you're interested of course."

Between him overlooking my awkwardness and his offer, my smile was hard to tame down. "You may be underestimating my serious lack of skill."

Ethan's voice was tinged with humor. "I promise no miracles, but my aunt has a few horses, very tame, and she appreciates it when I take them out to stretch their legs."

"Oh, they're family horses. I'm pretty sure once Logan finds out you'll have a new best friend."

Ethan sat back in his seat as someone approached, but kept his eyes on me. "As long as he brings you along, I'll consider myself lucky."

A plate was set down in front of Ethan.

"Thank you," Ethan said.

"Can I get you anything else?" the waitress asked.

"Uh," Ethan looked around the woman, "is the other meal coming?"

The girl looked confused, and then her eyes opened wide. "I am so sorry." She covered her mouth. "I'll go check on it."

She hurried away before I had a chance to ask about coffee.

Ethan slid his plate to the side. "I'm sure she'll be right back."

My hopes weren't high. Some people didn't know how to react to me, so they mentally moved me into an empty space. If someone was distracted or has met me more than once, things were golden. When Logan and Rider were around, they were able to take attention away from me until the other people became comfortable with me.

Ethan's fingers were drumming the table again, and he kept looking towards the kitchen. I almost felt sorry for him.

"You know," I said, "I think our waitress might be having a bad night."

"That could be. I'm really sorry about this." He looked around the crowded room. "It's supposed to be warmer tonight than last night, isn't it?"

"I'm not sure. I can check my phone if you want."

"Thank you. You check, and I'll be right back."

Curiosity made me watch him go, but when I looked up from digging my phone out of my purse, I had lost track of where he went.

When he came back, all signs of apprehension had vanished. "Let's get a change of scenery. How's the weather?"

"Cool, but warmer than last night," I said carefully as Ethan ushered me to the door. Outside I added, "It sets a bad example when a lieutenant walks out without paying."

Ethan chuckled. "I paid and even left a tip, although I admit, I thought against it."

"Where are we going?"

"Our first stop is around the corner."

"First stop. You're feeling ambitious." Around the corner, the aroma hit me. "Mmmmm."

"I figured a coffee shop would be a safe choice." Ethan opened the door for me.

The massive board of caffeinated beverages stood behind a long bar, music filled the air, and the place was packed.

"What would you like?" Ethan asked, leaning in close so he didn't have to yell over the noise.

For the first time, I was close enough to smell his cologne, which worked well for him, but his warmth made me lean a little further in, to tell him my order.

"Wait here?" Ethan asked.

"Sure." I watched him walk away, but this time, my focus was on the view, in an admiring kind of way.

He brought my drink and we went back out into the fresh air. Ethan took me on a winding trail around downtown. We talked about silly stuff mostly, he bought me dinner on the go, and our last stop was at a bakery, where we each chose a cookie.

After dinner, somehow we ended up holding hands, and after the bakery, it felt natural for me to reach for it again.

"So," Ethan said on our way back to my car, "this date went better than the last."

"It was a nice evening," I said.

"I thought so too."

The following silence wasn't awkward, which was a nice change.

We stopped next to my car.

"Are you free on Saturday?" Ethan asked.

"It's possible my mother might be over, so as long as work doesn't call, I am definitely free."

Ethan laughed. "Won't she miss seeing you there?"

"She's there to see my grandmother." It was only a little white lie; Mom would notice my absence, but she may appreciate the fact that I'd be on a date.

"You live with your grandmother?" Ethan asked.

"Yeah. After her last husband passed away, I didn't like the idea of her living all alone. I was looking for a new house, so the timing worked out well."

"Do you take care of her?" Ethan asked.

I laughed. "No, Gran is one hundred percent independent. In fact," I checked the time on my phone, and it was almost ten, "I'll probably beat her home."

"Well, if you're sure I'm not taking you away from your family, would you like to go hiking?" Ethan asked.

"That sounds like fun."

The words were barely out when he kissed me. He was hesitant at first, but when I fell into the kiss, he did too.

When he broke away, he asked, "I'll pick you up on Saturday?"

"Hmm, Saturday it is."

He opened my car door for me and waited on the sidewalk while I drove away.

CHAPTER

EIGHT

My cell phone rang around three am. Nothing good comes from a call at that time of night.

"Cassie," I answered.

"It's Hank, got another fishy death for you and Logan."

"Fishy how?" I asked, forcing myself out of bed.

"Some guy killed his girlfriend—"

"That's nothing new." I yawned and stretched.

"He claims a possessed necklace made him do it."

"Okay, that's new. A necklace?"

"I thought that would get your attention. They have him at the police station."

I called Logan, and his voice was chipper. It was too early for that.

"Hank already reached out," Logan said. "Call Rider. He's been useful on this case, and we want to keep him with us."

I've never called Rider in the middle of the night, but he answered right away and sounded alert. I have no idea how my partners did alert at three am.

"We have a lead," I said, "possessed necklace."

"Like the one in evidence?" Rider asked.

"Let's go and find out. Meet us at my house."

I hung up and pulled myself together enough to get dressed and go in search of caffeine.

"Morning, sugar," Gran said when I stumbled into the kitchen.

"Did I wake you up?" I blinked in the glare of the bright kitchen lights.

"No, I woke up knowing you'd need coffee," she said winking at me. "I have three tumblers ready."

"I love you, Gran." I wanted to sink into a chair and rest until my partners arrived. It was a nice thought, but my time would be better spent finding out if Hank had any details in the file for today's case.

The tablet wouldn't open for me. Apparently, a bleary-eyed attack on the password wouldn't work. Logan arrived in time to keep me from breaking the wretched thing on the counter.

"Go finish getting ready," Logan said. "I'd like a chat with Margaret before she turns in," Logan said.

I thought I was ready. How was everyone so awake in the morning?

"Sure." I went upstairs.

In my tired state, I had reverted to my old uniform of T-shirt, jeans, and boots. I changed into a better shirt and finished getting ready. Three-thirty in the morning wasn't pretty, but at least I was fully dressed.

Rider arrived while I was on my third cup of coffee. I grabbed another to go, and we were out the door.

THE ENTRY to the police station was open but empty. The officer behind the bulletproof glass buzzed us through without trouble this time.

Ethan stood in the middle of a flurry of activity. He was talking to a uniformed officer, but he waved us over when he noticed us. How had it not occurred to me that he'd be here?

He looked uneasy when we approached. "Agent Seale, and, uh, Agent Heidrich." He tripped over the greeting, and I didn't blame him. "And you are?"

"This is Agent Wolfe," Logan said.

Ethan blinked up at Rider, taking in his height. Standing behind me made him appear even taller in comparison. "Good to meet you. Let's go talk in my office."

I was uneasy, wondering why Ethan was pulling us into his office. The talks that needed to take place behind closed doors were almost never fun.

Ethan stifled a yawn as we entered the room. At least I wasn't the only one who thought being up at this time of the day was obscene.

He looked pointedly at me. "I'm not sure how this works." I could hear the frustration behind his voice.

Did he think I knew? "I think we treat each other the way we would anyone else."

"Right." Ethan looked like he was thinking that over. "I find it interesting that my suspect was not even at the station when I received a call saying I couldn't interrogate him." He aimed this at Logan and Rider, as though trying to exclude me from his irritation. "Would you all care to shed a little light on why the Department of the Treasury is interested in a local homicide?"

"You went out on a date with him?" Rider asked.

Shaking my head and smiling, I looked up at Rider. "Yes, but that was last night, we should keep work separate."

"Do I have to like him?" Rider asked as though we were alone in the room.

"We can talk about that later," I said.

Logan looked like he was trying hard not to laugh while Ethan looked resigned.

"Sorry," Ethan said, "bad start."

"No, what you said was okay," I assured him.

Logan took the lead. "We may be here for no reason at all. We'll have to talk to the suspect to know for sure."

"That's all I get?" Ethan asked.

"We need to talk to the man to find out more," I said, "then, if this incident has nothing to do with us, we'll try to get out of your hair. It's too early in the morning for the bureaucracy crap to get in the way."

Ethan's lips curled up, but it only lasted a moment. "Well, you all are not the only ones waiting. The DEA have been around for a few weeks, and they want to interview him. They weren't too happy when they were told to cool their heels."

Logan was watching the office through the window in the door. He was already bored with this conversation and ready to move on. Rider was looking everywhere, as though he was memorizing the office.

"Why is the DEA here?" I asked.

"Seems like they're always here these days," Ethan said. "There're rumors about a new drug hitting the streets."

"Here, and not in the city?" That didn't sound right to me.

"It's only a rumor," Ethan said. "As far as I know, no one has found anything yet. Here, or in the city."

"Can you tell us anything about the suspect?"

"The man killed his girlfriend in a rage. DEA is hoping to get a blood test soon. They think he's doped up. Since we found drugs in the apartment, it's a safe bet, but we only found the usual stuff." Ethan glanced at Rider before sitting back in his chair. He motioned for us to sit as well, but I was the only one who did. "We were told not to interrogate him. The thing is that he doesn't really need to be interrogated. He's been talking since we picked him up. We left him alone in the room, but we got down plenty before he reached the station."

"What did he say?" I asked.

"He admitted straight away that he killed his girlfriend."

I arched my eyebrows. "No trying to deny it?"

"No. We read him his rights, but he kept talking. He claims his necklace is possessed and made him do it. Prime candidate for a mental deficiency plea."

Logan came back around to the conversation. "Could be that's what he's trying for."

I looked at my partner and wondered what he really thought. "Anything else?"

Ethan stood. "That's the gist of it. It'll all be in the file, but I think you'll be able to hear for yourselves when you get in there."

"We're going to need the necklace when we talk to him," I said.

"I'll bring it up." Ethan gestured to the door.

Time to go see our suspect. It struck me that I was getting ready to walk into a room with a man that had murdered someone only a few hours ago. It didn't sit well mentally, but I tried to push away the oncoming anxiety of being in the same room with a killer.

"Agent Heidrich," Ethan said, as we left his office, "may I have a word with you in private first? It will only take a minute."

"Sure."

Logan chuckled, and I closed the door firmly on both my partners, knowing that it was no more private than if I had left the door open. With my partners' extreme listening abilities, they could walk across the room and probably hear every word we said.

Ethan cleared his throat, and he looked like he was thinking carefully about what he wanted to say. "Is this going to work?"

"We said no hard feelings if either of us had to cancel anything for work, right? Let's amend that to include no hard feelings for anything that might happen that's work-related, including treating each other like we would anyone else."

"Thank you for that." He looked tired but smiled. "It may be easier said than done, though."

The look made me want to curl my toes, so he might be right about that, but I plunged forward. "If either of us decided to walk off this case for the other, we would end with resentment. Especially since I don't even know if we have a case."

"You're right, and it may not be so bad working together." Ethan moved around to the front of the desk but kept a respectable distance. "You look nice. How do you look so put together in the morning?"

I tried not to laugh, but it filtered through my words. "Four large cups of coffee and a partner who made me go upstairs and fix my first attempt at getting ready."

Ethan coughed to cover his amusement, and then looked out the door while regaining his serious mood. "We probably shouldn't keep your partners waiting so long. Agent Seale looks antsy to talk to our suspect."

"He probably is, but then he always looks like that." Even standing still Logan looked like fluid movement on the brink of being released.

Ethan opened the door for me. "Thank you, Agent Heidrich."

"Yeah, that agent stuff is probably going to have to go," I muttered.

Ethan led us down a few halls, and we found two people arguing with an officer outside the interrogation room.

"You can't go in," the officer said. "I have my orders. You shouldn't have gone in there in the first place."

"It's not down to you to kick us out. We're doing our job," one of the agents said.

"And I'm doing mine," the officer replied.

It was one of those arguments among professionals where no one raised their voice, but you could tell by their stiff stances and glaring eyes that no one was thrilled with the situation.

"Excuse me," Ethan said and led the men down the hall, leaving the officer behind. Once he had them down the hall, Ethan gave us a nod.

Logan pointed to a door. "Rider, we'll have you in the viewing room. Make sure no one joins you, especially those men. They're DEA agents."

"How can you tell?" I asked.

"I can't imagine anyone else as eager to get into the room as these guys appear to be," Logan said.

Looking down the hall, one of the agents was glaring our way while talking with Ethan. The officer by the door was watching Ethan and the agents, looking amused.

The suspect began talking as soon as we entered the room. "You have to listen to me, it's the necklace. It did this to me. It's the reason I killed her."

Logan held up a hand to stem the admission. "Rider, mosey on in here for a minute."

I tried not to look puzzled, but I'm not sure I managed it.

"Look," the suspect began again as Rider entered the room. "If you listen—"

Logan held a hand up again and quieted the man down before turning to Rider. "You hear it?"

Rider looked like he was concentrating. "I hear many things."

There was nothing I could hear, but I seized the Path, holding back much of the current, to see if I could read what they heard.

"This one is a buzz," Logan said, "down low and away from the lights."

Rider walked to one of the chairs and then flipped it over. At first, I didn't see anything but a blurry concentration of greenish brown that clung to the Path, but once they pointed it out, I recognized it. Not only had the DEA come into the room, but they also bugged it. I'm sure this was against the law, but more importantly, it pissed me off.

Rider took the tiny device off the chair, inspected it briefly, and then handed it to me.

Aggravated, I marched straight out of the room and down the hall where Ethan was talking with the agents.

I held up the small device and scowled. "This is an obstruction of justice and infringement on the rights of the accused." I had no idea if any if that was true, but it sounded right. "We're supposed to be on the same side." The Path picked up a frenzy of emotion, guilt, impatience, anger; it all came at once and pressed in on me.

Rider walked out and gave a low menacing growl, his Path merged into the others before overpowering them. Instead of making me more uncomfortable, though, it rolled through me.

Everyone stopped to look at Rider, even me. A man nearly six and a half feet tall can garner a lot of attention when he's angry.

Rider took the tiny listening device from me and held it up with two fingers to show the agents. Then he crushed it. He rubbed his fingers together, flicked away specks of the device, and went back to the viewing room to watch the interrogation.

The Path around the agents diminished and shifted hesitantly, as though afraid to travel too far from its source.

"Damn," Ethan said, under his breath.

I stifled a grin, appreciating my partner's antics, and trying to avoid looking at Ethan's Path, I moved back to the interrogation room.

"Agents." Ethan held up a plastic bag. "Here's the item you asked for."

Logan took the bag and examined the contents through the plastic.

"Thank you." I flashed Ethan a smile, in case Rider had thrown him too far off balance, then Logan and I went back into the room.

The suspect was sitting in the bright lights with his hands folded in front of him on the table. He took one look at what Logan had in his hands and let out a scream while jumping into the corner. Blues, purples, and greens marred the room and yellows crushed their way through. It was beautiful and terrible at the same time. The intensity also had me damming the Path back to a trickle to have enough energy to keep going.

The interrogation room door had remained open, so the officer outside noticed the event and looked questioningly at us.

I shook my head, and he shut the door.

"Knock it off, Ed," I said.

Logan dropped the plastic bag holding the necklace onto the table.

"Keep that thing away from me." He stood trembling. "You shouldn't touch it either, keep it away."

"Why don't we start with what happened?" Logan said.

We left the bag sitting where it was, ignoring it. For Ed, the presence was like a weight—each time he shifted his gaze to us, it always landed back on that bag.

"Look I killed her, okay. That's what happened. Now get that thing out of here."

"Where did you pick this up?" Logan sat back on a chair.

Seeing what my partner was doing, I leaned against the wall. We tried to pull back from Ed in a way that would make him more comfortable with coming forward. It wasn't happening, though. The man looked like he was prepared to put down roots. Even his Path clung to the corner.

Logan nudged the bag forward a minuscule amount. "Where'd you come by it, Ed?"

Ed licked his lips. "A guy I know. He said it was fun. Said it would help me get what I wanted."

While they spoke, I drew up feelings of safety and contentment and tried to get the emotions to calm Ed. I may as well have been using a feather to knock down a wall, and I was left feeling shaky enough to join Logan at the table.

"Who's this guy?" Logan asked.

"Don't know him well. His name's Terry, but I don't know any more than that."

"What did you want from Terry?" Logan asked.

Ed looked at Logan with his forehead creased. "Man, I wanted what everyone wants. Money and an easy life, maybe a little to smoke up now and again."

"What else did Terry say about it?"

I continued to watch as Logan and Ed volleyed back and forth.

"I don't know," Ed said. "I don't know, get it out of here. Away from me."

"He must have said more."

"I thought it was a good luck charm. He talked as if it was some sort of drug. We were both wrong. That's not what it is."

"You believe in good luck charms?" Logan asked.

"It doesn't matter, that's not what it is."

"What is it?"

"It's possessed. He sold me evil bottled up."

"So you believe in possession?"

"No. I mean I didn't before."

"Now you do?"

"It's crazy, but I'm telling you." Ed slid down the wall and tried to make himself smaller. "That thing is possessed. You need to get it away from me."

"Why did you think it was a good luck charm?" I asked, trying to drag his attention away from the necklace.

"Terry said it would help me get what I wanted. He said it was good, and it would help me. I thought it would bring me luck, or help bring money into the house." Ed focused on me, but, inevitably, his gaze went back to the table.

"Tell me why you killed your girlfriend?" I asked.

"She—it was an argument, and she was yelling. I snapped. I lost it. I'm not even sure what happened. I don't even remember what happened."

"What made you think it was the necklace?" Logan asked.

Ed didn't say anything. He sat in the corner, pale-faced and sweating. It looked like he was trying but failing to look away from the plastic bag.

"What made you think it was the necklace?" I repeated Logan's question and reached for the bag.

"It... something came out of it." Ed's voice quavered. "It filled me up, filled up the room. Then it was over."

Not wanting to drag Ed down a bad Path, I didn't pick up the evidence. Instead, I leaned back and scratched my temple to let Logan take over the conversation completely, and I read from where I sat.

A range of colors swirled across the room. Memories of old Paths that hadn't worn away, along with Ed's additions to the tapestry. The necklace was encased in soft red halo.

Maybe traces of Ed's homicidal actions? I moved around, adjusting to view the necklace at different angles, but saw nothing beyond its own smooth glow.

I rubbed my eyes and leaned back. A red blaze flashed from under the plastic and winked out again. It was like one of the small sparks that flew away from welders, but encased. I moved again, trying to catch another glint, but couldn't reproduce the results.

Color rippled, and the Path flowed smoothly around the room; no matter which current I rerouted or layer that I peeled back, I couldn't find that dazzling light.

A rushed knock made me jump and the Path poured over me.

Gripping the table for support, I heard Ethan's voice at the door. "Can I have a word?"

I had a tenuous hold on my power, but, with a struggle, I anchored myself down long enough to force the torrent away. Weariness crept over me as colors went dreary.

Logan had been my partner long enough to know when I ran into trouble, and he waited at the table. Once I gave him a small nod and stood, he snatched up the evidence, and we left the room. Seeing Ethan made me put in the effort to appear alert, but I had to lean against the wall for support.

"When our friend Ed came into the station, he made a phone call right away," Ethan said.

I frowned, knowing where this leading.

Rider joined us in the hall, sticking close to my side.

Ethan cleared his throat. "The thing is, instead of calling his lawyer, he called his shrink, and the man's here to see Ed."

Logan crossed his arms. "Psychologist?"

"Psychiatrist, but in residency," Ethan said.

The groan escaped me before I knew it was on its way.

"What is the difference?" Rider asked.

"A psychiatrist is an MD, medical doctor." I gestured to the room with Ed. "Basically, Ed called for medical help."

"Is he injured?" Rider asked.

"Not exactly," I said.

Arms crossed, Logan looked at Ethan. "What's the decision on how to handle this?"

"Given his actions and behavior, I'm inclined to let the doctor in to see him." Ethan shifted and avoided looking in my direction. "When this comes to trial, it could cause trouble if we don't."

A hint of grin showed up on Logan's face. "How'd the DEA take it?"

"The agents weren't too happy, but they can get their drug test with the doctor in the room," Ethan said.

Logan relaxed and rocked back on his heels. "That puts us out of play. At least for now."

"Did you get what you need?" Ethan asked.

"Well, yes and no," Logan said. "With all his raving about the necklace, we'd like to get a closer look at it."

"It's a murder case," Ethan said, "so all of our evidence can be moved to the top of the heap for processing. It has to go to the lab, though. It's not an in-house job."

Inwardly, I winced. "Is there anything our office can do to help?"

Criminalistics laboratories were great, but I knew they would take time. The evidence would also be passed around. They would wear gloves and take precautions to avoid contamination, but with the type of work we do, the more people around it, the less we can get from it.

Ethan hesitated. "For as often as Ed mentioned this thing, if the case goes to trial that necklace is going to be involved somehow. If it's tested separately from the rest, and not in the state lab, it's going to look bad."

He wasn't wrong, but it wasn't an ideal outcome.

Ethan looked at me and I tried to make my face look neutral, but I'm not sure it worked.

"Now," Ethan said, "I know you all have pull, and you could take this thing out of here tonight if you really wanted to, but it might be better all-around if you leave it with us."

Looking at Logan, I could tell he wasn't interested in messing up Ethan's case for the necklace.

"He killed someone," I said. "We're not going to do anything that would jeopardize your work."

I hadn't realized that Ethan was tense until I saw him relax.

"Are you done with the evidence?" Logan asked me.

Feeling a dull ache settling in, I knew I shouldn't push myself further. "I could use a few more minutes, but I think I've done what I can for now. Maybe some caffeine will help." It wasn't likely, but a girl could hope.

Logan passed the necklace on to Ethan. "Are you sending Ed's doctor in now?"

"He has to wait for his supervisor. I'm not really sure," Ethan said.

I threw in the reasoning without thinking. "It sounds like he or she is under direct supervision. They must be early in their residency."

Logan eyed me.

I shrugged. "I knew a few people that were pre-med in college."

"Mind if we talk to some of the officers that were on scene?" Logan asked Ethan.

"Sure thing," Ethan said, "follow me."

Ethan introduced Rider and Logan to the two officers that made the arrest. The men looked like they had been keyed up, but had lost ground to fatigue. I stood well back, knowing that meeting me could make the introductions go downhill fast.

"Agent Heidrich, I'll show you where we keep the coffee." Ethan held out his arm, letting me go first.

I started towards the direction he indicated, but dropped back to walk beside him in case I went the wrong way.

Ethan took me to a small kitchen, more of an alcove really, and poured me a cup of coffee.

While I mainlined caffeine, Ethan held up the evidence bag. "It's an awkward-looking necklace, but I didn't notice anything about it that stood out."

The shape wasn't that important for me to see since there would be pictures somewhere that we could examine. For me, the Path was most important.

I feigned interest with itching to reach out to the Path and explore the thing properly. "Anything special about the design?"

"It's odd is all. Almost like an animal wearing a bird mask."

A uniformed officer came over. "Sorry to interrupt, sir. That psychiatrist's boss showed up and he's really anxious to talk to the man in charge."

Ethan looked resigned. "I'll be right there."

The officer retreated and I could hear him speak to someone down the hall.

Ethan cleared his throat. "This could take a while. Will you be here when I get back?"

"It's hard to say what my partners are up to, but there's a chance." I poured another cup of coffee, pausing long enough to add sugar this time.

"Do you think you and your partners will be taking over the case?"

I almost fumbled the cup. "The homicide?"

Ethan gave an imperceptible nod.

"We have an interest in a few of the details, but from what

I've seen, there would be no reason for us to be involved in the actual homicide investigation."

"Good to know." Ethan rubbed the back of his neck. "So we won't be working together?"

"We may bump into each other, but no, I don't think we'll be working together."

"Good to know."

Wondering if it was worth chancing the Path, I gestured to the bag Ethan was holding. "Is that being mailed to the lab tomorrow?"

"Driven there. Later today in fact. I'll make sure it gets to the front of the line." Ethan looked like he was going to say more, but the officer came around the corner again. "I'm on my way." Ethan said the words before the officer could speak. "It was good seeing you again, Agent Heidrich."

Before I could help myself, I grinned. "The agent thing is really going to have to stop."

In all, it hadn't been bad that our work bumped into each other. Sure, it would have been nice if there wasn't a dead body involved, but we can't have everything we want.

Ethan looked as though he might take my hand, but stopped. "We'll figure it out." Ethan joined the officer and disappeared around a corner.

I topped off my cup while listening to Ethan introduce himself. When I peeked down the hall, he wasn't in sight. Taking the opportunity, I sagged against the wall and closed my eyes. The coffee and sugar made me jittery, but it wasn't giving me any strength back. Real sleep was going to be needed if I was going to be useful. Why did I have to stay up so late last night?

My mind wandered back to Ethan and the kiss next to my car. Ahh, that was why.

It had been worth it.

The noise down the hall lowered, allowing Ethan's voice to filter through. He wasn't yelling, no one was, but the irritation in his voice was clear.

I couldn't quite make out the conversation, but I heard the word 'rights' and 'violation' from more than one mouth. When I knew my feet wouldn't fall out from under me, I moved down the hall to see what was happening.

Ethan was talking to a tall, overweight man dressed professionally. Due to his age, I figured he was not the resident, but the supervisor. The man's face was calm, and the words didn't have much in the way of heat, but I could tell he was less than pleased.

I felt bad for Ethan, but I was glad this wasn't my problem, and since I had drunk more coffee than any person should ever try to drink in a short period of time, I searched for a restroom.

When I found my way back to the room, the conversation was still going. Since the only inappropriate action had been taken by the DEA, and we had put a stop to that, there was no reason for this aggravation.

Maybe I could pull up the Path enough to share some calming emotions. Moving towards Ethan, I figured I'd find out fast. There was a desk close enough where I could sit and be effective but unobtrusive.

"Cassie?" The voice came from behind me, and it was familiar enough to root me to the spot. The voice lowered. "What are you doing here?"

Zander. Of all people, why did it have to be my ex? It didn't take much of a leap to figure out that he was the resident.

My jaw clenched, and I turned to face him.

"Zander, it's..." No, I wasn't going to say it was good to see him. The last time I saw him, he was trying to have me committed to a mental institution. Forcibly. "I didn't expect to see you here."

"I'm here for work. What on earth are you doing here?" The concern dripped out of his voice, making me want to cringe.

Trying to keep my face passive felt futile. "Work."

He stood a few inches taller than I did, and his hair was cut shorter than when I had last seen him. He looked professional, standing there with two cups of coffee and worried eyes watching me. Intently. I could feel him trying to locate a tremor or sign that I would lose grip with reality.

"You work at the police station?" Zander let a hint of skepticism into his voice.

"No, I am here for work. I work with the Department of Treasury." It was a defensive response.

There had been a few times when I had pictured myself running into the man I had once planned to marry. There were things I was going to say, but none of that was coming to mind.

Zander sat the coffee down. "Is there someone I can call for you?"

"For what?"

"The Department of Treasury?" Zander had the nerve to look put upon. "Cassie, I'm concerned for your well-being."

My mouth fell open. He thought I was delusional. How do you even respond to that?

"I was concerned when we were together, and I'm worried about you now. Your mother and your grandmother have the best intentions, I'm sure, but they—"

My face grew hot at the mention of my family. "Take your concern and shove it, Zander. I don't need it, and I don't want it."

"We need to pull you back into the real world, Cassie. I know that with your file, the Department of Treasury wouldn't hire you."

"What file? I have two speeding tickets from high school."

Zander looked down at his hands and appeared to study

them before looking back up at me. "After your mother took you away, I was distraught. She was feeding your delusions."

I crossed my arms and glared at him. My 'delusions' of Reading the Path. I hated him for not believing me. We were supposed to be happy together and to trust one another. When he proposed to me, I wanted to be open and honest about everything. It was stupid of me to be that trusting.

Clearing his throat, Zander continued. "Since I knew you were a danger to yourself, and perhaps those around you, I spoke with the psychiatrist at the facility we discussed."

"You discussed." The words had heat, but I kept them under my breath, wondering where this conversation was going.

He didn't look directly at me when he continued. "They made a few notes but suggested I reach out to the local police. Which I did."

"You did what?" The words came out loud and piercing, but I didn't care.

Zander held up his hands in the universal calm down gesture. "It was for your own safety. You were going down a dangerous path."

"You arrogant, pompous ass—"

"Is everything okay?" Logan appeared, but without his usual smile.

Zander barely paid him any attention. "We're fine. Give us a few minutes." He took my arm and tried to lead me away.

I drew myself back. "We don't need any time. We're finished here. This has been finished for years."

"Doctor Fin?"

Zander looked away from me, his concerned face turning impassive. "I'll be right there, Doctor Grant." He turned back to me. "May I call you? We can talk."

"Are you kidding me? No!"

When he walked away, I felt like kicking him as he passed.

Logan was silent for a few minutes while I tried to get a grip on my fury.

"Old friend of yours?" Logan asked.

"That. Was Zander."

"The ex?"

"Yes."

In the past year of being partners, bits and pieces of my life with Zander had come out, so Logan knew how things had ended.

"Wish I had known that before I walked up," Logan said

"Why's that?" I took a few steadying breaths of meditation. With the anger slipping away, my heart felt heavy. It's possible that I wouldn't have resented Zander so much if he hadn't made me doubt my own sanity.

"I might have had a few more words to say," Logan said, keeping his eye on the man.

That earned him a small grin. "Standoff at high noon?"

Logan relaxed and looked more like his usual self. "Depends on what he had to say. Ready to get out of here?"

"Definitely. Where's Rider?"

"He'll be done in a minute. Did you get anything from Ed's necklace?" Logan asked.

I sighed. "Mostly a headache. It has an aura, and there was a spark, but I have no idea what it was." I rubbed my head and tried to focus on the case. "It was there for a second, but I couldn't find it again."

"We've done enough here. I'll grab Rider so we can go to the office." I could feel the weight of Logan's eyes on me. "Or maybe back to your house."

"I'm fine," I said. "It's been a long morning is all."

CHAPTER

TEN

After Logan left, I looked around the office, trying to spot Ethan. Instead, I had more than a few officers discreetly shooting glances my way.

My face grew hot. I hadn't realized that Zander and I had drawn so much attention. I turned to go to Ethan's office and almost ran into him.

"Oh, sorry." I took a step back and smoothed my hair back away from my face. "Um, I was looking for you."

"It's my lucky day." Ethan sounded like he meant it. "Let me know if it's none of my business, but is everything okay with you and the doctor?"

My embarrassment grew to new levels. "Oh, yeah. It's fine. It was a..." I almost said misunderstanding, but the weight of that lie might cave in the ceiling. "It's fine," I repeated.

Ethan didn't look convinced.

Looking around, I tried to grasp a hold of a new subject and seeing the plastic bag in his hands, I figured the safest thing to discuss was the case. "Are there already pictures of this in the file?"

"It seems odd for so much focus to be on a thing this small." Ethan held up the bag to look through the plastic. "They haven't added pictures to the file yet, though. Do you want to take another look?"

I took the bag by the seal, but it was difficult to feign more interest when I couldn't pull up the Path.

Ethan cleared his throat. "Will I see you around the station?"

"It's hard to say for sure, but I doubt it. Someone else might come back to look this over." I indicated the necklace by rattling the bag around. "But unless something new turns up, we'll be out of your hair."

"Do you want me to stop by tonight?" Ethan asked.

I hadn't been expecting the question, and after Zander, I was thrown off guard. "I'm pretty sure, after the day ahead, I'll be horrible company."

Ethan looked skeptical and I was at a loss on how to make the conversation go any better. Gripping the bag in both hands, I could feel the sharp lines of the contents dig into my hand.

The florescent lights buzzed and one popped out. A charge of energy leaped from the necklace and I went rigid while it wrapped itself around me.

Dense emotion circled through me. Trying to get rid of it was like trying to move smoke.

Ethan looked down. "Tonight probably is bad timing. Sorry about that."

"No." Splitting my concentration wasn't working. "I mean yes. Tomorrow night?"

Ethan agreed but looked apprehensive.

The intensity of the sensation died down. A long thread of living Path stretched and then coiled into me until I felt it condense and settle into my core.

"Sorry, it's been a long day. I need to go." Shaking, I turned and walked away.

"Cassie?" Ethan called.

Inside my mind, I wasn't alone. There was a strong feeling of myself, but someone else had joined the fun.

"Yes?" Trying to keep my features impassive, I turned back to him.

"The necklace?"

Should I hand it back? The foreign entity flexed. Breathing became difficult and I broke out into a cold sweat.

"Ready to go?" Logan asked.

I jumped and turned to his voice. Ethan was a civilian, at least when it came to the Lost and the weirdness we faced day to day.

"Cassie?" Logan reached out to me, concern written across his face, but I stepped away. With my back to Ethan, and as low as I could manage, I whispered to Logan. "Something jumped out of the necklace."

Logan's features locked and he glanced at Ethan. "Is it empty now?"

Gripping the necklace hard in my hand, I tried to sense anything else. "I think it's empty. Did you touch it through the bag?"

"Several times," Logan said.

"Nothing odd?" I asked.

"Nothing." Logan reached out and took the bag. He cupped the necklace in his hand and squeezed it.

The conversation was too much of a distraction. Like a virus, I felt the intruder settle further. It was power and energy, but that was a thin veil that attempted to mask rage.

Internally, there was a struggle, as I tried anything I could to dislodge the new energy, but I was at a loss as to what to do.

Logan spoke to Ethan, but I didn't let myself be distracted.

The newness of the invading force began to fade as it became more established. I tried to rein my own power in and separate myself from the other. The new flow of energy slowed, allowing me to gain some ground.

Rider was next to me. I'm pretty sure he was talking, but I was concentrating too hard on my struggle.

"I have to get out of here." It's all I could manage.

I'm not sure what type of excuses Logan and Rider used, but we were out the door quickly. Rider opened the door to the truck to let me in, but I stalled as the film of energy masking the presence inside me shivered.

"Back," I said.

"You want to go back into the station?" Rider asked.

Logan was already in the driver's seat, starting the vehicle.

I gritted my teeth. "Back of the truck."

Why doesn't he listen to me, and why am I letting it bother me so much? Rider's slowness and lack of understanding led to aggravation, and the veil between the infestation and me slipped and rage spilled through. Closing my eyes, I tried to meditate, to put things back under my own control. The new power had found a crack, and it worked to pry that crack open.

I couldn't do this. Why couldn't I do this?

With the power of the Path, maybe I could burn this away. When I let my mind stretch, it ran straight into the alien energy. I staggered and someone grabbed my arm. Retaliation was the first thought that came to mind, but I stamped it down. My friends were here, and they could manage any threat. We were also in public, outside a police station. This was going bad fast.

"Logan?" I didn't want to lose control, but it was happening. "Logan. Tranq me. Lock me down. It's about to get through."

The internal frenzy searched for a target. Thoughts of

Zander loomed up and my foothold loosened. Fury mounted, and it felt good. I could completely abandon reason and let go. The anger and rage could take over. The thought left me giddy, and I felt myself lose more ground. Leaning against the truck, I closed my eyes and tried to steady myself.

"Logan?" I'm not sure if the words came out or if they stuck in my throat, shielded by the wrath. The last salvages of myself slipped away, and I was alone in the darkness.

Like a fever dream, shadows, shapes, and colors formed in the emptiness, only to fall away again.

WHEN I WOKE UP, it was to see a dimly lit room, and I was strapped down on a hospital bed. Exhilaration and thrill of reckless abandonment were evaporating, leaving a numb fatigue in its wake. I wanted to grab hold of that stimulation and explore it, keep it wrapped around me. The idea felt wrong and fragile, so I contemplated the reaction while staring at the ceiling. As the sensations ebbed away, memories of the police station trickled into my thoughts.

That power that jumped into me. What had it done?

More importantly, what had I done to my partners?

I licked my lips and kept my voice low, afraid of any response. "Logan? Rider?"

Doctor Yelton came into view. "They're downstairs." He shined a tiny bright light into my eyes.

I tried to cover my face, but again registered that I was strapped down. Last remnants of temper tried to spring forward, but it was swiftly swept aside by my own stability returning. Doctor Yelton took a step back but kept the light swinging back and forth in front of my eyes.

"They'll be staying downstairs until I'm sure you're stable."

"I'm feeling okay. A little tired maybe."

Doctor Yelton flipped off his light. "That's why your pupils turned into giant saucers. Because you're doing so well."

"I didn't know doctors were allowed sarcasm."

"Your friends have been harassing me."

"If you let them come up, they would stop harassing you."

He took a deep breath, getting ready to say something, and then the air rushed back out. I grinned at him.

"They were worse than useless," he said. "They can't restrain someone and treat them like glass at the same time."

I narrowed my eyes. The doctor raised an eyebrow at me until I dropped the glare and settled my features.

"I'm not glass." I wanted to add that I hated to be treated like glass, but the doctor was treating me like any other patient.

"I'm going to run a few more tests. If all goes well, Rider and Logan can join us."

He checked my pulse, blood pressure, drew blood, stared at my eyes, ears, nose, and throat.

"You're stupid and you suck at your job," he said.

"What the hell?" I yelled. That came out of nowhere. "Look, I'm not sure what happened, but you need to—"

"Good response," he said, shining the light in my face.

"What?" I said.

"Normal response to negativity. Maybe a little more aggressive than I would expect from you, but not bad. Sorry, it was another test."

My glower returned, but he finished his tests and looked at me expectantly. "If you keep glaring, I'm going to keep on the restraints."

Sighing, I tried to put on a calm face. "What happened?"

He leaned over and released my arms. "You and your partners will have to work that out. I treated you for incoherent mania, but you appear lucid now. We need to take care of your wrists."

Large purple bruises covered my arms. Treated like glass?

The doctor wrapped some sort of cool gel cast around each arm. They were rigid, but only a few centimeters thick.

"We took x-rays, and there are no breaks. These will help with inflammation. You seem to be bouncing back pretty well."

I swung my legs off the bed and sat up.

"But," Dr. Yelton put up his hand, halting me, "you're staying here tonight. For further observation."

"I'll be—"

"Fine? I know it will be. You'll be here, under my care until I say you can go. I couldn't forgive myself if I sent you home and let you accidentally hurt your grandmother."

That shut me up. The doctor knew exactly which buttons to press. I swung my legs back onto the bed, but messed with the controls, so I was sitting up.

"Wish I'd learned that trick last year," he muttered and walked away.

"Logan and Rider?" I called to him.

"Calling them."

"My tablet?"

"Later."

While I waited for Logan and Rider, I inspected the plethora of bruises. My arms had quite a few, along with my midriff. I could feel others on my legs, but I wasn't going to slide out of my jeans to check. That could wait 'til later.

More worrying now was the feeling inside. Is it possible to have vertigo of the mind? It was like there was a residue of the experience lingering and twisting up small parts of my thoughts. My worry began to evaporate as the feeling began to fade.

I was more myself when Logan and Rider entered the

room. They were hesitant and purposefully making slow movements. The doctor stood by, watching for reactions.

I blew out a breath. "Can you fill me in on what I missed?"

Rider and Logan both relaxed.

"I'm not rightly sure," Logan said.

Rider came over and lifted my arm, twisting it around, inspecting the cast. A soft noise escaped him, like a sniff. Was he smelling me again? I thought we were over the whole smelling me stage.

"I'll be down the hall if anyone needs me," Dr. Yelton said.

Logan thanked the doctor and turned to me. "Why don't you tell us what you remember?"

I couldn't tell if he was trying to 'handle' me. If he put on kid gloves, we'd have a problem.

Casting my mind back to the station I tried to pick out what happened. "It was the necklace. Did we take it with us?"

"It's on the way to a lab now," Logan said, "but we're keeping in touch with Ethan, and we'll have Clancy take a look once we get hold of it."

"Ed wasn't too far off base," I said. "When I looked at the pendant, I saw that glimmer in the Path, but then it disappeared so I couldn't pinpoint what it was. Stupid mistake."

"It is not your fault," Rider said.

"You're not telling me it was possessed?" Logan asked.

"Not exactly. What came out, I've felt something similar before. It's like one of the Lost." I struggled to put words to the idea. "It's like a part of one of the Lost, their power or essence. It was trapped in the necklace. When I touched it, what was there leaped out."

"What kind of Lost?" Logan asked.

"It was, or at least I think it was a minotaur. It was the rage of a full-blood minotaur."

"I am not sure I understand," Rider said.

"I think I do," Logan said.

I waited for him to continue without really wanting him to go on.

Logan watched me closely. "It sounds like someone ripped out the soul of a minotaur and crammed it into a necklace."

Closing my eyes, I rubbed my forehead. I knew what Logan was thinking. We've known someone who could pull out souls and release them. Vincent. Our absent partner.

"I'm not sure it's quite the same thing." I lay on the bed, watching the two men for reactions. "It wasn't like a full soul was trapped inside. It was a small portion of power."

"This does not sound good," Rider said.

"You mean a piece," Logan pressed. "Like someone tore a soul apart?"

"Vincent is gone," I snapped. "If he were back, we would know. He would have contacted us."

"Would he?" Rider asked.

"There are other Walkers," I said.

"Vincent himself said no other Walker had done what he managed to do to you," Logan said.

I glared at Logan. "He said that no one else had taken a soul out and stopped before killing the person."

Logan looked thoughtful.

"But his action of returning your soul is what caused it to fall to pieces," Rider said.

"I'm not sure," I said. "He was trying to fix it, though. He wasn't going to go out and try it again."

"If he was trying to fix you," Rider's voice was quiet, and he looked at his feet, "Vincent would not practice on you."

I wanted to close my eyes and ignore the idea, but that wasn't the way things worked.

My eyes met Rider's. "He's a friend."

Rider didn't flinch or look away. He looked at me for the length of a few heartbeats, and then nodded.

"Well," Logan said, "we'll get the necklace. Once the doc sets you free, you can check it out and maybe we'll know more. While we wait for the piece to return, we'll try to figure out our next move. It sounds like this case is a lot closer to one of ours than we anticipated."

I remembered Ethan asking me if we'd be working together. Turning the idea over, I realized my answer was the same. He'd be working the homicide and we'd be working an entirely different case. Those thoughts led to vague memories of what happened at the station after I touched the necklace.

"Um, the way we left..." I hesitated, not knowing where to go from there. Work and personal are things that don't usually mix when civilians are involved. "Did I, or we..."

Logan gave me a knowing look. "It's sorted. Lieutenant Parker believes that your run-in with the Zander had you out of sorts."

"Did you tell him who Zander was?" I asked, trying to bite back the panic in my voice.

"No, I only referred to him as the doctor, and that I didn't know what happened."

I frowned, but I guessed it was better than Ethan thinking I had lost my mind.

"How are your arms?" Logan asked, effectively changing the subject.

I wanted to know more about what had happened with Ethan. In fact, I wanted every word, but I didn't want to seem overly interested. "Sore. I don't really remember what happened after we left the police station. You all want to fill me in?"

Logan glanced at Rider and back to me. "I tranquilized you, and the two of us brought you here."

Rider laughed. "That is what happened."

"Did you know Jonathan and Paula are fighting?" Apparently, Logan was done with the conversation.

Was he bored or evading?

Since I wasn't too keen on our chat anymore, I let it drop. "I hadn't heard. It's been a while since I've seen him."

Rider settled into a chair.

"She doesn't like his new career move, so he has his hands full," Logan said.

After last fall, Logan's son had switched his area of study to criminal justice with a heavy emphasis on law enforcement. "Hopefully she'll come around. Has he..." I let the question die. I wasn't sure if it was appropriate to ask if a Lost had told a human what they are.

Logan filled things in smoothly. "She doesn't know. He's struggling with what to tell her."

Thinking of my experience with Zander, I understood.

"Susan and Gerald had dinner with Margaret," Logan said.

"How late is it?" I asked. "I should call her so she doesn't worry."

"I told her we'd be here at work pulling an all-nighter," Logan said.

"She didn't say anything about today, did she?" I would hate to find out that Gran saw this and worried.

"No, she said to go see the Palm Reader when you get the chance," Logan said.

"She said that the other day," I said. "I don't know any Palm Readers, but Gran mentioned it's in the city."

Logan rocked back and forth. "Sable called today. We have a message from her."

"Sable from MyTH?" Rider asked.

"Yeah, she wanted to touch base, and to give the gnomes some feedback."

"I think she has everything we know right now," I said. "Well, all the facts anyway."

"I'll give her a call in the morning," Logan said.

"In the meantime, can you ask Hank to check out the local minotaur population? We should see if anything odd pops up." If a soul was missing, then the minotaur would be gone.

"Yeah. If someone's missing, it's going to hit the Lost population pretty hard after last fall. I'll go talk to Hank." Logan tipped an imaginary hat and left the room.

I relaxed into the bed. "There are too many things piling up at once. I need to get my tablet and check a few things out."

Rider winced. "Not tonight."

"Sooner is better than later."

"In this case, I do not think it is. You need to rest." Rider came back over to the bed and picked up my arm, lifting the gel cast up to inspect it. "Maybe we should figure out a way to restrain you. A way that does not hurt."

"Are you planning on needing to hold me down again?"

"Who knows what will be necessary in the future?"

"It sounds like you need to keep the tranquilizers close at hand."

Rider's eyes darkened.

"The wrist is fine, Rider." I took back my arm.

He went back to his chair, looking like he was going to settle in there for the night.

"Are you sticking around tonight?" I asked.

"Yes. It will be an early morning anyway."

"There are dorms in another building. For agents and other workers that stick around."

"Here is better. In case—" He broke off.

After feeling the minotaur, he didn't have to tell me in case of what. "There are other hospital beds."

"Full."

"All of them?"

"Yes."

That sounded bad. "Things are busy, I guess?"

"The doctor said that two Lost broke bones on the Farm today, due to a fight. Another Lost that lives outside the Farm became ill. Agent Thompson said her spouse poisoned her. Another Lost had an allergic reaction. They are not sure to what yet. The others were gremlin attacks. The portal opened again."

"Hopefully that will stabilize soon. It's been months since it was forced open."

"It is not good to have gremlins running around." Rider didn't sound convincing. For some reason, he liked the gremlins and jumped at the chance of taking one of the calls. "The portals reopening make it easier to send them back, though."

Rider tried to get more comfortable in the chair. His long frame looked determined to hang over both ends.

"Can you ask the doctor for my tablet before going to sleep?"

He didn't even open his eyes. "Doctor Yelton said not tonight."

"That doesn't look comfortable."

Rider opened one eye and looked at me. He closed it again and tried to roll over in his chair. "It will work for tonight."

"At least take a pillow and some blankets."

Rider found a blanket in the wardrobe and forwent a pillow. After a few more twists and turns, he settled in. The chair lay back, but more than a few inches of leg hung over the footrest.

Rider's breathing slowed as he fell asleep. I gave it a few more minutes before getting up to go downstairs.

"The doctor will strap you back to the bed."

I froze to the spot. Rider had gone from sound sleep to wide-awake within two steps.

He didn't move, but I got back into bed anyway. I knew my sigh would be audible to the werewolf, but I made it a little louder than necessary to make sure the point got across.

CHAPTER

ELEVEN

T he next morning, when I walked into a conference room downstairs, it felt like pixies were flapping in my stomach. Hank, Logan, and Rider, I expected, but Kyrian was also sitting in on the debriefing of yesterday's incident. The conversation had started without me, and the room felt uncomfortably hot as I sat down.

I received a cursory nod, and the conversation continued.

Hank cleared his throat. "We haven't found a connection between the man in custody and our Lar, Bill, or to his three roommates."

Kyrian leaned forward at the table. "Except the jewelry."

I tried to get up to speed. "Are the necklaces the same?"

Hank answered. "Similar materials, but different idols are represented in each. The idols are not related in any way."

"Idols?" I asked.

"Depictions of gods. One coming from Africa and one from Central America."

"Where did Bill get his necklace from?" Kyrian asked.

I crossed my arms. "I never asked. It appeared to hold some sort of power, so I thought we should take a look."

"The other boys weren't wearing them, though," Logan said. "Nothing like it came up on the list of items found on the deceased."

"It could be that they both happened to have the same cheap jewelry," Kyrian said, "but it's out of place. Clancy will take a look at Bill's necklace today. We should have the other as soon as the lab is done." Her attention turned to me. "You said something jumped from the necklace?"

"Yes. I saw a trace of light," I said. "Logan held it before I did and it probably crossed half a dozen hands before it reached us."

"So why you?" Kyrian drummed her fingers on the table and stared at me as though she was trying to put her finger on what I had done wrong.

My heated response died when Logan jumped in. "There could be any number of reasons. Top of the list, she's a Reader. She can see things others can't."

Everyone else's soul was nice, shiny, and whole. Mine was shattered into pieces. Not that I was feeling bitter about the fact. If it was a fragment of a soul, it would probably find itself at home with the other pieces I contained. Vincent had unintentionally kept a piece of my soul when he returned it last fall. Maybe this fragment found the hole left, although I had a part of Vincent inside as well, filling that gap.

However, my bosses didn't know that my soul was splintered and my powers had grown out of control.

"It could have recognized something in her and made the jump," Kyrian conceded. "We'll have Cassie take another in-depth look when it arrives. You can inspect Bill's as well. Once Clancy is done with both."

"We checked Bill's the other day. It didn't have anything like this," I said.

Kyrian moved on. "Cassie, you said you saw a trace in the idol, and you mentioned a minotaur, uh, Path, I think. Go through what happened with us, from your point of view."

This was turning into an exercise in patience for everyone involved. I explained what happened, but hard facts were slim. Saying 'something' jumped into me that held the rage of a minotaur was met with a thousand questions. No one had any of the answers.

After I had described everything in detail, with many stops to answer questions and provide more details, I felt wrung out. Guilt also materialized. I gave all the details about the previous day, but I left off the lingering feeling that I wasn't quite alone in my own skin. That needed to be analyzed before I decided to let others know.

Kyrian looked, well, maybe not completely satisfied with the description, but at least content that she had what we knew.

"Hank, track down our lar, Bill, and ask about the necklace. Bring him in if we have to." Kyrian turned to Logan. "While you're waiting for that, go to yesterday's crime scene. See if we can find anything the police overlooked." Kyrian stood and looked at Rider. "Mr. Wolfe, I believe you are in training this afternoon. Join the others once you're done. Once we hear from Bill, find us a connection between the people or the purchases."

We murmured assent and followed Kyrian out of the room.

Rider disappeared to whatever training he had to attend, Hank returned to his electronic domain, and Logan and I went home. I needed a shower and fresh clothes, Logan needed to see his family, and we both needed a fresh perspective on the case.

Yesterday's clothes felt grungy, but food had priority when I made it home. Gran was gone, but when I opened the fridge, I found a sandwich that she had left for me, secured in plastic ware from straight out of the seventies. As a fleeting thought, I wondered if she had 'seen' that I would want the meal, or if she had assumed. Hard to say with Gran, but either way, I had food.

There was only time for one bite before the phone rang. Frowning, I looked from the sandwich to the phone. With a sigh, the phone won.

"This is Cassie." I tried to sound distant and hurried.

"It's Ethan."

Frantically, I tried to recall how I had left things last night. "Oh, I'm glad you called. I mean, uh, after I left so quickly, I was hoping you would call." That was way too many words. "I didn't want you to think that..." Why was I still talking? "Well, anyway, I apologize." I bit down on my lip to make myself stop.

Seconds of silence ticked by before Ethan cleared his throat. "This is more of an official call."

Crimson embarrassment crept across my face, and my words came out quick. "Oh, right, of course, what's going on?"

"Your office asked about gaining access to the crime scene."

"Oh, right. Yes, our boss would like us to take a look around."

Ethan's voice was purely professional. "I can meet you at the scene and take you and your partners through what we know. The DEA has been over the scene several times as well. If you'd like for them to join us, I can make those arrangements."

"I don't think we need the DEA there." I didn't know if Logan would want them there or not, but I didn't want Ethan to feel like he had to set up appointments for us. Besides, the agents we had met the previous night didn't instill me with a lot of confidence in anything they might do or say. "If you could walk us through the scene, though, we'd appreciate that."

"I'd be happy to." His sounded less rigid this time. "Meet you over there in, say, an hour?"

There was no way I was going anywhere without a shower, especially if it wasn't urgent. "Can we make it an hour and a half?"

"I'll be there."

"And, um..." If anything, my face grew redder, but he sounded distant, so I had to ask. "We mentioned getting together tonight?"

Ethan was silent for a few beats and my heart quivered, as though ready to sink. "It didn't sound like you really wanted me to stop by."

"I do." That sounded hurried, so I tried again. "Last night, work would have gotten in the way, but if you're interested, you could stop by."

"Work may keep me pretty late tonight. We should receive some test results today."

Damn. That didn't sound promising. "Sure, I understand."

"I could text you when I'm free, and if you're up..."

"Yeah." I felt a little better. "That sounds good."

Once we hung up, I called Logan and, after filling him in, I ran upstairs, sandwich in hand, and ate as I got ready. After my shower, I caught myself taking too much time trying to pick an outfit since we were meeting Ethan. As soon as the realization struck, I put on normal work clothes. Last fall that would have consisted of jeans and a T-shirt. Seeing Kyrian move up so quickly, take charge, and make big changes in our branch of the agency, made me take a closer look at my own career trajectory. So far, I wasn't aimed in any particular direction, but slacks and a button up shirt began to make regular appearances in my wardrobe.

On the way to the crime scene, I read out parts of the file from our tablet. The details along with the crime-scene photos painted a gruesome picture.

I pressed my hand to my stomach when I looked at the victim. "He beat her to death."

Logan glanced over at the picture. "No human was meant to carry the fury of a minotaur."

"Did I—" I stopped, not knowing where I really wanted to go with the question.

Logan filled the dead air. "You didn't hurt anyone."

"I don't remember much, but if you and Rider weren't there, I'm pretty sure I would have attacked someone. I was so... angry."

"Did the feeling start as soon as you touched the idol?"

"Before, actually. Zander had me ticked off before the energy jumped into me." I explained what it felt like after the alien energy settled into place and the rage began to build. "Do you think Ed felt the same way I did?"

"Hard to say for sure, but I don't think so. It jumped straight into you, which may have amplified the intensity. The necklace probably affected him, but I don't think anything entered him like it did you. Otherwise, it would have affected someone else at the station."

"It certainly felt intense."

"When you woke up, could you tell the energy was gone?"

"Gone?" The silence drew out again as I tried to figure out how to answer the question. The anger was gone. Everything seemed normal, except the small nagging feeling that I wasn't alone in my own skin.

"Put a rain check on that." Logan was eyeing the newly installed GPS device in the truck.

In the past, we made do with maps, and then Smartphones began to trickle in a few months ago. Once Kyrian took over, new tech rolled in, which led to a GPS system in almost every work vehicle.

It looked like we were a few blocks away, but I wanted to let the subject drop. "We have a civilian on the scene with us, what should we focus on?"

"Delving into the past should be avoided if possible. The police have the murder covered, so there's no reason to get a replay of events as they happened. We're looking for any signs of where the necklace came from, how long they had it and are there any connection to the kids that died the other day."

"Sounds good." Looking at the pictures of the crime had been bad enough. There was no way I wanted to see the scene played out, especially with Ethan watching over us.

Ethan was waiting in front of the building. "Agent Seale, Agent Heidrich."

Logan shook the offered hand. "I think we can lose the formality. First names are good for us."

My partner knew me so well. With Ethan wavering about tonight, there was no way I would have mentioned the whole name business, but really, who wants to be called agent all the time?

Ethan appeared to be okay with the suggestion.

"We're going up to the second floor, to the back-facing apartment on the left." Ethan led the way into the apartment and up the stairs. "The neighbors below called the disturbance in first. They could hear the argument through the floors. Before the police were on scene, the neighbors from across the hall called it in as well."

"Have the neighbors made any complaints about them before?" Logan asked.

"They've lived here about two years and no one contacted us about them before this incident. It's not the worst neighborhood around, but not the best either. People tend to mind their own business, and no one in the building seems to know anyone else. At least not when we ask.

"We had to kick the door in, but a new door jamb was put in this morning to keep people out." Ethan took down crime-scene tape that made a flimsy, but effective barrier to the apartment and opened the door.

I handed Logan a pair of disposable gloves and put on my own. While pulling them on, I closed my eyes and mentally moved to the edge of my mind. There was a feeling of something watching beyond that edge that made me uneasy, and I hesitated, unsure of what would happen when I crossed the chasm into the Path.

If I wasn't willing to access the Path, what was I even doing here? Forging forward, there was an unsettled feeling before the Path snapped into place. It dissipated before I could put a name to the sensation. Making sure I had a firm hold on my power, I stepped into the apartment.

"The incident occurred in the front room," Ethan said.

It was like stepping into another world. I've seen bursts of anger that sank hooks into the Path and remained in place, but this was a blight on the Path. Angry reds twisted around thick black waves, and although the Path flowed, the storm of emotion crashed back into itself and remained in place.

"It's a mess, I know," Ethan said, coming up beside me and looking around the room, "but I can tell you what we know and which areas are most affected."

Ethan must have mistaken my reading as being over-whelmed, which wasn't far from the truth, but mostly, I didn't want to step any further into the room. I was already being buffeted with the residue that poisoned the apartment. My own rage, or at least the rage that had filled me, hadn't been gone for long. What would happen to me if I stepped into this hell?

"Well, partner, any area in particular you want to start?" Logan asked.

Tearing my eyes away from frenzied mess was difficult since it dominated the room. When I found other flows of color, I regretted looking away.

I pointed to an area by the window before I let the meaning of the Path truly soak in. "Over there. I'm guessing that's where the girlfrien-, uh, the victim was found." It wasn't really a guess. The confusion of color left behind was concentrated in one small spot.

"Yes," Ethan said, "the body was discovered here, and our perpetrator was found in this room as well."

"Why don't you talk me through what happened, Ethan," Logan said.

With Ethan focused on Logan, I could concentrate more on the apartment.

Looking from the stormy mass left behind by the boyfriend and back to the condensed spot of fear, sadness, and spark of anger left by the woman, I felt overwhelmed. The intense fear and disorientation the woman felt was somehow more powerful than the rest of the room, where the fury might be permanently woven into the fabric of the Path.

It was too much. After taking one last calculating look, trying to take in the whole room without feeling, I pushed the Path away. I welcomed the muted dullness of color that came with the normal world.

Ethan and Logan were moving to the rest of the apartment. I stood not far from the door, which probably didn't look good from an outsider's point of view. In fact, it must have looked like I did nothing. Would Ethan think I was so affected that I couldn't go through the crime scene?

With great reservation, I went further into the room. Even without the Path, I could feel the remains of the fight, so I concentrated hard on the physical. Except where the fight had disturbed things, the room was tidy. Looking around, I found the small kitchen. It was dim and depressing, with no natural light, but it was clean, and someone had tried to make the room better with sunny canisters and curtains around a fake vinyl decal window over the sink.

Exploring further, I found Ethan and Logan in what might have once been a second bedroom, which had been turned into an office of sorts. There was a cheap desk and chair with a computer monitor, a small bookcase, and the rest of the seating was beanbag chairs and floor cushions. The room was fairly neat, but the smell of cigarette smoke and pot clung to everything.

While Ethan listed the drugs and drug paraphernalia confiscated, I took a closer look at the bookshelf. The titles made me roll my eyes. There were a few books on drugs, but other titles were things like, *The Healing Power of Crystals*, *Magik in Nature*, and an eclectic mix of books on secret societies, prophesies, and the end of the world. The book on mythological creatures piqued my interest, but when I flipped through the pages, I didn't discover anything out of the ordinary. There were a few photos on the bookshelf and on the desk, so I shifted my focus to them. Most of the pictures were of the couple, but a few contained what could have been friends or family.

Without looking up, I asked, "Do we know who's in the pictures? Could one of them be the person that Ed mentioned, Terry?"

"We're checking on a few. Ed hasn't been as talkative since speaking to a lawyer, so our trek to getting answers is longer. So far, no one by that name."

Concentrating on the smaller details in the photos, I discovered that Ed appeared to be wearing a chain around his neck. It might not have been the source of all this trouble, but it was the only photograph that showed him wearing any jewelry. The only other jewelry in the picture was a ring that his girlfriend was wearing.

"Were they engaged?" I asked.

"She was wearing a ring, but Ed stated they weren't getting married. No one else knows anything about an engagement either," Ethan said.

Logan looked over my shoulder at the photo. "I think I've seen all I need to. Cassie?"

"I want to take a few pictures in here, but otherwise, I'm done." I snapped a few photos of the books and the pictures and followed Ethan and Logan out of the apartment.

Once outside in the cool spring day, it felt like I could breathe easier. "Thank you for showing us around. I think the only thing left for us is a visit to the morgue to see the victim."

Logan didn't miss a beat. It wasn't a part or our plan, but you'd never know that from his reaction.

Ethan looked tense again. "Your office didn't mention that part. I can call the hospital to let them know you're on the way." He looked like he wanted to say more.

"Yeah," Logan said, "we'll be out of your way after that. At least until Terry surfaces. We'd appreciate a heads up if he does."

"You're following the drugs, like the DEA." Ethan's strained look dropped away. "We've given the DEA some office space while they're working here."

"I'm surprised they don't have a substation nearby," I said.

"I think we've been too small of a town until the past few years," Ethan said, "I'm sure it's crossing their minds, though. I have to get back to the station, but I'll make a call to the morgue on my way."

With a polite nod, Ethan left. Wistfully, I had hoped for a better goodbye, but we were on the job and Logan and I needed to get to the morgue.

CHAPTER

TWELVE

The room looked and felt the same, stark white and shiny metal with a clean smell. The staff was different this time, though.

"Howdy," Logan said as he strode into the room, "thank you for the help."

The man didn't get up from a desk in the corner of the room. "It's no trouble."

Logan smiled, which appeared to make the room brighter. "That's good of you. Could we ask you to wrangle up what this woman had on when she came in?"

"Sure thing." The man appeared unconcerned and uninterested in our presence, but he had caught Logan's smile. After tapping a few buttons on his computer, he left the room.

The victim was on a table in the chilled room. The small, tight ball of emotion from the apartment was fresh in my mind, so I only took a cursory look at the body, which was more than enough to roll my stomach. Moving away, I let Logan have more room while I waited at the desk.

Logan, letting melancholy slip into his features, inspected

the victim more closely. When the elf moved from happy to this, the room around him appeared to dim. There were times when I was with my partner that I could almost believe there was real elven magic.

I wasn't sure what Logan was looking for as he examined the woman, but I didn't want to ask, either. I was too afraid he'd show me, and I didn't want to spend more time here than necessary.

Still smiling, the helpful man returned and sat a box on his desk. "The clothes are in the large bags."

Watching Logan, he covered the woman back up but stayed next to her.

"She didn't have much on her. Here, these are the two smaller bags," the man said.

I held out my hand but kept an eye on my partner. It was almost as if he flipped a switch. The sadness washed away and he looked normal again.

The man dropped a plastic bag in my hand, and I turned my attention back to the items the woman had.

A small shock of energy flexed and jumped straight into me. My eyes widened as I looked down into two plastic bags in my hand. The smallest of them held the same ring that the woman had been wearing in the picture. My hand jerked back in delayed reaction and the evidence clattered to the desk.

"Shit. Sorry." I didn't immediately recognize that I had spoken out loud.

"It's no problem," the man said, picking up the dropped items.

The sorry had been a more general sorry, one to me and to my partner for my stupidity. The buzz like a flow of electricity raced through me.

"You've been a great help," Logan said, keeping his voice

jovial. "Will pictures of these materials and a copy of the autopsy report be added to the police file today?"

Assuming the energy would try to settle in the same way as the last, I put up all the barriers I could. The trouble was that living beings are more fluid than our physical bodies would leave us to assume. Plus, this bolted through me much faster than the last.

"It might be tomorrow for the preliminary autopsy, but some of the photos may be available later today."

"Thanks again," Logan said.

With my concentration locked inside myself, I barely noticed the glances in our direction when Logan led me out of the hospital with haste.

The force spread up from my core and wrapped itself around me, much like the previous energy had, but there was a difference in the feel.

"How are you holding up?" Logan asked once we were outside.

"I—" The shift of energy was throwing me off. "I think it's okay."

"There's nothing there?" Logan asked.

"It's there, but... I don't feel angry or ready to lash out. I'm working hard to keep it away, though."

Logan hesitated at the truck. "It's not the same as the last?"

"Yes and no," I said, "I'm not sure what it is. Stick me in the back?"

"No, up front."

My concentration was too fierce to put up an argument.

Logan drove as fast as he dared. He was practically vibrating with his need to go faster. He made a call, but I didn't pay attention to who he contacted. Every defense I set up was beginning to fall apart. The energy slipped over, around, and through every obstacle I put in its way. It was like trying to hold the wind.

"I feel—" once again, I was struggling to put the feeling into words. "I feel anxious sitting still."

"Anxious, not angry," Logan said.

My leg bounced and my hands felt jittery. "I need to move around." It was as if someone poured a hundred cups of coffee into me, all at once.

"We're almost to your house."

As soon as the truck stopped, I jumped out and paced. Logan ran around the truck and ushered me into the house where Jonathan met us at the door with a tranq gun in hand. He looked ready to dart me but showed restraint.

"I'm not sure what this is." I began to wear a path into the floor by quickly pacing the room.

"What's happening?" Jonathan asked.

Words flung themselves out of my mouth faster than I could account for. Jonathan got a quick rundown of the jewelry circulating, with shards of essence. The need to be active, and to do more than pace, was strong. I made my way into the kitchen and scrubbed down counters and appliances as I talked.

"Maybe we should call the doctor?" Jonathan asked when I stopped to draw breath.

"I feel great. Fantastic really. Oh, maybe we could go out for a run. Wait, you two don't run. I should call Rider over to go for a run with me." I grabbed the phone only to have it yanked from my hands.

"I'll call Rider. Jonathan, keep an eye on her." Logan stalked out of the room.

"Do you run?" I asked.

"No," Jonathan said.

"Cookies!" I didn't even cringe at the delighted squeal that came out of my mouth. "You all need cookies."

Jonathan and Logan sat uneasily and watched me mix and bake cookies. Waiting for them to bake was driving me nuts, so I cleaned everything in the kitchen that I missed when I cleaned it the first time. The floors were being erratically scrubbed when Rider arrived.

"Is she okay?" Rider asked.

"I'm great." Great was an understatement. "Let's go out!"

Moving felt wonderful, and each time I finished something and bounced to the next thing, a little thrill went through me. There was so much to be done and so much I wanted to do. There had to be something bigger, though.

"Can you tell a difference in her?" Logan asked.

Rider picked me up and sat me on my feet.

I wrapped my arms around him, giving him a big hug before slipping out of his arms and going into the living room. "We really should go somewhere. Have you traveled much since you've been here?"

Logan followed me into the living room. "Rider needs to take a look at you."

Logan looked worried, so I relented and turned to Rider. He looked me over carefully, but standing without moving caused me to fidget. I needed to move.

"Your heart is racing," Rider studied my face, "and your eyes look strange. What happened?" He gently took my bruised wrist and held it close for inspection. "Her smell is off again."

"I thought it might be," Logan said.

"My smell is off?" Standing still was almost painful, so I took my arm away and began to inspect every item in the room.

Rider followed me, as though trying to look me over. "You really should sit."

"Can't," I replied. "If I don't move, it's bad."

"Maybe we should use the tranquilizer," Logan said.

"No way." This felt great and I wanted to keep it.

"Do we know anything that acts this way?" Jonathan asked.

"Not that I can think of," Logan said.

While I was rearranging some of the smaller items in the living room, my world slowed. I could feel the newly held power retreating.

"We need to keep these things away from her," Rider said.

Normally that kind of statement would have aggravated me to no end, but I was too content to be disturbed. "That 'her' is in the room." I said it out of habit more than anything else. "It's not like I took it on purpose. Besides, we don't know what they are. It could be stored energy, stolen away."

"I don't think so," Logan said. "Seeing this makes me revisit our original idea. This isn't only energy. I think you're pulling in a part of someone. Part of them that has broken off and stored away."

"Did Hank find anything on a missing minotaur?" I asked.

Logan shook his head. "Nothing came up in the area."

The jittery feeling faded, and a part of me wanted that high back. As I slowed down even more, I began to realize what that meant.

"It's a drug." This time, I cringed at the excited little squeak that broke through.

Logan and Rider looked at me expectantly.

Once I felt confident my voice was under my control, I continued. "It leaks out and affects a person. Someone wears it and gets a little dose of what's inside."

"But when you touch it, you get the whole thing," Logan said, catching on.

"Right," I said, "maybe it has to do with my gifts. It jumps into me."

"All the more reason to keep you away from it," Jonathan said.

"Maybe," I said, "but now that we have a better idea of what's going on, I have a chance of controlling it."

Logan raised an eyebrow. "Control it?"

"Well, more like block it. I don't go around grabbing energy or essence out of everything I touch. Now that we know what to expect, I can try to come up with a way to block it. Maybe I can make its Path not enter my own."

"That might be possible," Logan conceded, "but we can't assume that yet."

"This could be the drug that the DEA is looking for." I yawned and didn't want to be standing anymore, so I sank into a seat. The more I felt like myself, the more tired and achy I became.

"She is returning to normal," Rider said.

"That's for sure." The almost overwhelming euphoric emotions died away with the rush I had experienced.

"Thanks for the help, son. You can take off. Put that tranquilizer gun back where you found it."

"Sure thing, Dad." Jonathan got up; he hesitated for a minute, but his dad motioned towards the door and he left.

"Is it gone?" Logan asked.

I rolled my shoulders, trying to expel some of the ache that was taking up residence in my joints. "I'm feeling normal. Tired and sore, but I feel like myself."

"That doesn't answer the question," Logan said. "Is the first one there?"

You can't keep things from your partner. The office and your boss? That was no problem. Logan and Rider deserved the truth.

"It's not like it's front and center. With the first one at least, I barely notice anything. The second will probably be the same. It's already settling in."

Rider radiated concern. "It did not go away? Can you make it leave?"

"I can try," I said, "but it's difficult to pinpoint. At first, the whole thing feels alien. I can tell it doesn't belong. Once the general effects are over, I don't really notice it anymore."

Logan and Rider didn't say anything, but they didn't look too happy either.

"Look," I said, "it's not like I'm hurt. It'll probably fade further away as time goes on."

"Could be," Logan said, "but keep your guard up. Meditation might help. Rider had a good suggestion, force it out if you can."

"I'll do my best." I yawned and stretched. My muscles felt like I had run miles.

Logan stood. "Get some rest. I'll be by in the morning to pick you up."

"Take some cookies with you. Rider, you too." It felt like I sank further into my chair.

Rider looked confused. "You will be okay on your own?"

"Sure, and Gran will be home in a while, and I might have company later tonight." As though to prove a point, I got up and went to the kitchen to divide out cookies.

Rider took a few and left looking reluctant.

Logan went out the back door. I could hear him chirp to Cici who responded by twittering back. The language of the fairies was not one that I was privy to. Not that they would talk to me anymore anyway.

When Gran came home, we talked before making dinner together. After that, she busied herself with a few chores before she went to bed. I was determined to stay up, at least for a while, despite my fatigue.

My computer called to me as a distraction. Pulling up my email, I discovered that Quin had been in contact the night before. Opening the letter, I felt bad getting it so late.

DEAR ANALA,

It was good to hear about your experiences with the shadows in the Path. It set my mind at ease. It has cropped up from time to time over the years, so I'm glad I don't have to worry on it any longer. I've never been moved into the future of the Path for more than a minute or two. I spend my time looking through the past. Have you wandered into the Path when a monument has been built? I spent hours the other day, watching one under construction. It was beautiful.

Your question about the blank spot in the Path has me intrigued. I don't know of anything that could leave such spots on the Path. I've never seen an area where the Path didn't flow. It makes me step back and wonder what type of person could cause the Path to disappear when they walked through? Whatever is causing it, I think you should leave it alone. I'll let you know if I find anything similar.

Sincerely,

Quin

I READ the letter twice before closing the laptop. Having another Reader to turn to was a treasure, but I do have to keep on my toes. Reading the Path had altered for me in the past year. I'm stronger, but I also have less control. On top of that, too much of my work was confidential.

CHAPTER

THIRTEEN

It was ten-thirty when Ethan texted. Not too late in the scheme of things. I replied, giving my address and letting him know that I would be up for a while longer if he wanted to stop by.

Before I had time to get nervous, he was at my door.

Despite the long day, it felt good having Ethan here. "Hi, come on in."

"I feel pretty lucky you were up," Ethan said, as I led him into the kitchen.

"I'm glad you came over." Once I grabbed some drinks and a plate of cookies for us, we sat at the table.

Ethan looked tired, but like me, he looked pleased with where he was. "You have a nice place."

"Thanks."

"Are we going to bother your grandmother?"

I grinned. "Not at all, Gran's used to me having people over late."

"She is, is she?"

"For work." Embarrassment was written in red across my

cheeks. "I meant that Logan and Rider sometimes stay late to work on a case."

"And what would she think of someone not work-related stopping by?"

"'Good for you.' I'm pretty sure that's exactly what she'd think." She probably would have added, 'it's about time,' 'good luck' or possibly even 'go for it,' but I wasn't going to throw that out there.

Ethan chuckled. "I look forward to meeting her." He was close enough that it was easy for him to take my hand. "I probably shouldn't stay long, tomorrow is bound to be another long day."

His hand was warm and it felt good entwined with mine.

"I'll bet," I said. "Still, it was good of you to stop by, even for a while."

"With our jobs coming together yesterday, I was worried."

"What about?" I almost held my breath, hoping I hadn't made a total fool of myself leaving.

"Well, you were upset. Logan said the shrink bothered you, but I thought I may have done, or said something." Ethan looked down, embarrassed.

"Sorry to make you feel that way. We shouldn't have to work together much, so it'll take us a while to get used to it."

Ethan frowned. "What happened?"

"With the psychiatrist?" I twisted in my seat, unsure about telling him.

"No." He held my hand and then slid up the edges of my shirtsleeve.

"Oh yeah."

"May I?" Ethan asked with his hands over the buttons on my sleeve.

"Um, yeah. I guess."

He carefully unbuttoned the shirtsleeve and rolled it up. He traced the edges of a bruise with his finger, which made me shiver. When he didn't say anything, I bit my lip, and then reached to push down the sleeve.

Why did I say that was okay? "It looks worse than it feels."

His brow furrowed, and when I had the sleeve back down, he took the other hand and peeked around the edges.

I sighed and took one of his hands in both of mine. "Work hazard. It's no big deal."

Ethan looked pale. "That may be harder for me to adjust to."

A lump formed in my throat, but I swallowed it down. "You've never picked up an injury on the job?"

"I keep trying to think of what situation would cause bruises like that. For someone to grab you that hard. Where was Logan? Or that other partner of yours?"

I had to admit that the bruises probably looked bad from his point of view, but trying not to get aggravated was difficult. "My partners were right there with me." I let go of his hand and leaned back. "And we all help each other, but the job isn't always easy."

He appeared to struggle with what to say, but I could tell his eyes were focused inward.

My frustration levels dropped when I realized he had more ugly images in his mind than the run-of-the-mill person on the street. "You see bad things, every day. I get it; it's your job to stop the evils in the world. It's my job too." He tried to interrupt, but I kept going. "But, sometimes things look much worse than they are. You know I can't tell you what happened, but remember, it's not all bad. Someone might grab hold of someone if they're scared or in pain, and it would cause as much damage."

Ethan seemed to think that over. "You're right, sorry."

My face was flushed red. There was so much I wanted to

say, and not all of it was friendly, but I liked Ethan. I could tell his mind had been striking out in bad places, but I also had to make him understand.

In the silence, I gathered my words together. "Before we decide to move forward from here, there are a few things I need to say."

Ethan looked like he was trying to bring his thoughts back to the light. "Okay."

"First, my partners and I, we look out for each other, but it's not their job to make sure that nothing ever happens to me. We all carry our own weight. Second, you have to understand that I'm not a woman with a nine-to-five work life. We both have jobs that are tough, and I have training, same as you. And this is so important for you to understand, I am not helpless, and if you ever try to treat me like I am, we're going to have issues."

Ethan's face was flush. "Anything else?"

"That covers most of it."

"Okay, my turn."

His turn?

He must have sensed I was going to break in, because he held out a finger, to wait. "You're right, in this job, your thoughts go to some bad places, and like it or not, I'm going to be upset when I see you injured. It's only going to be worse since you can't tell me what happened. Also, I don't know your partners at all, so yes, I may question what they were doing when you're black and blue, and they seem fine."

I crossed my arms but kept my mouth shut. How would he know if they were injured or not?

"And yes, I'm going to put your welfare above theirs." He held up a finger again, to hold back what I was going to say. "I really like you, and it's going to pain me to see you injured. But do not mistake my concern for you as an indication that I think you can't take care of yourself."

"Can I say something?" I kept my voice level.

"Two more things." Ethan's voice slowed. "You're definitely not an ordinary woman, which I think is why I like you so much. And I'm going to say and do the wrong things along the way. It's a fact that I've learned to live with."

I bit my lip to keep the corners of my mouth from turning up. "Anything else?"

"Yes." Ethan let out a steady breath. "I shouldn't have said or assumed anything about your partners. Now that I know you're okay... are they? Logan looked fine, but I didn't see the other one today. Agent Wolfe, right?"

I looked into Ethan's face and saw genuine concern. "Rider, yes. He and Logan are okay."

Ethan stood up. "I'm sorry about tonight. Seeing someone I care about hurt and not being able to do anything about it, well, it's hard to deal with."

Studying his face, I also stood up. "Too hard to deal with?"

We stood there, looking at each other and I could feel the question hanging heavy in the air.

One corner of Ethan's mouth turned up. "It's going to be a big adjustment."

The tension that had been building died away. "Yes and the fact that I'm amazingly clumsy isn't going to help matters."

Ethan stepped closer, and the look in his eyes made my heart beat faster. "I'm sure it'll take a lot of patience on your end to put up with me."

I inched closer and took his hands. "Patience is not one of my strengths. I have witnesses."

"Where does that leave us then?"

Eyes locked together, I wrapped my arms around him and

we kissed. He held me tight, and soon my eyes shut, and I lost myself in the moment.

That time stretched out and into the living room. After having to keep so much control over the past few days, it was almost a surprise that I could let myself go so completely. There was a hitch when he unbuttoned my shirt and saw bruises on my stomach. I froze, expecting a bad reaction, but he traced his fingers lightly over the skin, kissed me again, and seemed to forget the whole thing. When his phone rang a minute later, we stopped kissing to catch our breath.

The phone was in his pocket, but Ethan wasn't in a hurry to answer. Still, I knew our evening was over, which was probably for the best, even though a part of me wanted to smash his phone. It was the same part that was confused as to why we were wearing so many clothes, even with half of them on the floor, so it was best to ignore that inclination and lock it away for now.

"You are beautiful," Ethan breathed, giving me a kiss that was much more chaste.

He looked dreamy, but I gently pushed him up. "You should answer your phone, Lieutenant Parker."

"Was that a request, Agent Heidrich?" Ethan kissed me again.

I laughed through the kiss, and then broke apart. "I wasn't aware there was the option of an order. But now, you know, you can never call me Agent again while on the job."

Ethan sounded amused, but when he looked at the caller ID on his phone, he sighed and stood up. He was tucking in his shirt on the way to taking the call in the kitchen.

I stretched out on the couch and closed my eyes, wanting to keep hold of this feeling.

Unfortunately, I could tell from Ethan's tone of voice that he would be on his way out the door soon. Patting my hair, I tried to make sure it wasn't too bad when I went into the kitchen. Ethan looked almost put together. When he got off the phone, I had a plastic food bag with cookies waiting for him.

"Sorry, I have to go," Ethan said.

"Work is work." With a kiss, I handed him the bag.

"You didn't have to—"

"Gran would be horribly embarrassed if I didn't."

"Only if you told her," Ethan said, stowing the cookies in a jacket pocket.

"Trust me, she always knows."

THE NEXT DAY, Gran left early after giving me the warning to stay out or Rider's way, which was cryptic. Since Rider was my partner, I was not sure how it would be possible either.

Being alone allowed me to work through some tangled thoughts. It would have been wonderful if my sleeping mind had dwelt on my evening with Ethan, but the case was weighing me down. Last night, nightmares showed me blurry images of my partners having their souls ripped out and stuffed into jewelry that I wore. In the dream, I had tried to take the necklace off, but it clung to my skin.

The morning's coffee didn't wash away the dreams, so when the phone rang, I groaned and assumed it was bad news ready to ruin my day.

"Good morning, Cassie." Ethan's voice put a tremor in my stomach.

"Good morning." I was determined not to trip over my own tongue, making assumptions as to the nature of the call, so I stopped there.

"I overheard an interesting conversation this morning that I thought your team would be interested in."

Of course, it was work related. My entire life was work. "Sounds intriguing. What do you have for us?"

"I happened to walk by the offices of our friends at the DEA. They cleared out, leaving for Langston."

"I have no idea where that is. Why were they going there?"

"It's on the outskirts of the city. They mentioned a drug bust," Ethan said, "and you and your partners have taken a special interest in some necklaces."

"We have," I agreed, wondering how weird that sounded from his point of view.

"They mentioned that there was a bunch of jewelry there as well. That's probably not too rare with drug money, but it sounded like these were bagged up like the drugs."

My interest ratcheted up. "Have they already left? Did you hear anything else?"

Ethan let out a chuckle. "I thought you'd be interested, so I called you right away. They were leaving the office when I walked by. That's all I have."

"This is great, thank you, Ethan."

Ethan's voice dropped to a less professional level. "I'm sorry I had to leave like that last night."

"It's okay. I understand. Are we on for tomorrow?"

I could hear Ethan's smile through the phone. "The day looks clear. I'll pick you up around nine-thirty tomorrow morning?"

"I'll have my hiking boots laced up."

When Ethan and I were off the phone, I called Hank. We needed an all-access pass to a DEA crime scene and, as our handler, Hank always made sure we were well prepared and had what we needed.

Hank clicked away on his keyboard after I told him what I knew. "Access to the site could take a while, but if it's in the city, it'll take you over an hour to get there anyway."

"Luckily, the local team doesn't have too long of a head-start on us." I shot off a text to Logan and Rider, telling them to gear up for a road trip. "Is there anything in the system yet?"

"So far, only a prelim report. We know where they are and drugs are involved."

"How long ago was the bust made?"

"About an hour ago. Kyrian should be able to pull some strings to get you all in as soon as you arrive."

"Do you think she can get them to keep people away?" It was a long shot, but worth a try. "A clear site would be easier for tracking, but I've already ticked the DEA off once."

"With this late of a start, I doubt we can make that happen."

Another thought struck me. "Any way to get MyTH out there? They're close by, and at least we can learn what's happening on scene."

"They don't have badges." Hank paused in his relentless attack on the keyboard. "Actually, one person does. Let me talk to Kyrian and see if we can move in that direction."

Two texts came through, letting me know that Rider and Logan were on their way. "How did someone from MyTH end up with a badge?"

"They're only about ten years old, some sort of an offshoot of an older organization. The man who set it up came from AIR. Agent Gordon took early retirement to set up shop in the city."

"And AIR let him go off on his own?" I asked.

"I checked out the file once, and chunks of the report were redacted. Something happened in St. Louis around that time. MyTH was set up to oversee it, and AIR gave their blessing."

"Hopefully they can get Gordon over to the site. If he can, have Sable and Dr. Taylor meet us there as well."

"Will do."

"Thanks, Hank. Before I go, have you heard any updates about the minotaurs?"

"Everyone's accounted for so far. You'll hear from me soon."

It should have been a relief, but, as I hung up the phone, it made me wonder what we were dealing with. If all the minotaurs were accounted for, could we even be dealing with souls?

Hank got back to me once Logan, Rider, and I were on the road. MyTH was on their way to the site.

"Hopefully this will lead to another piece of the puzzle. We do not have much to go on yet," Rider said.

Glancing at Rider, I saw nothing that would make me want to move out of his way. Still, Gran wouldn't have given me the warning for no reason.

"True, and no suspects," I said.

Rider and Logan remained silent. I could have asked them if they still thought Vincent was behind this, but I chickened out, certain that I didn't want to hear their answer.

"So, what are we walking into?" Logan asked after a few beats of silence.

Grateful for the change of subject, I opened the file.

"Hank sent us a little more," I said. "The bust is joint work with local police and DEA. Suspects have been removed and are in interrogation. The last time they updated the file they were photographing and cataloging items on site."

"Anything about the jewelry?" Logan asked.

"Not a thing," I said. "Maybe they aren't connecting the two yet."

"Keep a close eye when we get there," Logan said. "Make sure nothing has slipped into their evidence bags before we have a chance to take a look."

"What are you going to do when we get there?" Rider asked me.

"Same as usual. It's a crime scene," I said.

"I do not think it is a good idea for you to be in the room until we know if the jewelry is active or not," Rider said.

"He makes a good point," Logan said. "We don't know what, if anything, we have here. It would be bad if you took in a bunch of energy from the Lost at a crime scene."

"I've been thinking about that." The implication that I couldn't handle my job made me twist in my seat. "Nothing seems to happen if I am near the items, only when I touch one of them, and it shouldn't be hard to avoid that. No one's going to be tossing around evidence."

Logan began humming to himself.

"Look," I said, "I can do my job."

"We know that," Rider said, "but we want to keep you safe."

Logan shook his head then continued to hum.

I took a couple of meditative breaths before responding. It really didn't help. "Are you going to be able to tell if something is in the jewelry without me? Have either of you been able to detect anything in the items?" Rider didn't answer. "Look, I'm not saying it's the best idea, but if the unexpected happens, I can at least hold things off 'til we are away from the scene. I managed to do that at the police station, and that was before we knew what to expect."

Logan's humming filled the silence for the rest of the trip. The ethereal tones rolled over me, taking my aggravation as it went. The GPS took us right up to the entrance of an apartment building. There were police officers mingled in with several agents with DEA stamped across the back of their jackets.

"Has the file been updated?" Logan asked.

Outside the truck, Rider took in the entire scene and appeared tense.

It took a few seconds for the tablet to refresh. "Nothing

new." Watching Rider's anxiety threatened to bring back my aggravation. "Look, take some tranquilizers with us, just to be on the safe side."

"I do not want to tranquilize you." He looked offended, but it didn't last long. Rider tensed, all anxiety seeming to flee, and he looked around the site.

Following suit, I took a tentative step into the Path. The dark recesses hidden beyond my mind shifted as I jumped the gap over them, and into the Path. Rippling waves of emotion streamed widely, but it was punctuated by holes that held no glimmering traces and dulled the areas around them.

Goosebumps broke out on my arms. "We're in the right place."

"Good to know," Logan said. "I grabbed some tranqs. Let's scoot on in there."

"Scoot?" I looked at my partner in surprise.

Logan grinned. "Cowboy lingo."

Of course it was.

Rider rolled his head on his shoulders, grabbed a tranquilizer without looking at it and put it into his pocket. Logan took the lead and I followed behind, but everything was out of balance and had me moving slower than normal. When I damned up the Path, reading only a tiny trickle, most of the effects died away. There were blank spots to avoid which caused my trail to wind. Rider followed my zig-zagging path. I'm not sure if he could sense what he was avoiding, or if he was trying to cover the fact that I looked ridiculous.

There were a few agents outside. One guarding an official truck with two other men taking notes, and another few moving to and from the apartment. Two officers guarded the yellow crime-scene tape around the yard, keeping a close eye on the neighbors that were smoking and watching the show with interest. Rider's nose wrinkled up. Hopefully, the cigarette smoke wouldn't hide the scents we needed to track.

Each agent took notice of our approach, making sure we knew they were watching. Logan flashed a badge as we approached the officer standing watch over the door. The guard inspected our badges, taking more time than I thought the occasion warranted. Finally, after looking at each of our IDs, he let us through.

Even with the people outside the apartment, it was over-crowded when we entered the room. Two men tried to bar our progress further, but our badges wiped away the protests.

"Make a big bust and all the feds come out of the wood-works," someone muttered. "Where were these guys last week?"

Seeing the holes in the Path was making me edgy, and I wanted to turn to tell the man exactly where we were last week and where he could shove his comment, but Logan intercepted and brought us further into the room.

"Telling that fool anything isn't going to help you or him," he said in a low voice.

The argument was on the tip of my tongue, but he was right, so I let Logan steer me further into the room and straight into Doctor Taylor. Literally. I bumped into him from behind and I was apologizing before I even recognized him.

"Good to see you here," he said quietly. Taylor hadn't taken his eyes off a door in the hallway and I could hear a heated discussion coming from the other room.

"Who's in there?" I asked.

"Gordon's in there with some DEA agent that tried to kick us out," Taylor said. "And what you're looking for is in that room."

FOURTEEN

That was enough for Logan. He tipped an imaginary hat at Taylor and walked into the room. Rider was caught in indecision. He followed Logan, but then stopped and watched the door, much like Taylor.

When Taylor looked at me, I shrugged. "Logan will sort them out." Under my breath I added, "One way or another." I meant it for Rider's ears, but both he and Taylor relaxed.

"Is Sable here?" I asked.

"No, only Gordon and myself," Taylor said.

"Rider, do you want to see if you can pick up anything while we wait?" I asked.

Immediately, his eyes darted around everywhere and moved in circles around the room. It was a difficult task with this many bodies. A few people grumbled, but I caught their eye and gave them my best glare. I didn't make any friends, but I was an unknown quantity, as was Rider, so no one spoke out too loudly. The room had the stuffy, sticky feeling of too many people in one area. There was no objection from me when someone reached around me and turned on the AC.

"What's happened so far?" I asked, trying to keep my voice low.

"The place has been dusted and inventoried. Some of the drugs were being moved off scene when we arrived. Gordon put his foot down and holed up with the lead DEA agent to tell him off. I'm not sure what it accomplished."

"It bought us some time at least. They didn't move any of the jewelry?" I asked.

"No, but they moved quite a bit of meth out."

"Rider?" I didn't have to raise my voice. His ears picked up everything. "Can you try to tell if any of our evidence walked off?"

I saw Rider nod and walk into the room where Logan had disappeared. I guess he was getting a good scent off the items in question. When someone yelled, I followed my partner inside but found Rider blissfully ignorant of the man's attention. Even with the voids cutting through the sliver of Path I was watching, I could tell the jewelry was what we were looking for. With so many pieces together, even from here I could feel the energy radiating from them.

"It's here," I said quietly.

Rider perked up and went to the jewelry while a man continued to yell at him. Logan and a balding gray-haired man that I assumed to be Gordon, watched the angry man.

"Don't touch it," I whispered to Rider, knowing my voice would break through the other noise to reach him.

Rider rolled his eyes, a move he'd recently picked up from me, and hovered around the plastic folding table that held our evidence. He paced back and forth, and then breezed past us, out of the room and on the trail.

This only upset the man further. "What the hell does he think he's doing? You all can't—"

My patience had reached its tipping point. "Excuse me, we can and we will. You are?"

He brought himself up to his full height, ensuring that he stood taller than I did. "I'm Special Agent Wilson of the DEA, and this is my crime scene."

I heard someone scoff from the other room. Apparently, some of the local officers weren't too thrilled about the joint task force.

"I think we've heard enough for now." Logan didn't lose his smile, but his eyes looked hard as they settled on Wilson. "Let's get the place cleared out."

Gordon was keeping silent. Trying to ignore the feeling that the blank spots in the Path were trying to fold in on me, I held out my hand and introduced myself. "I'm Agent Heidrich."

Gordon peered at me, hesitating only momentarily before shaking my hand. "It's a pleasure to meet you. I'm Agent Gordon." He shook my hand, but our introduction was interrupted.

Gordon might not have minded meeting me, but I wasn't so lucky with the other agitated man in the room.

Wilson honed in on my motion like a shark and swore at me. "Who the hell do you think you are? Walking in—"

Trying to keep my cool wasn't working. "Agent Wilson—"

Wilson's face turned redder and stepped closer to me. "That's Special Agent Wilson. Don't you forget it!"

Trying to rein in my anger, I took a long look at Wilson. The man was too close, but there was no way I was backing up for this jerk. Even when people were put off by my shattered soul, I had never encountered anyone on the job that acted this unprofessional.

Logan moved up to the man, speaking in a calm voice.

"Special Agent Wilson, why don't we go for a walk and discuss this situation."

While Logan tried to pacify the man, I watched reds and oranges pop onto the Path, and then wrap themselves tight around Special Agent Wilson.

Wilson's Path melded into a cloudy shade of red as blackness snaked in and I almost took a step away. The bright glare flaring up on his hand was what grabbed my attention.

His hands balled into fists. "Why don't you and your team go—"

"He took evidence." The words popped out of my mouth before thinking.

Any sense of restraint Wilson may have had broke. Open palmed, his hand slammed across my face. Shock ran through me almost as fast as the stinging pain in my cheek.

Logan broke his cool. Even had I not been in the Path, I would have sensed the explosion of aggression that jumped from the elf. In the Path, the usual golden color that surrounded Logan burst away, replaced by anger so violent that it etched into the room. His features looked sharper, which was a clear indication things were about to get bad.

Before I could fully take in the situation, Doctor Taylor was there. In a blur, he twisted Wilson's arm behind his back and tipped him forward enough to shove him into the floor. Rider was at the door. I'm not sure if he heard what was happening or felt Logan's anger. I caught his eye, and he took a step into the room, but I held up a hand to have him wait; there was already too much confusion. Rider was going to object, but I waved him away. He leaned against the door-frame.

Logan stood unmoving while he bottled up his flare of fury. He looked strained while trying to regain his composure.

Trying to steady my own anger didn't take the heat from my voice. "The ring on his finger needs to be taken off."

Without losing his grip, Taylor reached down, slid the ring off, and held it out for me to take.

Some part of me wanted it. I wanted to open the Path and let that tiny piece of the Lost jump into me.

My heart nearly skipped a beat and I shivered before taking a few steps back, bumping into the wall. Taylor took his eyes away from the agent for the first time and watched me as Logan took the ring.

Wilson sputtered, went slack, and his breath sounded as if he had run his out-of-shape body through a marathon.

I ignored the look from Taylor and addressed the man on the floor. "Special Agent Wilson, it's time for you to step aside and pull yourself together."

The man had hit me, I didn't retaliate, and now it was too late. This realization did nothing to temper my anger. "Or should I have the good doctor here escort you out?"

Taylor managed to pull Wilson to his feet, even though it looked like the agent outweighed him by more than twenty pounds. Without waiting for an answer, Wilson, looking confused, was led to the door. Rider left without saying anything. Taylor said a few whispered words to Wilson who nodded, more towards the ground than at Taylor. Taylor dropped Wilson's arm and followed him out of the room.

Wanting to make sure the man was far away from me, I stepped out and watched Wilson leave. Everyone bagging evidence very carefully kept their eyes away from the men leaving. Concentrating on the Path, I couldn't see a void, but the last smear of rage that had surrounded Wilson fell away.

"Moron," I said, not bothering to keep my voice down.

Back in the room, Logan was handing an evidence bag over to Gordon.

"So this is what we're after?" Gordon held the bag up to the light.

"That's it, or at least part of it." I gestured to the plastic table holding many pieces of jewelry.

Gordon turned the bag around in his hands. "Does the bag dampen the effects?"

I glanced towards the door. "We don't really know yet. Everyone that's responded has been wearing the ring for a while. Agent Wilson could have put on the piece hours ago." I glanced towards the door again and nailed down the source of my anxiety. "Maybe Rider should try to spot if anyone else has a souvenir?"

"I'll talk with him," Logan said on his way out the door.

"Are you ready for us to bag evidence?" Gordon asked before Logan left.

Logan glanced at me before addressing Gordon. "If you can get us started, then that would be great."

Gordon agreed, and Logan left, to be quickly replaced by Taylor.

At the table, Gordon took a few pictures before pulling out some evidence bags. "What do we know about these items?"

We had approval from AIR to work with MyTH, and Gordon was technically an agent with clearance, so I filled them in on what we knew so far about the jewelry. I stayed across the room while Gordon and Taylor bagged each piece and set them back on the table. It was interesting how each one of them checked the seals on each bag multiple times to ensure they were firmly sealed.

"Do we know if this is all of it?" Gordon asked.

I couldn't tell if Gordon was asking Taylor or me.

"I'll be able to look around more once what we have is out in the truck." My skin felt itchy being this close to it. I wanted to walk over and put my hands on each piece of jewelry. I was already leaning against the wall, so I couldn't back further away. I was about to walk out when Rider reentered holding a box.

"Any other pieces picked up?" I asked.

"One more and I think another piece or two left earlier. I am not sure if it was before, during, or after the authorities entered the building." Rider dropped the box on the table and reached out to grab a bag.

"Wait," I said.

Rider drew back and looked at me impatiently.

"Let's wait until Logan gets back," I said.

Rider stalked to the other side of the room and then paced back to the table. We weren't sure how the Lost would react to the fragments in the jewelry, but I didn't know how to say that in front of the others.

Gordon looked at Rider. "We'll finish bagging each item. Why don't you help Agent Heidrich check out the rest of the place?" He winked at Rider.

Since I didn't know Gordon, I didn't want to leave him alone with the evidence. "It might be easier once the apartment is cleared out."

Gordon went back to work. Rider paced around the room, throwing jittery yellow streaks onto the Path.

Watching my friend, I worried. "Rider?" I reached out to him to stop his pacing, but he shook me off. Nothing from the room appeared to be interfering with Rider, but his Path was becoming more vibrant, and increasingly wild. "Rider, I think you should slow down."

Gordon continued putting the evidence away, but Taylor was now watching Rider pace. Taylor waited until Rider had walked across the room again before slowly approaching, which caused the werewolf to issue a low growl. Taylor stepped back and Gordon, after a quick look, moved away and put his back against a wall, putting space between himself and Rider.

Rider moved quicker and he looked lost in his thoughts.

"It's not the jewelry, but there's definitely something wrong." It was said more to myself than the others. Feeling anxious, I stepped in front of Rider, blocking his way. "Rider, stop for a second."

Rider reached out and grabbed my arm in a vice-like grip. His fingers elongated and claws dug into my skin. Looking into his eyes, my heart froze and I stopped breathing. Rider's normal calm and curious eyes were gone, replaced with an intensely animal presence.

Rider's wolf showed through. It was the first time I'd seen it, and nothing in those eyes looked like they knew me.

"Get out of my way." Rider's voice was soft, but the menace it contained made the hairs on my arms stand on end.

Rider's eyes narrowed and he tossed me aside. There was barely time for me to think when I left the ground, but true panic jumped in when I landed on the table.

FIFTEEN

My body tensed as I slammed into the table. Tiny bits of essence flew straight into me. Before I could really think of options, I ripped through the Path and molded it into a shield around myself. I could feel a few alien bits of energy ratcheting around in my body. The new essence wasn't mixing well with what had already claimed me as home. As other pieces began clinging to my shield, I put as much focus as possible into keeping it up. This was becoming more and more difficult with the chaos of the room.

Rider attempted to rush over to me, whether to help or throw me again, I wasn't sure. For the second time today, I had Taylor to thank. He barred Rider's advances.

Rider looked like he was trying to get himself under control and he didn't lash out at Taylor, but it also looked like he was losing the battle.

Gordon came over to me to try to help, but I shuffled away from him, further into the wreckage of the table. I wasn't able to articulate the warfare going on inside.

Gordon took the hint and backed off. "What the hell is happening? Is this the jewelry? He didn't touch them."

It didn't take Taylor long to come to a conclusion. "It's meth. It looks like he's hopped up on meth."

"Isn't he a werewolf?" Gordon hissed the words, trying to keep his voice low. "A tweaked-out werewolf is not ideal in a small room."

"In any room," Logan said.

Relief flooded me when I heard my partner enter. It didn't last long however—my bubble of protection wavered. Logan could handle Rider at least, and I could concentrate on my own issue.

Rider turned his head to Logan and back to the others a few times. His Path was becoming gray and muddled with the greens and browns of his non-human side.

"Confusion. Paranoia." I couldn't form complete sentences, but I would be damned if I wasn't going to help.

Doctor Taylor looked ready to launch himself against Rider. Fleetingly I thought, how stupid can you get? I've seen Rider beat a demon to death. I'd hate to see what he could do with a man like Taylor.

Logan was prepared. He took out his tranquilizer and actually threw the dart at Rider. It didn't put him to sleep, but it took a little of the wind out of his sails.

Logan turned to Taylor. "This isn't going to last long." He glanced at me before he continued. "How do you treat meth?"

"He needs an opiate. I have some in my med kit." Taylor looked hesitant to leave.

Rider was calm enough for Logan to reach into his pocket. Logan took the tranquilizer that had been meant for me and drove the point into Rider. Rider was on his feet, but his Path looked sluggish.

Logan looked at me again before turning to Taylor. "Bring everything you have."

Taylor left the room at a run while Logan stayed between Rider and the door.

"What's the situation over there?" Logan asked me.

Rider was shaking his arms and rolling his shoulders, burning through the tranquilizers.

I leaned against the wall, watching the blurs of light roll around on the enclosure keeping them at bay. "Take care of him."

Rider was wearing down the carpet again by the time Taylor came back. Taylor had a bag in one hand and a needle in another.

"What's his metabolic rate?" Taylor asked.

"Fast," Logan replied. "Why isn't the meth out of his system?"

"It must be in the air. We need to move him out of here."

"Dope him up and we'll get him into the truck," Logan said.

"Will it hold him?" Taylor asked.

"Those things will hold a rampaging chimera. It'll hold him," Gordon said.

Logan took care of Rider while I immersed myself in my own issues. I struggled to maintain my shielding and watched tiny bits of sparkling light trying to break through the shield. Almost breaking my concentration, I heard a scuffle, but when I managed to look beyond my shield, Rider was calm, and Logan took him away.

"Watch over her, but don't touch her," Logan said as he left the room.

"The meth indicators were clear earlier," Gordon said. "We shouldn't get a higher concentration after it's removed. I'm going to poke around more." He left Taylor and me alone.

Taylor crouched down and watched me from a short distance away. I looked at him, but my focus was internal. Weariness settled in as I burned myself up to keep those bits of energy from reaching any further. Even the essence that had jumped into me were being burnt out through the effort.

"I've seen looks like yours on battlefields." His gaze was intense.

I didn't answer. If you looked at me, you'd see me sitting there, doing nothing. However, my grip was slipping. I'm not sure what would happen if everything jumped into my system at once. Could I handle that?

"Can you tell me what you need?"

I wanted Logan here, but I had Taylor for the moment. He was a doctor, maybe he knew how to help better than we did. I closed my eyes, trying to think of anything useful.

"Not sure what she's going to need, but we have an idea about what's happening." Logan stood nearby, which made me feel stronger. "That jewelry holds fragments of the Lost. She attracts it to her, like a fairy is attracted to plums. My guess is each and every one of those necklaces and rings are empty now. Did you keep them off ya?"

"Mostly," I managed to say.

"Well, let's get you out of here." Logan came towards me, but I backed away along the wall, clattering through our evidence on the way.

"They're here, surrounding me." I shuddered. "If they jump, a raging elf won't help."

Taylor lifted an eyebrow and looked at Logan.

Logan answered his unasked question. "She's afraid they'll jump from her to us, and she's right, it's possible." Logan squatted and watched me. "Any way to get rid of them?"

Feeling myself drain away, I made the only decision I could

to keep everyone else in the room safe. Looking straight into Logan's eyes, I said, "Be ready."

Before he could form a response, my barrier crumbled.

My body went rigid as everything punched into me. Power whipped together. My own essence felt drained but began to revive as it joined the rolling turmoil. Whatever mores my shattered soul had made in my body were ripped away as it mixed with the new fragments that were swarming into me. I went slack and couldn't move.

The reaction wasn't only internal. The Path around me didn't fall away, but instead it began to fight. Empty spaces in the Path broke out around me, trying to erase traces of my presence from the room. The Path didn't want evidence of me removed. I had been there and it knew it, so it struggled to sweep the empty spaces away.

As I watched, Logan's face appeared. He moved me into a flatter position on the ground. Taylor also appeared and looked like a professional at work. My vision clouded around the edges, but I saw Taylor lean over me with a stethoscope. If I could have spoken, I might have protested when he ripped a few buttons off my shirt, but he was completely clinical in his examination. He listened closely to my heartbeat.

A familiar feeling crept over me as my vision clouded over completely. I could fall away, out of this existence and into the next. I'd taken that route once before and I wouldn't let it happen again. Sweat broke out as I made an effort to stop the aberrant activity of my soul. The confusion inside slowed, but I could no longer tell what was foreign energy and what was my own. Maybe they were the same now?

Bright blobs of Path danced above me when I was moved. My mind refused to stop reading. When I closed my eyes, a falling sensation met me, and I jerked them open again. I couldn't leave, too much would be left behind.

CHAPTER

SIXTEEN

Time passed in lurches, and occasionally I heard voices, some familiar, and some unknown. I had no idea where I had been moved to, but I felt safe each time I heard Logan's voice.

Reality bent when I went from working to keep my eyes open, to trying to close them. People asked me questions, but I was having a hard time sorting through their words. My skin felt dry and stretched, but relief came when a lulling sensation spread over me.

There was blissful darkness until arguing woke me up. Everything was too bright when I opened my eyes to an unfamiliar room.

"You sobered me up for this?" A young man, maybe twenty, looked mad, and all his anger was directed at Taylor. "You're the damned doctor."

Taylor spoke through gritted teeth. "You're the one with firsthand experience."

"How the hell am I supposed to know how one of the Lost is going to be affected by energy?"

"She's not a Lost."

"Don't be retarded, dude." Even through his agitation, he sounded like he jumped from an 80's version of a Californian, getting ready to catch the next wave. "That elf told me what she can do. If you had read my research, you would know that having that much of an aberration could only be caused by the introduction of DNA that doesn't exist naturally in homo sapiens. On top of that, she hasn't ingested any drugs."

"It acts like a drug in the system," Taylor argued.

"Drugs are chemical compounds. This is not. Not knowing the parameters or extent of her ability, I cannot adequately judge her capacity to ingurgitate the power. Seriously, did you get your medical degree from the pixies?"

Taylor rubbed his forehead and muttered. "Christ, you're such an ass."

"Which is a well-established fact. So I'll ask again. Did you seriously bring me around for this?"

"Look, you little shit." Taylor grabbed the front of the man's T-shirt. "We need research. Take yourself into your little lab and Frankenstein this problem together. We want to know where the jewelry came from, what is anchoring the energy, and then I want you to get in touch with your dealers and find out where the hell this stuff comes from."

"Dude, I can't go to my dealers with this? Unless you're going to suck it up and start writing me scripts, the dealers stay out. If I turn narc, my supply dries up."

"Just get to work," Taylor said, dropping the shirt and turning away.

The man gave Taylor the finger. With his back turned, Taylor couldn't possibly see it, but he stiffened all the same. The man blinked and looked panicked, but he was able to duck out of the room before Taylor could turn around.

With the newcomer gone, Taylor came back over to me. In

his agitation, he didn't immediately notice I was awake. When he looked at me, I glanced at the door and back at him.

Taylor took out his penlight. "That was Neil. Never mind him. Follow the light with your eyes."

I did as I was told.

"Tell me how you're feeling."

"Dazed," I admitted. A squelchy, bloated feeling squirmed through my system, but it felt like it was coming from the Path, not a physical symptom. "I'm not feeling myself at all. Where am I?"

"You're at the MyTH offices in the infirmary."

"Is Rider okay?"

"He's fine. He had some mood swings for a while, but he metabolized the drugs quickly once he left the apartment."

"There was that much meth in the air?"

"Not when we got there, but Gordon found a supply hidden in the duct work. When the AC was turned on, it was blown throughout the crime scene. That was also our cover story for taking you and Rider out of there the way we did."

"Is Logan okay?" I asked.

"It never fazed him. He's with Gordon now at the local PD. The DEA is getting an earful; leaving the drugs in the vents was sloppy work. We took out the evidence AIR needs."

"Rider said some left the apartment before we got there."

Taylor checked my pulse. "They found it pretty quickly. Two items were mixed in with the drugs removed earlier in the day. At least that's what we were told. I'm going to draw blood."

Taylor tied a piece of plastic around my arm, and I cringed at the sight of the needle.

"Anything you want to tell me about the bruises?" he asked. "The old ones I mean."

As he stuck the needle in, I looked at the patchwork of

bruises, new and old. There was also a large fresh bandage.

"Job hazard," I said as I tried to puzzle out the new injury. "Doctor, what happened to my arm?"

"It's Taylor," he said, "Your partner ripped through the skin. He's in another room while we finish up blood tests. I wasn't sure if you wanted him in here right away."

"If he's not cracked out, let him in," I said.

Taylor hesitated. "We'll confirm the blood tests are clean before he comes in. Even without drugs, werewolves are known to become dangerously aggressive without provocation."

A flash of anger took hold and I had a sense of churning inside, but I turned it aside and managed a normal tone of voice. "It sounds like you have issues with werewolves. Is that prejudice? From someone working with the Lost?"

Taylor's forehead creased, and he sounded serious, if not offended. "No, it's been my experience with them. I've been lucky enough to have a few call me friend in my lifetime, and I learned their habits."

The conversation was becoming too weighty for me and my anger fizzled away, so I coerced myself to smile. "My gran would chop off his tail and put a stop to his sugar supply if Rider acted like that."

Taylor laughed. He looked good with a smile on his face.

"And believe me, she'd know about it. Probably before I did. Speaking of which, can we wrap up here so I can call her?"

"I think we're done for now."

Taylor handed me my phone and left the room with vials of my blood. Paranoia bubbled up, but it dissipated quickly. What could he do with my blood?

Gran picked up on the first ring. "Darlin' I am so sorry."

It was good that I didn't have to fill her in. "I'm okay. How much did you see?"

"Enough to know that you might be dinged up."

"It's not that bad."

"There was another thing, but I don't know what it means."

"Maybe it will make sense later on. What was it?"

"It was you, but at the same time, not you at all."

My hair on my arms raised and I broke out in goose-flesh. "Was I doing anything?"

"No, it was you, but something else at the same time."

The thought wasn't comforting. "Will the 'something else' go away?"

"I'm not sure..." she trailed off.

"I'm sure it will make sense when the time comes." Trying to sound upbeat was becoming hard work. "Everything okay at home?"

"We're good here. Susan and Gerald are with me, and we're baking lemon bars."

I told her to have fun and then we said our goodbyes.

My thoughts were becoming less muddled, but more cluttered as worries and questions took up space. Being alone in the room gave me time to reflect on the situation, but I wasn't sure that was a good thing. How many little pieces of essence had rushed into me?

I sat up and closed my eyes. Spinning like a whirlpool, my entire being felt like it had been torn apart. Worse yet, it felt like I wasn't the only one whirling.

My eyes snapped open.

The vertigo didn't leave, so I carefully laid back on the bed and focused on my surroundings. First, the ceiling, then the remaining room. The walls were padded, which made me shiver. Had they thought I would hurt myself?

That idea was thrown aside before I spent too much time worrying about it. We had rooms like this at AIR. Maybe it was built this way to muffle sound or protect a Lost that wasn't sentient and didn't want to be trapped in a room.

When I felt ready, I sat back up. Noticing I was wearing a hospital gown gave me the motivation I needed to get out of the bed.

Looking for my clothes let my mind wander back to the small room at the crime scene. Agent Wilson smacked me and Rider threw me across a room. What would have happened if I had been on my own facing that?

I blamed those thoughts on my unfamiliar surroundings. AIR agents had partners, which helped ensure that no one had to face things like that alone. By the time I found my clothes, I was ready to crawl back into the hospital bed. Instead, I put on my pants and shoes, but my shirt was missing a few buttons, so the gown stayed on. Since I hadn't found my tablet, I settled for a pen and paper to take notes. The paper already had print on it, but when I glanced it over, it looked like my own medical readouts, so I didn't feel bad about using it.

The notes didn't get far before Rider came into the room.

Tension I didn't know I had began to unravel at the sight of my friend. "I take it your blood work is clear?"

Rider picked up my bandaged arm when he reached me. "The drugs are gone." He inspected my arm from every angle, moving himself more than the arm. "Doctor Taylor has said that my blood is clean."

"Call me Taylor." Taylor strode into the room and stopped when he saw me. "I wasn't expecting to see you out of bed." He looked like he wanted to say more, but instead grabbed a chart. "How is everyone feeling?"

Rider shrugged and didn't look up from his inspection. When he was apparently satisfied, he set my arm back down and looked around the room.

Taylor watched him walk around the room, and then he turned to me.

"What did you keep in here?" Rider pressed the padding on the walls.

"Most recently, a griffin." Taylor didn't take his eyes off me. "Angel, a co-worker, spotted that it had a damaged wing. I treated the wing and we took her home. And, how are you feeling?"

"I feel okay." The response was automatic.

Taylor raised his eyebrow.

I sighed and tried again. "Physically, I feel fine. A little sore, but nothing serious."

"And, outside the physical. Has everything worked through your system?" Taylor asked.

I squirmed uncomfortably, unsure of how much to say.

"Your reactions, according to your partners, are different this time." Taylor appeared to take my non-response as a response. "We need to closely monitor your behavior and reactions."

"We?" I asked.

Taylor smiled. "Mostly your partners, but also myself while you're here. If you request, I'll forward the records on to your doctor as well, but not without your request. Whatever details you can tell us might be able to help."

He couldn't tell work. At least not more than they needed to know.

That made my decision easier. "As far as I can tell, it's all there. It doesn't go away."

"I thought it might be. We should go over this in detail when you're ready, but first, I'd like your permission to add this to Neil's research. I know he'll be able to help."

"The kid that was here earlier. He sounded like a hyped-up surfer and looks like he's barely out of high school."

"He's older than he looks. Unfortunately, he's a genius. Even worse, he knows it."

SEVENTEEN

While I was on the phone with Kyrian, Logan arrived. The conversation began with Hank, but our boss broke in and left Hank taking notes in the background. Keeping all personal details to a minimum, I gave them both an overview of the day. With that taken care of, and a borrowed shirt from Taylor, Logan and I ventured out of the infirmary and into the offices of MyTH.

"Taylor has given us the run of a conference room down the hall," Logan said. "He and Sable will be joining us soon. How are you feeling?"

After glancing up and down the halls, I let Logan know where I stood. He looked worried and didn't ask any questions, which wasn't like him.

When we reached the room, I made a point not to fall into the nearest chair, even though my body was protesting the fact that I was on my feet. "How did things go at the police station?"

"Well, the local PD and DEA are steamed, mostly at each

other, but they're out inspecting the crime scene. Special Agent Wilson wanted to talk to you."

"I was hoping he'd be off the case."

"I told him you'd rather talk to a rattlesnake right now, so he sent along his apologies. They're using the meth as an excuse for his behavior like we did. He's been stood down from field work for a week, but he's minding the paperwork, which is almost as bad as being off the case."

Knowing Logan's aversion to anything relating to paperwork, I grinned. "A horrible fate, I'm sure. Anything from the people they arrested?"

"Gordon and I interviewed them but came up with nothing. They said the pieces of jewelry were good luck charms, given to them."

"That doesn't sound like they're being used as drugs. Who would give that to them?"

"They were definitely being sold as a drug and an expensive one at that. One of the men being charged told us they had a test batch, and they worked. Some had a few bad side effects, but a few users experienced things they couldn't explain. They had their trinkets on when they were arrested."

Bad side effects was an understatement from where I was sitting. "We have the pieces now?"

"They're on their way to the office, along with most of the ones we collected. We're hoping Clancy can give us news. Gordon is meeting with Kyrian, so he took charge of them."

"Most of the ones we collected?"

"The evidence the police moved out before we arrived is being tested here. I'm told there's a smart lad taking care of it for us."

Getting near those things wasn't high on my priority list, but the thought of someone handling them didn't sit well with me. "The person isn't affected by them? Wilson couldn't have been wearing his for long, so some of them could be more potent."

Logan studied my face before answering, but I wasn't sure what he was looking for. "I checked things out. They've got it covered."

The old elf looked tense, so I shifted our focus. "The people arrested, who gave them the jewelry?"

"They couldn't say."

"You mean wouldn't?" I asked.

"No, I think it was couldn't." Logan leaned back in his chair. "They didn't have any issues talking about the jewelry, since it wasn't technically drug-related. Their lawyers suggested they'd earn some good will by giving us what they knew. They couldn't remember who gave it to them. We'd have to bring Darla in to know for sure, but I'd bet an ear tip they weren't lying."

Darla had been AIR's retired truth detector, and there was no one better, but she wouldn't come in if we already assumed an answer.

"Were they too high to remember?" I asked.

"Maybe. One girl thought someone used them as payment, but she couldn't say for what."

"Anything else?"

"I grabbed this out of the truck for you." Logan slid over the tablet that I had been using for this case.

"Thanks." I set the device aside, not bothering to turn it on.

"You sure you're okay?" Worry was etched across Logan's face.

"I'm frustrated. This case seems to be getting nowhere."

"Hank is tracking our victims back home to see if they lead to any of our suspects."

There was a rap on the door, and Sable entered the room carrying a large stack of papers. "We have some information."

She slid packets to us and sat down. "Neil has found a few things of interest."

Taylor and Rider came in, grabbing a packet on their way to their seats.

"Is this for the case, or..." I trailed off, not wanting to ask if it was for me. I had given permission to add my issues to the research, but I didn't like the idea of sitting around a conference table discussing it.

"This is limited to case knowledge," Taylor said, "nothing else."

"What does 'Dummies Guide' mean?" Rider was reading the top page.

Taylor grimaced. "That little shit."

"I am sorry about this." Sable's face was red, but I wasn't sure if it was from anger or embarrassment. "Neil is—" She stopped and looked like she was reforming her words. "He doesn't deal well with strangers. Or Taylor."

Taylor was scanning the remaining contents and didn't respond.

Logan chuckled. "We can ignore it."

Taylor closed the document, looking more resigned than cross. "Neil was able to review the evidence collected today. Your offices allowed us to experiment with four items. From initial findings, it appears that these items are used to anchor some form of energy. There are residual traces of electromagnetic energy."

Rider looked hopeful. "So it is energy stored; not part of a soul."

"What is a soul?" Taylor asked. "Everything is made of energy. We can't rule out that this isn't some fragment of a Lost trapped."

Logan looked thoughtfully. "But without a soul, the Lost would die. We haven't had any suspicious deaths."

"That's the overlying problem of our initial searches," Sable said. "Hank and our team as well were looking for suspicious deaths. When a soul gets removed from a body, the body can live on for a short time."

"Vincent mentioned that." I didn't want to drag his name into this, but I drove on. "The person wastes away and dies."

"Exactly." Taylor flipped through a few pages. "The Lost community perceives it to be a natural death and doesn't report anything suspicious. They note fewer of their number when visited."

"You've found deaths?" Logan leaned forward and flipped through pages.

"We've discovered fourteen recent deaths by natural causes," Sable said.

Rider shuddered next to me. "Over how long?"

"Approximately three months," Taylor said. "At least two of those appear to be actual natural causes, but we have no way of knowing without examination. Even then, I'm not certain we'd truly know."

"Says here we've lost a minotaur." Logan looked pointedly at me before looking back through the list. "A gnome, two pixies, a fairy, two trolls, a changeling, a gremlin, and a witch."

I frowned and tried to find the area he was reading from. "That's not twelve."

Logan pursed his lips and took out his phone. "The others mentioned aren't Lost. I need to make a call."

"Humans, not Lost?" Confused, I watched Logan walk out before returning to my search. "Why?"

Towards the end of the report, I found what I was looking for. A list of names, the reported date of death, and their species: gnome, two pixies, fairy, minotaur, troll, changeling, gremlin...

"How did we find out about the gremlin?"

"Neil has his ways," Taylor said, sounding reluctant.

I read on. There was another troll, a witch, and then my heart froze.

A psychic.

My gaze jerked from Taylor to Sable and back down, trying to find more context to the list. "How do we know the humans ended up dying because their souls were taken out?"

"With these people, nothing has shown up in autopsy reports, but not many were autopsied. The others had suspicious circumstance around them. Like Am, there was no indication of illness, but the Lost reported an unexplainable feeling in the area around the home, or site where the body was found." Taylor's voice sounded harder than it had before.

"Someone is targeting the Lost?" Rider asked.

"It's not only Lost on the list." My voice was raised in my panic, but I didn't waste the breath to apologize for snapping.

"Which you seem far more concerned about." Taylor's voice was thick with animosity, but his face was impassive.

Fury clawed its way up out of the disaster or my soul. Fear and worry exploded into anger and I moved slowly to my feet, glaring at Taylor. "How dare you."

Rider moved in front of me, and I tried to push him out of the way. It felt like I was trying to move a wall. My veins filled with fire and crushing rage. All sense of myself was shunted aside.

Taylor had also risen. He was studying my reactions, but I saw accusation written across his face.

Vertigo rolled over me and I felt off balance, but I let the anger keep my stance. "You don't know me. Each person on that list—"

Rider grabbed my face and made me look straight at him. "This is not you."

His eyes bore straight into mine. I wanted to knock him out of my way to get at Taylor.

At the same time, I cringed at the thought. This was Rider. No part of me should want to shove around my friend. Grabbing hold of that feeling, I stared at Rider, anchored my thoughts to him, and began the struggle to pull myself out. The fury danced below, trying to keep hold, but I didn't, and couldn't, let it take control.

My muscles felt used beyond their ability, but it was me again. I gripped Rider's arm and he dropped his hands. I'm not sure what he saw, but he relaxed and dropped his gaze. Rider looked confused but kept eyes on Taylor, since Taylor hadn't sat down.

"I need to examine you. Now," Taylor said.

"You stay away from me," I snapped. Feeling rubbery and worn, I sat before I could fall. I didn't look at Sable, and I decided to ignore Taylor completely.

Exhaustion kept the panic from rising too far.

"Rider, there are psychics on the list." My voice matched my mood.

Taylor moved towards me. "The—"

Rider let out a low growl before Taylor could say anything else. Rider's low rumble filled the room and left me feeling like nightmares waited in the shadows.

The room was motionless even after the sound faded.

"When did you last speak with Margaret?" Rider's voice didn't hold a trace of the menace he had unleashed.

"I spoke with her a few hours ago, but Gran doesn't hide who she is. And Mom, oh God." Panic crept back in my voice. I hadn't talked to my mother in over a month, but Gran had recently talked with her, right?

"You're a Reader in a family of psychics?" Taylor's voice was low and held remorse, but I ignored him.

Logan came back in the room. My fear was on display, but I didn't bother trying to hide it.

"Margaret will be staying at my house for now," Logan said.

I let out a slow breath, but the tightness in my chest didn't go away. "Is anyone checking on my mom?"

"Your mom is pretty closed off about what she is," Logan said.

"Only after my dad died. When she was younger, she was good at what she did. That's hard to hide and even harder to forget."

Logan already had the phone back out. "We'll ask Hank to get someone to keep an eye on her until this gets sorted out."

"And your family?" I asked.

"Jonathan's handling it for now. He'll keep them safe."

Logan didn't shut the door behind him, but he moved far enough down the hall that I couldn't hear what he said.

"Cassie, I'm sorry," Taylor said. "I didn't mean to imply—"

"That I thought humans were more important than the Lost?" I glared at Taylor. "I'm pretty sure that is exactly what you meant."

Taylor cleared his throat and spoke more formally. "You're right. I should not have assumed anything. I apologize."

I wasn't comfortable with his solemn attitude, but I tried to let go of the last threads of anger. "You didn't know. And I shouldn't have gotten so agitated."

"Speaking of which. May I?" Taylor waved a penlight he'd been holding.

"May you blind me repeatedly?" I sighed. "Go for it."

By the time Logan returned, Taylor had checked my pulse, listened to my chest, taken my temperature, and of course, shined lights to check my pupil dilation.

"Hank has someone on the way. They'll keep an eye on her," Logan said.

I finally relaxed.

Logan didn't leave time for a thank you. "The Lost and anyone with an ability outside of the normal is being targeted. The office has begun their own search, and they are going to try to pinpoint areas with the highest risk of being affected. Teams will be moving to those areas soon. Sable, I think they'll ask MyTH to help work through the city."

"I'll talk with Gordon and call people in," Sable said.

After Sable left, Logan looked around the room and frowned. "I feel like I've missed something in here, but we need to move on. We need suspects."

Taylor, already sitting back down, cleared his throat. "Neil has a list on page twenty-seven that should help us."

Rider sat back down, and we all flipped to the page Taylor mentioned.

The list was much longer than I suspected. Some of these types of Lost I had never heard of and several had subcategories listed. There were human abilities here as well.

"Has there even been an alchemist in this country?" Logan asked.

"Neil is thorough," Taylor admitted. "He's allowed for the possibility that anything could be around without us knowing."

The word 'Walker' jumped out at me from the list. I expected it to be there, and I tried to concentrate on the others, but my eyes were drawn back to the word again and again.

The list of demons was extensive and most of the words, if they were actual words, were unpronounceable, but a few of the names I knew. Demons weren't beasts of the underworld, but I could see where people got that idea. Like other mythological creatures, they come from other planes of existence.

Their home dimensions, at least the ones I knew about, resembled different forms of Hell. They come to our world through portals, like the other Lost. Demons, along with several others on the list, aren't allowed to be brought to this world intentionally. That doesn't mean they aren't around, but it's hard for them to remain inconspicuous, so the likelihood that one of them was behind this wasn't high.

"What are the little numbers next to some of the names?" Rider asked.

"Footnotes," Taylor said. "If you turn to the next page, you'll see a matching number."

"That's a lot of notes," I said.

"It looks like most of them are 'would likely consume energy rather than use in this manner,'" Logan said.

"Most of the demons fit that bill." Under my breath, I added, "It could take a lifetime to track everything down."

"We're going to attack this from multiple angles." Logan didn't look up. He was busy crossing out names and making marks. "We're going to narrow down this list and concentrate on the most likely. The notes will help us. We'll also go at it by following the case. There are drugs, money, and connections to be made."

"I've tried to get Neil to contact some of his dealers, but he won't give them up," Taylor said.

This was the second time I had heard of Neil's dealers. I thought about asking why Neil had known them, but decided I wasn't sure I wanted the answer.

I rubbed my temples and stared blankly at the paper. "It does seem like it would be easier to trace back the drugs, even if we don't have names. There have to be links to the people arrested today. There's also the merchandise itself."

"It's all cheap jewelry. It could have been picked up anywhere," Logan said.

"Yes, but there was a whole lot of it on site today, probably purchased all at once, and my guess is, it wasn't a jeweler buying it. If it was all bought from the same place, we should be able to track the purchase."

"And the purchase should have been larger than what we saw today," Rider said. He too was making notes on the page, or at least making marks on it. It didn't look like English.

"Why larger?" I asked.

Rider took time, appearing to think through his response. "They were a payment. These are possibly new and unique, at least for drugs. I do not believe they would all be given away."

"That would make it easier to trace. While Hank looks for connections between people, we'll ask him if this type of purchase could be traced," Logan said.

"We could ask Neil to look into the same, if you want," Taylor said.

I noticed Logan's eyes flick towards me. "We should let him concentrate on what he's doing now." Logan dropped his pencil and looked over his notes. "The people we've met who take this don't realize it's a drug. At least they don't think of it that way. Once Hank finds us a name, we need to follow this up the food chain, to find a source."

"Paper trail?" The ex-accountant in me came out. "Should we follow the money?"

"These people paid in product, that may not help you while following the drugs," Taylor said. "You need someone moving around the same circles as the product."

"Neil?" I didn't bother trying to cover my skepticism.

"He would only get someone through the door and be a guide. Neil is too young, too inexperienced, and too closely connected to the wrong people." Taylor's words didn't sound like insults, only facts. "Someone else is going to need to meet these people."

"Going undercover in the city's drug scene?" Logan asked. "I spread my face around the police station and spent too much time with the criminals for that."

Looking confused, Rider looked up. "Undercovers?"

Logan grinned. "When you go undercover you pretend to be someone else and infiltrate from the inside."

Rider looked like he was thinking that over before going back to work.

"Although, that's not really what this needs to be," Logan said.

"I think you're right," Taylor said. "Someone attending a few events might be enough. I was thinking Rider, but..."

It took a lot of effort for me not to grin. "That leaves me."

CHAPTER

EIGHTEEN

Logan crossed his arms and leaned back into his chair. "Are you sure you want to volunteer? Margaret will have my ears if anything happens to you."

I tried to downplay the fact that I was excited about the idea. "I'm assuming you all won't be far away."

"Maybe we should send someone else in with you," Logan said.

"Should I go with her?" Rider asked.

Taylor cleared his throat. "You might work better in surveillance. She'll have Neil. Whether he likes it or not, he can be an important tie to the right communities, and he's good at figuring his way out of tight corners."

I cringed. The thought of relying on someone like Neil didn't inspire a lot of confidence.

"Neil and I don't see eye to eye on much of anything," Taylor said, "but I would trust him in this. The kid's a lot of things, but he's loyal above all else. He might not admit it, but he would sell his dealers out before he would anyone in this room."

That didn't settle my thoughts about Neil, and I could tell that Logan didn't like the idea either.

Putting Neil out of my mind, I focused on other areas of the job. "So, where would I be going? Clubs, or dropping by people's houses?"

"There could be a bar or two involved," Taylor said, "but the parties are where you'll need to be. They always move around, and they're hard to get into. You have to know the right people."

"And the way you've been talking, Neil knows them all." There was an edge to Logan's voice if you listened hard enough.

Taylor sighed. "He does, and that's our reality. The larger dealers set up private parties. Sometimes, they even show up."

"Why would they get that close?" I asked.

"I wondered the same thing," Taylor said, "and Neil told me what he knew. They never sell, consume, or hold any drugs at the parties, and they probably have an exit strategy. It's not a large risk because they've set up the event and it's private. Neil thinks it's worth it for them because they get to see their top sellers and top buyers. They watch, and they have other people watching. They know who they're dealing with on both sides of the table."

"How many big dealers do you have in the city?" Logan asked.

"Neil has access to two. He never talks to them, only their..." Taylor waved his hand around as though trying to push aside words that weren't quite what he was looking for. "I guess they're employees? Other dealers, anyway. But he recognizes the bosses when they show up."

"Before we move any further, we need to talk to Hank. Maybe he's found a connection and we don't need to mess with any of this." Logan didn't sound too hopeful.

"I'll talk with Neil to see if anything will be happening over the next few days that would be useful for you," Taylor said.

"It's late, but if Cassie's got the doc's sign off, we have a chance to sleep in our own beds for the night," Logan said.

"We're in uncharted territory," Taylor said. "The best I can suggest is get some rest while you can, but I think you need to be under observation until we know the side effects."

My eyes narrowed at Taylor. "I have plans tomorrow, and I don't intend on missing them unless we move on the case."

"Maybe Logan or Rider could—"

"No way." Take one of my partners on a date? That would be humiliating, not to mention hard to explain. "Besides a few bruises, there's nothing physically wrong with me."

Logan drummed his fingers on the table. "It's a hike, right?"

"Um, yeah." Hearing my personal life up for discussion didn't exactly make me comfortable.

"Let me talk to Ethan. He can be on the lookout for anything odd," Logan said.

I leveled my glare at Logan and crossed my arms, trying to keep everything inside pushed down, while hiding shaky hands on the outside. "You're going to ask Ethan to what? Watch out for mental instability?"

Logan leaned back. "We could tell him you hit your head while on the job, and he's probably already heard about the drugs."

My breath caught.

Logan hurried on. "The drugs at the bust. Cops talk; if he hasn't heard that some agents got a healthy dose of meth, he'll hear it soon. I thought he could keep an eye out for mood swings. Look, I know how you feel about this, but sending you out into the wilderness with Ethan thinking everything is okay, isn't an option."

"Will he be able to handle the situation if it goes wrong?" Rider asked. "There will be no one around."

My mouth went dry, and I turned to Rider, gaping at him.

Rider met my gaze with a level, but not an unkind look. "How would you feel if you began to act odd, or attacked him and caused an injury?"

I slumped in my seat and tried not to look too upset. "I'll cancel." It came out as a mumble.

"Or you could change your plans." Logan sounded way too cheerful, and when I looked up at him, he was grinning. "Instead of roaming the countryside with the risk of getting hot and sweaty and possibly hurting someone, you stay in and follow doc's orders, watch some movies, and let Ethan keep an eye on you."

Thinking that over, I frowned at Logan, but I sat up straighter. "Let me tell him."

Logan frowned. "You'll undersell it."

It felt like I was bargaining for freedom and losing. "No one goes on a date with a permission slip from their partner."

"That depends on the partner." Logan looked at my expression and tapped his fingers on the table. "You tell him, but either me or doc sits in to make sure he knows what he needs to."

"To my side of the conversation only."

"Deal."

<hr>

"I AM SO SORRY ABOUT THIS." It was probably the third time I'd said it since Ethan had arrived, but I couldn't seem to stop. "You really don't have to spend all day over here if you'd rather do something else, like see sunlight."

"Spending the day with you is the highlight of my week. We can go in the backyard if we feel the need to see the sun."

Thinking about the fairy in the backyard, I grinned. "Maybe."

"And this time, I know what happened, which I think will be a novelty."

"That's true." I couldn't look at Ethan when I said it.

"Well," he said, a little less optimistic, "at least I know the important parts."

"You do. *And*," I stressed this part, "because you're here today, I don't have to spend the day with the doctor or anyone else watching over me."

"I thought your grandmother might be around," Ethan said.

The smell of baked goods was almost unnoticeable now that Gran had moved in with Logan's family for the duration of the case. This morning I had hoped to talk with her in person, but I had no luck.

"I thought she'd be here too, but she's away from home for a few days."

"Well, I'm happy to be of service and keep an eye on her granddaughter." His grin was adorable, but short-lived. "I heard it was a mess on scene."

"It wasn't pretty, that's for sure. Rider must have stood next to a vent, and the DEA agent that was taken out wasn't in the best of shape."

"So," Ethan sidled up close to me, "how long do I get to keep you under surveillance?"

He was so wonderfully warm. "You have me all day."

It was a great day. We told stories about growing up, laughed, and got to know each other better, I think, than our scheduled hike would have allowed. While cooking dinner together, it felt completely natural for him to touch my arm or hand, and I found any excuse I could to put myself in close contact with him.

Later that evening, we found ourselves in my room wrapped up together. It had been a long time since I had been this close to anyone, and while we undressed each other, I could tell he wasn't comfortable with the new bruises or injured arm, but he didn't say anything to ruin the evening.

The evening went by in naked blissfulness. When my phone rang at six-thirty the next morning, I was still wrapped in Ethan's arms and reluctant to move away, but the phone wasn't magically moving to me, and I didn't want to wake him more than I already had.

"Morning." I made it to my feet, but Ethan took my hand and gently pulled me back next to him.

He didn't have to try very hard to get me to stay.

"It's Logan. We're making plans and I needed to check in with you to see how you're doing."

"I'm good. What type of plans?"

"The doc wants to do another checkup."

I groaned but didn't interrupt.

Logan chuckled. "I told him you'd be thrilled about that. As long as everything looks good, this afternoon, we're sending you out with Neil."

It took a little time for that to sink in and I sat up, blinking. "It's Sunday, I wouldn't think it a very big day for clubs or parties."

"It's not, but Neil seems to think you'll have better success if you meet some people today. Tomorrow's the actual event. I'm not thrilled with the idea, but he's right. Think you'll be ready by eight?"

I bargained up, giving myself two hours to get ready. "Eight-thirty?"

"I'll grab Rider and we'll meet you at your house. Pack for a few days at least. Neil said he sent you a list."

"Why did Neil send a list?"

"He said we'd get it wrong."

We hung up, and after I had checked the time, I stretched out next to Ethan.

"Morning," Ethan said, wrapping an arm around me and pulling me to him.

My laugh turned out to be more of a giggle, but I was too happy to be embarrassed by it.

"I take it you're back to work today?" Ethan asked.

My emotions were a jumble of excitement and worry coming at me from work and my personal life.

Who knew I would ever have a personal life? "Yeah, I have to get ready."

"Five more minutes?"

"Only five?" I asked.

Ethan nuzzled my ear. "I'll take every minute I can get."

Letting out a contented sigh, I leaned back into him, enjoying the comfortable feeling of my bare skin against his. "I wish we could take longer, but I have to pack."

Ethan leaned up on an elbow, keeping his other arm wrapped around me. "Going out of town?"

I rolled over and looked up at him. "Yeah, it sounds like it'll be for a few days."

"A few days of clubs and parties?"

Seeing unease in his eyes, I tried to keep it light. "You make that sound like a lot more fun than I'm expecting."

He relaxed some and followed me when I rolled out of bed. While getting ready, we found ways to stall and be near each other. Conserving water by showering together failed since we took our time. I was running a brush through wet hair and had my suitcase on my bed when I opened up the list Neil sent.

"I should go," Ethan said, "and get out of your hair."

"Gran would be upset with me if I let you out the door without breakfast. This will only take a minute."

Ethan wrapped his arms around me from behind. "And what would she say about being here for breakfast?"

I scrolled through my email until I found a packing list. "Mostly, she'd say, 'Good for you, make sure he eats before he leaves.'"

Ethan laughed and I sunk back into his embrace, enjoying the moment.

"What's that?" Ethan asked.

"Hmm?" I looked down at my phone, and my face turned red. "What the...?" I stepped away and read the list. The least embarrassing thing on there was the skirt that hugged the right places.

Fumbling with my phone, I began pacing and forwarded the list to Taylor, asking him if this was some sort of joke.

The reply was faster than I expected but slower than I hoped. *Sorry. Jeans, T-shirt, sneakers. Nothing new.*

Sighing with relief, I looked up and found Ethan leaning against the wall with his arms crossed.

He wore a smile, but it didn't look natural. "Anything I should be worried about?"

"No. Someone has the sense of humor of a twelve-year-old." I handed him my phone, with Taylor's text showing, and went to my closet.

"Doesn't sound like the usual work attire." He sounded better than he looked.

I raised my voice while I rummaged around my closet. "Actually, besides the shoes, it's pretty much all I wore last fall. This is more to blend in with the crowd, though."

"I hate to see what list your partners were sent. The word 'chaps' comes to mind."

I stepped out of my closet to see Ethan, and he looked like he was trying not to laugh.

"Logan is very into Westerns," I warned. "Don't mention chaps, spurs, boots, or Stetsons, or I may be facing them on a daily basis."

Ethan chuckled, and I returned to my closet and chose a few items. I threw them on top of my suitcase and returned for more. Once I had a handful of clothes and everything I might need from the bathroom, it was a huge mess.

I turned my back on the mayhem. "Let's go get breakfast."

He looked at the case and back to me, then back to the case again. "Not great at packing, are you?"

"What are you talking about?" I escorted him out of the room to get breakfast. "I was finished in three, maybe four minutes."

"Yeah, I think that's part of my point." Ethan pulled me in for a kiss. "I'm going to make breakfast. You, go upstairs and pack."

"It's—"

"Upstairs." He kissed me again before turning me around and nudging me towards my room.

Mentally, I ran down a list of everything I might need for four days, folded everything neatly, and met Ethan back down in the kitchen where eggs and toast were waiting.

Even better, there was coffee.

"I'm really happy you came over last night," I said.

"Yesterday morning," Ethan corrected, "and so am I. Give me a call tonight after work, and let me know when you might be free again."

"Believe me, I really wish I could, but I'm not sure what our plans are. I'm pretty sure I won't have access to my cell phone for a few days. Let me see your phone." He handed it over, and I opened the contacts list. "I promise I'm not being nosy." I grinned at him, inwardly thankful that he didn't seem worried. "I'll make sure you have Logan's number and Rider's though. In case..." I stumbled over my words while handing his phone back to him. "Well, in case you need to get through to me."

"They get to keep their phones?" Ethan asked.

I bought some time to think it over while getting more coffee. "Lieutenant Parker, I'm thinking that you must be very good at your job with the questions that you ask."

"It's a habit. If you can't say anything, though, I understand."

"Parts of it probably won't matter if I talk about them." I drummed my fingers on the counter and stirred the sugar into my coffee. "As long as you don't tell anyone else. From what I hear, cops gossip more than I suspected."

"My lips are sealed."

"I'm going to be going into places without Logan and Rider."

"The clubs and parties?" Ethan asked with his eyebrows raised.

"I probably shouldn't have mentioned that part, but yes."

"And your partners are not going with you because..."

"Logan has talked to some suspects. It's too risky for him to be anywhere pretending to be anyone else. And Rider... well, he stands out. We need to blend in."

Ethan looked like he was thinking over his words carefully. "You'll be alone?"

"No, someone else will be with me, but Logan and Rider won't be far away either."

"You'll be wired?" He looked troubled about the wire as much as the rest.

"I'm not sure what the plan is yet, but I'm not going anywhere, or doing anything that will cause someone to want to check me close enough to notice, even if they strap a tape recorder to my back."

Ethan looked tense.

I put my hand on his leg and softened my voice. "You're thinking too far in the wrong direction again. I'm not going in, guns blazing, ready to make some big arrest. I'm slipping in, seeing a few faces, and walking back out again."

He tugged gently on my arm, and I moved over and sat on his lap.

"No arrests?" he asked.

"None."

"You won't be alone?"

Neil counts, right? "Someone has my back."

"Am I worrying too much?"

"Always."

"Am I being overbearing?"

"Completely tyrannical."

We were both smiling through our kiss.

HEATHER DEAN WILLS was escaping an abusive relationship and hiding out in the city. Considering the mass of bruises and cuts that I had collected over the past week, it was a good cover. She was smart but went down the wrong trail early in life. Heather had no real friends in the community beyond her adopted cousin Neil, and she was one of those people that could really thrive if the world would stop kicking her down.

Neil couldn't say why that was important, but he insisted the data pointed in that direction. I would be able to slide into his circle because I was an occasional druggie with the track marks to prove it.

It's a good thing I'd had so much blood drawn in the past year.

If I thought too long about who I was and what I was doing, I'd only make myself nervous, and I didn't need to be. I should be able to read the Paths and follow this thing back in no time. I had a werewolf and an elf backing me up, not to mention MyTH. Besides, there was a tingle of excitement to the whole thing, and I wasn't backing away.

I think getting Neil's buy-in was hard. I'm not sure what type of threats or bargains Taylor made, but in the end, Neil had agreed to bring me into the world of drugs and dealers.

When we were introduced to Neil, Logan tried to call the whole thing off. Neil was stoned, and he didn't care if I was going with him or not. This didn't instill me with a lot of confidence, but I couldn't sit around and wait for new evidence to fall into our laps.

By two-thirty, Neil and I were out the door, meeting up with a few of his friends. Given the fact that Neil was glassy eyed, I got behind the wheel. He wasn't talkative, which didn't make for the best company.

An hour later, we were walking up the stairs to a second-floor condo. The exterior of the building was meticulous, luxury cars littered the parking lot, and I felt horribly out of place in jeans and a T-shirt.

"What are we doing here?" I hissed before we reached the door.

"Chill, man. You've got to, like, relax."

"If you're screwing around again, I swear I'm going to make you regret it."

"This is the place to be. You've got to, like, throw out your stereotypes and prejudices. Besides, I don't want to screw this up any more than you do." He sounded much soberer during his last statement.

Before I could say anything else, he was knocking on the door.

My mouth almost gaped when the door opened, and I was introduced to Pat. She was a tall, beautiful African American woman that was as meticulously put together as the decor.

If I hadn't been nervous before, I was now. Then a strange thing happened—after about twenty minutes of Pat being standoffish towards me, I began to fit in. At first, I didn't notice it, but Neil stealthily led the conversation to highlight everything about Heather that Pat might relate to in some way. The abusive-relationship cover story came in handy, and I wondered if it had been hand tailored for Pat. As far as Pat was concerned, Heather was her, two years ago, and she couldn't wait to give me advice.

A few hours later, I found myself in Pat's BMW, with Neil in the backseat. She made a stop and left the car running in front of a house.

"Want anything?" she asked as she got out.

Neil stretched out in the back seat and laid down. "Nothing hard, man. That shit can hold off until tomorrow night."

"You're going to the party?" Pat sounded surprised.

"I'm like, hosting my cousin. It's the only way to make sure we get the best."

"Do they know Heather's coming?" Pat asked.

"Oh man," Neil said. "You think that will be a problem."

"Who knew someone so smart could be so dumb. Don't worry Heather, I've got you." Pat winked at me and went in.

"You're in." Neil sounded almost sad.

"Already?" I asked.

"Pat is a VIP wherever she goes."

"She's pretty cool."

"Yeah man, she's great. Too bad work's involved now."

"I'm not sure why you're in any of this, but I'll try not to mess it up."

"Oh man." Neil sprang up in the seat. "You were like, awesome. I couldn't even believe the shit you all were talking about. You were totally Heather."

"Thanks, I think I'll take that as a compliment. We've got company," I added, seeing Pat come out with someone else.

"Oh, yeah, that's short dude."

No one introduced our new passenger when he got into the car, so I only knew him by the name Neil gave him. Since I wasn't going to call anyone short dude, I avoided using the name completely.

On our way back to Pat's, my role as Heather led me into the metaphysical. It wasn't part of my cover, but I stuck my foot into it and had to incorporate the mystical. Pat drove us past a strip mall, and I spotted a neon sign lit up in the shape of a hand with an open eye in the palm.

"It's a Palm Reader!" I was so excited that I almost forgot I was Heather. "We have to stop."

"Dude, not cool," Neil muttered from the back seat.

CHAPTER

NINETEEN

"Is that like a psychic?" Pat asked.

"Yeah." Feeling embarrassed, I looked out the window.

"You believe in all that fortune-telling stuff?"

Thinking of Gran, I grinned. "It's fun."

"I knew there was a reason I liked you." Pat turned into a parking lot and turned the car around. "Let's go."

Neil leaned forward from the backseat. "Really?"

"Hell yeah. Sit back, smart boy, some things can't be explained."

"Huh." Neil slumped back in his seat.

"Most of these people can't predict that you shouldn't walk down Defoe Street in the middle of the night, never mind that the cops don't even go there until morning. But every now and again, you find someone that knows their shit. You boys wait outside." Pat jumped out of the car.

I noticed Neil's face when I closed the door, and he looked like he was mentally trying to solve a hard problem, so I left him to it.

The brightness of the day was cut off when we stepped inside, along with the traffic being hushed in the dimly lit room. The walls were lined with scrolls of parchment in other languages, detailed drawings of a person's hand, and pictures or mirrors covered with black fabric. Scattered around were relics, old pottery, statues, and candlestick holders. I recognized a statue of Shiva and one of Buddha, but the rest were lost on me. The only items that looked new were cluttered around the front counter. Miniature Buddhas stared at me from by the cash register. Pat was as excited about seeing the palm reader as I was by the time we were greeted.

The woman that approached us was wearing a green sari. She wore jewelry in her hair, thin golden ropes leading to small jeweled medallions. It set off the golden tones of her skin and looked beautiful nestled into her dark hair. Her voice was lightly accented.

"Good afternoon, my friends, my name is Fatima Jain. May I assist you today by showing you what awaits you in the future?"

"This is exciting! Yes, we both want to know what's coming," Pat said.

"One at a time, please, unless this is a group or couple reading." Fatima lifted a curtain to a small room off the main store. "The inner eye gets clouded when there are too many people."

"You first." Pat nudged me towards the door, and when the curtain dropped, an enchanted ambiance greeted me.

Fatima lit a candle, a bright beacon, and she asked me to put a hand down next to it. As I sat down, butterflies flapped in my stomach. What was Gran expecting me to see here?

"Fortune telling is a gift brought to us from India." Fatima's voice became more heavily accented. "The gift spread throughout Asia before moving to the western world. In reading the lines on your palm, we see the past, present, and future. We see the mingling of these states and how they affect one another.

"There are those who would tell you that palmistry can be learned. That its secrets can be unlocked from a book or words from another. This is untrue. True palmistry is a gift from the gods. Those who are ordained to possess these gifts must dedicate themselves to the path, or forever walk the realms of uncertainty."

"What does that mean exactly, dedicate yourself?" My voice came out lower than intended in the dim room.

Fatima smiled at me. "No matter what lies in your fate or mine, in the past, or present, it is my duty to help those that seek to peer into their futures and speak the truth."

My arms broke out in goose-flesh. as I laid down my palm next to the candle.

"We will start with the Heart Line. Relationships in the past, present, and future." Fatima traced a line through my palm. "I see here that you were in love in the past, but it ended in pain. It is important not to let that pain guide you into your future. You have held it close to you in the past, which has caused you to miss out on new relationships. It appears that presently, you are trying to shed some of that past pain. You have several prospective relationships moving towards the future. If you allow your past strife to continue forward, you will choose poorly."

Most of this stuff I already knew. The fact that she knew it from looking at my hand was unnerving, but I hardly think Gran would send me here for my love life.

"Lucky girl. There is more than one path to relationships that will lead to happiness."

She lost me on that one. I don't see my personal life ever becoming that complicated.

"Unfortunately, each way has its own complications and pain." Fatima squeezed my hand and looked at me. "But that is always the case with love."

That part, I believed.

"Next, we will look at your headline. This helps us take a look at how your mind works." Fatima traced another line on my hand. "I see stagnation of your intellect in the recent past, but in the present and the future, you will add to your stores of knowledge. This isn't unusual for someone your age. You will gain great knowledge from what you do, but also from unexpected sources. Your mind spent some time in apathy, but is now growing."

Which told me nothing beyond I had moved to a new job, and let's face it, all of my sources of new knowledge were unexpected.

"Your stubbornness can cause strife for others, but that appears to be fairly balanced with your intellect and your ability to know when to speak the truth and when to hold your tongue. Although, the stubborn nature leads the way a great deal of the time, and that's not always a bad thing."

I would like to say I could argue against that one, but that would be a lie to me.

"This is your lifeline, which tells us of your physical heath and events that disrupt our lives in—" She grabbed my hand tighter and twisted it around, looking at it from many directions.

I leaned forward. "I've not encountered this before. You— this says you have died recently." Fatima twisted my hand again, pulling it closer to the candle. "It says you've died twice. There have been several cataclysmic events in your past and present. So much pain feathering out and you have even greater turmoil in your future." Fatima blinked her eyes rapidly, closely examining each little branch of my lifeline.

"There are three places where your lifeline rolls over on itself, to become you and not you at the same time."

Wait, had Gran said that?

"Things become confused here. It's almost as if you are relocating, but—" She narrowed her eyes and looked confused. "But you're not at the same time. Looking at your lifeline with your travel lines only confuses the matter further. The trip that is not a trip will become of great importance.

"You have ominous lines that affect your lifeline again." She was so caught up in what she was reading that she dropped her accent completely. "Interesting to see the clouding of the lifeline, but to see the future beyond that. Do you die again? Does that cloud your future? There are relics and other items, of course, that can do this. They can alter your path, remove obstacles and move you into a better future. Is this the effect of such a relic?" She dropped my hand and inspected her own, before looking at them at them side by side.

Fatima was silent for a while, which only built the anticipation I was feeling. Travel, but not travel, death twice in my past. I knew I died last fall, but twice?

I cleared my throat. "Did you say I'll die again?" I asked.

Fatima looked up at me, not really seeing me. She blinked a few times until she was actually looking into my eyes. Her cheeks turned red. "I am so sorry," she said, regaining her accent and removing her own arm from the table. "You have a very interesting palm. It is unique, and I let my professional curiosity get the better of me. Please forgive my rudeness."

"It's no problem," I said quickly. "Did you say I was going to die?"

"Your future is clouded. I see injuries, relocation, and possible death before, of course, the inevitable death. There are many events in your future that could lead to perilous outcomes. Many Paths will open themselves to you. Choose wisely moving forward. Don't rush to judgment or rush a decision."

"Is there anything I should be doing now? I mean, for the immediate future."

Fatima swallowed hard. "Keep your friends close, beyond that, I can say no more that would help."

I stood when she did and looked at my hand. Keeping Logan and Rider close went without saying, but what she had said about my future shook me. Everything else had been so accurate, so was her prediction of the future going to be the same?

Pat was led back into the room, practically vibrating with excitement. Lost in thought, I looked around the shop. Had Gran wanted me to hear all that? Could things change?

Several items in the shop seemed to sing out. There was a long thin piece of clay that looked like a stick. When I reached out to touch it, little warning bells pinged me from the Path, even though I had it closed tight. No touching, got it.

Was that the type of item that Fatima had mentioned? One that can change the shape of the future?

Right, time to get a grip here. Even if Fatima was the real thing, which I suspected, then I had a little warning, but the future was still the future and it's all coming towards me. Nothing I can do, but be prepared.

Other peculiar items in the shop seemed to clamor for my attention, causing me to feel jumpy. After a stroll around the shop, I found that around the register looked like the safest place to stand. Little Buddhas in bulk and the other items sitting out here looked safer to inspect. On the wall behind the counter, some pictures weren't covered up. Family maybe. There was one in particular that stood out, with Fatima and a man embracing each other. There was a familiar look in his eyes, but I didn't know him.

"That is my betrothed," Fatima said from behind. "My family is very old fashioned, and they have only recently allowed the union." She laughed. "Not that it would have stopped us."

Pat was very quiet, but not altogether unhappy. While she paid, I looked through the glass facing of the counter.

My heart sped up, and my breath hitched. A tiny silver pendant of some unknown Indian god stared up at me. The case had a few different gods, all silver, and all the same size as the pendants we had in evidence.

Maybe this was why Gran sent me here.

"These look interesting." I was amazed my voice was steady.

"They are beautiful, are they not? It is said that they bring luck." Fatima took one out to show me.

I was very careful not make contact with the pendant, but I looked closely. "You know, I could use a few gifts for some friends."

As Heather, I ended up having money for five after paying for the reading and had them wrapped and placed in a bag, which I held carefully by the handle.

The sunlight was blinding after the dimness of the shop. My eyes took time to adjust before spotting Neil by the car, looking dejected.

"That was intense," Pat whispered on our way to the car. "How about you?"

"That's a good description."

"You think she's the real deal?"

I looked back at the shop and said, "I think she is."

"Me too, but don't say anything to Neil. He's too smart for his own good and gets all weird if he doesn't understand everything. But I guess you know that."

"Yeah." Heather would know, but I had no idea what she was talking about. "My lips are sealed if yours are."

THAT EVENING, Pat took a pass on the drugs, giving me a knowing look, so I felt free to do the same. After she had gone to bed, I got to work.

Neil opened one of the packages that Fatima had wrapped for me and almost dropped it. "Dude," was all he said. Then he placed it on a table for me and appeared to forget about it in a haze of pot smoke.

Concentrating on the little figure didn't give me hints that there may be a fragment of a Lost inside. Taking the next step, I closed my eyes and went to reach for the Path. Waiting for me were hundreds of flecks of light, glittering, wanting to be seen, and they stood between the Path and me.

Some of those were pieces of my own soul, right? Was I still me?

Trying and failing to shake the unnerving feeling, I stretched over the milling shards of soul and opened my eyes to a world of incandescent color.

I spent the next thirty minutes depleting my energy, trying to find some spark in the necklace pendant.

Neil was the one who reminded me that I might be pushing too far.

"You're like, pale and shit. Are you getting a contact high or what?"

There was a fizzy feeling running through me, so I dropped the Path. Seeing the colors turn even more muted than usual, I thought the contact high wasn't far off.

Ignoring Neil, I reached out tentatively.

"That's a bad idea, man." Neil watched, but didn't try to stop me.

"You know I'm a girl, right."

"That's pretty obvious. But Taylor's going to kill me if I bring you back broken."

I rolled my eyes. "Too late to worry about that."

The silver was cool, and while I had braced myself to add yet another shard of soul to the horde, nothing happened. "Humph. Nothing." I carefully unrolled the other trinkets, each one cool to the touch, but void of a companion soul shard.

Sighing, I stowed them all away. "We should go soon."

"Sure, man, the couch is comfy, and I need a few more minutes. Short dude will be back soon."

"Hey man, I'm not short," said the guy ambling back into the room with a bottle of tequila.

"You're shorter than me, which makes you short dude," Neil said.

I laid my head on the arm of the couch and watched Neil drink and smoke dope.

PAT COULD PROBABLY WALK into any club, bar, or party in town, which worked out great for me because it was her influence that got me onto the list for the party. It was naive of me to think that would make things easy. Pat dropped her car off with the valet, but the man on the door was one of those people that took an instant dislike to me.

"She's on the list." Pat jabbed a finger down on his clipboard.

"No ID, and it's obvious she doesn't belong here." The man sneered at me.

My aggravation caused a flurry of activity inside me, and it amazed me that no one noticed.

"Wait here." Pat strode into the massive structure. Within two minutes, a man came out and waved us in. Before the door closed, I heard the doorman being chewed out for upsetting a VIP.

At the door, our cell phones were confiscated, and since Logan and Rider had remote access to mine, I was feeling a little lost without it.

The music was loud, there were loads of people dancing, and you only had to walk a few feet into the room to see that drugs were being passed around like candy. Pat jumped straight into the mix. Someone dropped something into her mouth as she hit the dance floor.

"Look," Neil said quietly, "don't take a drink from anyone but me and keep your hand over it when you're not drinking." He sounded sober enough that I didn't hesitate to agree. "I'll keep you in sight, but we have to mingle."

Neil handed me a drink, gave me a joint, and then disappeared.

CHAPTER

TWENTY

My plan was to pull up the Path and take a look at things from the fringes of the party. This could work in the ballroom, where the lights were dim, the noise was loud, and everyone was dancing, but the other rooms would be difficult.

Watching everyone dance made me feel conspicuous, so I drained the glass Neil gave me and met Pat on the dance floor. It had been so long since I'd danced that I felt thoroughly embarrassed, but each time I turned around, I was dancing with a new person. What better way to fit in and meet people? We barely had to talk.

Neil showed up long enough to pass me another drink, and I left the dance floor with Pat. There was no telling what she was on, but she didn't sit on the sidelines long. When she went back to dance more, I stayed put. It was time to get to work.

"What's a hot little thing like you doing over here?" Arms reached around me from behind.

Adrenaline hit my system. My skin dropped a few degrees, and I broke out into a cold sweat. I could feel the man's breath on my face, and I cringed. He trapped my arms in a bear hug before I could react.

My mind worked frantically trying to figure out what Heather would do, or what I should do to get out of this.

"There is a hit of X here with your name on it," he said into my neck.

"I'm not an X kind of girl." I tried to keep my voice light.

"I could change your mind." He moved one rough hand down my side.

This worked out well for me because he had to loosen his grip, which allowed me to pull, at least partially, away.

"First time here?" The man laughed, and I could tell he thought this was all in good fun.

Still, he had a strong grip on my arm, and he didn't look ready to let go. "Making a scene can get you tossed out. Let's go have a chat. I can tell you all you need to know."

"No thanks, I'm good." Trying to break his hold on me was becoming a futile effort. "Besides, I need to go meet up with my friends."

"I'm not seeing any friends here," the man said.

"Leave the girl alone."

Vincent?

My face turned red, embarrassed at being caught like this, and I searched for the face that came with the voice.

The man didn't look away from me. "Mind your business."

"Back away." Vincent walked out of the shadows.

He didn't look at me, but I couldn't take my eyes off him.

I knew I was safe now, but my stomach twisted into tighter knots, and it was a struggle to keep calm.

"Shove off," the man said, not letting go of my arm.

Vincent reached out and held the man's shoulder.

The man's eyes widened, and he dropped my arm while

trying to move away. "We were only having a bit of fun. I don't—"

The man dropped to his knees.

Vincent's face was blank, and he didn't let go. When the man's eyes closed, I tried to pull Vincent away, afraid he would kill the man.

Looking into my eyes for the first time in months, Vincent let go. I couldn't detect a trace of emotion, but I noticed that Vincent had a thin scar angled across his temple. I stared at him, unsure of what to say. What do you say to a man you cared about when he returned without telling you? I wanted to scream at him or hit him. I wanted to hug him and ask him where he'd been. I wanted to take him out of the party and find out everything that had happened, but where would I start?

"Dude, you gotta step away." Neil kept his eyes on the ground and tugged at my arm. "Come on, Heather, we've gotta move back into the party. The party is the party, the fringes are bad news."

Impassive as ever, Vincent looked down at Neil. "Go away."

Neil bobbed his head nervously. "Sure thing, man. Only, I don't go without her."

Vincent's eyes pierced mine. "She stays."

My glare was instantaneous. Did he seriously *tell* me to stay?

Neil cringed. "Yeah, no problems. I gotta stay with her, man."

Vincent closed his eyes for a few seconds, and then looked back at me. "He's with you?"

"Yes." I emphasized this by taking a step slightly in front of Neil, shielding him from Vincent.

"You both need to go." Vincent looked away, back into the crowded room.

"Are you serious?" I didn't know what else to say. He saved me only to turn around and piss me off.

"Don't draw attention to yourself and don't look for me." Vincent walked away.

"Wait," I called.

There was a hesitation, but then he moved out of sight.

My chest tightened. There had been no chance to say goodbye when he left last fall. There hadn't been time. Tonight, though? He walked away without provocation, and he wasn't rushed.

After that, the party was too loud. There were too many bodies pressed together having a crazy, drugged-up experience. Before, I hadn't noticed the driving energy of people and music. Now, even with the Path closed, I could feel the giant swirling mess that was this party.

"So yeah, new rule. Stay away from the edges of the party. That dude was seriously scary. Did he kill that guy on the ground?" Neil asked.

"I don't think so." I swallowed hard and didn't bother looking down. Simmering up, another fragment tried to press itself out. I stamped it back down and tried to do the same with my thoughts of Vincent.

Neil moved us back into the party. "It's about time for you to do your crazy voodoo shit and then get the hell out of here."

"Right," I said dully. "Crazy voodoo shit."

There was a job to be done, and this party was our best chance to find what we needed. I could blow that if I followed Vincent. Sadly, I wasn't convinced I made the right choice. Wanting to get this over with, I grabbed Neil's arm for support. He bobbed to the music and ignored me while I opened up the Path and looked across the party.

I wasn't far off the mark when I thought the party might look psychedelic. Purples, blues, reds, browns, and blacks swirled together while yellows exploded and dissipated. The Path was as high as the people fueling it.

One bright, tarnished golden spot stood out and drew me forward. I dropped Neil's arm and tracked the brightness, only to find an elf who was watching the party-goers.

Turning around, I scanned again, looking for another target.

When nothing stood out, my mind latched to my former partner. Vincent being here couldn't be a coincidence, which made me tense. Wouldn't we know it if he was here for an assignment? Considering we didn't know he was in this world, there was a chance the answer was no. I'm not sure what hurt worse, the possibility he came back and went to work without telling me, or the possibility that no one knew he was here and was wrapped up in this case, but on the wrong side.

Trying to dislodge the thoughts, I focused on finding other clues. If he was involved, we'd find out.

Figuring someone high in a drug-dealing organization would sit and make people come to him, I moved around the room. My attention was caught near the bar close to the dance floor. This bar not only held booze but an assortment of drugs behind the counter. The bartenders, slash dealers, were working together smoothly to take care of their customers.

With samples at the bar, I assumed the dealers weren't far away.

Neil made a subtle gesture to someone who melded into the party. Neil's dealer wasn't my target, so I ignored it. A man, maybe in his mid-thirties, drew my eye. Well, not him, but his Path was interesting to watch. It was amazingly clean; he was covered in a shimmering yellow, with no traces of any other color. I'd never seen anything like it from a human.

Stepping away, I found a place where I could watch him without being as obvious.

"Neil, do you know that man?" I asked.

"Sure, man, that's Indian Dude," Neil said without looking.

"Indian Dude? As in, he's from India? You can't call him that. Does he have a real name?"

"Everyone has a real name. It's not always best to know them." Neil bounced to a throbbing base, looking as though he wasn't paying the least bit of attention to me.

"What does he do?" I asked.

"You ask questions that I won't give answers to."

"So he's a dealer?" I said softly.

A flicker of annoyance crossed Neil's face. "Luckiest man in the world. That's what he is. I've seen cops walk right past him to snag someone else. He gets the high payers too."

"Interesting," I said under my breath, lost in thought as I watched him.

A person approached and the dealer's Path welcomed the person in. The shimmering current parted and curled around the newcomer as though giving a welcomed hello.

"Look," Neil said, "I'm getting too sober. If I go find a guy, can you keep yourself out of trouble?"

"Sure." I looked away but kept the Path in my periphery.

"You can't sit here and watch people while doing nothing." Neil passed me a cigarette and a joint. "Smoke one or the other, I don't care which. I'll be a few minutes."

The glassy look in Neil's his eyes faded. Along with his speech changing, he looked more aware of what was around him.

It was the wrong place to ask, but I did anyway. "Why don't you ever stay sober?"

Neil dropped his gaze and ran his hands through his hair.

He looked uncomfortable. "There's only so much anyone should think. Light one of those, I'll be back." He walked into the crowd. Someone instantly sidled up beside him, and the party swallowed them up.

Choosing to keep myself as drug-free as possible, I chose the cigarette. I tried not to cringe at the taste.

People might think that watching one man should be easy, but trying to be stealthy about it was harder than it looked, and I wasn't doing the best job of it. At least the man wasn't moving around.

"Since when do you smoke?" Vincent stepped into my line of sight.

I had been concentrating so hard on my target's Path that I had missed him come up.

I pointedly took another drag. "Why do you care?"

"Cassie—"

Looking around quickly I said, "It's Heather, least you could do is remember my name." It was said louder than necessary in case someone heard my real name.

"Right," he said quietly, "Heather. I'm Will by the way."

"Lovely." I rolled my eyes and tried to look around him. "Well, Will, I'm a little busy here. Besides, I don't hang out with idiots who don't understand the concept of a phone."

He sighed and shifted a little to the side. My target was back in my line of sight, and it looked like I was looking at Vincent.

Someone else approached the man, but instead of the Path welcoming this person, it turned them away. The Path urged the approaching person a few steps to the right where they tripped and fell. When he got up, the newcomer looked confused and walked off.

"Look," I hissed, "it's not the time or the place for a reunion." I was trying to wrap my brain around what I had seen. People and objects affect the Path, not the other way around. Was the dealer even human to have a Path move around him like a sentient being?

"I agree, but you forced my hand."

"Forced your hand?" I blushed, thinking of the man Vincent had taken down. "Whatever. You did your rescue thing, now run along."

"If that's really what you want."

"What I wanted was a call, at least to let me know you were safe. Don't worry though. Mutual friends will be in touch."

"Mutual friends? You're not doing this on your own?" he asked.

"Of course not." I jabbed the cigarette into an ashtray harder than necessary.

"They sent you in here?" He struggled to keep his voice low. "Into this?" Vincent's blank mask broke and I saw tiny hints of emotion. His forehead creased and his eyes narrowed as he looked around the room, as though expecting to see Logan or Rider in the crowd.

Ignoring my target, I turned to Vincent. "How long have you been back?" Trying to keep my voice low was a struggle.

His only response was to glare harder.

"They aren't here. How long?" I demanded.

"Dudes." Neil approached walking stiffly and looking around. "Chill the hostility. This is a place of party, man."

"Back off," Vincent said.

"I told you, he's with me," I said.

"Have they lost their minds?" Vincent's muscles tensed. "You've always been reckless enough, but you had someone to rein you in."

I could feel my face reddening. The anger was drawing up a rage that I knew I couldn't control.

The black in Vincent's eyes began to grow. A sure sign of his anger. "By the number of bruises you have, I figured you stepped into this on your own."

Feelings of the minotaur rushed forward, trying to take control. "You have no right—"

Vincent's voice lowered and he leaned in. "That elf made me a promise."

"Look, dude," Neil interrupted, "I'm not sure what's going on, but you need to mellow and back off."

"You're right." Vincent took a step back. The shadows in his eyes were the only indication of anger. "You won't see me again."

My anger was doused with cold fear and the piece of soul that had reared up fell into the pool of others. "Are you serious?"

Vincent's face was pure indifference.

"I..." What could I say? I scanned his face for any traces of emotion. There was a time when I could read him effortlessly.

Apparently, that time had passed.

TWENTY-ONE

"Tell me, Will, who is your friend?" The man with the interesting Path had approached while my attention was on Vincent.

I caught a flash of fear in Vincent's eyes. Maybe I could learn to read him again.

"She's no one." Vincent's voice was as deadpan as his face.

My stomach churned at Vincent's words.

"Nonsense! It's fantastic to know that you are capable of having a friend. Even one that responds to you with such fiery spirit." The interloper had the calm look of someone who feared nothing. The strange Path around him was actively trying to push Vincent and me away, but it was ambivalent towards Neil.

Vincent's Path cut through like a knife. My own Path responded with brute pressure. I was a Reader, dammit, and there were no Paths that could turn me away.

"I am Jinendra, but you can call me Jin." Jin had a thick accent. He spread his arms out wide when he spoke as if trying to draw us all in. His Path persisted in doing the opposite.

"Jin," Vincent said, "this is Heather and her friend..." Vincent looked blankly at Neil who watched the party. "This is Heather. We knew each other briefly last fall."

"It is a pleasure to meet you, Heather. Perhaps we will do business in the future. Any friend of Will's is a friend of mine." He turned to Vincent. "I have one last trade, and then we must leave." When he walked off, Vincent went to follow him, but I put a hand on his arm.

When Jin was out of hearing distance, I moved closer and kept my voice low. "I don't know your involvement here, but the others think you're a suspect. This looks bad." I'm not sure I could handle it if Logan and Rider were right about Vincent's role.

Vincent leaned so close that I could feel his breath. "And you?"

"Up until a few hours ago, I thought you wouldn't make me wait months to learn you were alive. You can't ask me to guess about this."

Vincent's eyes clouded over. "You didn't know?"

"No one knew, and now you're here." I gestured to the mass of people.

"That's not—" He looked around. "Even if I'm not the one doing this, it doesn't mean I'm not to blame. Go home and stay safe."

"You know I won't do that." Lost were being killed, there was no way I could leave.

"Even though that's who they sent you here with?" He gestured to Neil who was nervously hovering nearby.

"He's harmless."

"That's the problem."

Responding would probably only make things worse at this point. There was no way to tell him everything we were doing, or everything that I wanted to say.

Moments of silence slowly slid by before Vincent broke it. "I wish I could say I'd call."

"I'm not sure I would believe you if you did. We'll see each other, though. Soon." I emphasized the last word. In this case, we were moving towards the same spot. It would have been a comfort to know if he would be on my side when we reached that point.

Vincent took my hand and gave it a gentle squeeze.

A white-hot fire of energy bolted through Vincent and me. The small piece of my soul that he carried merged us together. The turmoil of emotion that his appearance brought felt magnified.

My heart raced. I grabbed the edge of the table and jerked myself away from Vincent. Every single spark of soul surged, clamoring, racing, and fighting to move to the forefront.

"What's wrong?" Vincent went to reach for me again, but I backed away.

The chaos inside became a struggle, and trying to grab hold of it was like trying to stop a tornado. My concentration needed to be inward, not with Vincent. Who knew what was inside me, ready to take over?

"Shit." Neil's scared voice came from next to me. "You're you, right? Man, you gotta be you."

"I'm me." The last thing I wanted was for Neil to think I couldn't keep myself together.

"Okay, so like, you got all upset right?" Neil tore through his pockets.

"Does it matter?" I snapped.

"Right." Neil opened a bottle of water and dumped a fine powder into the bottle. "So like, drink this. Fast."

I hesitated and tried to think this over, which caused my attention to waver. A large, dark, chunk of soul detached itself from the rest and tried to take over. A promise of ancient power and control came with it.

But I had power, and I was determined to gain my own control.

"It's all we can do here." Neil's voice was pleading as he put a water bottle in my hand.

"Sure," I mumbled and drank.

"What the hell, Cass?" Vincent's words were an acrid whisper.

"Shit, man, he looks ticked." Neil moved closer to me. "We gotta get out of here."

Before Neil could go anywhere, Vincent grabbed him by the shirt and yanked him up, nearly lifting him off the floor.

"What's wrong with her?" Vincent's voice was low.

I tugged on Neil's shirt. "Doesn't matter. Drop him, we have to go." When Vincent didn't move, I lowered my voice. "You are a distraction that I can't handle right now. Let. Him. Go." A twinge of guilt followed the harshness of my voice.

But it worked. Vincent let go and stepped back. Neil wasted no time dragging me out of the party.

My heart clinched when I reached the frigid night air outside. Once again, Vincent and I parted ways without saying goodbye.

Neil passed a ticket to the valet, my muscles relaxed and more importantly, the clamoring began to slow. My own soul fragments began to move forward while the intruders began to swirl before settling.

Contentment rolled over me like fog, and Pat's car drove up.

Finally able to pay attention to the world around me, I nestled into the seat. "Hmmm." The pleased sigh came with a smile that I don't think could be pried from my face.

"Is it working? It sounds like it's working. How do you feel?"

"Hmmm, I feel... good." Streetlights flickered past. "Where are we going?"

"I don't know what the hell happened in there, but I think it's time to take a step back."

"Take a step back?" My voice came out in a drunken slur.

"Those were some bad dudes. Whatever you needed, I hope you got it, because we can't go back."

Sweat began to pour off me. "Right, take a step back."

Vincent, I thought. He's here, he's alive.

Lights became brighter, or maybe there were more of them as we drove across the city. I watched the skyscraper-sized hospitals blur by us.

"Are we going to the office?" I asked.

"Dude, Taylor is going to kill me for tonight. Unless your partners get there first."

I laughed but covered my mouth to stifle the flow.

Neil gave me a worried look. "I'm not sure they'd be wrong after giving you those pills, but man, it was go with the flow right? I did what I had to do."

"Right." I tried to put on a serious face, and follow what Neil was saying, but the words weren't sinking in.

"It was necessary. They can't fault me for that, right?"

"Right," I repeated, sinking further into the soft leather.

Neil's anxiety levels were ratcheting up, but it flowed over me.

"Yeah, but the party was intense, man. Besides, Taylor said your own partners had to tranq you in the past."

I nodded and closed my eyes.

"So we agree," he said. "Okay, we can do this. Stand united and all that shit."

"Uh huh." Some of Neil's words finally worked their way through my euphoria. "What are you talking about?"

"I had to chill things out." Neil's concentration on the road was intense. "So I thought some pams would to the trick."

I laughed again. "I have no idea what that is."

"Anti-anxiety. Doctors prescribe it. It's all good."

I went back to staring at the lights.

"And the, uh, amount of heroin in the pills was minuscule. And it worked. I mean we left the party, you're all chill, and no more trouble."

"Heroin?" I repeated.

"I've seen trouble with Indian Dude," Neil continued. "Trouble rolls off him like oil, only to land on everyone around him, and you looked ready to lose your shit. We had to get out of there."

"So, I'm on heroin?" It sounded really bad, but with the drug coursing through me, I couldn't make myself get worked up over it.

"So we're good right? Stay united?"

The intensity of my feel-good mood began to gradually fall. "Sure."

When Neil parked the car, I opened the door and let my legs swing outside, but I had no interest in getting up. The cool air soaked into my skin and I became enamored with the sharp clouds that my breath made in the air.

Neil came around and leaned on the car door. "Maybe we should have driven around more. You look like you're flying way too high."

Somewhere in the dark, I heard a car door slam shut. My legs bounced and I looked around, expecting to find that Vincent had followed us. It wasn't until I saw Logan that I remembered we'd been nearby all night.

"Did you see him?" I asked Logan.

Rider appeared and wrinkled his nose. "What is that?"

"What's what?" Neil asked running his hand through his hair.

"That smell. All the smells." Rider covered his nose.

"Always the gentleman," I said. "Did you see him?"

"Let's get inside," Logan said.

"But it's so comfortable here," I argued.

Neil stepped back. "Maybe I should get back. Take Pat's car to her and make sure everything is good at the party."

"No." My voice was sharper than I intended. "I know you saw him. You're coming with us." My mind tried to twist that around. I'm pretty sure I wanted to stay outside, but we needed to talk. In the end, the need to talk outweighed everything.

Taylor met us in the hall and looked Neil and me over. "What did you take?"

When I didn't say anything, Taylor turned to Neil.

Neil tried to be noncommittal. "Nothing much."

"Time to sober up," Taylor said.

"Past time," Neil agreed.

Taylor looked taken aback.

Standing was taking way more effort than it was worth, so I meandered down the hall, knowing that the chairs in the conference room wouldn't be too far away.

Taylor sighed. "Grab some water for both of you, and then I need the names. Everything. Cassie, let's go to the infirmary for a while."

"No way, we have to go over stuff." I looked up and down the halls trying to find a familiar door. "Besides, I feel great. Conference room?"

It looked like he was going to argue, but decided against it. Instead, he led the way.

This time, I didn't mind taking the seat closest to the door.

I fell into the chair and let it swing back and forth, then, leaning far back, I stared at the ceiling while everyone settled in. As soon as Neil sat the water bottle in front of me, I snatched it up, thanked him, and drank half the bottle.

"What did you all take?" Taylor asked again.

"Look, man, she was drawing attention to us. It was like... intense. It was intense enough for Indian Dude to come over."

"Jin," I corrected.

"I shouldn't know his name." Neil leaned in, put his elbows on the table, and rubbed his temples. "I should walk around unnoticed. Once dealers notice you, bad shit happens."

"We're in the dark," Logan said.

"So we split up at the party, but I kept an eye on her. I watched her to make sure she was okay, but then, all of a sudden, she wasn't okay. She wandered into someone doing X. She reacted like a champ, but it was the other scary dude that saved the day. I'm pretty sure he killed the dude on X."

I rolled my eyes. "He didn't kill him, only knocked him out."

"Are you okay?" Rider asked.

I waved my hand towards Neil to change Rider's focus.

"Where were you?" Logan asked Neil.

"I was on my way over there. Nothing would have happened, I swear. The scary dude beat me to it. At that point, I thought that we needed to check out of this place and bounce. I stuck to her for a while, but then she started eyeing the dealers. Not just any dealers, though, Indian Dude—"

"Jin," I corrected again.

"Whatever," Neil said. "Point is, I stepped away for a minute to pull myself together, and when I came back, she was fighting with the scary dude who saved her. He looked ticked off, too. I thought things might get rough. Everyone was noticing, but they kept arguing. And that dude runs with Indian Dude."

"Jin," I corrected again.

"Jin, the dealer?" Logan asked.

"Yeah," Neil said.

I was able to concentrate enough to gather my question together. "How long has he been around here, working with Jin?"

"I noticed him about three months ago. He worked his way up fast," Neil said.

"Three months." My cloud of tranquility disappeared, and I fell back into the real world.

The real world sucked.

"Anyway," Neil said, "dude looks ticked and then Indian Dude comes over. That was harsh, man. How do you explain to a dealer why you're arguing with his man? Only thing is, the guy introduces her to Indian Dude. Called her Heather and everything. Like they'd known each other. I practically crapped myself at that point. So Indian Dude walks off, and the other guy starts to follow, but she stopped him."

"It's not as bad as you think," I said, staring up at the ceiling, "and it's Jin. Can you please call him by his name?"

"You asked him point blank if he did it! Straight to his face and all. He leaned in real close and said something. I didn't know what it was, man, but it shook her up. Shit turned worse and I thought she was, you know, losing herself. So I doped her up and got her the hell out of there." Neil stopped. He breathed as if he'd been running.

From his point of view, it probably wasn't that far off.

"Cassie, is that what happened?" Taylor asked.

"Pretty much." I drew myself up into a passable sitting position and looked at Logan and Rider.

"Why would you fight with a stranger?" Rider asked.

"Because, it wasn't a stranger." I rubbed my temples thinking how bad this looked for Vincent. "Sorry Neil. I should have told you I knew him. He's been missing for almost six months." I watched as Logan's eyes narrowed. "He used to be one of our partners."

TWENTY-TWO

Without reading the Path, I could feel anger boil up. It filled the room and rolled my stomach.

"You are telling us that Vincent was there tonight?" Rider asked.

"I was hoping that one of you saw him coming or going into the party," I admitted.

"We didn't," Logan said.

"So the guy you were fighting with, he's your partner?" Neil's voice was wounded.

"He was my partner. Our partner really," I corrected. "We haven't seen him in almost six months, though."

"You think he's here undercover?" Taylor asked.

Logan said the words I was dreading to hear. "I think he's behind this."

Neil sagged back in his seat. "So, we're looking at an AIR agent, or possibly an ex-AIR agent."

"What makes you think he's behind this?" Taylor asked.

I tried to avoid getting frustrated with the turn in the conversation. "I know you all think he's guilty—"

"He's a Walker," Logan said. "He's one of the few people we know of who could be capable of tearing a soul into pieces."

"I didn't know Walkers could do that." Neil leaned forward. "Walkers were on my list because they take souls."

"Vincent shredded Cassie's last fall," Rider said.

Taylor looked at me. "He shredded... but—"

I frowned. "Because he's able to, doesn't mean he's doing this."

"What did he say at the party, when you asked him?" Rider asked.

"He said that even if he didn't do it, it doesn't mean he's not to blame." I'm not sure if Vincent was helping himself or hurting himself with what he said.

"He could be lying," Logan said.

"If it were you or me, I would agree," Rider said. "But he said this to Cassie."

"Not everyone thinks of a friend in the same way you do," Logan said.

"I think he meant what he said. Look, we know Vincent. If he thinks he's to blame, he'll try to fix it. No matter what the costs." My stomach flip-flopped, and I looked at Logan, pleading for him to understand. "I don't think he did this."

"I don't know Vincent," Taylor said, "but from what you all have said, I don't think you can trust one thing over the other. You need more."

Logan looked down at his hands. "Maybe Taylor's right. We should gather more details. Find out what he's been doing for the last six months."

Reluctantly, I agreed. It was the smart thing to do. Get the whole story and make an informed decision. It wasn't my choice, but it was the right choice.

"Let's talk about the dealer, Jin," I said, changing the focus away from Vincent. "What can you tell us about him, Neil?"

"Dude's super lucky. I've never seen anything like it," Neil said.

"What do you *notice?*" Taylor asked.

Neil leaned back in his seat and looked at the ceiling, and then he closed his eyes and launched into an explanation. "All dealers deal with risk. You have narcs, rival dealers, and others in their organization that want more money, more status, or who plain want to take over. Then there's the drugs themselves. Addicts die all the time, but too many dead druggies isn't good business."

"That doesn't make Jin anything special," I said.

"Yeah, but about a year ago, Jin was like the other dealers," Neil said. "Anxious, careful, and paranoid. He got busted, but they let him go. Not long after that, he became untouchable."

"What do you mean untouchable?" Logan asked.

"Stuff rolls off him. For a while, everyone thought he went narc, but no one else got busted, so things went back to normal, only Jin's risks went away." Neil looked like he was turning the thought over in his mind. "Actually, it's more like they went around him. Bad shit that should have rained down on Jin dropped on people around him. Other dealers don't mess with him anymore. I've seen people that wanted to hurt Jin in a bad way, only to have badness bounce back. Not like Jin does them in, but weird accidents happen to them after something should have happened to Jin."

"What makes you think he isn't a narc?" Logan asked.

"The facts don't add up," Neil said.

"How is it you notice all this and no one else does?" I asked.

Neil shifted uncomfortably in his seat and looked up at Taylor. Taylor nodded.

"This doesn't go in any report," Neil said. I could feel his anxiety whip around the room. "It doesn't leave this room."

He looked each one of us in the eye as we agreed.

He shifted in his seat again. "It's what I do. I see everything, add up the facts, and get the answer."

"That sounds simple," Rider said.

Neil let out a noise of frustration and tossed himself back in the chair.

"His IQ is off the charts," Taylor said. "By that, I mean he can't be tested. We've tried, but he sees things, even in the tests that no one else does. He got his first Ph.D. before he could vote. But got kicked out of his first three colleges."

Neil crossed his arms. "Professors don't like to be told they're wrong."

"They don't like to be told they're wrong by a kid with an attitude problem. Anyway," Taylor continued, "he sees what other people miss. He makes connections even when he can't explain why the facts add up the way they do."

Neil rolled his eyes. "I know why they add up that way. I just don't know how to explain it to someone who isn't me. And no one is me. It is what it is. The facts are there, and they fit together. In this case, Indian Dude is untouchable."

"I saw his Path which might help explain." I stretched out and gathered my thoughts. "The area around him flexes and moves like nothing I've seen. It's almost as if the Path around him is inviting to some people, but discourages others from coming near."

"I'm not that familiar with Readers, so I'm not following," Taylor said.

I liked talking about what I do, so I sat up straight and filled him in. "The Path is an overlay to our world, which I read. It's like a ripple of running water, but it's everywhere, covering everything."

"Do you see this all the time?" Taylor asked.

"No," I said. "Readers have to open themselves up to it. Everything leaves traces as we move through the world. We leave marks on objects we touch and the air we walk through. The Path is almost like a memory of that mark left behind. It picks up on emotions, and occasionally intent. The stronger the emotion, the longer the Path holds onto that impression. Some Readers can pick up a Path and follow it back through time to find its origin."

Neil's eyes widened. "Dude, you can time travel?"

I grinned. "Not exactly. I stay put in this time, but the Path shows me the past."

"So you could follow my Path back to my home?" Taylor asked.

"Not if you drove," I said. "Cars tend to muddle things. They move too fast for the person to make a lasting impression. If you were *really* angry while you drove, maybe, but it would be difficult. If you walked home, especially if it was every day, the imprint would be worn into the Path, and I could follow it."

"You say some Readers. Do different Readers do different things?" Neil asked.

I frowned, thinking back on everything I had said. "There aren't many Readers on record, so it's hard to say. I've spoken to a Reader who is much older than me but is only now beginning to follow Paths for any distance. She can, however, read intricacies of the Path that I have never noticed before."

"We should probably keep that much detail off the record as well," Logan said, eyeing Neil and Taylor.

Taylor agreed, but Neil wasn't done. "What you do and what you have described doesn't add up."

"I'm sure we could say the same about you," Logan said to Taylor and Neil.

"There's more to it," I agreed, "but from what I understand, most Readers in the past have had these skills. And it's these skills that let me see the abnormalities in Jin."

Taylor looked at me like he had when we had first met, like he was studying me.

Logan leaned forward. "Does this mean he has the ability to move the Path around him?"

I thought that over before shaking my head. "Anything that alters the Path uses effort, which affects the Path. His fingerprints would have been on it somewhere."

"So the Path was acting cognizant in this case?" Neil asked.

"Cognizant? Are you sure you're you?" I asked, stealing his words from earlier.

"He's sobering up," Taylor said.

"And it sucks," Neil muttered.

Not knowing how to respond, I moved on. "I'm not sure if that's the right word. I'm not sure the Path itself was aware."

"I'm not understanding everything here," Taylor said. "How does the Path decide to turn someone away on its own, if it's not aware?"

"I've never seen anything like it," I admitted, "but it would move to draw some people towards Jin. But I saw one person approach him, and his Path worked to keep the person away."

"When Jin came close to you, what happened?" Rider asked.

"I didn't feel the inclination to move away," Neil said.

"His Path flowed around you and didn't try to affect you," I said. "If I hadn't been Reading the Path, it probably would have moved me away. I could see it trying to. Vincent on the other hand, well, the Path tried to make him go away as well, but he sliced right through."

"That is probably the Reader in him," Rider said.

"I thought he was a Walker," Taylor said.

"When he broke up Cassie's soul, he ended up with a piece of it," Logan said.

"Is that normal for a Walker?" Neil asked, leaning towards Logan.

Logan didn't answer.

"If he is breaking apart other souls, would he have a piece of each?" Rider asked.

"It's hard to say." It was an awful thought and one I didn't want to dwell on.

"How are Vincent and Jin connected?" Taylor asked.

I twisted in my seat again. "No idea."

"Is Jin even a suspect?" Rider asked.

"I think that depends," Logan said. "Are there any Lost that could have a Path like Jin's?"

I sighed. "I've never seen anything like this Path."

"We know wearing the jewelry affects people," Logan said, "based on what type of soul is trapped."

"You think he was wearing a piece of the jewelry." It wasn't a big leap.

"I'm fairly certain of it," Logan said. "Who is suspected to have been killed by this?"

Neil rattled off the list.

The number of people that had fallen to this monster was alarming. "I've seen the Path of all of them except the telepath. None of them look like Jin's, and I doubt the telepath would look the same either."

"There are other Lost around that won't report deaths. Some are here illegally, others are private, and others don't have the capabilities to report such a thing," Taylor said.

Neil was staring into space. "It adds up. Jin has been untouchable for months, but I had it wrong. Untouchable is the wrong word. Well, it's the right word, but there was another word I used to describe it. Luck. The man is lucky."

Logan's eyes grew wide. "That can't be. There are none around here."

Neil snorted. "Those little bastards could be all over the place and we wouldn't notice. That's the point. They're Lucky. They're untouchable."

"Who are they?" I asked irritably.

Neil smiled smugly but didn't say anything.

"Leprechauns," Logan said sadly. "He's got a leprechaun."

I watched Logan carefully. "I haven't seen any records that leprechauns exist." How does he know this stuff?

"Man, you are dense," Neil said. "Haven't you figured it out yet? Everything is real. We have griffins living in caves off the river. Gremlins pop in and steal metal. Mermaids swim in the ocean and even in some lakes. Werewolves, vampires, sphinx, you name it and it's out there somewhere. How do you not know this already? Hell there's even a drag—"

"Neil, stop being such a little shit. We get it." Anger filled Taylor's words, but fear and anxiety rushed through the room.

"Whatever, man." Neil pushed his chair away from the table and stalked out of the room.

We ignored him, except Taylor, who watched him go.

"Okay," I said, "Jin may have a leprechaun soul on him. The other souls didn't last long, but it sounds like Jin's been this way for a few months."

"He could have the whole leprechaun somewhere," Logan said.

"How would he have caught one?" Taylor asked.

"They're almost impossible to catch," Logan said. "They're faster than gnomes, can't be trapped, and they have luck on their side. You physically have to pick one up to catch them, and with their history, they don't allow that."

"What is their history? I mean the real history, not pots of gold at the end of the rainbow?" I asked.

"The real and the myth collide too much to know for certain," Logan said. "One of the oldest legends talks about three leprechauns dragging a man into the water. The man caught one, and supposedly, the leprechaun bargained for its freedom by agreeing to grant the man three wishes. The man became a king. Some say he got his wishes and let the leprechaun go, others say he kept it in a cage, hanging in a dungeon after it stopped granting wishes. Knowing human nature, my guess is it died in its cage."

I cringed. "That's awful."

"It's not only humans that would have locked one up. There's a lot of people, elves included, that always grasp for more. Anyway, word got 'round, and people were trying to hunt leprechauns. Stories of gold only made the attempts more frequent."

I wrapped my arms around my stomach, feeling ill at the thought of small people being hunted like animals.

Logan started to sound far away and he looked lost in thought. "The thing was, only the one was ever caught. For a while, it's said that the leprechauns taunted their hunters and played cruel jokes on them. And who could fault them for that? Then they disappeared. Occasionally, there are rumors of kids spotting one, and they've popped up in records a time or two in the past few hundred years, but nothing concrete. I've never heard stories of one on this side of the world."

"Maybe this is where they disappeared to," I suggested.

"Does their luck ever run out?" Rider asked.

Logan crossed his arms. "If Jin has one, the leprechauns' luck ran out. At least for the one he has."

"It could fit," I said.

"From Neil's reaction, I guess it fits better than other options," Taylor said.

"If only one man, hundreds or even thousands of years ago ever caught one, why would it be possible now?" I asked.

"You broke through the Path that moved others away." Rider looked away from me. "So did Vincent."

"Should we try to go talk to the leprechauns?" I asked. "If they're around, they could have seen who did this."

Taylor and Logan looked at each other for a few beats.

Logan's face matched the seriousness in his voice. "If there are leprechauns, we need to keep them out of it. Keep the government out of their business. The last thing we need is a bunch of politicians trying to gain luck."

That was the first time Logan had hinted about the government trying to use the Lost. If he were worried, though, why would he work for AIR? I put it out of my mind. Better to concentrate on the trouble we already had.

"Okay," I said, "we can't be sure of leprechauns. They stay out of the reports and we leave them alone."

Logan appeared to relax, which made me think I should be more cautious about what I put in any of my reports.

"If Jin's Path is always like this," I said, moving us back on track, "he has to have a steady supply of whatever is causing it, or he has power himself. People around him have to know more."

Logan frowned and leaned back. "Someone does know." He looked at me, worry in his eyes. "But you'd better call Margaret to see if she has any warnings before you talk to him again."

TWENTY-THREE

Despite Logan's concerns, I didn't think Vincent would be any trouble. Jin, however, gave me the creeps, so I wanted to stay far away from him.

Gran was worried when I called her, but she was at a loss to know why. The only thing she could tell me was, "Don't go see the artwork." Hearing the misgivings in her voice, I took the advice to heart and promised not to look at any paintings or drawings.

After talking with Gran, I knew I needed to talk with Ethan. Calling him was more difficult than I expected. Thinking of Ethan made me feel guilty, which was ridiculous. Worse yet, thinking about Vincent being back made me feel guilty. There was no reason for either, so I buried the emotions in my mind and ignored them.

Once I heard Ethan's voice, it became easier to keep that guilt hidden away. His relief from hearing from me was noticeable, and once I'd spoken to him, I knew I needed to see him.

However, there was too much to do. Buoyed by speaking with him, I went back to work and attacked our case head on. I wanted to get this wrapped up, even though we didn't, or at least I didn't, have a suspect in terms of who was killing the Lost.

Jin knew, though.

For someone that didn't want to know anything about his dealers, Neil knew loads about Jin, and once persuaded, he tracked down more.

After finding Jin, it only took patience to find Vincent. Patience was a virtue that I didn't have, so Rider and Sable worked together to trail our ex-partner for a few days.

Meeting Vincent had to be done in public, and we had no idea who else around could be involved in the case. This meant I would be going in blind, and I needed someone other than Neil with me. We debated using Rider, but in the end, a Native American man almost six and a half feet tall would draw attention. That would have been okay, but he also hadn't been in this world long and missed subtleties, and some social interactions stumped him.

Thanks to me, Rider was getting used to sarcasm, but beyond that, he took a lot of things at face value.

Logan was out, along with MyTH, and we discussed other AIR agents, but in the end, it was too risky. The agent would be human, almost all of them were, and they would find out more than any of us wanted them to in the official file.

In the end, we settled on Jonathan. Logan had been teaching him to fight. As an elf, he was strong and fast, he was working on his degree in criminal justice, and he could be trusted.

Logan also mentioned that his son needed some breathing space from his fiancé, Paula. Apparently, their relationship was in a downward spiral, which I hated to hear.

I had hoped that we could go pick Jonathan up so I could catch up with Ethan for a few minutes. For some reason, I really wanted to see him again before I went any further into the case. Instead, Jonathan was driving my car over. It made sense, we needed another vehicle, and getting Jonathan here faster was better.

To make up for not getting to see him, I called Ethan again and later that night, we even chatted by video.

Early the next morning, Rider joined us, while Sable let us know when we could 'accidentally' bump into Vincent.

The moment I stepped into the restaurant and saw him, pixies fluttered around my stomach.

I closed my eyes and opened myself to the Path, then stemmed the roaring tide into a small stream of rippling emotions. Besides Jonathan, no one's Path looked too agitated or eager, although I avoided reading Vincent altogether. No one looked intensely focused on anything. I hoped that meant that no one was listening, but I knew it would be silly to assume. Once satisfied, I dropped the Path, allowing the otherworldly overlay to disappear.

Trying to convince my stomach to stop wobbling wasn't working, so I plunged in. "It's nice to bump into you like this, William."

Vincent grimaced and muttered, "I should have known." He looked torn between leaving and telling me to leave.

I slid into the booth beside him, not giving him the chance to get up, while Jonathan sat at a table nearby.

Vincent didn't bother with preliminaries. "If I asked you to stay away?"

A small part of me had wanted him to ask for help, or at least confide in me now that we were away from Jin's people. The hurt I felt must have shown on my face.

"Not like that." Vincent put his elbows on the table and buried his face in his hands, looking more frustrated than I'd ever seen him. "Not like that." He sighed heavily. "You're working what I'm working." He straightened and sat back, looking composed. "It wouldn't matter if I asked you to stay away. I know you too well for that."

"You're right, it wouldn't help at all." Taking a hard look at Vincent's face, the new scar stood out. I lifted my hand to trace the mark and stopped. It wasn't my business.

"I don't know what you're working. You haven't told anyone. As far as AIR is concerned, you disappeared in the line of duty." I kept my voice low. Jonathan would be able to hear everything, but others in the diner would need to strain to overhear.

"If you're here, and showing up where you're showing up, you've found the jewelry," Vincent said.

Bells on the diner door jingled. My nerves rattled, as I looked up and I opened the Path to see the newcomer. The couple that entered looked like they were Gran's age and they didn't show signs of hostility in any way. After another scan of the room, I dropped the Path.

"It looks like you've gained more control," Vincent said. "I'm still trying to work out how to fix what I've done."

"Is that why you're with Jin?" I asked. "Are you practicing your new-found skill on the Lost?"

Vincent's expressionless face didn't change, but it paled. "Do you really think it's me?"

"No," I admitted, "but it's not only my opinion that counts."

"Rider?"

"No, Rider's taking my side."

"Logan?" Vincent tensed, and I could see the trace of hurt in his eyes.

"You haven't left him much choice."

He swallowed. "I didn't expect Logan to think I would

purposely hurt the innocent. We had been getting along before I left."

Sorting through the tangle of emotions that Vincent brought up was starting to override everything else. The case, I thought firmly, focus on the case.

"We need information," I said. "We need to know if Jin is dealing this stuff, and who's supplying him."

"Jin will kill anyone who gets too close, and it won't be quick. You have to stay away."

"I have to?" I should earn some type of medal for not raising my voice.

"I shouldn't have said that. I should know better." There was a trace of tension in his eyes. "Okay, I know you're not going to leave town, and it's too dangerous for any of you if you don't know what's going on. All of it." Vincent glanced at his watch. "But Will needs to be somewhere soon, so there's not enough time now."

"Look, we need to move on this," I said.

"We can meet later today. Four-thirty in Hampshire Park; there's a lake. Meet me on the northeast side of the boathouse, near the lake. I'll be at the second bench you see."

I wanted to argue but settled for a disgruntled sigh. "I'll be there."

There was so much I wanted to say and to ask, but neither of us spoke. The silence was awkward, which we rarely had to deal with in the past. I moved to slide out of the booth.

"Wait." Vincent reached for me, but hesitated and let his arm drop to his side.

I really wanted him to take my hand.

Okay, I should feel guilty about that. Embarrassed by the thought, I could feel my face turn red. Think of the case and only the case.

We were both at a loss as to how to proceed, and the silence continued.

"Stay safe," I said. "We'll have all the time in the world to talk after this is over."

"Sure. Stay safe," he repeated the sentiment but sounded distant.

Jonathan joined me, and we left the diner. The truck was a few blocks away, so I had a few minutes to pull myself together, and after seeing Vincent again, a few minutes may not be enough time.

"Oh, no," Jonathan said.

Looking up, I saw two men blocking the sidewalk in front of us.

The Path roared free with barely a thought. Not the small stream I usually viewed, but the raging river of power.

Why hadn't I been paying attention? We had already turned a corner or two so the diner would be out of sight.

I looked around, seeing two people crossing the street and two men following us. None of them looked friendly, and there was nowhere to run.

"Three sets of people," I murmured softly. "We can't lead them any further towards the truck without announcing that we're not civilians. How many can you take?"

"Three, maybe four."

Jonathan and I had never worked together, and there was no time to make a real plan. "You take the two behind us, and I'll take the front. Get the two in the middle as best we can. If they pull guns, disarm first."

My stomach clenched. Wrestling with the Path, I began to bend it. Jonathan turned around to cover the two men behind.

The men in front of us moved forward.

"My boss said Jin took an interest in you." The man wore a T-shirt advertising a heavy metal band and looked at least ten years older than everyone else. "We can't touch Jin, and we can only follow his man, but we can take you. The boy can stay because no one said anything about him. But you? We need you."

There were no guns in sight, and no one looked too worried about what we might do.

"Ready?" I asked Jonathan under my breath.

"Yeah." Jonathan's breathing sounded measured, but his voice betrayed his doubt.

"Now." It came out louder than I anticipated, which announced my massive uncertainty.

Jonathan was virtually silent. The men in front of me froze in confusion before scrambling to their pockets. I slammed together the Path in front of me, creating a solid, invisible wall in midair. It burned through my energy, but they never knew what hit them when I shoved the wall forward as fast as I could. They fell back, tripping when the wall smashed forward. When they hit the ground, they were thrown further away. Cloth ripped, and I heard a bone snap. A blow to the face broke my concentration, and the solid air fell apart.

I staggered back clutching my eye as pain radiated out. I barely noticed Jonathan darting to another target. The man was ready to throw another, but I found his Path. The man must have been a bundle of nerves when he had crossed the street, because his Path was thick in the air. I hardened the trail behind him and yanked him back into the street. As he flew back, I saw the gun, and it was aimed at me.

Mentally reaching out, I tried to draw enough energy to make the air solid again.

Why did I make the first wall of the Path so big? Nothing was pulling together fast enough. The trigger was pulled as the gun was smashed away by a kick. The crack of the gun was unreal as the sound reverberated between the buildings.

Jonathan's fist met the man's face and the gun clattered to the ground. I took a shuddering breath and looked around. After another punch from Jonathan the man crumpled, and Jonathan launched himself at the man in the street. It didn't take long for him to fall.

The men were down, but stirring.

"We have to go." I was shaking.

Moving to a man that had managed to get to his knees, Jonathan was ready to attack again.

"Hey!" I tugged Jonathan's arm, ready to drag him away.

Jonathan swung around, punching before thinking. His eyes widened, and I saw him pull the punch as it reached me.

I collapsed in a heap, with the air knocked out of me. After a few panicky tries, I was able to suck in a breath.

"No, no, no." Jonathan's face blanched.

I tried to talk but only managed a wheeze.

Without another word, he scooped me up. Any protest I wanted to make went out the window, when I saw the pale panicky face of the elf carrying me.

The tightness in my chest lightened and I breathed easier. "I'm okay." I tried to reassure him further, but he looked caught in his own world of panic.

Rider and Logan were running to meet us, but Jonathan didn't seem to notice them. Jonathan's focus was on running straight for the truck. His dad grabbed his arm and stopped him dead. Jonathan's head whipped towards him. Rider snatched me away, and Jonathan's gaze snapped back to Rider. Logan unceremoniously yanked Jonathan's arm behind his back, knocked his feet out from under him and pinned his son to the ground.

CHAPTER
TWENTY-FOUR

Rider was putting me on my feet while Logan murmured in his son's ear. I heard a few words, but the language was unfamiliar. Rider patted me down.

"Were you shot?" Rider asked as he manhandled me. "I smell blood."

"It's not mine."

Rider walked around me checking every inch to make sure there were no new holes in me.

I stood clutching my stomach. Rider moved back in front of me, and this time, his eyes were on my face. From the pain, I was sure there had to be a spectacular bruise forming.

"We're taking Vincent in now." Logan's voice was rigid.

"We should leave." I tried to sound firm through all my aches. "Those guys—"

"Go get the truck." Logan tossed me the keys, which bounced off me and landed on the ground, and he dragged Jonathan to his feet.

Jonathan remained pale, but the panic was gone.

"We can't take him in. We'll blow his cover," I said.

"He did this!" Logan yelled, his voice going colder and higher pitched as his face elongated and his ears rolled out to points. His eyes became slanted and looked larger, much too large for his face. The destructive strength behind Logan's alien appearance made me take a step back while an icy feeling of dread spread through my body. Rider angled himself in front of me and tried to get me to move further away.

I took a few steadying breaths. "Someone was following him." I was afraid using Vincent's name would shove my partner over the edge. "They decided to follow us. I wasn't paying enough attention and didn't notice them." I groped around for the right words, but I couldn't find anything else.

Even through the alien vestige he now displayed, I could tell Logan was struggling. His hands were balled into fists, and he looked as though he was poised to run and hold himself back at the same time. I wanted to move closer to try to pull up enough dredges of the Path to lighten the atmosphere, but Rider wouldn't budge, and I didn't think I was strong enough to move the Path.

Logan closed his eyes and began to shrink in upon himself. His ears rolled back, and slowly, his face returned to normal.

The ice in my stomach melted as my partner began to look more like himself.

"Let's leave." I managed to keep my voice steady, but my hands were shaking.

Logan agreed and tried to steady himself.

Rider picked up the keys, handed them to Jonathan, and then motioned Jonathan away.

Jonathan took a nervous look at his dad before going to the truck.

Rider's hand remained in my way, refusing me to move any closer to Logan.

"Let me through," I said.

Rider didn't respond and kept a watchful eye on Logan.

"I can—"

"No," Logan interrupted me, "he's right to stand in the way. I lost control, and I shouldn't have. But when I heard that shot?" Logan leaned against the building. "If Jonathan had..." Logan took a shuddering breath and looked like the words were too hard to say. "And then I thought about what I would have to tell Margaret if you were shot."

Logan's pain was palpable in the air. We stood silently while he reined in his emotions.

"You know, your son kicked ass out there today," I said, trying to lighten the mood. "He's the reason neither of us was shot."

"His first real fight," Logan said approvingly. "He didn't lose it like I did today?"

"No." I wasn't sure how to avoid telling him what made him panic and run, but Logan saved me the trouble.

"It's good he was partnered with you when it happened. Did he do that?" Logan asked motioning to my face.

"Wait, what?" Rider dropped his arm and looked from me to Logan and back again. "No, why would he?"

"He didn't," I said. "He hit me in the stomach, but pulled his punch in the end."

"But—" Rider started.

Logan grinned and held up his hands as the truck approached. "I could tell he hit her because no one was shot, but he was panicked. He never would have hit her on purpose, but he's never been in a fight before. He'll learn from this and do better next time. He did better than his older brother too, but then he was surrounded by other elves. Garashem would be proud."

"Older brother?" My brain was working hard to make sense of that confusion.

Logan's grin faded. "Never mind, only a passing thought. I don't want to hear the name come up from either of you, especially in front of the kids."

"Sure." Concern for or about what might have happened to Logan's family overrode my confusion. "But—"

"It's a story for another time," Logan said with more force than necessary.

I agreed, still confused, but I knew there were areas of darkness in the elf that I should never try to see. They were buried within his golden Path.

Logan appeared to relax. "Thank you."

Jonathan parked the truck beside us, and Logan climbed in. I moved to the cab, but when I looked back, Rider was staring at us, looking puzzled.

I smiled back. "Come on, my friend, let's talk about Walkers and elves and why they shouldn't kill each other."

IT DIDN'T TAKE LONG to fill everyone in, but there was a lot of time spent getting set up for my meeting with Vincent at the park. Logan wanted to make sure that every area was covered and that no one would follow us in or out.

I tried to cover the giant purple bruise spreading across my face, but it surpassed my skills with makeup, which didn't come as too much of a surprise. I found a thrift store and grabbed a pair of sunglasses with a large frame and lenses. The woman behind the counter gave me a concerned look and asked if I was okay as I checked out. When I retrieved the glasses from the bag later, I found a card for a woman's shelter. I worried about what others may be seeing when they looked at me, but then I tossed the thoughts aside. It was all part of the job.

It was too early to stop at the lake. At this point, the entire area would be under surveillance. Logan, Rider, Jonathan, Sable, Taylor, and a few other MyTH employees were watching everyone who entered and exited to ensure an attack like this morning wasn't repeated. Jonathan, Logan, and Rider were all placed close enough to the action that they should be able to hear everything.

Since I needed to stall for time, I parked at the art museum on the other side of the park. I flinched when I looked at myself in the visor mirror. The glasses would be large enough to hide some of my face, but there was no mistaking the bruise. I folded up the visor and my car door opened.

A gun was leveled directly at my face and I stopped breathing.

"Let's not add to the damage," Jin said.

A wet cloth went over my mouth and nose. Trying not to breathe in, I struggled to move away until cool metal settled against my temple. I gasped and fell away.

SHADOWS SHIFTED until blurry images appeared. My head pounded and my mouth was dry and tasted like chemicals. I tried to lift my hand to wipe my hair out of my face, but I couldn't move my arms. Shifting in my chair, I felt coarse ropes digging into my skin.

"Are you awake?" Vincent's voice was low but clear.

I blinked and lifted my head. It took some time before my eyes cooperated and I focused in on Vincent.

His face was unreadable. "I was worried he killed you."

My brain was groggy, and it took its time catching up. Vincent and I were tied up, facing each other in chairs.

"I should have made you go home," Vincent said.

"You know you couldn't have made me go." I stared at my restraints, but my mind was too cloudy to try to figure out what to do about them.

"You wouldn't have liked it. You would have hated me, but I should have done it anyway. If Logan and Rider had known about Jin, they would have helped," Vincent said.

There was always a way out, I only had to reach for it. Closing my eyes, I concentrated on pulling open the Path.

Sharp pain exploded behind my closed eyes. It felt like a cleaver had been wedged into my brain.

"No!" Vincent yelled.

I think I screamed, but I couldn't tell what was happening beyond the pain. I wanted to crush my head between my hands, anything to stop the feeling of being ripped in two. The Path was beyond that pain, which made it beyond my ability to reach. Mentally, I drew back, and the pain began to subside. There was a feeling of gaping chasms of nothingness replacing the pain. Sagging, I stared at the ceiling trying to catch my breath.

"Are you alright?" Vincent's voice was panicked. "You've got to answer me."

Breathing heavy I asked, "What was that?"

Watching Vincent from the corner of my vision, I saw him sag in his chair.

His voice shook. "That was the void. Or a piece of it anyway."

With all the time I had spent with Vincent last fall, I had never heard his voice carry so much fear.

I looked up and watched Vincent. "What is the void?"

"One of the nightmares that live between the worlds. It's roving areas of nothingness." Vincent took control of himself again. "If it touches you, it will consume you. Not only your body and mind, but your entire existence will be gone."

Never existed? "That's not possible." If I believed that, why was my heart beating faster?

"Which is why only Walkers survive long stays between the worlds."

"We're not between—I mean we can't be there. Where are we?" Trying to think through the rising panic was difficult. I looked around, eyes darting from object to object, trying to take in all of my surroundings at once.

"We're in a basement," Vincent said. "When they brought you in, I sensed the void, trapped. It's on your head somewhere."

My eyes opened wide. "They brought this thing from between the worlds? They strapped it to my head?"

What could I do without the Path? Tears threatened to form. I leaned back again and squeezed my eyelids as tight as I could. I wouldn't cry over this, not in this place. Holding tightly to the arm of the chair, I tried to calm myself. There was no way I was going to survive this without a cool head.

"Don't—" Vincent swallowed hard. "If you don't try to tap into the Path, I don't think it will hurt you."

"And if I do try for the Path?" I didn't look at him, afraid to see his response.

"I think it will consume you," Vincent said.

"How is this even possible? You wouldn't do this."

"I didn't do this, but I have an idea who did."

The door swung open. Vincent kept his gaze straight ahead, but I turned to see Jin.

"Look at the two of you getting along so well," Jin said, pulling the door closed behind him. "I'm glad that you have had this chance together."

"What do you want?" I spat the words, eager to turn fear to anger.

Jin ignored me. "You know, William, I began to trust you.

You were the only one to have enough skill to get close to me without being turned away. You've also shown me you could kill a man with a touch, so I know what you are."

Vincent's face betrayed nothing.

"Unfortunately, to protect my business interests, I must know more." Jin went to the door and knocked twice.

A skinny pale man entered the room. After a signal from Jin, he took out black, zippered, wallet the size of a paperback book. He moved around behind me, where I couldn't see, but Vincent could.

Watching Vincent's face for a clue to what was going on wasn't much help. The only reaction was him closing his eyes momentarily, as though preparing himself.

The skinny man moved up beside me and tied a piece of plastic tight around my arm. My heart skipped a beat, and I looked from Vincent to our captor. Jin's eyes were firmly on Vincent.

My arm was being wiped clean by a damp white wipe smelling of alcohol.

"We are of course, hygienic," Jin said. "The doctor here makes sure of that."

"Gee, what a relief." Showing sarcasm had to be better than yelling or crying, right?

The doctor had a needle. When he held my arm, I tried to pull away. Whoever had trapped my arms had done a good job, but I could still twist them around.

"That will make things worse." The doctor kept quiet, but there wasn't a trace of fear or anxiety over what he was doing. He gripped my arm tighter and repositioned it.

"Stop." Vincent's voice was strong but emotionless.

For that, I was thankful. If he could hold together, so could I.

The doctor looked up, and Jin held up a finger. The doctor moved back behind me.

"What do you want to know?" Vincent asked.

Jin moved in front of Vincent once more. "Everything. Anything that could cause trouble for my family, my business, or my employees."

"Injecting me with, whatever the hell is in that needle, is going to be a huge mistake," I tried to keep my voice level, but my fear slipped out.

I couldn't see his face, but I heard Jin sigh, and he shook his head. Jin whipped around and slapped me across my already bruised face.

Biting back the pained noise wasn't possible, but I balled up my fists and strove to end my cries quickly, working hard to pull myself together.

Jin waited until my fists unclenched. "You will stay quiet."

"Don't touch her again." Vincent's voice held a dark edge.

Jin looked unfazed. "We are doing this the nice way, William. Don't make us go the hard way." Jin motioned to the doctor again.

The needle was in my arm before I had time to react.

Fear and anger pushed me over the brink and an internal whirlwind formed. "What the hell is this stuff?"

The doctor sat the now-empty needle aside. "This will cause temporary central sensitization."

"What?"

The doctor leaned in while removing the tourniquet around my arm, and lowered his voice for my ears only. "Any pressure, such as those ropes digging into your skin, will cause pain."

I didn't bother to whisper. "Why?"

"In less than an hour, his slap will be like a baseball bat. Without causing physical damage, he can do it again."

240

TWENTY-FIVE

Pain without damage. Turning that thought over and over again in my head only worked to increase the activity of the unsettled masses inside.

Vincent's hands were gripping the arms of the chair, but his voice was flat. "You didn't ask anything."

Jin let out a long, sad breath. "Asking now does no good. I have to believe the answers you give, and she will provide that assurance."

"Injecting her was a mistake." Vincent looked around Jin to include the doctor who was leaving the room. "For both of you."

"I'll be back shortly," Jin said. "Cedric will keep you two company."

Jin left and was replaced by a large man that stood by the door, watching us.

Looking widely around the room for anything that might help us, some means of escape, got me nowhere.

I watched Cedric for a while, wondering if there was any

hope there, but Jin wouldn't have left him watching over us if there was a chance he'd help us.

The soul fragments were shifting, wanting to reach out through me. One of these had to be useful, right? Who knew what was there?

Who knew what would happen if I let one of them take over?

Vincent's face remained impassive, but his hands twisted around, testing his restraints.

Twisting my arms didn't do anything, although it did hurt more. Were the ropes rougher against my skin? It had to be my imagination, but I stopped moving.

I looked at Cedric again. Could we get him on our side? "You must have the most boring job in the world."

He smirked but didn't respond.

The look on his face made my skin crawl. He was enjoying this. "Are we allowed to talk?" I asked.

Cedric's only response was a grunt.

Vincent's eyes looked straight ahead, but I don't think he was really seeing me. His pupils looked like saucers.

"Vincent?" I've seen him go down this path a few times before. I glanced at Cedric again but plunged forward. "Can you get out of here?"

"No." His voice was hollow.

"No you can't, or no you won't?"

"Both."

My face began to throb in time with my heartbeat. "Why can't you go? You could get help."

He blinked twice and focused on me. "You're suggesting I go between the worlds, strapped to a chair?"

For once, I was thankful I couldn't really read his expression. "Right, stupid idea."

Nothing in the room, no way to go for help, and the Path was out of reach.

The cuts on my arm ached dully.

Closing my eyes, I inspected the throng of souls. Most pieces were my own, which was good to know.

"Don't." The demanding tone Vincent used made me look up.

"Don't what?"

"You cannot go through the void."

I raised an eyebrow and frowned at him.

"That wasn't a challenge." Vincent's voice was firm, but he backed off a little.

"I'm not taking it as one," I said. "I don't like being told what to do, but I'm not stupid. You said it wouldn't work, and I trust your judgment."

Closing my eyes again, random souls jostled their way forward. Trying to sense what type of Lost they had once belonged to, had my mind spinning and I chased after one shard. Down I went until it felt like smashing into a sheet of ice. As I fell, a burst of energy was able to urge itself forward.

No, no, no! I had to stay me. That I was sure of.

My body felt like it was speeding up, but I was sitting still. Anxiety crept over me, urging me to move. A sensation of someone else looking at the world with me became unnerving.

Pain bloomed everywhere. Each bruise and bump, each rope digging into my arms and legs. Everything.

Feeling the spike of pain, the little scrap of energy retreated to the group of others, allowing me to gain control.

The need to move died away, but the pain stayed.

Looking at Vincent, I could tell he had noticed the change.

"Burst of adrenaline." Did that even make sense? "I think it kicked the drugs in faster."

"You're a bad liar."

I tried to hide the strain I was feeling. "The explanation is close enough."

All those little pieces, but none of them merged. They didn't seem sentient, yet they all felt like they wanted to have their own chance out.

After being torn to shreds, only a small bit of their nature remained. It's no wonder they wanted out to feel the world again.

"What?" Lost in thought, I had missed what Vincent said.

"I don't know what the drugs do." He looked pained. The blank slate that he used to shut out the world was cracking.

I hesitated, not knowing if it was better for him to know or not. In the end, Vincent's imagination could probably get much worse than any drug.

"It's temporary." I swallowed hard and tried to keep my voice light. "Mostly, it's going to make me cry without being hurt."

Vincent was gaining his composure, but he stared at me, waiting for the rest.

"It lowers pain tolerance, that's all." I didn't even want to think about what this was doing to Vincent. "It's going to look like I'm hurt, without them actually having to do anything to me."

There was silence apart from Vincent's arms twisting under their ropes.

I ground my teeth together and shoved the misery into the farthest reaches of my mind. Feeling around the room without opening the Path, I received a taste of Vincent's hostility, which was like venom in the air. It was candy to a few shards of soul, and the minotaur pushed me aside before I had the chance to ground myself. In a frenzy, I began pulling up at the ropes, straining to break out. Agony in my arms combined with dread that it would only get worse, allowed me to gain control.

My head lolled down and I didn't bother lifting it up. Small pieces of soul crowded me, my body was tormented each time I moved, and Vincent was going to be forced to sit here and watch what they did to me. Despair was coming around the corner, straight for me. A person can only take so much broken.

Crying would only cause more pain and anger for Vincent, so my eyes itched with unshed tears.

There was Gran to think about, Logan, Rider, and all the other Lost that might be taken so that Jin could do business.

There had to be a way out of this. "The thing on my head. Is it like the jewelry? A small part of the whole?"

Vincent didn't say anything.

When I looked up, his eyes were completely black. He looked as lost as I felt.

Gritting my teeth, I tried to think of anything else besides what I was feeling. "Look, if we are going to get out of here, I need to know more."

There was silence.

"You owe me."

Vincent flinched.

It was a cruel thing to say, especially in anger, but I had to drag him out of himself.

I shifted in my seat and the ropes burned into my arms. The drugs had truly set in.

"We're out of time." I hated myself before the words were out. "Do you want me to die in pain tied to a chair, or die fighting to get out?"

Vincent closed his eyes.

"I'm sorry, but they are taking Lost along with humans with special abilities, including psychics." My own words caused tears to flow.

"Your family?" Vincent spoke softly.

"Gran has moved in with Logan. Mom is discreetly

protected by AIR." I sniffed and tried to rein in the crying. "The Path is there, I can feel it. I need information if we are going to get out."

Vincent looked up and kept his voice slow and steady. "This is nothing like the others. It is a small piece of a whole, but even a small piece will devour you if you try to pass through it. You can't make this go away."

My heartbeat ratcheted up as my discomfort grew. "Jin has answers we need."

Vincent went stony. "Jin will die screaming."

Cedric chuckled, and I looked over, surprised to see him in the room.

I turned back to Vincent. "We're taking Jin in. Does he wear a piece of his own jewelry?"

"We don't talk about that." Cedric sounded alert.

"Around his neck," Vincent said.

Cedric rapped on the door, which opened a crack, and Cedric said a few words to someone outside.

I lowered my voice and kept an eye on Cedric. "About Gran. If I don't..." My throat tightened, and I couldn't finish those words. I looked at Vincent, making sure he understood what I wasn't saying.

He had a small, sad smile. "We'll have all the time in the world to talk after this is over."

The only way I could fake hope was through my words. "Of course we will.

The ropes dug into me like knives. Looking down at my arms, I wondered how it could be that they weren't bleeding.

"It's now or never." My vision began to blur with tears that I had no chance of stopping.

Closing my eyes, I searched around. Even inside, pain dominated. Before I could find that little sliver of void, I had to shove as much of my torment aside as possible. Things were only going to get worse. When my mind was able to separate the misery, I moved towards the Path, careful not to reach for it. The souls lived here, but they gave me no trouble, they wanted to see outside, not be trapped in my mind.

The emptiness sat there, directly between Path and me. It was such a small sliver of a thing. It felt like I should be able to move past it, but trusting what Vincent said, I didn't try.

There was talking in the room, but I ignored it, knowing my chance to reach the Path was slipping away.

Instead of trying to go through the void, I pulled. It remained resolute in its tiny prison. Souls began to clutter around me, but I kept my concentration on the target and tugged harder until it sprang free—much like the piece of the minotaur soul and the many others since I started to absorb the blockade.

Cold darkness spread through me. My veins felt like they were covered in fire and filled with ice. My voice locked up as shadows moved in, dimming the aches in my body. Only the feeling of being trapped in an infernal darkness remained.

A part of me wanted to curl up into a little ball, letting the void stretch out and continue dulling the sensations, but the Path was within reach. I wanted to live in the light of the Path, over the darkness of the shadows.

Bright color burned away the shadows when I plunged myself into the Path, and then opened my eyes to our captor.

It was a different world. The roaring Path was here, but there was contrast that I had never seen before. The darker shades made the colors of every flow more vivid in comparison.

A beautiful yellow-green glow swirled around Jin, remaining independent, but without straying away. New shades to the Path showed me what was lurking close to Jin. Knitted tightly around him, a poisonous blur of greed and hatred appeared to be in a battle with joy, and everything was coated in dull misery.

If this was a leprechaun soul that Jin had stolen, it was hiding Jin's malice, even from himself.

Jin looked around the room, alert as the glowing Path around him urged him towards the door. Jin raised a hand. Pain ripped through my arm and coursed through my body when Cedric bore down.

My scream tore through the room. In agony, my system burst into overdrive, trying to deal with more pain than I thought possible. Lights popped behind my closed eyes, and my cries continued as Cedric strengthened his hold.

The darkness of the void, strong and unsettled, began to fill me again. My scream stopped as feeling and the Path became eclipsed. The torment remained, but bearable enough to take action.

Jin was checking Vincent's bonds without touching him. He must have assumed the threat came from Vincent, which was almost always a smart bet.

Reaching out along the Path with an odd sense of detachment, I took Cedric's Path, strengthened it, and wrapped the shimmering orange and green strands around his throat. It didn't take me long to let go, leaving Cedric choking. Gripping air in front of me and making it solid, I slammed it straight into Jin.

Vincent looked murderous with flat black eyes when Jin crashed into him.

Before Vincent could do much harm, I connected my own Path with Jin's necklace. The energy jumped to me.

It was a horrible mistake.

The new essence scorched the darkness away. It moved around me with more fluidity and felt more solid than any other soul, including my own.

The Path around Jin was bled into the poisonous concoction that was his life, but an emptiness had begun eating his Path away. He was also draining away into Vincent.

"No!" I yelled.

Vincent paused and Jin shifted himself away, obviously drained; Jin stumbled into a wall. Vincent's mouth tightened, and he turned his gaze on me.

"He will die suffering." Vincent's voice was much like the frost thawing in my veins.

"His Path is collapsing in on itself. If you pull that into you, I don't know what will happen." I stopped and took a shaky breath. "I'm not going to lose you again."

Vincent's face softened until he turned his eyes back to Jin. Jin was pressed against a wall, trying to catch his breath.

We needed to be free. The new soul was crowding me and all the other pieces, but it was also pouring luck.

There was a noise behind me, but I ignored it, knowing that it presented me with no immediate danger.

Cutting through the ropes sounded like a good idea, but I wasn't sure I could control that Path with such pinpoint accuracy. If I cut through more than rope, things could turn worse.

The chair didn't look like a much better option. I took a close look at Vincent's bonds, then a close look at mine, or at least those of mine that I could see.

Luck was on my side. If there were ever a time to work miracles with the Path, this would be that time.

An alarm went off in my head, and I looked up to see Jin staggering towards me. With such a strong, early alert, I easily tossed him aside, shoving him into a wall. Jin bounced off the wall and fell to the ground. Seeing that his Path was almost gone, I worked fast.

Twisting fine strands of the Path together was easy, but I was working with air, which was having a hard time keeping an edge to cut through the rope. After the second attempt, I looked at the rope itself. Like everything else, it had a Path, so I grabbed it and yanked it tight.

Screams tore through me and the Path of the ropes fell out of my grasp.

Stupid, stupid, stupid idea. Once again, I expected to see blood running down my arm. How could this hurt so bad without breaking the skin?

Taking shuddering breaths, I tentatively took the Path of the rope again, and instead of pulling it, I unraveled.

I had never done anything like it. The rope frayed, but it cut into my skin to a point I couldn't handle.

Crying, I stopped. Even with luck, I felt defeated.

"I don't know what you are doing, but stop doing it to yourself." Hints of emotion on Vincent's face, ones others may miss, howled his anger at me.

I tried to catch my breath. "It may not hurt if I tried it on your ropes."

"Do it then."

I couldn't muster enough energy to get aggravated by his tone. Instead, I poured it all into the Path while I was able. Working as carefully as I could, I unraveled the Path of the rope. My early warning system wailed.

Jin's Path was gone, and I was burning out.

Putting as much effort into it as I could, I coerced the Path of the rope apart. All the threads jumped and frayed until Vincent was able to pull free.

Retreating from the Path wasn't as difficult as I imagined it would be. The noise in my brain dimmed, but the Leprechaun soul recognized the imminent danger. "We don't have much time."

Vincent took a knife out of his boot and he was cutting his bonds when the house and ground shuddered.

The Path was going to have its revenge on Jin. It didn't care if we were in the way.

"I'm not sure this luck is going to hold out if the house falls on us," I said.

Vincent moved to me, and I grimaced as he cut the rope, causing fresh waves of pain, but it wasn't as bad as before.

A pipe burst in the corner, pouring water into the room, and then the house stopped shaking.

If that's all he got for imprisoning a leprechaun and stealing its luck for months, I was going to have to get vengeance on my own.

"Can you walk?" Vincent asked.

Without thinking, I agreed. "I've got his luck. I think we can get out if we move."

Getting up, I saw Cedric on the ground, and my stomach tried to revolt. His face blue, eyes bulged, and he held his neck as though trying to pull away what he couldn't see.

The chair scraped across the floor as I fell back into it, almost knocking it over.

I had killed him.

"You need to move," Vincent hissed.

"Right." My eyes were locked to the body.

Vincent moved into my line of sight and knelt down to look directly at me. "You have to deal with that later." His voice wasn't unkind, but there was a dull edge to it. His eyes were normal again, something I spent months thinking I'd never see again. "Get to the door."

There was no reason for me to look back now. Memories of Cedric, dead on the ground, were branded into my memory.

I staggered in the direction that held a hope of escape, and the house moved again. Vincent strode over and wrenched open the door. Glass broke in the house above. It surprised me that the door even opened. I thought it had been locked.

Vincent stood aside, and I grabbed the door-frame to steady myself.

Back in the room, Vincent advanced on Jin.

"No, Vincent!" I tried to sound stern, but it came off as desperate.

Vincent hesitated. The wall around Jin trembled and exploded outward, covering Jin with debris.

Again, Vincent moved towards the man.

"Please, we have to go." This time, Vincent ignored me.

Vincent leaned over Jin. I'm not sure what he said to him, but when he reached out to touch Jin, I reentered the room.

"You will not touch him." My own anger boiled over, not needing the wrath of the minotaur. "You will not pull his soul out."

Vincent stared at the man on the ground. "If he can't die between the worlds, at least his soul will."

"And you?" The need to leave was crumbling. I was pushing my luck too far. "You will always carry a small piece of him with you."

"It's a small price to pay."

"How do you think that will make me feel?"

Vincent turned to look at me. A joist twisted and cracked before falling free. Another followed while he stared, the blackness in his eyes retreating.

"We may be too late already. I'm going to be seriously upset if I die down here next to him." I was trying to make light of the situation, but in truth, I was convinced we were about to die.

Vincent backed away from Jin and his hands clenched and unclenched repeatedly.

Water and worse flooded the room from broken pipes. Something sounding like a wall hitting the floor above us was followed by drifting dust. Sirens could be heard in the distance.

My luck stirred when Vincent moved beside me. He reached for my hand but stopped before touching me. Remembering what had happened when we touched in the club, I understood the hesitation, but things couldn't get much worse. I took his hand and it nestled warmly in mine.

Luck urged us to the stairs, but even fighting through the pain, I was moving slowly.

"You're going to hate this," Vincent muttered. He picked me up, trying to be gentle. "Tell me where to go."

Every part of my body that was pressed into Vincent felt like spikes being driven into my skin. The nightmare I held, fighting with the new soul, managed to spread through me and dull my senses once again.

Directing Vincent upstairs, we found a perilous jumble of falling walls and debris. He maneuvered us through the back door and into the cold night air. Vincent slowed when we were out of the house, but I urged him further away.

So many things could happen in earthquakes. The house was on fire and gas lines could be burning, but I had a nagging suspicion that this was different.

When I told him he could stop, I leaned my head against Vincent's chest as we watched the house sink into the ground. Emergency crews in front were yelling to move back as the ground cracked. Their lights lit up the night and reflected off the white houses along the street.

When everything stalled, the house was nothing but a tangled heap of sticks, shingles, and stone. In front of the house, someone talked loudly about sinkholes, and they began evacuating the rest of the street. I was confident that everything else on the street was safe.

TWENTY-SIX

"We shouldn't stick around here." My mind was fuzzy, but dealing with the police right now wasn't high on my to-do list. "We can go through a neighbor's backyard and circle back around to the street."

Vincent didn't move. "I don't think we should be seen around here."

"I'm not sure what time it is, but most of the houses look dark. No one is going to help us if we wake them up to use their phone. There are people here, and maybe we can borrow a cell phone to call."

Vincent moved into the neighbor's backyard.

"I can walk." I didn't relish the idea, but I didn't want Vincent packing me around after what we had been through.

Vincent didn't even slow down. "When we're further away."

Listening to his heart beating steadily was a distraction. Right now, I think the worst thing for me would be to think about what had happened. The rhythmic thump helped me let everything fall away and allowed my mind to float in an exhausted haze.

We moved quietly between houses. Vincent put me back on my feet, and we watched the flurry of activity from the darkness between houses.

"Are you sure you want to go out there?" It looked like he was focusing on the emergency vehicles.

I scanned the people that had come out of their houses. "I'm sure. I want away from here the fastest way possible."

Vincent put a hand on my face and looked into my eyes. For this rare moment, his face looked soft. Worried, but real. The real Vincent.

Mesmerized, my foggy mind clutched at this new distraction. Vincent's hand moved up, and he ran it through my hair; his gaze followed, so I shut my eyes and concentrated on his hand moving over me. It snagged in my hair. I whimpered. Whatever drugs they gave me should never have been made.

Did I seriously whimper? In front of Vincent?

Avoiding everything was apparently not the right answer. It was time to let my brain move again.

"Sorry." Vincent kept his voice low, but it was tinged with concern. "But I need to get this accursed thing off your head."

"It's okay. You caught me off guard." For once, I succeeded in keeping my voice level and normal when I wanted to.

Vincent took away a hair clip, with a small jewel sitting among beads. He turned it over and over again in his hand.

"It's gone." Vincent looked down the street at the remains of the ruined house. "I need to go back."

"Don't." I ignored the sensation of my heart being squeezed.

"Even that small fragment could wreak havoc in this world. I'll borrow a phone on the way and call Logan. I'll let him know where you are."

"You don't have to go back."

"It has to be done." Vincent's face was already hardening and looked as though his mind was focused on the task ahead.

"I have it."

"You have it? Where?"

"It's inside me."

Vincent frowned and took a step back. "I don't know what you mean, but I am sure you're mistaken."

"You said I couldn't move past it. So I... I don't know, absorbed it."

Vincent's face went blank. "You took that into yourself?"

"It is. With all the others."

"Others?"

"Do we have to do this now?" I was standing, but only brute force and stubbornness kept me on my feet. There was also fear about lying down. With the drugs running through my system, it sounded like a nightmare.

"It's not having any effect?" Vincent asked.

I gritted my teeth. "It's minding its own business right now. Now, can we please get out of here?"

"If it's safely contained—"

"It is," I snapped.

Vincent grinned. "You still get cranky when you've worn yourself down."

"I am NOT cranky." I cleared my throat and tried to keep my voice level. "And I've worn myself down saving our asses from a collapsing house, and..." I wavered, my thoughts taking turns into bad places. "Did that really happen?"

"We can't think about that now." Vincent took my hand gently. "We're not through the night yet."

Right, don't look back. "By now, Logan and Rider are probably searching the city door by door."

"And you know how much they're going to love seeing me

again." Vincent's eyes were darting from one shadow to another, and I sensed his apprehension.

"They will," I said. "Well, once they know you're not a crazed killer."

"Let's get you out of here."

We drifted out of the darkness and out into the street. With each step, I moved slower. I hung back and let Vincent borrow the phone. Someone kindly stopped taking video of the burning house long enough for Vincent to call.

Vincent took a few steps away from the phone owner and made the call.

He didn't look thrilled when he was off the phone, but he looked polite and thanked the person for their phone. Instead of taking his hand, I took his arm, using it to help support myself, and we walked away from the house of nightmares.

There was nothing for either of us to say. As bone weary as I was, with phantom pains springing up each time I touched anything, or even when my clothes pressed too tightly to my body, I could say nothing.

I made it almost two blocks before stopping.

"Let's go to the corner," Vincent said. "We can meet the others there."

It looked like such a long way. Forcing one foot in front of the other, I made it to the corner on my own steam. I wanted to sit down when we got there, but I knew if I sat down, I wouldn't get up. At least not on my own. So I stood, leaning against Vincent, and watched the sky grow light with an early morning glow.

When I felt Vincent's body tense, I knew my partners were in sight.

I looked up, and almost cried when I saw them. It was over.

Logan came around from the driver's seat and Rider rushed out of the passenger side and dragged me into a hug.

I didn't have time to phrase the word no, but my scream sent the message, and Rider let go. Vincent grabbed my arm as lightly as he could when I stumbled back.

"What has happened?" Rider was putting off waves of unease.

My teeth were clamped together, trying to quell the agony, but I managed to shake my head.

Vincent looked strained trying to help me stay on my feet without holding me too tightly. "They called it 'central sensitization.'"

"Are you certain of that?" Dr. Taylor had a bag in his hands.

I had never been so happy to see a doctor.

"I don't know what it is," Vincent said, "but that's what they said the drug caused."

"Move her into the back," Taylor ordered.

I tried to protest when Vincent lifted me off the ground, but I only managed to wince and grit my teeth.

When I saw the emergency hospital bed strapped down in the back, I managed more. "Seriously? Is this necessary?"

"More than I thought." Taylor looked impatient standing by the truck. "Put her on the bed."

"At least set me down in the truck and let me do it myself." It was the only way to keep a touch of dignity.

Vincent hesitated, but sat me down and moved to get in the back.

"Oh no you don't." Logan grabbed Vincent's shoulder. "You're going to tell us exactly what happened."

Taylor put a stop to any argument that Vincent might have made. "She'll be better off, and I'll work better with only myself back here."

Logan kept his hand on Vincent's shoulder, but he was watching me. "Is she going to be okay, Doc?"

"We need to get back to the office as soon as possible." Taylor had dodged the question, which left me unsettled.

When they closed the door, the sounds of the world became hushed, and I laid back in the bed. The only thing that kept me awake were the bolts of pain that ran through my back.

"I need to know everything that happened." Taylor was already checking my heartbeat. "This is going to hurt, but I'm afraid it's a necessity. We don't have the equipment to cover this." He strapped me down so I wouldn't roll off as Logan sped away.

I closed my eyes hard, trying not to scream again.

"Details, Cassie." Taylor had a needle, ready to start an IV.

I cringed away. "It's what Vincent said. A drug that causes pain." If ropes could feel like knives, what would a needle do?

"Did they say what the drug was?"

"No." I closed my eyes.

"Cassie, I need you stay awake a little longer. Where did they inject you?"

I looked down to my arm.

Taylor looked over the injection site. "I'm going to try to numb your arm for an IV. What did they do after they injected you?"

"They went away for a while."

"Tell me when it hurts." Taylor wiped a liquid on my arm that started cold but then turned my skin to putty. He pressed my skin in a few areas to test the pain, and then inserted the IV.

"And when they came back, what happened?" Taylor asked.

There was no way I was going to take myself back to that place.

"I'm sorry, Cassie. Try to think about what they did that might have caused any trauma."

When I moved my thoughts back, I started crying and shaking. Why did he have to do this? Breathing became difficult.

"Okay. It's okay. Stop. Your friend knows what happened?"

God, he did know, he had seen it all. My cries were on the verge of sobs.

"Calm down, Cassie, you're safe now. I'm going to give you medicine that's going to dull the pain, and help you sleep."

Swallowing hard, I tried to get myself under control. My only comforting thought was that my partners couldn't see me here, at my breaking point.

Taylor gave me a shot through the IV. The pain was there, but I began to relax bit by bit until I fell asleep.

TWENTY-SEVEN

As far as I could see, there were flecks of broken glass twirling through the air. Each piece was its own dazzling color, and they appeared to be playing roughly, or maybe fighting, but without smashing one another. Some of the larger pieces moved out of the way, as others approached and refused to take part. I sensed another piece, larger than all the others combined, but I couldn't see it anywhere.

Logan was always humming a song. I had no idea what it was, but it had been beautiful, and I tried to hum it now while watching the glittering display.

The recklessness they displayed began to die away and everything slowed. Like dandelion seeds, the colors moved lightly, but steadily.

A few changed course, and before I could react, they slammed into me.

Bolting up, I expected to feel the shards, but they were gone. Taylor was there, already trying to get me to relax and lie back.

Logan had been sitting next to the bed, but now he was standing next to me.

"Howdy, partner. It sure is good to see you awake."

I frowned and looked around the room.

"The doc said he'd have you on your feet in no time."

I closed my eyes. The pain was gone, my muscles felt like a knotted mess, but even that was a huge relief. Dull aches I could manage.

"Can you tell me how you feel?" Taylor asked.

The question took some contemplation, but in the end, I opened my eyes. A large part of me had wanted to ignore him and stay insulated behind closed lids. However, the world doesn't work like that.

After clearing my throat twice, Taylor gave me some water.

"I feel much better." Even after the water, my throat felt raw.

"That's good to hear. I'm going to put pressure in different areas. Tell me when you feel pain."

Taylor went to work. He squeezed my arms and legs, and put pressure on my stomach and face. In each spot, he pressed lightly, then harder. In a few spots, I told him about the muscle aches but assured him it was nothing like before. The only exception was the injection site, which caused spasms of pain to radiate out when touched.

"Vincent filled us in on the case." Logan kept his voice level, but no trace remained of that musical tone that elves usually have. "He didn't give too many details about what happened in the house."

I didn't even acknowledge Logan's unasked question. "Where is he? And Rider?"

"The doc didn't want us crowding you. Do you want me to send Vincent in?"

My heart jumped into my throat and I shook my head. Little beeps I hadn't noticed before sped up.

"Don't worry. You don't have to see anyone you don't want to." Logan sounded like he was extremely careful with his words. "Is there anything you want to tell me?"

I looked at my partner for the space of a few heartbeats, and then I looked away. "They made him watch." I swallowed hard. "I mean, I got in the way, everything went to hell, and because of that..." I stopped. "I don't want to see anyone."

"It's raw now. It'll get easier with time, but you know he doesn't think that way. We did our jobs and did them well. That's all we can do."

Taylor interrupted and asked more medical questions—well, if you can call questions about swallowing a piece of the void medical. Who knows, maybe it was for Taylor. Once he was assured that I wasn't being eaten alive from the inside, he wrapped up for a while. He didn't have any questions about the leprechaun, only the void, which had settled down. For the short time I'd been awake, the leprechaun soul was what gave me trouble.

Once the doctor was done, Logan picked up where he left off. "We might want to discuss what to put on the official reports."

Work. I could latch onto that and move forward. "Yeah, I can do that. If you bring me the tablet, I can work on it."

Logan grinned. "I didn't mean right now. It can wait 'til tomorrow."

"I don't want to sit here all day and do nothing. My mind needs to work."

"Ethan's called a few times. Might be good to hear another friendly voice."

My heartbeat ratcheted up again. "He doesn't know that I was... gone, does he?"

"I didn't tell him or Margaret anything."

"Maybe I can call him back tomorrow."

"Okay, how about some company? Rider's pretty worried. Maybe he could come in and visit? No work talk. And nothing about the past few days."

"What day is it?" There had been no sense of time in the basement.

"It's been about thirty-six hours since we found your car in the parking lot. You spent a good chunk of that here, though. Resting up."

I felt behind, which didn't sit well with me. "You need to fill me in with what's been happening. What have I missed? Have we moved any further in the case?"

Logan raised a hand to stem the flow of questions. "You haven't missed anything. We'll fill you in tomorrow. For today, though, no work talk. I'll make sure Rider sticks with the same."

Seeing Logan's resolve, I agreed.

"It's good to have you back," Logan said. "I'll send in Rider."

Rider was a giant bundle of nerves, but those fell away after a few minutes of talking. He stuck to Logan's rules, so we mostly talked about what we were going to do after the case. There were lots of hikes we could take, and we talked about renting a kayak, though neither one of us had ever tried one. I explained the concept of an amusement park to Rider, and when he understood the concept, he was geared up to go. We moved the conversation to families, Rider wanting to know if Gran and I could teach him to bake something. He didn't really seem to care what. Around that time, I closed my eyes.

Images of Jin, Cedric, and Vincent were mixed up and thrown through my brain. My eyes flew open and I bolted up in bed. The room was dim, but I searched every corner until I found that I was alone.

At least almost alone. Vincent was in a chair, moved far enough away from the bed that someone might say that he wasn't sitting with me. I watched him sleep, looking uncomfortable in the chair. He had to be as tired as I had been, although with Logan's probable interrogation, he may have been even more worn out.

Letting him sleep was the best thing I could do. Besides, what could I say? Asking him if he was okay was a stupid question, and how do you ask someone how bad off they are?

Luck was on my side, so I was able to slip out of the room undetected. I wandered the dim, silent halls, feeling better for moving around after such a long time in bed. A few dull banging sounds became louder the closer I came to the end of one of the halls.

My good fortune led me to a refuge in the one place that no one would think to look. I found Neil's lab.

"Get the f—" Neil started, turning around. "Oh, it's you." He turned back to the table.

The smell of pot was stale in the air.

Neil picked up a small hammer and hit a piece of metal, flattening it more with each strike. "Taylor's going to be ticked you're in here. Or out of bed at all." He dropped the hammer and moved to one of the many computers that littered the room.

I moved to a chair close enough to see what Neil was doing. "I won't tell if you won't."

We sat in silence for a while, and Neil worked on whatever it was he was working on. Computers and machines whirred. Neil clicked the keyboard and mouse every now and again. It was relaxing in a way. I didn't have anyone looking over me, worried about what might happen or what I might do.

"Want to see something cool?" Neil asked.

"Sure," I said.

Neil moved away from the computer screen, and I took a look. There was a map on the screen. "Watch here." There was a glowing spot on the screen. In a few seconds, it grew brighter and brighter until it was almost blinding to see. Then it went back to a dimly glowing spot.

"What was that?" I asked.

"Portal." Neil sat back in his office chair and watched the screen. "A permanent portal to be precise."

"That looks pretty close to a populated area. I didn't know there were any permanent portals around there."

"I don't think anyone's supposed to know. I mean," he picked up a joint, then changed his mind and set it back down, "the area is cordoned off. It's like the government is keeping this one secret."

"The government keeps all the portals secret. Does AIR know about it?"

Neil lit a cigarette. "It's in their system, but they don't monitor it. It's like they purposefully keep it off their radar even."

"How come your system sees it?"

"My system sees the unseeable. I built it from the ground up, and it goes everywhere and sees everything."

"That's impressive." More than impressive really, it was a good thing he's on our side. "You know what they're doing with the portal?"

"There's nada in the system. Paper trail only."

We sat in silence for a while longer.

"Sorry about the drugs, man, at the party I mean," Neil said.

"It was probably for the best," I said.

"What happened with Indian Dude was messed up."

"It was."

"You coping?"

"Getting there, I guess. Going back to work will help."

Neil turned to his computer. "Almost time to face the world again." He stared at the little dot for a while, then powered down the screen.

"Almost." I wasn't quite ready to face the day.

Neil smoked another cigarette, and we sat in silence for a while.

"I see you're forgoing the hard stuff today." I indicated the cigarette.

"Don't tell Taylor. He'll like, try to make a big deal of it, and it's not like I'm turning all straight-laced or anything. I've taken enough stuff tonight to keep my brain pretty mellow without checking out."

"Finding a balance?" I asked.

"I see what I see, and then people want it explained to them. Sometimes there's not even words to cover the jumps my brain makes. By the time people finally understand, if they ever do, I'm so ticked off I can hardly stand it. Taylor gets it, though. He knows it's hard."

"Everything seems hard lately." I sighed and got to my feet.

"I'm getting that," Neil said.

We reentered the world together, Neil showing me the way since I hadn't paid too much attention as I roamed the halls. Although the halls were empty, all the lights were on, which I guess meant the day had begun.

Neil and I turned a corner and saw Logan and Vincent talking. They both looked up. Vincent took a step towards us, stopped, and then spoke with Logan again.

"What do you think?" I asked Neil. "Do they look upset?"

"Nah, you've got a free pass with them."

"I could use one of those. You're the smart one. How do I get them to hold my free pass until I really screw up?"

"If I could figure that out, Taylor and I wouldn't fight so much."

"Maybe. As much as you all may fight, I can tell it comes from a good place. Maybe one day you won't clash so much."

"Maybe," Neil said.

Deciding it was best to get over my reluctance to talk to Vincent, I walked up to them.

Logan smiled. "Morning. We're getting together in the conference room to plan our next moves. I think Taylor wanted to see you, but we'll wait to get started when everyone's together."

Neil slouched around behind me while Logan talked.

"Sure," I said. "I'll see you all soon."

Neil kept me between him and the others, but he stayed nearby to show me the way back to my room. It's sad when you start thinking of a hospital room as your room.

Taylor looked up when I entered. He looked at me for a few seconds before turning back to the computer. "I'd like to go over a few things with you this morning. Did you sleep well?"

"Dude," Neil said in a low voice, "if that had been me that disappeared, his face would be all red. And there's this vein on his forehead that pops out."

"Neil," Taylor said, raising his voice, "can wait for us outside."

Neil closed the door on his way out, and I took a chair near Taylor, deciding that I wasn't getting back in the bed.

"Is it me, or did Neil look sober?" Taylor asked.

"Trust me, any time he is sober, don't make a big deal about it. At least not right now."

"Did he talk to you?" Taylor asked.

I shrugged noncommittally.

Taylor's eyes looked brighter. "Having a friend that isn't an addict or a dealer will be good for him. I'd like to go over a few things this morning."

There were really only a few things. He took the usual vitals and did the same pressure test on my skin he did the day before. Except for around the injection site, nothing hurt. Even the muscle aches were fading.

"Physically, I think you're good to go," Taylor said, "and when you're ready to talk to someone—"

"No." It came out with more force than necessary, so I backed off. "At least for now. I want to focus on work right now."

"I understand, but don't keep it bottled up too long. Let's get to the conference room."

"Thanks."

Down the hall, Rider and Logan were already in the conference room. Vincent wasn't far behind us. I noticed Neil appeared to duck behind Taylor when Vincent entered the room, and after Vincent sat down next to me, Neil chose a spot that positioned himself as far away from Vincent as he could at the table.

Taylor started us off. "Sable's out on one of the farms. One of our tenants had a problem with a neighbor." The air around the table became uneasy, and it wasn't lost on Taylor. "It's nothing she can't handle. She's not alone, and no one is hurt."

"We're all worried we're going to find the next person hit. It's time we figured out our next move," Logan said. "We have more information, but we don't know what Jin knew."

"But we know what Vincent knows." Rider looked past me to Vincent.

I cleared my throat. "I'm not sure I'm up to date on everything."

Vincent blinked a few times slowly, then, through a mask of stone, he turned over what he knew. "As soon as I returned, I reached out to a friend in the West Coast office. She told me about rumors of a new drug floating around the Mid-West. It was a little too close to home for me."

My stomach quivered. Vincent had called a woman from his old office but never contacted us. What did that mean? Before I could get too worked up over it, I rolled the thought to the corner of my mind. That corner was getting a little crowded, but I'd worry about it after the case.

"They put me to work, undercover. I uh." He stumbled over his words. "I thought it better not to contact the Mid-West office, and my office, my old office. They were going to take care of that part for me. So I stepped into a new life and worked my way up through the ranks. I discovered Jin was selling something that wasn't a drug, but worked like a drug. When I first started working for Jin, he was expanding out. He called it a designer drug and sold it to the highest bidders. He began to trust me and kept me around more often. That's when I discovered there were actually two different products. The good stuff that didn't burn out went to friends and family, and the rest went to anyone willing to pay cash, but they didn't last."

"So the most potent stuff is the stuff he didn't sell?" Taylor asked.

"I didn't get the impression he gave it away. He charged everyone. He trusted me enough to include me more. I was going to meet the one who made it all possible and learn more about the process, but uh..." Vincent trailed off.

"But I showed up," I continued for him.

There was a hint of a flinch. "I should have called. I wanted to, but I thought this way was better."

I held a hand, stopping that conversation. "The case."

Vincent's surprise couldn't be hidden from me. He knew

the old me, but he didn't know the woman that stayed up reviewing case files and was always early to work, even when she had to drag a tired elf along behind her. Vincent didn't know me now.

"Dude, you discovered more working for Indian Dude," Neil said. "You said, even if I'm not the one doing this, it doesn't mean I'm not to blame. That doesn't add up with what you've told us so far."

Vincent stared at Neil long enough to make Neil slump down in his seat, looking uncomfortable.

"Before I ran into Cassie, I discovered what the drug was. I'd seen its effect on some people. Souls had been taken out and anchored into objects. Some objects only held traces, which were sold to those who could afford them. Others held together longer, and those were sold to family. It was Walker work." Vincent's thoughts seemed to turn inward. "Last fall, I reached out to Walkers that I knew. I tried to figure out how to work through what I had done to Cassie. That sparked the idea for someone."

"Good call, Neil." Logan crossed his arms and watched Vincent carefully. "So we have a Walker pulling out souls of the Lost. Any ideas about who this could be?"

"I know three people with the ability, but I haven't tracked them down," Vincent said. "It takes time."

"How much time?" Taylor asked.

"It could take months," Vincent said. "They may not even be in this world."

"We don't have that kind of time," Logan said. "Too many lives are at stake. And whoever is doing this is here."

I leaned forward and rested my arms on the table. "I have an idea of where I'd like to start. Right now, I have a lot of luck on my side, and I need to give it back to the leprechauns. They had to have seen him."

"Dude." Neil's eyes went wide. "I'm not sure that's the best idea. You may need that luck."

I shook my head. "I know, but it's not mine to keep. Besides, I saw what it did to Jin when it caught up with him. It wasn't a pretty sight."

Neil snorted. "Indian Dude had that coming."

Vincent and Rider nodded in agreement, which helped Neil's confidence. He sat up straighter anyway.

"Cassie's right," Logan said, "giving it back is the right thing to do. She'll have to use a little luck to return it, but maybe they'll help us."

"We also need to find every friend and family member that has one of Jin's little trinkets." It gave me the creeps even saying his name, but it couldn't be avoided.

"You don't think they'll run down on their own?" Logan asked.

"No, not if they're like Jin's. Most of them hold that little shard of soul. It doesn't have anything keeping it together, so it dies away." I shuddered at the thought, but took a steady breath and moved forward. "What Jin has isn't a larger chunk, it's the whole thing. One solid soul. Who could say how long that would last?"

TWENTY-EIGHT

Neil, doing more calculations and analysis than any one person should ever be able to manage, found a likely place for me to find a leprechaun. As far as AIR was concerned, we were running down a lead, which was true overall. AIR and MyTH were working together to hunt down anyone who Jin might have sold souls to. Although they weren't sure why we wanted them, the police and DEA were collecting anything that might resemble what we were looking for.

It felt good knowing so many people were working on this. Hopefully, that meant that none of the jewelry fell through the cracks.

My two partners turned into three now that Vincent had joined us. MyTH helped us gear up for hiking and camping in rugged terrain, and we were off to find the leprechauns.

For the first three hours of our journey, I used the tablet to update our case file. It caused me to run into a few difficult decisions on what should go on permanent record. In the end, I skipped around, telling the parts I was willing to think about and ignoring the rest. I wanted to ask Logan what I should say about Jin, but he held up a finger for me to wait, and then pointed to the eye of the device.

Logan was becoming more and more concerned, or dare I say it, paranoid, about what the office might be tracking. Or maybe he was only more vocal about it, now that we had been partners in the field for a year. As my mentor, Logan could be trying to get me to pay more attention to everything that went on around us.

I caught up with Gran and let her know I missed her. She told me that I needed to take Vincent to the Palm Reader. Also, that I was to ignore the old coot in the woods. It was the first time I had truly smiled in days.

Logan hummed, although sometimes he moved back and forth between humming and singing. I asked him if he wanted me to turn on the radio, but he declined.

The track of land Neil sent us to was in the Ozarks. The countryside was beautiful, but I was already dreading the hills. Logan left the paved road and roamed down a gravel one, which turned to dirt before he parked the truck.

We were unloading our gear and my phone rang. Ethan's name appeared on the screen.

"I'm going to take this." I walked away from the truck. "In private."

"Hi," I said, walking down the road, "I'm glad you called."

"That's a positive start," Ethan said. "I've seen some stuff cross my desk in the past few hours that put me in mind of you."

"The jewelry?"

"Yeah. We'll be on the lookout. Does this mean that your case is winding down?"

"We're getting ready to talk to a witness. If they saw

anything that we can use, we should be able to wrap things up before long."

"That's good to hear, I was hoping we'd have the chance to get together again, soon."

"I wish I could say yes." Going out with Ethan, forgetting about work, Vincent, and everything in between, sounded wonderful. "Unfortunately, I am getting ready to walk into the wilderness, and it's possible I might not walk back out for a few days."

Ethan's cheerful mood came through his voice. "I never pictured you as a camper."

I laughed and the muscles in my chest loosened up. "Neither did I, but we do what we have to for the job."

"That's the truth."

"If you want, I can call in a few days, once I've reached civilization again."

"I'm already looking forward to it. Good luck catching your bad guy."

"Thanks."

Walking back to the truck, I saw that the team was huddled around a map. Unless it was GPS, with a little blinking dot on a trail, I'm pretty sure I wasn't going to be much help. When I came up beside them, Logan insisted that he show me where our starting point was, and which direction we were traveling.

We grabbed our gear and with Logan in the lead, we walked into the forest.

And we kept walking. Logan and Rider were good for updates on pace and how far we'd walked. After the third mile, the terrain became more difficult to navigate. It didn't help that I suggested a different direction, but since it came from the extra soul I was carrying around, we figured we were going the right way.

"It's getting dark," Vincent said about a mile later.

I wasn't about to complain. There was enough light to see by, but I was done for the day. Logan began putting our camp together while Rider checked the surrounding area.

Vincent was surprisingly adept at camping. We decided on no fire for the night, but they sent me out for wood in case we needed it, and as many twigs as I could manage for the cook stove.

I didn't have high hopes of twigs being able to cook anything, even if I brought a tree's worth back to camp, but I took their word for it and went into the woods.

Our team really didn't feel like a team anymore. All evening, everyone went about helping with the camp, but much like during the drive here, and the hike, there wasn't any discussion. You'd think, sitting around the stick-fueled cook-stove (which worked better than I ever expected), that a team would talk. There would be stories, and someone would say, "Remember when" and everyone would chime in with their own memories.

Everyone acted as if they were afraid to say anything, although it could be that I was the only one that felt that way. Maybe this was what things were supposed to be like when you were trekking through the wilderness.

Or maybe I was hoping for an instant reunion.

The night closed in when I went to find the hammock Logan had set up for me. It was a tight line, about chest level between two trees. After staring at it for at least a minute, I attempted to get in, and probably looked ridiculous, but there was no way I was going to ask how to jump into one. Once I managed it, though, it was more comfortable than I thought. I slipped into the sleeping bag, without falling out, and fell asleep listening to the sounds of the woods at night.

THERE WAS A BLEAK, cold chasm below me, and I was dangling from a rope. The air felt moist and burned my throat with each breath. The darkness began to shift, and someone lurked in the murky distance. Below me a whirlpool formed. My grip tightened as I was moved with the flow of the swirling shadows. My muscles felt weak, and the chill air began to settle into my bones.

The gloom underneath lurched and the rope grew taught as if someone was taking hold of the bottom. My breath came faster which scoured my throat even worse, and my muscles protested as I made them pull my own weight. I struggled up until my hands turned slick with blood. In a vain effort, I looked up, hoping to find anything to grab onto. There was nothing. Realizing I was climbing to nowhere, my lifeline frayed and became thinner even with my hands wrapped tightly around it.

When there was nothing but a thread remaining, it snapped and I fell. Hands from the shadows grabbed me and shook violently. Afraid it was Jin or worse, I tried to lash out. My muscles were weak, but I'd be damned if I was going out without a fight. I threw a punch.

"Cassie," Rider whispered, "wake up."

"Cassie," a voice hissed and drove the chill even deeper.

I reached out to the warmth of Rider and opened my eyes.

My hand was clamped around his arm. After reassuring myself it was Rider, and I was safe, I was able to pull away.

"Are you okay?" he asked, keeping his voice low.

My night vision was pretty good, but I looked around, and it played tricks on me. Across the dark camp, there was the shade of an old man who stepped around a tree, disappearing. Swirls of pitch night were opening up around us. Resisting the urge to reach out and grab Rider's arm again, I closed my eyes and took a few steadying breaths.

When I looked again, the camp was normal. "It was a bad dream." The night had grown chill, so it was no wonder my dream was full of cold. "Sorry to wake you up." I tugged up the sleeping bag and buried myself inside.

"Would you like to talk about it?" Rider asked.

"I'm okay. It's been a lot all at once is all." I'm sure my voice was muffled, but I was equally sure that Rider could hear me. "Good night, Rider. Thank you for waking me up."

"Good night."

In the morning, I felt grungy and without the option of a shower, it didn't make for a pleasant morning. At least there was coffee.

We hiked further into the woods.

"Is this how *Deliverance* started?" I asked around noon.

Vincent chuckled lightly behind me.

"Nah, we need banjos for the beginning," Logan said.

"Oh, right." Feeling a twinge of good luck, we moved west and followed a creek. Once we were back on track, I picked up my line of conversation. "So, what you're saying is, we've jumped into the middle of the movie. I'm not finding that comforting."

Logan and Vincent laughed. After the previous day of silence, it was comforting.

"I think it looks like the movie you showed me last Halloween," Rider said. "Dale and Tucker?"

"Wait, does that make us the college kids?" I asked.

Rider laughed, and at least for a short time, we felt more like a team.

With my encouragement, we crossed the water. Shortly after that, I called for a halt.

The trees were sparser here, but we would be in good shape for setting up camp.

"You think this is the spot?" Logan asked.

"For camp I do." I tried to nail down the feeling behind the decision, but it radiated from everywhere. "I think the rest of today's hike needs to be on my own."

Rider and Logan stopped and looked at me.

"We do not know what is in these woods," Rider said. "It is better if we stick together."

"Do you really think the leprechauns will come near me with three other people around?" I asked.

Rider began to object.

"Or with even one other person around? They haven't been seen in centuries. The best chance we have is for me to go on my own."

"She's right." Vincent didn't even look up from setting up camp. "She's got luck on her side."

"Luck will only get her so far, there are smells out here. Of predators." He glared at Vincent. "What do you think they will do when they sense Cassie?"

Vincent grimaced and looked up at Rider. "Would you rather have us wander around out here for nothing?"

"Yes, if it means she stays with us," Rider said.

"She goes on alone, but not far." Logan added to me, "And get back here before it gets dark."

"Right." I checked over my water supply and food while trying hard to ignore the fact that they'd argued about me going when I had already made the decision. In my mood, it was best not to linger. "I'll see you all soon."

When it came to distances, I was the worst. There was no way for me to judge how far I walked, but I kept a steady pace and moved where my inner guide suggested. There was a small clearing by a stream where I stopped, sensing that now I had to wait. The water rushed by and the breeze blew gently. It wasn't the kind of feeling that you got at a fairy homestead or a gnome hill, but it was a pleasant place to sit.

So many things can go through a person's mind when they have time alone with nothing to do. Thoughts that I had been determined not to think about had been stuffed into small corners of my mind and were now stumbling out. The easy ones, my job, Rider, Logan, and Gran, flew by fast. My mother and my ex took up some time, but those had been squashed down so long that it was their natural state to be ignored.

Thoughts of Vincent were becoming densely tangled into the case, but it was memories of pain and fear that knotted things up. There was guilt there as well. I should have spoken with him after the night with Jin. He was probably as bad off as I was, but I was keeping him away.

Crap, I was crying at work. Who does that? All those thoughts had to be rolled up and crammed into their hiding places.

Concentrating on the sounds of the forest and running water helped to clear my mind. How many people can say they've been truly alone, possibly miles from anyone else? The surprising answer is, almost no one. People may think they're alone, but all types of beings lurk in out-of-the-way places.

After spending some time tuning into the world around me, I spotted three examples.

There was no one to tell me what a leprechaun looked like. What I had expected, the little people in green that you see on posters at St. Patrick's Day, were so far from the truth that I wondered who had dreamt them up.

Two people, around three feet tall, watched me. The third was taller than I was and made little alarm bells go off in my mind. The tall man stared at me while smoking a pipe. He faded away into the woods. It was unsettling, and I breathed easier when he disappeared.

The remaining two weren't wearing green as one might expect, or even red, which Logan had said was what the older version of leprechauns wore. Instead, they wore brown, and while their hair was redder than my own, it grew in a tufted way around the head, neck, and face, suggesting they weren't actually of Irish descent.

I was pretty sure they were a type of Lost, maybe one that came here hundreds of years ago and became trapped. But it's hard to say what might have originated in our own world.

The two continued to stare. I didn't make a move beyond looking from one to the next.

TWENTY-NINE

When the luck nudged me to do so, I spoke, the words forming without much thought on my end. "Something was taken from you, and I've brought it back."

One of the two disappeared, but returned quickly with a third person of the same size and shape.

"Uh, someone came and took something from you. I've brought it back?" I hadn't intended it to be a question, but I wasn't sure what I was doing.

"They always come looking." I'm not sure if he was talking to me, or to the others.

"For hundreds of years we go unnoticed, but to a few of our choosing," another said.

"Now two discover us," said the third.

The first one who spoke continued, "Always looking, but you say you are returning."

"What is it that you want in exchange?" the second man asked.

"More than we are willing to give, and more than she

deserves." The third person clearly didn't like me; I think he was male, but it was hard to say for sure.

They stopped speaking. They stayed well away and appeared to blend in with the trees if I took my eye off them. I waited a moment, reveling in the fact that I was meeting leprechauns.

The second soul wasn't helping me out now, so it looked like I was on my own. "I'm not exactly sure what I'm supposed to say. I don't want anything and what I have isn't mine to keep."

"Nothing in return," the first one said.

"Well that's not true," the second said.

"She will ask for more than she deserves," the third said again.

"Well," I continued, "I'll give it back no matter what. It doesn't belong to me, but I would like to ask a few questions if you are willing."

"Information can be expensive," the first one sighed.

"Is it worth the luck?" the second one asked.

"We should take what's ours and throw her back," the third said.

I really didn't like the sound of that. "The one that did this. He killed one of you and stole the soul away. I want to know if you saw him. If you know who he is, or if you have any clue, I'm trying to stop him from doing this to any others."

"She wants to help us," the first said.

"What she says may be true," the second said.

"She might want more from the thief than he is willing to give," the third said.

"That's not our concern," the first said.

"She can do what she likes," the second said.

The third crossed his arms. "What she says could be true."

It sounded as if the third was agreeing with the other two,

which may have been a signal. All three stepped out into the open but stayed well out of reach.

"What should I call you?" I asked.

They hesitated and looked at each other.

"You'll give us what was taken?" the first asked.

"She has the stolen luck," the second said.

"You'll return it unconditionally?" the third asked.

I nodded, afraid to speak. We really needed to know, but the soul had to go back, no matter what.

"The man who came was like one with you only more," the first said.

"His darkness grows to greater depths," the second said.

"He takes what is not his and walks where no one travels," the third said.

"Do you know what he looked like?" I asked.

The first stamped his foot. "Tall like your friend."

"Blond like the elf," the second said.

"Hair long like yours," the third said.

I opened my mouth to ask more, but the first leprechaun stamped his foot again.

"She means to trick us," the first said.

"She means what she said," the second said.

"Be patient," the third said.

Somewhere along the way they reversed roles. The three working in unison baffled me.

"I don't want to trick you." They gave me a description to work with. Between Vincent and the AIR data banks, I'm sure we could come up with some leads. Besides, who wants to tick off a leprechaun? Their good luck could mean bad luck for me if I got on their bad side. "Who should I give the soul or the luck to?"

All three blinked at me and rocked on their feet as one.

"She means to give it back," the first said.

The second one blinked in awe.

"You would be willing to hand over the luck?" the third asked.

"It's not mine," I said again.

"You must give it to the one it was stolen from," the third said.

"Is he alive?" My heart jumped. "The other Lost died within days or even hours after what this person did. We can save him?"

"We don't know of the Lost of which you speak," the second one said, "but our friend did not survive."

I slumped, "I was hoping..." Taking a deep breath, I forged on. "Let's give him his luck back."

"Even though he's gone, you're willing to give it back?" the first said.

I had a sneaking suspicion that they were working together to try to catch me in a lie. "Yes."

"We'll take you." The third uncrossed his arms and walked into the woods.

I hurriedly stood and followed. Even with luck on my side, I lost track of them from time to time, so one fell back and stayed with me. The trails they took were for people three feet tall, so I became caught up in the undergrowth and trees on the way. When I walked into a small clearing, I could tell we were close to their home. There was a cave entrance a few feet away, and the entire area felt more alive than any other place I'd been. There were similarities to the homes of other Lost that lived in the wilderness, but somehow this was more vibrant. They took me near the cave and pointed to an area on the ground.

I took a few steps and stopped. "I'm not sure what to do."

"The luck will know." It was possibly the first one again, but I had gotten them mixed up, so it was hard to be sure.

As the sun sank below the tree line, I closed my eyes and concentrated inward. The leprechaun soul gave me the feeling that it was crowded, but it vibrated with relief.

It was home.

With a little hint from the luck, I knelt down and put my hands to the ground. The shards of all the other Lost stuck to my own soul, but the leprechaun had never attached itself like the others. With a little concentration, I felt the warm yellow-green glow flow from me and into the ground.

It left an uncomfortable emptiness behind. I didn't move and stared at the spot for a while. It wasn't until one of the leprechauns stood eye to eye with me that I snapped back to myself. It was the closest one had ever come.

I remained still and watched him closely. "I suppose without the luck, I'll never see you all again."

He winked at me. "Everyone has a little luck." He reached out with his finger and drew what felt like a circle on my forehead.

"What does that do?" I asked.

"Always asking questions," he said. "It marks you as safe. It doesn't mean that you'll see us, but our kind will see you and know you are friend to us."

He moved back to stand with the others.

Before I could stop myself, I asked, "That man I saw earlier with you, the tall man, who was he?"

"Always questions," the first said.

"Even when they make no sense," the second said.

"There was no one there, but you and us three," the third said.

I started to reply, but they shook their heads, so I thought better of it. The sun had set, and shadows were merging together with others to build the night.

"I don't suppose you know which way I need to go?" I asked.

"We will lead you out." The three moved as one and walked into the forest.

There wasn't much choice but to follow, and I knew they wanted to lead me as far as possible from their home.

"I'm having trouble seeing anything," I said after running into a tree branch.

"It's dark," one of the leprechauns said.

I'm pretty sure they were randomly picking directions to walk.

I laughed. "Yes, it's dark. Luckily, my friends can see very well."

"The wild one and the elf," I heard someone say from around my waist.

"They have good hearing too," I said.

"We are almost where they can hear you, but not us."

"You all really didn't see someone standing there when we met?" I asked.

"With luck, you can see what others miss," someone said.

"Even we do not see him. Only his passing. She could not have seen," someone else said.

"Unless he wanted to be seen," said another. "It is time we go."

"I can't tell you how happy I am to have met you all," I said. "I'm sorry it was under these circumstances."

"Be well, Cassie Heidrich."

I didn't hear them leave, but my surroundings began to feel drab and empty, so I knew I was alone again.

They hadn't told me which way to go, so I assumed it was the direction they had been taking me. It took me two steps to walk into a tree. Pain jumped up my arm from the injection site when my arm rubbed across the tree bark. I was going to have to talk with Taylor about that spot and see why the pain was still there.

I had decent night vision, but the darks appeared darker here. Rubbing my arm lightly, I took two steps back from the tree. My foot caught on a root, and I fell to the ground.

"Yep, luck is gone," I muttered.

There was no way I was going to get anywhere on my own, so I called out. "Rider! Logan!"

An answering call sounded far away. I stood up and dusted off. When I heard a twig snap, I looked up, expecting Rider.

An old man stood closer than I expected. The moon hit him in a way to make his features stand out.

"Who are you?" I took a step back. "I saw you before."

His beard and hair were long, but they didn't have the unkempt look of a man who might be living off the land.

Why, why, why, did I have to think about *Deliverance* earlier?

"They marked you." The man was at ease. "That is a rare occurrence indeed."

He didn't seem threatening, but the whole situation was eerie, so I stayed on my guard.

"I think it's rare anyone even sees them." Chancing it in the dark, I closed my eyes briefly and reached out to the Path. This couldn't be a coincidental meeting.

When I opened my eyes, the Path was a mass of brilliant white. That brilliance rushed forward, caused pressure all around me, and then threw me out of the Path.

"No peeking," the man said.

I gasped and staggered back, bouncing off the tree. No one had ever pushed me out of the Path before. I didn't even think it was possible.

"Who are you?" I blinked as if my eyes needed to readjust to the night.

"I am me, and no one else." His voice was higher pitched, almost like an old woman instead of an old man.

Time to raise the bravado. "Look, it's been a long day. What do I call you? Are you human or Lost?"

"I'm as human as you." He laughed hard.

"What's your name?"

"My name?" The man let out a chuckle. "My name! It's been so long since someone's asked me that."

I edged around the tree, away from him. This was too weird, even for me.

"What do you want?" I asked.

"Ah, yes, yes, I wanted to see."

"See what?"

"To see if you were the one."

"The one what?" I was able to take a few more steps back.

The man didn't move, but there wasn't any more distance between us.

"I needed to see the one that is you," the man said, "and I was the first!"

I crossed my arms. "I'm me, and you're you. Glad that's settled."

"Yes, yes, that is settled." The man was gone. He didn't hide behind a tree, or walk away, or anything. He simply disappeared.

I took a few more steps back, trying to look everywhere at once. All around, shadowed shapes loomed. I was hesitant to reopen the Path. The first time in days I had used it, I had been kicked out. It didn't bode well for my confidence, but my need to know outgrew my anxiety about using the power.

There was nothing. No trace of anything. I ran through the shimmer raging forward to see the past and the Path the man had left behind, but there was no trace.

An intense fear took hold. It was too dark to move quickly,

but I tried my best to put as much distance between that man and me as possible.

"Rider! Logan!" I tried to keep the fear out of my voice, but I failed miserably.

When Rider ran into view, he was breathing heavily, even though he was used to running long distances. He came over to me and I hugged him without thinking, relieved not to be alone.

"Is everything okay?" Rider accepted the hug until I drew away. "You were supposed to be back before dark."

"I got wrapped up. Quick, can you take me to where I fell back there?"

Rider looked unsure but walked in that direction.

Logan bounded into view and followed us. "What were you thinking, girl? We were worried sick."

I flapped my arm at him, intent on Rider.

Rider circled an area. "You fell here."

"Can you tell what else was here with me?" I asked.

"Nothing." Rider walked in increasingly larger circles. "I smell nothing else in the area. Were they here, did you see them?"

Sighing, I turned to go and promptly lost my footing in a hole. Logan managed to keep me standing.

Gran told me to ignore the old coot in the woods. Maybe this is what she meant. I regained my balance and took a last look around. "If I can manage to stay on my feet, I'll explain on the way back."

I told them the story of the leprechauns and giving back the soul of their friend. I didn't tell them I had been marked since I wasn't sure what it meant. It also seemed personal in a way.

Then I explained about the old man.

When we walked into the campsite, there was a fire going. Vincent jumped up and met us at the edge of the firelight.

"You took your time." His face didn't hold its usual blankness. Swallowing hard, he looked me over, assessing any damage. I'm not sure how he expected to find anything among the mass of old bruises.

Somehow, he managed to look closer than I did. He grabbed a first aid kit and doctored cuts on my hands.

"I am going back for Cassie's bag." Rider melded into the woods and was gone.

"Wait up," Logan said, "there's someone else out there. We shouldn't travel alone."

CHAPTER

THIRTY

"We're not alone out here?" Vincent inspected my hands, cleaning scrapes as he found them.

My hands heated up every time he touched them. "Uh, yeah. He appeared, talked like a madman, and then disappeared without leaving a scent or Path behind." I relayed the rest of my adventures in the woods.

Vincent inspected my hands far longer than necessary.

"So," I said after describing the Walker who stole the leprechaun's soul, "is it someone you know?"

Vincent dropped my hand and repacked the first aid kit. He gathered the trash from the Band-Aids and cleaning wipes before he finally spoke. "Yes, I know who it is."

"And?" I said after it was clear he didn't want to move on.

"And, it's a friend of mine. I guess he used to be anyway."

"A friend of yours is doing this?" I asked.

"Yes." Vincent, finished with the trash, checked the rest of the campsite and he kept moving, refusing to look at me as we spoke.

"Any ideas why he would do this?" I tried to choose my

words carefully. Since I share a soul with him, I knew Vincent better than most, but only who he was on the inside. Now I was discovering that I didn't know anything about his life.

"I talked to him last fall. I wanted to know if he'd ever seen anything like what I had done." Vincent's voice dropped and he stopped moving. "He asked me details, wanting to know exactly what happened. He dragged out every last thing about what I did to you. He hypothesized with me. About what could be done to reverse it, what we could do in the meantime, and what could be done if any of those little pieces escaped."

"Escaped?" I made the leap without him having to say the words. "You two discussed storing parts of a soul into objects for safe keeping?"

Vincent jabbed sticks into the fire. "He knew it could be done with whole souls, but until last fall, no one even knew it was possible to fracture a soul, at least not to that extent. Now I see he wanted to try splintering a soul."

I sat on the ground nearby and watched him stoke the fire. Now I understood what he meant at the club and why he felt responsible. A part of me, a large part, wanted to comfort him, but yelling was also an option roaming through my mind. Both were wrong at the time, so I sat.

"I couldn't be sure it was him. That's why I was working with Jin," Vincent said.

"Now that we know, we can all move on this." Logan stepped into the firelight with Rider close behind, holding my bag.

"You didn't try to find the leprechauns, did you?" I hoped for a distraction.

Rider glared at Vincent. "You could have saved us time and trouble by letting us know before this. What happened with Jin did not need to happen."

"We couldn't have let him keep that soul," I said. "It didn't belong to him, and it was our job to bring it back."

"It didn't have to happen the way it did." Vincent's voice was low, and he didn't meet anyone's eye. "I agree with the wolf on that. I should have left Jin out of it."

"What's done is done." Logan's voice was firm. "We need to move forward on this now, not dwell on which way the centaur twitched his tail."

"You're one-hundred-percent sure that your friend is at fault?" I asked.

Vincent winced. "Ex-friend."

"This moves you off the case," Logan said.

Vincent looked at Logan, surprised. "There's no way you'd find him."

"Who is he? You will tell us where he is," Rider demanded.

"His name is Cole. I don't know where he lives, and we don't have the kind of time needed to track him down," Vincent said.

"What are you suggesting?" Logan asked.

"There are... channels that I can go through." Vincent shifted uncomfortably. "They're not pleasant ones, but I'll be able to set up a meeting."

"Then what?" Logan asked.

Vincent didn't look away from the fire. "Then I kill him."

"No!" The detached way he said this threw me off guard. "You can't kill your friend. Besides, we need to take him in."

"Walkers don't wait around for portals," Vincent said. "We can step between the worlds and disappear for life."

"That doesn't mean you have to kill him." There was no way I could let Vincent kill someone close to him.

"We can try to find a way to stop him. Vincent can arrange the meeting, and we can be there as backup." Logan's eyes flickered to me and then back to Vincent. "Is there any way possible you could talk him into coming in?"

Vincent's voice was cold. "Walkers don't get brought in. The knowledge of what we do isn't shared. If a Walker goes down, he goes down and out."

"We know what you can do." I worked to keep my voice soft, not wanting to upset Vincent further.

"You know a part, and you three know more than most." Vincent stood and looked at Rider and Logan. "But AIR knows what's useful for them and nothing more."

Logan and Rider nodded as though that fact was the most obvious thing in the world.

I felt uncomfortable. How much of myself had I put into the files? I was willing to bet it was more than these three combined.

"So what do we do?" I asked. "We can't kill him."

Vincent and Logan looked at each other, grim expressions on their face.

"We don't go around killing people." There were many things I wasn't sure about, but this wasn't one of them. "It's not what we do."

"It's not what you do." Vincent made it sound like I was naive, childish even.

I stood up and glared at him. "It's not what any of us should do! Not if there's an alternative."

"You don't get it." Lines of fury broke through Vincent's features. "This is a Walker. There is no nice way of making him come with us or go away. It ends in death."

Trying to keep in mind that Vincent had to be upset about the thought of killing Cole, I tried to rein myself in. "It doesn't have to end that way."

"She's right." Logan wasn't looking at either of us. "We have to find a way to try to take him in."

"Any ideas on where to start?" I asked in a rush, before anyone could interrupt.

"That's not a smart decision." Vincent's voice was beginning to escalate. "You know the wrong person could end up injured or worse if we try to take him alive."

Rider let out a low growl. Turning, I expected it to be aimed at one of us. Instead, he stared into the woods. We went still and Rider silently moved to stand beside me.

My ears felt strained in trying to hear what had agitated Rider, but there was nothing. The dark night stood still. Not a twig broke or leaf rustled. The forest sounded dead.

A cackle sounded out around us. To me, it sounded like it came from everywhere at once, and it was the same voice that the man in the woods had used earlier.

Logan abandoned the firelight, moving faster than I would have thought possible. I took a step closer to the fire and watched in the direction Logan disappeared. Rider glanced at Vincent and something unspoken ran between them before Rider also disappeared into the night.

"Gran said to ignore the old coot," I yelled at his retreating.

Vincent strode around the campsite. With a jolt of fear, I thought he too was going to run off.

Instead, Vincent doused the fire. "Start packing."

My heart beat fast; there was no way I was going to argue. I threw things in bags, but Vincent was more methodical in his breakdown of the camp. Vincent caused the fire to run low but still give us enough light to see by. Every few minutes, I would stop and peer into the night.

Staring at a tree, just outside the firelight, it almost looked as though someone was standing out of sight, only a small portion showing.

A hand landed on my shoulder and I jumped and spun around.

"It's okay." Vincent's voice was soft, a vast contrast from our fight. He reached around and took the bag I was stuffing.

"I know it is," I lied.

He shifted a few things around in the bag and somehow it looked more organized. "The important things should always be easy to reach."

"I thought we were in a hurry," I said.

"They need to be in easy reach, especially if we're in a hurry."

Looking around, I saw that the camp was almost packed away.

"We're going to leave Rider and Logan's bags here, and we're moving towards the truck." Vincent poured water and then tossed dirt over the remainder of the fire.

"Shouldn't we take their stuff with us?" I asked.

"Rider will find their stuff. I'm not sure we could carry it anyway."

I stared unseeingly into the night. "I don't feel right leaving Logan and Rider behind."

"They'll look out for each other and catch up soon."

It still didn't feel right, but this had to be the old man Gran had warned me about, and she didn't seem too concerned. I hefted the bag onto my shoulders and buckled the straps while my eyes adjusted to the dark.

Vincent had his gun out, and he was trying to look everywhere at once. He was also getting ready to trip over a fallen tree.

"Let me lead. I need to be of some use." I could have taken out my gun; that is if I had brought it. We were returning a leprechaun soul, not chasing someone down, so I had stupidly left it behind.

We didn't get far, when I heard a twig snap to the left. It was Rider's way of letting me know he was there; Vincent, however, must have missed that memo. He heard the twig snap and aimed in that direction.

"It's Rider, you idiot," I said.

Rider walked into my range of vision, but Vincent could see next to nothing in the woods. He kept his gun leveled in Rider's direction.

Seeing a gun pointed at someone made me nervous. "If you shoot Rider, I'm going to be really mad."

Rider snickered softly and moved closer. "We did not find anything."

Vincent lowered his gun.

Rider continued, "Nothing. Not even a whiff in the air. Logan agrees with Vincent, it is time to leave."

"Great, get Logan and let's go," I said.

"He is picking up a bag, and I will go back and do the same. We will be circling wide around you as we travel."

My nerves ratcheted up. "What happened to sticking together?"

"We will be in sight of you most of the time, but in the dark, you might not see us. We also have our signals. Logan wants us to keep our perimeter wide since we believe there is only one person out here with us."

After Rider was gone, Vincent and I didn't move for a while. I was listening intently for some sign of our other partners, but unless they wanted us to hear them, there would be no noise.

Vincent shifted the bag on his shoulders. "Let's go."

I looked around and one tree looked exactly like another. "I have no idea where we are."

He positioned me in what he said was the right direction.

I moved again and kept my voice low. "You can't see, but you know which direction to go?"

"I have an excellent sense of direction," Vincent said, "at least in this world."

"But not between worlds?"

"Sense of direction doesn't exist between worlds, at least not in the way you mean. Most of the time, though, I can move in and out quickly."

"Quickly, yeah," I muttered.

Vincent was silent for a while. "I should have called."

Understatement. "You really should have. But," I tried to lighten my tone, "you've apologized, and the past is past."

Through some sort of silent agreement, we stopped talking. Neither of us was able to walk through the woods silently, but we strained to hear over our own noisy steps.

It was impossible for me to tell how long we walked, but when I felt worn to the bone, I stopped. It had been quiet for so long, I had almost forgotten why we were still moving.

"Why are we stopping?" Vincent asked, but I could tell from his voice that he was as tired as I felt.

In response, I dropped my bag and leaned against a tree.

"We should keep moving," Vincent said, but his heart wasn't in it.

Rider and Logan joined us.

"Any sign?" I asked, yawning wide.

"Nothing," Logan said.

"It was toying with us," Vincent said.

"Yeah, but I'm not sure we should stop for long," Logan said. "Get some rest while you can. I'll keep watch."

"Aren't you going to need sleep?" I asked.

"I can go longer without sleep. Don't mess with the hammocks," Logan said, "and stick close together. I'll be out of sight."

The only thing that convinced me to move away from the tree was that my sleeping bag was nearby. I felt cold and damp from the spring night air, and my sleeping bag felt light as air. I was skeptical it would keep me warm, but too tired to care much.

"I guess this means we're sleeping on the ground?" I had my 'bed' for the evening under one arm, and in the dark, I was trying to find a place to sleep. None of these things made sense.

"Over here. There is space enough for all of us, and the ground is not too uneven," Rider said.

After stumbling over to Rider, he took my sleeping bag and rolled it out on the ground before putting his own down next to it.

I sat down and scooted into the bag. "How do you avoid snakes sleeping on the ground? And spiders?"

Vincent let out a harassed sigh and tossed his bag down next to me. "You don't."

I stopped moving and looked at him in the dark. "No, really, what do you do?"

Rider chuckled on the other side of me.

Vincent settled in next to me. "You weren't worried about this last night."

I yawned. "We were in hammocks. That's different. You're up in the air."

Rider laughed again.

"That's not funny," I said. "How do you keep them out?"

"Don't worry, Cass." Vincent's voice was already growing lighter as he slipped into sleep. "Rider and I will keep them away."

"Right." I zipped the bag up as much as possible while still being able to breathe. "I believe that."

"DID your grandmother really call me an old coot?"

I jerked awake and looked around. The sun hadn't risen,

but the dark was peeling back to make way for it. Sitting on a fallen tree, the old man was smoking a pipe and watching me.

"What?" I sat up and looked around. Rider and Vincent were sound asleep beside me. "Did you scare us off tonight because I said you were an old coot?"

"Ah, ah, ah. You said it. That is different."

"No, she said it, I repeated it." The only way my partners weren't waking up had to be that I was dreaming. I yawned and relaxed. "Right now, the names I'd call you would be much stronger."

He laughed and kept laughing until he wheezed.

"Do you have something to do with the Lost being killed?" I asked.

The laughter died down and the man sighed. "Always with the killing." He looked around and bobbed his head as though consulting an audience. "In a way, yes, and in a way, no."

"So, you are involved?"

"For this one, no, for all of them, yes." He sounded sad but no less odd.

"That makes no sense. Do you know who's behind stealing the souls?"

The man gave me a look that clearly indicated that he thought I was the crazy one. "You ask what you already know? Huh." The man waved the hand holding his pipe around at me. "Waste of breath. Too young, too slow, too stupid, and wastes time. Not a good start."

I leaned forward further. "Did you call me stupid?"

The old man looked away and muttered again.

"Fine. It was a dumb question." I shifted around and dislodged a rock from under me. "Do you know where he is? The Walker doing this?"

"As your new little friends tonight said, information is

valuable." There was a gleam in the man's eyes, which began to take on a reptilian look.

I had a flicker of uncertainty, but let it die. "Whatever. I'm going back to sleep." I slipped deeper into the sleeping bag.

The man chuckled. "Tell the Walking Man about the Palm Reader, and tell your grandmother I said hello."

I poked my head out of the sleeping bag. "What?" There was no one around. "Definitely an old coot."

Beside me, I could feel movement. Peeking out of the sleeping bag, I saw the same dim light from my dream. Beside me, Vincent was asleep, half out of his sleeping bag and mumbling. Despite my fatigue, I smiled. Who knew he talked in his sleep? My interest in the revelation was short-lived when I realized he wasn't dreaming so much as having a nightmare.

While staying in my sleeping bag, I scooted across the ground and sat up next to him. Our last few days together were rough, but he'd been on his own for months.

Not wanting to wake Rider, who was snoring a few feet away, I leaned closer and nudged Vincent's arm. "Vincent."

I couldn't make out what he was saying, or if they were words at all. I spoke as softly as the first time but nudged a little harder. "Wake up."

His hand shot out and clamped onto my arm and his eyes popped open, showing far too much black.

Right, not a morning person, I thought, trying not to wince.

"Cass?" Vincent sounded disbelieving and kept his voice low, but once he focused on me, he loosened his grip.

"It looked like you were having a bad dream," I said, watching his eyes grow lighter.

"Christ, Cass, I could have killed you." He sounded more tired than angry.

I laid back down and let my eyes drift closed again. "Rider

did the same for me last night. Our waking hours have been bad enough. There's no reason to stay asleep if it's more of the same."

Vincent's lack of response caused me to drag my eyes open again, and I watched him stare into the early morning sky.

"Do you want to talk about it?" I'm not sure I wanted to know the answer, but I had to ask. "Letting it out might make it easier to sleep."

"You first." There was an edge of sarcasm to the suggestion.

I thought that over and a knot formed in the back of my throat. "That's fair, I guess." Vincent looked surprised, but I kept going. "But not out here."

Rider twisted around beside me and soon stretched out.

"You've never been camping have you?" Vincent asked, raising his voice to a normal level.

"Not until this week," I said.

"Even as a kid?" Vincent asked.

"Hmmm, my mom and camping?" I mocked, thinking that over.

Next to me, Rider laughed. "That would be interesting to see."

"Yeah," I said, "I can't put together the words mom and camping."

"And no one else took you?" Vincent asked.

"I was probably too young when my dad was alive." I tried to picture him, but I couldn't. "I don't really remember. And my step-dad was about as outdoorsy as my mother."

"We spent the night in the woods last fall," Rider said.

I rolled my eyes. "I'm pretty sure getting strung up by goblins doesn't count."

Rider laughed and sprang to his feet.

"Where's Logan?" I asked.

"Making coffee," called Logan. "We need to move out. I'd like to get to the truck by the end of the day."

"Do you think he, or it, will be back today?" I asked.

"I'm not going to guess," Logan said. "He doesn't leave a Path, smell, or tracks? He's seen only when he chooses to be seen? He forced you, possibly the greatest Reader ever, out of the Path? We have no idea what he is, and we're not sticking around to find out."

"Right," I grumbled, trying to motivate myself to get up. "At least it means a shower tonight." Getting up was a battle I wasn't expecting. "And a bed." Every muscle ached. "Why do people do this to themselves?"

THIRTY-ONE

Logan was back to his usual jovial self by the time we reached MyTH, but it baffled me how he managed it hiking all day, and then driving 'til after midnight. When we reached the rooms Sable had set up for us, I stripped down and took a shower hot enough to scorch my skin. While water poured over me, I daydreamed about being able to sleep in an actual bed.

When I stepped back into my room, I found Vincent, already cleaned and dressed, waiting for me. Drowsiness was beaten back when my heart sped up.

"Sorry if I startled you." Vincent was standing near the door, and I could tell he was trying to keep his face blank, but signs of fatigue and unease stood out for me.

"No, it's okay." I cleared my throat. "I thought you'd be asleep by now."

"We need to talk first."

"Okay. Want to sit?" I motioned to the only chair in the room.

"No, this won't take long."

Inwardly, I groaned, and it was like a breeze blowing through all the small fragments of souls. "Okay."

"What happened at Jin's can't happen again."

At the mention, a tremor started in my hands. "You won't hear an argument from me."

Vincent's hands clinched. "What I mean is that I would have told him anything. You were there because they wanted me."

"That's not your fault."

"There are people: humans, Lost, and Walkers that are worse than Jin."

"I'm sure there are." Did he have a point, or was he trying to scare me?

"I've made enemies with a lot of monsters."

"And you think one of them might come after me?"

"That's not going to happen."

I rubbed my temples trying to revive my tired brain. "So, they're not going to do anything?"

"My transfer to the Mid-West is permanent now. We can be co-workers, partners, and even friends, but we can't go down the path we were moving towards last fall."

My hand dropped to my side. "Oh." I didn't know what else to say. On one hand, I wanted to roll my eyes at his arrogance and tell him I was seeing someone, but in truth, it felt like my heart was being squeezed.

He looked tormented. "I've seen horrors in this world and beyond, but watching them hurt you was—"

"Don't." Cold blood pumped through me. "I don't want to think about that." I hadn't realized I had backed up until I hit the wall.

Vincent looked stricken but strode across the room. "I wasn't thinking."

"No." I held up a hand and moved down the wall, towards the bed. "I'm okay, tired is all."

He stopped and looked at a loss for what to do. "Let me find Rider."

"No, it's okay." I tried to make my voice even and sat down on the edge of the bed. "I'll be fine after some sleep."

Vincent appeared frozen in indecision, which I didn't think was possible for him.

Dammit, I was not the person who gets scared and backs up into a corner. I wasn't sure if I was trying to prove something to Vincent or me, but I made myself walk over to him.

"I'm sorry, Cass."

He didn't pull away when I took his hand and gently led him to the door. "I understand what you're saying and why you're saying it. If you don't want to be anything more than friends, then that's what we'll be."

"It's for the best."

Next to the door, I looked at him as though memorizing his face. With my free hand, I traced the thin new scar on his temple. When I let go of his hand, he gripped mine tighter and took a step closer.

"You know," I said, "I never thanked you for getting me out of that basement."

"You're the one that got us out."

"It's possible that neither of us would have gotten out without the other."

Vincent studied my face. "Are you sure you don't want me to find Rider?"

I knew he was looking for signs of distress, so I tried to keep neutral. "I'm sure."

"Do you want me to stay?"

My heart skipped a beat over the implication, but then I

thought about Ethan and glanced away. "I think that would move us off in the wrong direction."

Vincent looked like he was going to say more, but I broke in first. "We should really get some sleep." I gave his warm hand a final squeeze, and then stepped away. "Sleep well."

"Goodnight, Cass."

Alone, I climbed into bed, but when sleep came, so did the nightmares.

The third time when I jolted awake, I gave up, got dressed, and began the morning search for coffee.

Even though I was up early, there were others awake before me. A team had brought in a centaur in need of medical attention. The centaur had been patched up, and I found Rider with him in the hall. The centaur had bandages around his flanks, but beyond that, he looked great. Incredible in fact. His torso and forearms were tanned which blended seamlessly into his brown coat. There wasn't a hair out of place. He could have been going to church instead of a doctor's office.

At least he could if centaurs went to churches.

Rider waved me over, and the centaur looked up at me, smiling, but his mouth twitched, turning it into a grimace. The centaur pawed at the ground with his front foot, and I took a step back.

Crap, it was way too early for this. Sometimes, meeting new people really sucked.

The centaur reared back and yelled. By the look on his face, I thought it was probably a good thing I didn't know his language.

Rider planted himself firmly between the centaur and me, pressing both of us back. "Cassie. Leave."

"What?" Streaking from crankiness to pure anger in record time, I crossed my arms and glared at the centaur.

It's not supposed to be like this.

Shards bubbled up inside me, and one of them lanced its way out.

Rider looked back at me. "You should go."

I felt lighter, bouncier, and more awake, but most of all, I felt absolutely thrilled at the idea of a fight.

My glare turned into a smirk. "This is going to be fun."

"Stop now!" Rider's demanding voice rolled over me, but the centaur stopped dead.

The hair on my arms stood up and I laughed. The souls, including my own, twisted around.

"I wasn't expecting it to be you two kicking up the fuss," Logan said from down the hall.

I laughed again, and my voice caused my skin to crawl. "Oh, and the elf. This is going to be fun!"

"It's not her, Logan." Rider looked worried.

"That's not playing fair." Anger became effervescent, bubbled to the surface, and then I launched myself at Rider.

Rider grabbed my hands, which were aimed straight for his eyes. My knee went up, but didn't make contact, so I threw myself back. Logan's arm went around my neck in a choke-hold; Rider held my hands.

"What do we do now?" Rider leaned down and looked at me, eye-to-eye. His brown eyes sparkled so much that they practically glowed.

With Logan holding me firmly, I couldn't look away, but the soul overriding my system tried to flinch and pull back all the same. There was definitely an animal lurking behind Rider's eyes.

"I don't know," Logan said. "What set her off?"

The flinch and that tiny slice of fear allowed my own soul to gain a foothold.

Rider gestured back towards the centaur, who was looking

confused and embarrassed. "She looked very tired and the centaur..."

"Had his first encounter with her." Logan sounded resigned.

Using the foothold, I pushed back that small, but horrible little chunk of soul. Once I gained control, my muscles turned watery, and I sagged. My whole body felt heavy.

Logan shifted his hold before I could choke myself out on his arm and Rider let go altogether.

"You good?" Logan sounded hopeful but wary.

Things were not supposed to turn out this way. "Yeah." I tried to get my muscles under my own control.

Rider cleared his throat. "That was—"

"Take care of the centaur," Logan said.

Rider hesitated but left with the centaur.

"I think I need to sit down." It was an understatement. My body was exhausted. Mentally, it had already been a long day.

When Logan let me go and I sat down, back against the wall, depression welled up. How could I do my job if my partners had to worry when I was going to attack them next?

Logan crouched down next to me, silent for a few heartbeats. "Do you know what that was?"

I closed my eyes and leaned back. "No." I listened to my breath go in and out. My heart felt as if it fell lower with each exhale. "I'm sorry, Logan."

He took a seat beside me. "We're not doing a good job of keeping you safe."

"That's not your job." I sniffed and didn't bother opening my eyes. "It's not Rider's either."

"It looked like you found your way back. On your own again," Logan said.

"This time." My heart felt like it hit a rocky bottom. I had attacked Rider, my best friend, all because I couldn't keep control of myself.

"If you managed to take control over that, well, I think things may be getting better," Logan said.

"It doesn't feel like it from my end." I clasped my hands tightly together on my lap. If I lost control at the wrong time, what would happen to my partners? I let out a shaky sigh. "I think—"

"You've had a long couple of days. Too long really." Logan cleared his throat. "I don't have the details about what all happened, but there was enough to know that you should have taken a few days off after you—well, after we got you back."

"You're taking me off the case." I had meant it as a question, but it came out as a deadpan statement.

Logan grinned. "For a day, maybe two. We've got some stuff to track down and we can get by. You can go home and get some rest."

"Everything okay?" Vincent asked. His face was blank as he approached, but I could see there was a hint of wariness in his eyes.

I didn't take the time to read what he was feeling. "Vincent can fix this." My heart began to rise and I took to my feet.

"Fix what?" Vincent asked.

"I don't think it works like that, Cassie," Logan said, "and I don't think we should risk it, even if it were possible."

"Risk what?" Vincent asked.

"Your friend, he took all these souls. All these little pieces from who knows what and you can take them back."

"Release them from what's holding them?" Vincent asked.

"No, release them from me." I breathed faster, excited by the prospect of gaining some semblance of normalcy, but a part of me was trying to rein that enthusiasm back in. "You can take them and let them go, wherever it is they need to be."

Vincent reached out and took my arm.

"Don't," Logan warned.

"I'm not sure what's going on." Vincent was looking at me intently, as though trying to peer into me to see all those Lost floating around.

"Those souls your friend smashed up," Logan said, "they stay where they're put when most people touch them, leeching out a little over time. But when Cassie touched them, it seems they found a more permanent home."

Vincent's grip on my arm hardened. "Are you okay?"

"They slip out from time to time," Logan said, "trying to take some sort of control."

"How many?" Vincent didn't take his eyes off me, and my eyes were glued to his.

"It started with one," Logan said. "The next was an accident."

Vincent relaxed a little. "Two? Do we know what they are?"

Logan let out a resigned sigh. "There was an incident at a drug bust. We went to confiscate our evidence, and things didn't go so well. Cassie was knocked into a table covered in the stuff. She kept them off as long as she could, but there's only so much a person can do."

"The count?" Vincent's voice could cut diamonds.

"Our best guess is north of fifty." Logan sounded sad, but I had hope.

"Is it possible," I asked, "to take the others and leave mine? Or take them all and strip off the extra?"

Vincent visibly paled. "It's not an option."

I blinked and stared, waiting for more.

"Look, Cass, I'm sorry." Vincent looked at Logan. "You were right, it doesn't work like that. There's nothing I can do."

"It's okay." Logan sounded understanding, but there was a

trace of sadness mixed in. "It's not the kind of thing we'd want to experiment with."

My chest seized up. "Right." I looked down the hall, not wanting either of them to see my disappointment, but I didn't think I could hide it for long.

"Maybe we should talk, Cass? We could go for a walk," Vincent suggested.

I feigned a smile and turned back to face them. "No, it's okay, I understand. I had to ask, right?"

"I'm sorry," Vincent said.

"Don't be." I looked him in the eye and tried to sound as sincere as I felt. "It's not your fault."

Vincent looked away. "If I hadn't hurt you last fall, none of this would be happening."

"Which you more than made up for when you saved us from dying at the hands of a vampire," I said.

"She's right you know," Logan said. "You saved both of us, and who knows how many more."

I had never been so relieved for my partner's back up.

"And only a few days ago, you got me out of that basement. Any debt you think you owe me is gone." My breath shuddered at the end. I had to get away. "You boys don't have too much fun without me."

"Where are you going?" Vincent asked.

Walking off, I waved over my shoulder, not wanting to face them again. "Home."

I stopped in the bedroom I had used, grabbed my stuff, and thought about calling Gran to let her know I would be home for a day or so.

I'd also ask her if she knew the man we had run into while camping.

My bag was packed, full of laundry, but instead of going to

my car, I found myself at the clinic. I knocked on a few doors before finding Taylor in his office.

"Are you leaving us?" Taylor asked, noting my bag.

"For a day or two, but I'm sure you all can keep my partners on their toes while I'm gone. Before I leave, who, or what lives out on the property you sent us to?" I asked.

Taylor tried to make his face unreadable, but after spending a few days with Vincent, I could read Taylor's hesitancy. "Is this an official question?"

"Off the record."

He looked at me appraisingly before answering. "Well, now we know leprechauns are there."

I hadn't even thought about the fact that MyTH would now know about them.

"Not that we'll let that get around." Taylor was fast to assure me. "To the south, a few elves live at the edge of the property. There's a pixie refuge and another gnome hole. A witch lived there for a while, but she moved out. I think that's all."

"That's a lot of woods for no fairy homestead," I said.

"There was one, but they asked to be relocated. I think the pixie population aggravated them. They left not long before the witch."

"So there's not a man living out there?" I was hesitant to ask. I was unsure who to tell about the crazy man in the woods without looking crazy myself.

Taylor looked alarmed. "There's someone living out there? I'm pretty sure Neil did a sweep recently. There was nothing we didn't expect."

"Neil did a sweep?"

"Infrared satellite." Taylor was suddenly very interested in his paperwork. "I hope everything else went okay out there. How's your arm?"

I didn't let him change the subject. "I think we should have Neil do another sweep."

Taylor led the way reluctantly, and we found Neil exactly where we expected to find him, in his lab. He was lying on the sofa staring and doing nothing.

"Dude, get the hell out of here." Neil's words didn't have any heft behind them.

"Fairies have more self-control than you," Taylor grumbled. "Time to wake up and earn your paycheck."

"What do you need?" Neil asked.

"Infrared," Taylor said, "of the south-central property. Our campers spotted someone out there."

"Dude, the campers must have been smoking something good," Neil said. "There's nothing out there."

"The campers weren't smoking anything. We need you to check." Taylor kicked the couch to rouse Neil.

"Dude, don't diss the furniture."

"Get up." Taylor's fuse was getting shorter.

"Look, man, I snagged satellites while they were out there. I watched them the whole time. They ran into nada." Neil stood and loped over to his computer. He brought up satellite imagery onto a wide—screen monitor on the wall.

"You checked on us while we were out there?" I asked.

"Dude, you're like my partner and stuff. Gotta catch your back," Neil said.

I blinked and looked at Taylor. He looked as surprised as I felt.

"The whole thing was recorded. There's like nothing there." Neil brought up the recording and fast-forwarded through. There was nothing but us on the tape.

"Strange," I said.

"Did it do anything to you all?" Taylor asked.

"Nothing," I said.

"I wouldn't be concerned," Taylor said. "No one else out there appears to have seen anything out of the ordinary."

Fairies and a witch had moved out—I wondered why they left, but I kept the thought to myself. I had bigger things on my mind. I'd have to ask Gran about the man.

"Thanks, Neil, I'm going to be gone for a day or so, but I'm sure I'll see you around again," I said.

"Drive safe, I'll be in the clinic if anyone needs me," Taylor said.

After Taylor had left, I turned back to Neil. "I'll see you in a few days?"

"Dude, what about the jewelry, I got that shit unraveled." Neil got up and paced.

"What do you mean unraveled?"

"Okay," Neil said, "this Walker Dude snags someone's soul. That's some nasty shit right there. But instead of getting rid of it, he shoves it back into the person's body, and leaves it all cut to pieces. But Walker Dude doesn't stop there. He pulls out the pieces. So like, there's a bunch of them. He puts the shards in jewelry to keep hold of it."

"The jewelry holds on to it somehow, but we assumed that part."

"Man, it can be anchored to anything, not only this. You could anchor that shit to a Ho-Ho if you wanted to. Not that a Ho-Ho would do you much good. You'd eat the thing and the shard would go into you all at once. Not great for a long-term high." Neil left his computer and went to a small fridge under a table. The table was covered with chemicals and beakers. "Damn, I'm out of chocolate. Chocolate would like, be the shit right now."

"Neil," I said snapping my fingers at him. "Focus. How are the souls anchored?"

"Oh yeah." Neil left the fridge open and went back to his computer.

I closed it and joined him.

"This stumped me at first, but it's so simple." Neil opened a file with enough symbols that I had anxiety flashbacks about college chemistry.

"That doesn't look simple," I said.

"But it's o-natur-al," Neil said. "It's plants and shit. I gotta admire the man. He even has hemp in the mixture. Anyway, this stuff mixed together anchors the soul but allows the effects to slip out. When the soul isn't whole, it gets used up. When it is whole, like Indian Dude's—"

"Jin," I corrected.

"Right, Indian Dude's was whole. A whole soul doesn't get used up, because it's like, a living thing on its own. Kind of its own perpetual energy source."

"So when you anchor a whole soul, it can be stored indefinitely?" I asked.

"In theory."

"You said it could be anchored to anything?"

"Yeah, the plant mixture was found in my research. They've used it for ages. There's even a little stone dude in the basement display of the art museum. I took a field trip to see it. There's a soul trapped in there. Someone must have ticked off a Shaman dude and got shoved into the little stone statue. I took some pictures, but he comes out all blurry."

"Can you put together an object for us? One that could hold a soul?" I asked.

"I'm already a step ahead of you," Neil said, grinning. "I did a trial run to test the theory. I picked up a few statues, but the dude at the shop didn't have much of a selection. Most of his stuff was concrete. But when I found this beauty, I knew it was the perfect one for us." Neil beamed and held out an oblong mound of greenish tinged rock with a carving on top of the stone.

It was cute and I wanted it.

"It's a sea turtle!" I wanted to sound professional, but there was a bit of girlish squeal in there. "And this little guy would hold a soul?" It fit easily in the palm of my hand.

"It's solid granite, which is what the little statue dude in the museum is made out of. From my research, it's a good choice of stone. It sat in the herbal bath while you were gone; now it's good to go. The turtle's yours to keep, though, soul or not. I made another, but it's kind of boxy. Good enough for the others."

"Thank you, Neil, I love it!"

CHAPTER

THIRTY-TWO

"Morning, Gran." I turned the granite sea turtle over in my hands, feeling the smoothness of its shell and the rough underside.

"Mornin', sugar." Gran's familiar southern drawl lifted my mood, even if it was over the phone. "It's good to hear from you."

"Then you'll like my news. After spending some time in the woods, I was thinking about coming home for a day or two. Sleeping in my own bed sounds wonderful."

"That is good news. Did that old coot bother you in the woods?"

"I almost forgot about him. He didn't like that you called him that." I thought about that a second. "Oh, wait, that was the dream. I did bump into him, though."

"Dreams." Gran half-snorted half laughed. "That old man is full of tricks."

"Was that part real then?"

"I wouldn't put it past him."

"Who is he?"

"Someone I knew a long time ago."

"Oh. He said to tell you hi. At least I think he did. He was a little, um, off. I told Logan not to worry about him, though."

"Well, I knew he wouldn't be a bother out there. Any other place or time and Logan would have the right of it."

"How did you know him?"

"We went out a few times." Gran hadn't even hesitated.

I stopped in the hallway. "If Logan was right to be worried, does that mean he's dangerous?"

"Darlin', I wasn't always a grandmother or even a mother." Gran sounded almost wistful. "Like your Walker, he was never any threat to me."

"He's not exactly my Walker." I didn't immediately notice that I sounded as wistful as Gran.

"That man will always be your Walker. Speakin' of Vincent, did you take him to the Palm Reader?"

I dropped my bag and leaned against the wall, eyeing the exit a few yards away. "No, I thought I'd tell him and give him directions. He can find the place."

"Things don't end well that way." Gran sounded serious this time. "I don't know what you've been up to in the city, but I know you've had a rough week. I think a few more days there will be good."

"You really think so?"

"At least take him to see that Palm Reader and decide from there."

Not what I wanted to hear. I slid down the wall and once again found myself sitting on the floor. "The man in the woods said I should take him there too."

"Oh." Gran sounded almost embarrassed. "I didn't expect that old fool to be helpful."

I turned the turtle over again in my hand, but my thoughts

were on Gran and her old friend. "After all these years, do you think about him?"

"There's somethin' about the wild ones that stick with you." Gran was quiet, and I could tell she was thinking about him, or at least who he had once been. "Still," she added, more strongly, "I loved your grandfather, and we had a good life together. Shorter than I would have liked, but good all the same."

"You should look him up sometime. I could take you down to meet him."

"Well, now, I'm not exactly the woman I was back then."

"I think he'd like who you are now."

"I'll have to think on that." She said the words, but it sounded more like she was dismissing them. "But for now, you take your Walker out."

"Maybe I'll see you in a few days then?"

"You take care of those partners of yours. They're going to need you."

It wasn't until we hung up that I realized she had avoided my question.

The thought of a few days off was nice, but maybe work was better. Vincent wasn't taking time off, and he'd been through as much as I had, and maybe more. He'd been on his own for months. If he could forge on, so could I. The past was the past, and whatever had happened could stay locked away; besides, seeing what had happened this past week, tomorrow could only be better, right?

Holding the sea turtle up at eye level, I looked at the glints of green and the intricate pattern on the shell. It's hard to believe that this little turtle could hold a soul, but then Jin's necklace had been smaller and it had held the leprechaun. That small bit of power Jin was using had constantly renewed itself.

It hadn't been his power, though. What if it had been his soul on the outside?

"I have been looking for you." Rider was striding towards me.

Looking up, I swallowed hard, thinking about what I had done earlier in the hall. Before Rider reached me, I scrambled to my feet. "I'm so sorry for what happened earlier."

Rider stopped in front of me looking worried. "Is that why you are leaving?"

"Logan thought I might need a break."

"Do you need a break?"

I ignored the question. "Gran says I need to stay."

"That is settled then. She is not wrong." Rider picked up my bag and waited for me.

"I really am sorry about earlier."

Rider shrugged. "It was not you."

"I wish I could believe that. So, is the team meeting?" We walked back to the room I was using, but without being in a rush to get there.

"Not now. What is that in your hand?"

"It's a present from Neil." I held it out for Rider to see.

"It is a good carving."

"I thought so too. What are we doing if we aren't meeting?"

"Logan is speaking with Hank. Vincent is meeting with Taylor."

"Oh, is Vincent okay?"

Rider seemed to think about this for a minute. "Vincent is troubled and worried."

"So normal?"

"Yes."

I grinned. "Well, Gran said I need to take him somewhere. When we get back, though, maybe we can see if the conference room is free."

"I will find Sable and ask." Rider's words came out in a rush.

"Thanks. You, uh, take your time." Rider and Sable? Good for him. "Vincent and I may need a while."

After returning my bag, it was easy to find Vincent. I went to the clinic and knocked on a few doors before someone answered in Taylor's office. Behind the door, Taylor looked harassed, and Vincent showed traces of disapproval.

"I can come back later," I said.

"No," Taylor said the words too quickly. "Mr. Pironis and I have reached an impasse in our discussion. Would you like to see me?"

"Vincent actually," I said. "Gran wants me to take him somewhere."

"He's all yours." Taylor was practically throwing Vincent out the door.

Vincent's mood didn't change after he followed me out.

"Everything okay?" Realizing it was a stupid question, I was fast to clarify. "With you and Taylor I mean."

"Yes." It was Vincent's only reply.

"Okay." If he didn't want to tell me, I wasn't going to pry further.

We walked outside and it was strange to see that the day was only getting started.

"I thought you were taking time off," Vincent said, his voice staying level and unbothered.

"That has to wait."

That appeared to agitate Vincent more.

"What's wrong?" I asked.

"I don't think I said there was anything wrong," Vincent said.

Moving around to the driver's side of my car, I frowned at

Vincent. "You don't have to say anything when you scowl at people."

Vincent didn't immediately get into the car. "I do not scowl at people. At least not to anyone that you might notice." He settled into the seat and kept his eyes forward.

"Since when does that bother you?"

"Where are we going?" Vincent said, ignoring the question.

I rolled my eyes and drove out onto the empty street. "Gran wants me to take you to see a Palm Reader I met a few days ago."

"A few days ago we were in the wilderness."

Gripping the steering wheel tighter, I worked to keep my voice steady. "I met the Palm Reader the day before I ran into you."

"You should be taking time off. If Margaret had any idea what happened in the past week, she wouldn't have you on this errand."

"Have you met my grandmother?" It wasn't even worth keeping my voice steady. "If she knows it's for the better that we do this, she's going to have us do it. Besides, why should I take time off? You've been right next to me the whole way, and you're at work."

"I have not been next to you the whole case. It seems there are large chunks of information that no one has decided to fill me in on."

I pulled off the road and into an almost-empty parking lot. "What are you talking about?"

"We should go to wherever you are taking me and get this meeting over with."

"No." Either he wanted to start a fight or he really didn't want to be around me. "Not until you tell me what's going on. Everything was fine this morning."

"Except it wasn't, was it? How could you not tell me you're taking in souls?"

"Oh, for pity's sake. When should I have told you? When should any of us have told you?"

"We spent three days wandering in the woods with not a lot to say."

"Oh, right, one day after being kidnapped and—" I shuddered, but barreled on, "and everything. Yet, I'm supposed to think about all you might have missed in the past six months?"

"This is different, Cass. What you're doing shouldn't—"

"What I'm doing? Are you kidding me? Do you think I'm actively absorbing these things?"

His fury might as well have been etched in stone and naked for the world to see. "Since I have no idea what's happening, how could I know one way or the other?" Oddly, for once, his eyes were crystal clear while he argued, no darkness crept in. "When you took the void in, you had to work hard to make that happen."

"That one was different. I have no idea why, but I told you that night that it was playing well with all the others."

"Was I supposed to guess based off that? That night, of all nights? There were other things on my mind."

"You and I haven't worked alone on this case. If we had, I assure you, everyone would have made sure you knew. You were completely uninterested in anything else that might have happened since you left, why should we pinpoint this one, unless you needed to know?"

"That's not fair. I was working while I was gone."

"And the world stops because you're working? You're working so you can't call and let us know you've made it back?"

"Amy was supposed to let you know." His voice held a burr that I would expect from Rider, not him.

"Who the hell is Amy and why should she have told us? Why wouldn't she tell us if she was supposed to?"

Vincent dropped back into his seat and stared out the window. "She's someone from my old office."

"If she's with AIR, why wouldn't she have told us?"

He let out an infuriated breath but didn't say anything.

"Vincent, why wouldn't your office tell us? And did you call them?"

He didn't say anything for a while, but when he spoke, it sounded like he was choosing his words carefully. "The night before I left, you and I had gotten close. I knew how I felt when I met you, but I assumed it was because of what I had done. It wasn't a feeling that I had expected you to reciprocate."

His words broke apart some of the anger that had been building around us.

When I prompted him to continue, the venom was gone from my voice. "What does that have to do with your office?"

"Before I came here, Amy and I had gone out once or twice." His words were wary. "It was nothing serious, but it was a relationship of a sort. I wanted to call to end things appropriately with her before contacting you."

What was I supposed to do with that? We weren't dating last fall, but we were definitely toeing that line. Then I thought about the whole thing together, then and now.

"Did you tell her about me when you called?" I asked, pulling out a few more details.

"I was honest with her." Vincent avoided looking at me.

Should I be upset about this? I mean, yes, a part of me hurt, and a part of me was angry, but did I have a right to be?

Maybe. "Are you telling me that you asked your ex to call us and tell us you were back after you told her, what, that you wanted to see me?"

Vincent didn't say anything.

"That's the stupidest thing I have ever heard." My voice was a mixture of anger and laughter.

He frowned. "Amy and I had barely seen each other. It was nothing serious, and we were both very clear on that up front."

"Yeah, right. Judging from her reaction, I'm pretty sure you were clear, and she agreed."

Once again, he didn't say anything for a while. "Is that what you did last night?"

Well, I may as well tell him, right? "That's different. I'm seeing someone."

"Oh." He looked like he was trying to think of what to say. "Is it serious?" His voice was flat, and for once, I was glad for that.

"We haven't seen each other long, but yes, it's getting serious."

"That's good." It sounded like the last of his anger had slipped away. "You deserve to be happy."

"I was happy with you."

He finally looked at me again. "I'm sorry, Cass, but that can't happen."

"So you said." I hurried on before he could read too much into that. "I'm good right now, though. I'm not sure how this got so turned around, but tell me why you're upset. I promise you that had you and I worked alone, you would have been told. I mean, once we actually started working together."

"What difference does it make if we're working alone, together, or with Logan and Rider?" It sounded like he was struggling to keep the edge out of his voice again.

"Together, Logan or Rider would have dealt with it if anything happened."

"Dealt with it how?" Vincent asked.

"I don't know. Tranquilizers seem to do the trick, although

Neil figured out that anti-anxieties and heroin work well." I meant it to lighten the mood.

"Christ, Cass, what are you letting people do to you?"

I slumped back in my seat, tired of the whole thing, with Vincent, the job, everything. "You don't know what you're talking about. I was joking about Neil. He didn't know what else to do and being around Jin scared him."

"That I understand at least. But if people are drugging you, then we have a problem."

"Would you rather I hurt someone? They only had to tranq me the first time anyway. And before you suggest differently, they absolutely did the right thing. Not only did I attack them, but I also did it in public." I had attacked my partners. What the hell was wrong with me? I sniffed and tried not to tear up.

"So they're not drugging you?"

I looked out the window. "If they need to, they will. I've asked them to."

"You can't let people do that to you."

I glared at him. "We do what we do for a reason. You make it sound like I'm blindly going around and saying drug me, please." Flashes of Jin's doctor jabbing me with a needle flashed through my mind, but I clenched my eyes and drove it away. "It's not like a stranger on the street. It's Logan and Rider. I trust them."

"What do you think I would have done to them if they drugged you in the woods?"

"Nothing!" I yelled. "Do you have any idea how furious I would be if you ever did anything to either of them?"

"I have some idea, yes."

"You're only aggravated because we didn't tell you right away."

"Do you know how infuriating you are?"

This was getting us nowhere. We were quiet for a while. I

tried to see things from Vincent's point of view, but I got nowhere.

"I shouldn't have said that." Vincent's words were grudgingly said, at best.

"I'm sure you're not wrong."

"Huh." The response was sarcastic, but I guess that was better than him being so angry.

I took a few meditative breaths. "Is this really what you're upset about?"

We sat in silence. After two minutes, I let out an exasperated sigh, which turned out sadder than I intended, and started the car again.

"I've made things worse again," Vincent's voice was monotone.

"Because we argued?" I asked, leaning back in the seat again.

"No, although I'm sure that doesn't help matters. Cole is tearing apart souls because of what I told him, and now, I see what it's doing to you."

I turned that over in my head before I responded. "You're not accountable for what he does. You have to know that."

"It's not only that." The corners of Vincent's eyes and mouth tightened and his voice dropped. "I let Jin meet you. It never should have happened."

"I was there to find Jin. He would have met me with or without you."

"He wouldn't have taken you and used you the way he did."

I really wanted to tell Vincent to stop talking about it, but he obviously needed to. Instead, I ignored my instinctive reply and took his hand. "I've done the same thing, blamed myself for tracking you down, knowing that neither of us would have been caught if I hadn't."

Vincent squeezed my hand hard. "You know that's not—"

"My fault? It's no more my fault than it is yours."

While the minutes ticked by, he held onto my hand like a life preserver.

Eventually, he put his other hand over mine and held tight. "I keep wanting to ask you if you're alright, but it's a stupid question."

"I don't think either of us is okay." I thought about that, trying to find a way to soften the sentiment. "But I think we will be." It would be so easy to sit like this with Vincent all day, but that wouldn't be right or fair for either of us. "What do we do now?"

"Now?" Vincent appeared to think about the question. "I should apologize for not calling, for getting angry, and for about half the things I said."

"Only half?"

The corners of Vincent's mouth twitched up. "Fair enough. Almost everything."

"That sounds better."

"And you?" Vincent asked, relaxing.

"Me? No, I'm pretty sure I meant everything I said." The whole atmosphere felt lighter, and it was easier to tease.

"Did you call me stupid?" Vincent took one hand off mine and loosened his grip with his other hand.

He was leaving it up to me if I wanted to take my hand away. "No, I said what you did was the stupidest thing I've ever heard. I could get second opinions, but things don't look good for you there."

"You're probably right." Vincent looked less weighed down.

Smiling, I pressed my hand more firmly against his. "I don't think I said it before, but I'm glad you're back." Then, somewhat reluctantly, I let go and looked around. The day had run away from us.

"Next time, I'll call."

"Promise you will, no matter what?"

"I promise."

"I'm holding you to that."

I had forgotten how long the drive was, but we had plenty to talk about. By some unspoken agreement, we avoided any topic that was too serious. We talked about Rider, Gran, Logan and his kids, and a few other people from the office. It felt good to take a step back and think about other things. Sometimes, it was hard to remember that life existed outside of work. Moments like these helped.

THIRTY-THREE

We found a parking spot about a half-block away from our destination.

"Did Margaret say what we need to do here?" Vincent asked, getting out of the car.

"No, but I had my palm read last time, and I think the woman's authentic."

"I didn't know there was such a thing." Vincent held the door open for me.

I lowered my voice as the sunlight was cut off. "Neil seems to think that everything exists somewhere."

"I'm not sure I like that kid."

"He's not so bad," I said. "He's young and seems lost, but he's a good person at heart."

"So, I should get a reading?" Vincent asked.

"Maybe. She also sells the same jewelry that Jin was using." Seeing the look on Vincent's face, I hurried to add details. "It's empty, though. Nothing in there."

"Good day," said someone helping another customer. "If you have an appointment with Fatima Jain, the Palm Reader, she will be with you shortly."

"Thank you," I said.

"There's so much stuff in here," Vincent said, keeping his voice low. "How did you find anything?"

"It's at the front counter." I led the way and squatted down to look at the shelves. "I bought a few of them at random and they were all empty."

There was no response. When I looked around, I saw that Vincent was standing, looking behind the counter, instead of the case.

I saw that he was focusing on the photos on the wall.

"What is it?" I asked. When I looked back at Vincent, his eyes were flat black. "Vincent?" I couldn't keep the worry out of my voice.

"It's Cole." His voice could drop the temperature. "We're leaving now."

I looked at the picture of Fatima and her fiancé and then left the store.

Back in the car, I sat there, not wanting to believe it.

"We need to go," Vincent said.

Noting that his eyes remained flat black, I sighed and drove off.

"She was so nice," I said. "I don't want to believe it's him."

"Who is she?"

"Fatima, the Palm Reader. The way she talked about him, I know she loves him." I sniffed. "Her family had finally given them permission to get married."

"She might be a good person, but that is definitely Cole, and we know he isn't."

"How could she not know what he's doing?"

"You know what I do, and you continue to work with me."

My mouth fell open and I looked at him. "Are you serious? You are nothing like him."

"You don't—"

I saw the signs that he was going to argue with me, so I cut him off. "If you dare try to start an argument with me again, especially about this, I'm going to douse you with honey and leave you in a pixie field until the case is over."

He opened his mouth and shut it again. Shaking his head, he tried again.

"You heard me," I said. "You are nothing like him. There's no way you would kill for money or power or whatever kick he's getting from this."

When I next looked over, Vincent's eyes were mostly back to normal, so I relaxed. Back at the office, we met with everyone in the conference room.

"He is seeing the Palm Reader, and we know where she is. It should be easy to find him," Rider said.

"We could follow her until she leads us to him," Logan said.

"No," Vincent said. "Paper trails are fine, but we leave her out of it."

"It might be faster to follow her," Logan said, "or follow the paper trail and her."

Vincent's eyes narrowed slightly, but I could see that he was pulling back his inclination to be angry. "Walkers don't have many attachments. The ones we have are left alone and separate, at least unless they're fool enough to jump into the fray."

Logan leaned back in his chair and crossed his arms. "Those sound like Walker rules. We'll do what we can, but—"

"You don't understand." Vincent leaned forward, and his eyes swirled with tinges of darkness. "He will pull the world down around us if he suspects that we might even have a passing interest in her. If the wrong Walker found out, any attachments we might have could be used as leverage against us."

"We find another way." The way Rider said it wasn't a demand or a suggestion, but a statement of fact.

When Logan looked at me I nodded, and, knowing he was overruled, he went on. "Okay, we find him a different way. Now that you know he's here, in the city, would you be able to track him down."

"Yes," Vincent said, "but I think Hank might find him faster."

"If you give me the data, I could track him if you'd rather." Neil looked anxious about speaking up. He fiddled with the rock in front of him. "You'll have to tell me what I can and can't use to find him, though."

Vincent looked surprised. "That might work better."

"We can start moving on that after we're finished here," Logan said, "but we'll need a plan for once we find him."

"We're facing the problem of him jumping into the void," Vincent said. "We need to ensure he'll never do this again. There's only one way to do that."

Logan shook his head. "We go in with the intention of bringing him in alive. That is nonnegotiable."

"Cassie blocked the demon from his powers last fall," Rider said, "maybe she could do that again?"

Taylor's eyes widened. That part had been left out of the file.

"No." Vincent didn't raise his voice, but it came out demanding. "Cole would pull her soul to try to stop her."

Having my soul sucked out wasn't high on my list of fun things to do.

"We need to attempt to bring him in. We don't go around killing people," Logan said.

"I think I have an idea for that," I said. "Let's look at what he's been doing. He pulls a soul from someone, and eventually that person withers away. He puts the soul, or a piece of a soul into an object a person would wear, like jewelry, and when worn, the person gets a small dose of what's there. Neil, will it hurt to pass around the stone?"

"No." Neil passed the stone to Logan. "This is meant to stand the test of time."

"When it's a whole soul, it can sustain itself," I said. "I'm not sure we could do this, but what if Vincent takes Cole's soul? We could put it in an object like the one Neil has."

"Would that not eventually kill Cole?" Rider asked.

I was on less stable ground here. "I don't think so; if we kept the object with Cole, his soul would be self-contained, but he would only have access to the small parts that leak out." I looked at Vincent. "I think that would sustain him. Keep him alive, but keep him basically harmless. Then we could take him in."

The room was quiet. I shifted in my chair while everyone mulled over the idea.

Finally, Logan spoke up. "It sounds like a good plan. Vincent, you know more about Walker powers and their effects. Will Cassie's idea work?"

"This has never been done before, so there's no way of knowing." Vincent leaned back in his chair. "It's a sound theory, though. Keeping his soul nearby should keep him alive. He may have limited use of his power, but it would be minimal. He shouldn't be able to capture souls or jump between the worlds."

"We would be relying on Vincent pulling the soul of a friend," Rider interrupted. "Will you do that?"

"Ex-friend," Vincent corrected. He looked up at Rider. "He's killing people. People we're supposed to protect. I don't think we have any choice."

Rider gave Vincent a sad look.

"What about the object?" Logan gestured to the rock that Rider was inspecting.

Neil looked more confident in this area. "It's made to anchor the soul." Neil walked everyone through the research he had told me about earlier.

While he talked, I sought out the turtle in my pocket. I didn't take it out, mostly because I didn't want to pass it around, but I reassured myself that I hadn't set it down somewhere.

I noticed that Logan gave Taylor the briefest of skeptical looks, but Taylor nodded, and Logan didn't raise any objections.

Vincent didn't appear to want to touch the stone when I shifted it towards him, but he slid it over to Taylor.

"Thank you, Neil," Logan said. "This looks like excellent work. We have the who, what, and how that we need in place to meet him."

"It would have to be somewhere we couldn't be seen," I said, "but if we ask him to meet in the middle of nowhere, he's going to know something's up."

"Chances are, he'll know anyway," Vincent said. "He'll come."

"If he will meet, then you do not have to hide your intentions, correct?" Rider asked.

"I don't think it will be necessary."

"What did you have in mind?" I asked.

"The MyTH property, where he took Am." Rider looked at Taylor. "We would stay away from the gnomes, and we would need permission to use the property."

"We can look at some maps," Taylor suggested, "and find a good meeting spot. If you think he'll show up out there."

"He'll be there," Vincent said.

THIRTY-FOUR

It baffled me that Cole agreed to the meeting. The next evening, we found ourselves in the country on the top of a hill, in the middle of the woods.

We stood behind Vincent, letting him take the lead. I couldn't get a good look at Cole when he walked up the hill, but I saw his Path clearly. Dark purples swirled around black cords. Encased were small cores of other colors shifting and moving, but always being drawn back down. The remains of his victims that he hadn't yet released. Chills swept up my spine as I watched the mixed swirl of color around Cole.

"It's been a while," Cole said as he approached. "I guess by our surroundings, and our company, this isn't a casual meeting."

"It's not," Vincent said. "I didn't want to believe that you could do this."

"Have you been able to help your girl yet?" Cole looked at me and winked.

Vincent balled his hands into fists. "Not in the way you mean."

"I've been able to help mine," Cole said.

I was caught off guard by the response. He was helping Fatima in the travesty?

"What do you mean?" Vincent asked.

"Her family wouldn't let her be with me, and it was tearing her up." Unlike Vincent, Cole didn't try to hide his emotions. My mood boiled at his indifference. "I tried to get around it, of course, go the easy way, you know. But in the end, her uncle took a shine to me."

"You worked for him and received the family's blessing," Vincent said.

Cole shifted from one foot to another. "You know you can't take me in."

"And you know I have to try," Vincent said.

"You've really changed. This girl has muddled your mind." Cole sneered in my direction before turning back to his friend. "The Vincent I know would have gone straight for the fight. Kill first and ask questions later."

Vincent shook his head. "That's not the way it works, and you know it. We take away only what needs to be removed."

"And now you think I need to be removed," Cole said.

"You're killing innocent people."

"The Lost are no more innocent than they are people."

It took a large amount of restraint not to give Cole a piece of my mind. Logan had the stone box and I hoped he was ready.

"You can't continue like this."

"Let's get on with it then!" Cole lurched forward and tried to grab Vincent.

Vincent dodged out of the way. "We don't have to do this. We can talk this out."

"I've helped so many people," Cole snarled. "You have no idea."

He launched himself at Vincent. Vincent grabbed Cole's outstretched hand. They stopped moving, but in the Path, I could see their struggle. There was a sway in the energy around each man. It was like a churning tide, the energy flowing back and forth. With all the sparks of souls trapped inside him, Cole had the upper hand. Slowly, Vincent's aura began to drain away into Cole.

"No!" I yelled moving towards the two.

Cole was taken off guard and Vincent was able to regain some ground. Without thinking, I grabbed Cole's arm as soon as he was in range. Little sparks of life leaped from Cole, eager to be free of him. He looked stricken as their power left and he shoved me to the ground. When he looked up, he saw Logan and Rider moving forward, more cautiously than I had been.

Cole's eyes turned black, and a grin broke across his face. "Time to take this to a more private location."

Picking myself up off the ground, I reached out again towards Cole. He took a step away and jerked Vincent towards him, locked arm and arm. There was a rapid buildup of energy around them and the Path began to twist.

They were going between the worlds.

I wasn't letting Cole get away that easily. I certainly didn't want Vincent to be swept away between the worlds with him. The traces of their Paths stood out, but they twisted with the Path surrounding them, ready to move out of this dimension.

I grabbed the familiar imprint of Vincent. Forcing power through, I made his Path solid and firmly locked it in place. Cole was more difficult. His Path tried to escape my grasp, but I wouldn't allow it. Refusing to think they might be gone, I slammed even more power into my work, making Cole's Path solid. Holding on tightly, I wrenched them back from the energy that Cole had amassed to make his escape.

Both men stumbled and they broke apart. Before Cole could get his bearings, Rider was on him.

When Rider hit him a second time, Cole was knocked to the ground. From there, Cole reached for Rider's leg.

Logan took Cole's foot and dragged him back, as Rider retreated. Cole kicked out and jumped to his feet when Logan let go. Cole's hand clamped around Logan's arm.

My heart spasmed when Logan's essence poured into Cole. That sunny golden energy was racing away. Vincent yelled out before slamming into the two of them, breaking them apart.

Cole was too strong, so I decided to bring him down a notch. I jumped into the fray, grabbing hold of Cole's arm. The remaining souls of the Lost, at least those not tethered down, jumped to me. When I tried to reach for Cole's soul, I realized I was no Walker. I could see it and even feel it, but it was his soul and it wasn't budging.

"You stupid bitch!" Cole squeezed my arm while I clung to his.

THIRTY-FIVE

I could feel myself weaken quickly. The specks that belonged to the Lost tried to stay with me, but they were being dragged in as well. Then a fragment like fire and ice shifted.

Cold poured through my body and Cole's black eyes widened. He tried to pull away, but I bore down harder. That cold, dark piece of the void was retreating from me. Cole swung his fist into my side and we broke contact.

The damage was already done.

The void had come out of me, but it had not passed into Cole. It was out.

The small piece hung in the air at the top of the hill. The world paused as though taking a breath, and all eyes were on the tiny ball of darkness that lingered in the air. A small breeze picked up. Within seconds, the air turned wilder, pulling at our clothes as it dragged past us. Soon, the wind roared through and was sucked into the dark mass. I could see the little spot grow larger.

Images and emotional vines of the Path were also being

sucked in. Cole and I were the closest to the whirling mass. I could see the terror on his face as we clung to each other.

Managing to take few steps away was all I could muster; the strength of the object was too strong. With Cole's help, we managed to push a further step away before being overpowered and we began to slide the other way. We each tightened our grip and tried harder, but we weren't having any luck. Cole looked across the clearing, then at me, and I could see his fear.

When he let go, I tightened my grip, but he easily pried himself away from me. He spoke, but the sound was lost, and it was too late.

I watched in horror as Cole was torn apart before my eyes. There was nothing left of him.

As the void fed, it became stronger. My mind went blank after watching Cole disappear, but it sprang back into action when I felt myself being dragged in. Looking around, I could see that my friends were having the same problem.

Panic welled when I swept the clearing for Logan. Had he been pulled in? Rider was further away. It looked like he was trying to work his way over to me, but I could tell he would never make it. With each step he took, he slid closer to the void. Vincent was on the other side of the clearing, trying to maintain his footing. He was yelling, but the sound, like everything else, was lost in the swirling mass.

In the Path, I tried to tie myself to the ground. Shoving energy down, I rooted to the spot. The void tugged, and ties to the Path wavered while my mind groped with what could be done.

An indistinguishable barrage of words came from behind me. A large chunk of granite sped past my head and sunk into the depths of the void. I held my breath and wondered if throwing the box in would do anything?

Nothing happened.

My mind groped again for a solution. What could we do? Would the world be swallowed completely?

Feeling a hand on my arm, I tried to turn, but the strength of the force in front of me wouldn't allow it.

Logan yelled in my ear, but only part of the sound reached me. "... wrap it... girl..."

Wrap it up. Maybe he meant the Path. The little pearl of void that started this whirlwind had been trapped in me, and it held pretty well. Was it possible to do that again?

The last time I absorbed the void it had been a struggle, but it had held together like any other soul. There was no way to absorb the monstrosity now; it would tear me to shreds.

If I could re-anchor it, like our original plan, it might work.

Gripping hard, I took the sea turtle out of my pocket. Holding the smoothly worked stone in my hand, I concentrated hard on the Path.

My root of power was strong, doing its work to keep me grounded. Rider was sliding dangerously close to the tempest that the void had become. Working fast, I made a wall of air around myself, but it was torn apart, and the power fell into the void.

The idea of trying to block the Path of the whirlwind was tossed out as well; the energy would be sucked up. How could all this happen?

The pull of void was becoming stronger as it gained more fuel from the Path and the world around us. Vincent was pulled closer. Rider didn't have much more time either. I had to act.

The Path roared past and I grabbed hold. Strings of emotions and memories slowed. Past and present images of the Path melded together, but their trail to the void stalled while real-world objects flew by.

Holding the stone, I concentrated on the unwavering root

of power holding me to the ground. When I stepped forward, it moved with me, and my foundation stayed strong. Concentrating hard on the Path of the chunk of granite in my hand, I managed to stop it from being dragged away from me.

My next step brought pain. Was this what Cole had gone through?

This would have to be close enough. The void had to create a Path of its own, even if it destroyed it as fast as it was being created. Reading its Path, I targeted an area and drew it to me. The pain grew greater. Without thinking, I pushed part of the Path into the real world, anchoring my body down. The pain lessened, and the void grew nearer.

I yanked on the Path of the void and wound it around my turtle. The granite soaked it in. It didn't take long before the void rushed into the turtle. I guided it forward. The pull of the void lessened. The Path stilled first. Then the outside world quieted as I guided the last vestiges into our rock.

Turning the stone repeatedly in my hands, I searched for leaks. Once I was assured our turtle would hold, I shoved away the Path and looked around for my partners.

I felt jittery. The air was motionless, but having spent more power than I had expected, I was wavering. Vincent heaved himself off the ground across the clearing. Rider was wide-eyed. There were ruts in the ground where he had been dragged forward. Logan moved around from behind me. It looked like he was talking, but there was nothing but the rush of wind filling my ears.

Logan reached out to inspect the turtle. It was hard for me to release my grip on the statue, but once I did, I knew I didn't want to hold it anymore.

The struggle was over, but my body wasn't so sure. I have to say, I was more than a little relieved when normal sounds returned. Vincent looked shaky when he reached us. He gave a cursory look at the turtle before trying to pull me into a hug. I returned it the best I could, but I was stuck to the spot.

The Path was no longer open to me, but when I looked down, I could see its familiar shimmer engulfing my feet and legs.

"What is it?" Vincent asked as he walked around me.

"It's the Path." My voice was as shaky as I felt. "I'm not sure how it happened. I needed to hold myself down."

"Can you step out of it?" Vincent asked.

I tried to lift my legs, but they weren't budging. Exhaustion was clouding my mind, but the Path shining brightly in the physical world fascinated me.

Rider came over and laid on the ground, inspecting it from the ground up. He eyed it for a while before reaching out and touching it. His finger sank through.

Vincent ran his hand over the surface, but it remained solid for him.

"It's like glass," Vincent muttered, watching Rider.

Rider experimented with the substance. He pushed his hand through in a few different areas, then took my foot and pulled it out. He freed the other foot, and we all inspected the results. There was not a trace of Path left on me, but it remained locked to the ground.

I sat down next to the shimmer. It wasn't flowing the way it does when it overlays the world. I closed my eyes.

"You think you should be doing that now?" Logan asked. He was squatting down next to the new creation.

My muscles were weak, and I was starting to feel numb. "I know it needs to be done."

He looked reluctant but didn't voice another objection.

I closed my eyes again, and stretched out, over the swarms of soul fragments, and into the Path. "It looks the same. Let me try to move it back to its original form."

It wouldn't budge. When I added more power, the world appeared to shudder and sparks flared in my vision. It was a good thing I was already sitting. When I laid my hands on the solid Path, I could feel it had sprouted tendrils and rooted itself into the ground. Getting out of the Path was a strain, and when I opened my eyes, I was surprised to see that I hadn't fallen over.

"It's firmly in this world," I said. "I'm not sure what to do with it."

"We're on MyTH property," Logan said. "I think we can cover it up and leave it here for now."

"It doesn't belong here," I said. "Are we comfortable with MyTH taking it?"

"Good to see you thinking it through." Logan looked up at Rider and Vincent. "What do you all think?"

"I think that we should keep this," Rider said. "We do not know what this could be used for."

Logan looked to Vincent for his opinion, but Vincent was staring into nothing, looking lost in thought.

"First thing we'll need to do," Logan said, "is to dig this up. Rider, are you good for a few more hours?"

"I am fine," Rider said.

"Good, I'll call Jonathan and have him bring us a few shovels. Vincent." Logan spoke a little louder when Vincent didn't respond. "Vincent."

"Yes, I'm good for a while longer," Vincent said.

"Good, you can drive Cassie home," Logan said.

There was no use arguing; I wasn't sure I could stay awake long enough to help. Reaching out, I drew my hand along the creation of the Path. What could this be used for? It was beautiful, but what would we do with it?

Vincent offered me a hand. "Come on, Cass, I'll take you home."

I blinked at the hand before deciding I could make it as far as the truck. He helped me to my feet. I swayed briefly before catching my balance.

"What do we tell work?" I asked.

"We stick to the truth, but this," Logan indicated the solid Path, "stays out of it. Also, there are no such things as leprechauns." Logan eyed Vincent before continuing. "Also, I think it's better all around if we say Cole wasn't a Walker. He can be an unknown."

"Thank you," Vincent said.

"Don't thank me yet," Logan said. "You've both got mandatory psych evaluations coming up."

"What?" My anger didn't have much chance to rise amid the exhaustion.

"Nothing I can do about it. After what happened to the two of you, it's protocol. Go home and get some rest. We'll get together soon to debrief."

I wanted to say something, but I had no idea what was left to say. Vincent tried to lead me away when I remembered.

"The turtle," I said, "I'll take care of it."

Logan turned the turtle over in his hands. "I thought we might leave this in the hands of MyTH. Neil seems to know a lot about how this thing works."

"All the more reason for us to take it," I said.

Looking reluctant, Logan handed the chunk of carved granite over to me. "For now, but we'll talk more about this later."

A wave of vertigo rolled over me when I took the turtle. Luckily, I was holding Vincent's arm, so I stayed on my feet. Once the feeling passed, I put the stone in my pocket and walked away with Vincent.

THIRTY-SIX

In the truck, it was a struggle to stay awake, but I knew I needed to, at least for a while. It was dark, except for the occasional passing car, and it was quiet except for the rush of the wind.

Once we were a few miles away, I broke our silence. "I'm sorry about Cole."

"He wasn't my friend in the end." Vincent's voice was low and tinged with regret.

"I think he was, though. Deep down."

Vincent shook his head but didn't say anything.

I knew if I didn't tell Vincent now, I might never tell him. "We were being sucked in." I tried to be careful with my words, so it came out slower than I intended. "Cole was closer, and he saw you across the clearing. We were holding on to each other, but... I think he thought he was pulling me in, so he let go. I tried to stop him, but he made me let go of him."

Still, Vincent said nothing.

"I'm sorry." I wasn't tearing up over the man that had

killed so many Lost, but I felt remorse for the loss of the man Cole must have been when he had been friends with Vincent.

Vincent took some time before replying. It looked like he was digesting that information.

"Thank you for that," he said.

For a while, I watched him out of the corner of my eye, looking for signs of mourning, then for any emotion, but he was a blank slate. Dropping any pretense, I twisted in my seat and looked at him directly. Only then could I see the slightly down-turned lips and the creases around eyes that were brighter than normal.

"I'm not sure what you did out there tonight," Vincent said, "but you have to be tired. Why don't you get some sleep?"

That was an understatement. "I wanted you to know about Cole, and make sure you were okay."

Vincent swallowed and looked at me briefly before turning back to the road. "Get some sleep, Cass."

I watched him for a while, but at some point, my eyelids closed and I was sound asleep.

When Vincent woke me up, I was more tired than I had been. How could that even happen? When I slid out of the truck, I used the door to steady myself.

"It's going to be nice to sleep in my own bed again," I said as I wavered on the way to the door.

"Are you going to make it inside?" Vincent asked. "Maybe I should see you in."

"What are you talking about?" I asked. "Aren't you staying here?"

Vincent hovered. "There's a hotel nearby in town. I'll go there for the night."

"Don't be ridiculous," I snapped, opening the door. "All your stuff is upstairs in your room." In my mind, even if he only lived here a short while, it would always be his room.

"My room?" He sounded amused by that.

Still, he locked the door and didn't argue.

"Help yourself to anything," I said. "Gran will be home tomorrow, now that we know no one is after her."

"I'm sorry I started all this."

"You know it's not your fault. We all know that. You are not responsible for what Cole did."

Vincent kept a close eye on me on the way upstairs, but he didn't say anything.

At my door, I hesitated. "There's something I wanted to ask."

He looked wary. "Okay."

"When Cole tried to pull my soul," I stopped, swallowing hard at the thought, "he sensed the void shard coming out and he was scared."

"Of course he would be," Vincent said. "He knew what it was and what it can do to a person. Taking that in would swallow him from the inside out."

"Wouldn't he have had to taken it once, to put it into the thing Jin used to keep me from the Path?"

In the dim light of the hall, I could see Vincent trying to think that over. "It couldn't have been him," Vincent said cautiously. "There's no way that a Walker could have taken a part of the void. I didn't think anyone could."

"So, someone else was helping Jin?"

"It's possible, but we know Cole was the one killing the Lost. The void isn't a living thing."

"True." I leaned against the wall next to my door. "We can talk it over with Logan later. Your room is the way you left it. Now that you're home, Gran is sure to want to ask you if she can dust. I think she's been itching to do that."

"It's your house." Vincent looked at the room down the

hall. He looked upset, but my sleep-deprived brain couldn't work out why.

I shrugged. "It's your room. Get some sleep. I'm sure Logan will have work for us tomorrow."

Leaving Vincent in the hall, I shut myself in my room and then kicked off my shoes. Knowing that my clothes were grubby, I threw them off, before falling into bed.

"Do you think the tree will be okay at your place?" I asked Rider as he drove me home.

"It is amazing how much it resembles a tree," Rider said. "Logan agrees that it is the best place for it until we figure out something different."

When I had spread the Path into the ground to tether me down, it had branched out. Once it was unearthed and flipped over, all those tendrils resembled a tree, and the base that had wrapped around me looked very much like a trunk.

"Gerald did a good job of painting it," I said.

"He is talented. I understand that you have plans later today," Rider said.

"With Ethan, yes," I couldn't keep the enthusiasm out of my voice, "but it's you and me this Sunday."

"Would you like to bring him with you when we get together?"

"Really? I thought you didn't like him."

"He is your friend, but I do not know him."

I beamed at Rider. "He's not the same kind of friend that you and I are. Maybe we can all get together another time, unless there's someone you want to invite."

Rider shifted uncomfortably in his seat. "I am still uncertain about how those types of relationships work here. I do not think I am ready."

"Well, when you are, or if you want to know anything, you can always ask questions. In the meantime, though, Sunday's for us."

Rider seemed pleased by that. "Have you spoken with Ethan about anything that has happened in the past few weeks?"

My good mood plummeted. "I haven't talked to him much in the past few days. Besides, our work is confidential."

"There are things that are not, though. I thought since you have not spoken with anyone, you might talk to Ethan."

"I've only been seeing Ethan for a few weeks. There's no reason for him to know."

Rider was quiet and I searched for a way to change the subject. "How's work?" It was a lame question, but it would move us away from talking about me.

"When you and Vincent return to work, it sounds as though Vincent will be my new partner."

"That'll be interesting."

"Does it seem odd to you?"

"No, you and Vincent have worked together before," I said.

"Most of the agency is human," Rider said. "Yet, the Lost and those with special abilities are paired together, leaving the humans to themselves."

"The luck of the draw I guess. Clancy works with everyone."

"This is true."

"Oh, Ethan's here early," I said as we drove up. "Gran's not home, but you're welcome to come in. You can keep Ethan distracted while I run and change."

"Is Vincent home?" Rider asked.

"No, he's out looking for an apartment." I slid out of the car when Rider stopped and greeted Ethan at the door. "Sorry that you had to wait." I opened the door to let them both in.

"It's my fault for getting here so early," Ethan said.

"Early is good," I said, "and it'll give us more time together. First, though, I need to change. I'll only be a minute."

I dashed upstairs but slowed down when I reached my room. Maybe Rider would have a chance to get to know Ethan a little better if I left them alone for a while. I changed into jeans and a T-shirt, but grabbed a long-sleeve button-up shirt to go over it. It was a warm day, but this time of year, you never knew if that was going to last. After I put on my hiking boots, I took the time to brush my hair.

It was only when I ran out of things to do that I checked the time. Eight minutes. It would have to do. I bounded down the stairs but slowed when I saw the two men. Rider looked serious, and Ethan looked troubled.

"Everything okay?" I asked.

"I believe so," Rider said, as though nothing was out of the ordinary. Only, he didn't look me in the eye. "I am going to visit Logan. Do you mind if I leave my car here?"

"It's no problem," I said. "I'll see you out."

"No," Rider said a touch too quickly, "I do not want to hold you two up."

He left before I could protest. The back door shut and I turned to Ethan. "What happened?"

Ethan seemed to come out of a reverie. "What? Oh, it was nothing. Guy talk is all."

I put my hands on my hips. "I didn't think Rider knew what that was."

"I think it comes naturally. You look nice today," Ethan said, obviously trying to change the subject.

They obviously didn't want to tell me what happened, so I let it drop. "Thank you."

"Are you sure you want to go hiking today? We could do something else if you'd rather."

"No way," I said. "You have no idea how much I need to get out and away from everything."

"If you're sure," Ethan said.

He sounded uncertain, which made me worry. "Um, if you don't want to go..."

Ethan smiled, closed the gap between us, and then took my hand. "I'm looking forward to it."

Then he kissed me.

Want to read further?
Stolen Sight (AIR Series Book 4)

COMPLETE WORKS

Complete works by Amanda Booloodian:

AIR Series (In Reading Order)
Stonecoat: Novella 0 (AIR Series Book 0)
Shattered Soul (AIR Series Book 1)
Redcap (AIR Series Book 2)
Broken Paths (AIR Series Book 3)
Stolen Sight (AIR Series Book 4)
Fenrisúlfr: Novella 3.5 (AIR Series 5)
Fractured Worlds (AIR Series Book 6)
Reliquary (AIR Series Book 7)
Never-Ending Nightmare (AIR Series Book 8)
Krampus (AIR Series Book 9)
Eclipsed Pathways (AIR Series Book 10)
Void (AIR Series Book 11)
Marked Soul (AIR Series Book 12)

AIR Series Box Set

AIR Series Books 0-4: Welcome to the Farm
AIR Series Books 5-8: Conspiracy Theory
AIR Series Books 9-12: Redacted

Spellbound Murder Series

Oath Bound (Spellbound Murder Series Book 1)
Grim Magic (Spellbound Murder Series Book 2)
Fallen Witch (Spellbound Murder Book 3)

Spellbound Murder Box Set

Spellbound Murder Complete Trilogy

AIR Series Audiobooks

Stonecoat: Novella 0.5 (AIR Series Book 0)
Shattered Soul (AIR Series Book 1)
Redcap (AIR Series Book 2)
Broken Paths (AIR Series Book 3)
Stolen Sight (AIR Series Book 4)
Fenrisúlfr: Novella 3.5 (AIR Series 5)
Fractured Worlds (AIR Series Book 6)
Reliquary (AIR Series Book 7)
Never-Ending Nightmare (AIR Series Book 8)
Krampus (AIR Series Book 9)
Eclipsed Pathways (AIR Series Book 10)
Void (AIR Series Book 11)
Marked Soul (AIR Series Book 12)

Spellbound Murder Series Audiobooks

Oath Bound (Spellbound Murder Series Book 1)
Grim Magic (Spellbound Murder Series Book 2)
Fallen Witch (Spellbound Murder Book 3)

ACKNOWLEDGMENTS

Special thanks to all my family, who are my biggest supporters in my writing. Adria Waters provided excellent feedback. Along with Christina Benedict, she provided support and encouragement along the way, especially when I became hesitant. I'd also like to thank Hadena James, who consistently encourages me to move forward.

The Columbia Writers Group provided me with different viewpoints which were beneficial throughout the process. The Editing company BubbleCow provided detailed comments that assisted me in making several points of the novel in a new light which I appreciated greatly. Thank you to Frankie Sutton, my editor, for all of her assistance. Deranged Doctor Design provided me with a wonderful cover design.

I also want to thank my parents for reminding me I can do anything I set my mind to, and my sister Tamera who is always supportive. Many, many other family, friends, and acquaintances have been incredibly supportive. Thank you all.

Most of all I must thank my husband for his continued reassurance, inspiration, and assistance in all my writing endeavors.

About the Author

Amanda Booloodian lives in Missouri with her loving, and often times peculiar, husband. She has been passionate about the written word throughout her life. Now, much of her spare time is spent at the computer, delving into worlds accessible only through vivid imagination. In warm weather, when she isn't pounding on the keyboard, she can often be found wandering through the wilderness. Occasionally she gets it into her head to SCUBA dive or to sit back at home and make wine, which can have interesting results and inspire her writing.

You can find out more about Amanda and her writing, including upcoming releases, on www.Booloodian.com. You can also find her on Facebook: Amanda Booloodian - Author and Instagram: AJBooloodian.

www.ingramcontent.com/pod-product-compliance
Lightning Source LLC
Chambersburg PA
CBHW072200130726
47910CB00011B/1733